CODE OF THE WEST

Books by Aaron Latham

Code of the West

The Ballad of Gussie and Clyde

The Frozen Leopard: Hunting My Dark Heart in Africa

Perfect Pieces

Urban Cowboy

Orchids for Mother

Crazy Sunday: F. Scott Fitzgerald in Hollywood

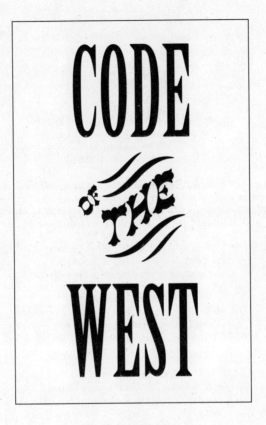

CODE OF THE WEST

AARON LATHAM

BERKLEY BOOKS, NEW YORK

A Berkley Book
Published by The Berkley Publishing Group
A division of Penguin Putnam Inc.
375 Hudson Street
New York, New York 10014

This is a work of fiction. Names, characters, places, and incidents either are the product of the author's imagination or are used fictitiously, and any resemblance to actual persons, living or dead, business establishments, events, or locales is entirely coincidental.

Book design by Ellen R. Sasahara
Cover design and illustration by Honi Werner

PRINTING HISTORY
Simon & Schuster hardcover edition / April 2001
Berkley trade paperback edition / May 2002

Visit our website at
www.penguinputnam.com

Library of Congress Cataloging-in-Publication Data

Latham, Aaron.
Code of the West / Aaron Latham.—Berkley trade pbk. ed.
p. cm.
ISBN 0-425-18513-3
1. Triangles (Interpersonal relations)—Fiction. 2. Texas—Fiction.
I. Title.

PS3562.A7536 C6 2002
813'.54—dc21 2001056467

PRINTED IN THE UNITED STATES OF AMERICA

10 9 8 7 6 5 4 3 2 1

To Lesley–my Revelie,
my Lifts Something,
my Guinevere

NOTE

The Age of the Cowboy is part history and part mythology. In this respect, it resembles the Age of Arthur, where fact and fiction ruled on twin thrones. In the Arthurian legend, historic names are mixed with mythical stories and impossible adventures. Invoking this license, I chose as my heroes a man named Goodnight and another called Loving. Of course, history knows a real Charles Goodnight and an actual Oliver Loving who really founded the Home Ranch in Palo Duro Canyon, but much of what I have written about them is made up. I tried to signal their dual real and unreal natures by giving them last names from history but first names out of my imagination. My Jimmy Goodnight is as real as Arthur and my Jack Loving is as unreal as Lancelot du Lac. Another name–an especially unlikely one–is also out of the history books: the outlaw Gudanuf. And there was a real cowboy strike.

BOOK ONE

QUEST FOR LOVE

1

Late 1860s

Jimmy was seventeen years old and nervous before the dance. He was tall, skinny, and awkward. Looking out at the world through a single knothole, he saw an ugly sight in the mirror: his eye patch. He asked himself: If I was some girl, would I wanna dance with a patch like that there? His scowling reflection shook its head. But then he saw himself smile as he remembered how hard his cousin Rhoda had worked giving him dancing lessons. She had only come up to his waist. He had felt like a big old clumsy buffalo dancing with a graceful deer. After all that effort trying to learn to polka, he wondered if he would actually work up the nerve to ask a girl to polka with him. Maybe he should just ask Rhoda. But it might embarrass her, and who wants to be embarrassed? Besides, she might turn him down. He told his mind: Just shut up!

When everybody was ready, all dressed up in their Sunday-go-to-meeting clothes even though it wasn't Sunday, the whole family climbed aboard a wagon dragged along by two plodding plow horses. Aunt Orlena was dressed in a long grey dress and grey bonnet. Uncle Isaac wore his baggy black suit, which was beginning to turn brown, and a black string tie. Cousin Jeff had on a black suit, too, newer than his father's, but even baggier, bought with the expectation that he would grow into it someday. Little Rhoda and littler Naomi looked pretty in blue flour-sack dresses and pigtails. Jimmy, who didn't have a suit, was ashamed of his butternut homespun pants and shirt, but he was proud of his new bandanna, which was fire red.

Jimmy wished the team would pull faster and stir up a little breeze. It was hot on this July night in the middle of Texas. Everybody said this summer was shaping up to be the hottest and driest in memory.

Even at this slow pace, the horses were lathered. They had worked hard all day in the field and must be tired. Now that he thought about it, Jimmy figured they had earned the right to plod slowly.

The wagon followed the road that led to the dreaded Weatherford schoolhouse, but Jimmy didn't mind because school was out for the summer. The closer they got, the more crowded the road grew, the more the little girls giggled, and the more nervous Jimmy became. When the wagon reached the school, the playground, which tonight would double as the dance floor, was already busy and noisy. Children were shouting and laughing, and the fiddles were tuning up. The sun was just setting, making even butternut look almost golden.

When Jimmy was getting out of the wagon, he tripped on something and almost fell on his face. He hated his own clumsiness. He hated the heavy clodhopper farmer's boots that weighed him down and made his feet feel like heavy hooves. How was he going to be able to dance? He longed for the lightness of his moccasins with the long fringe trailing out behind like a kite's tail. He could dance in *those.* But they were long–

No, Jimmy told himself, don't think about the past. It was too painful. Recalling his lost moccasins would just lead to remembering other losses, unbearable losses. Just think about here and now. But here and now was troubling, too. He couldn't dance. Not really. Not these dances.

Rhoda and Naomi ran off to be with other little girls. Cousin Jeff slouched off to look for his friends. Aunt Orlena and Uncle Isaac moved off to join the other adults who were busy talking about rainfall and crops. Jimmy kept the plow horses company. He didn't really fit with any group. He wasn't quite a member of the family, wasn't quite white in the eyes of many, wasn't quite right either, was too big for grade school and too dumb for high school. So he talked to the plow horses.

"O Great Goddogs, thank you for pulling the wagon," Jimmy said softly in the Comanche tongue. "I'm sorry you have to stand here. I know it must be boring, but at least there are two of you. You can keep each other company. There's just one of me."

Then Jimmy realized that several of the kids had noticed him talking to the horses. They were looking at him funny. Now they really thought he was crazy. He nervously started to put his hands in his pockets, but discovered that they were already there.

As the air darkened and cooled, Jimmy noticed individuals melting together into dark clumps. He saw girl clumps and boy clumps, big-kid clumps and little-kid clumps, farmer clumps and farmers' wives clumps. Then a clump of musicians started playing a tune, and the other clumps started breaking apart and reforming.

Drawn by the music, Jimmy moved closer to the musicians: two fiddlers were seated in leaned-back wooden chairs with cowboy hats perched on the backs of their heads. They looked to be in their twenties. A young woman about the same age played an upright piano. Jimmy wondered how she had gotten it from her living room to the playground. An old man probably in his seventies was playing a harmonica.

Jimmy rocked back and forth to the music, trying to work up the courage to ask somebody to dance. By the light of a full moon—assisted by several lanterns hung from trees—he studied the couples on the dirt dance floor. There were teenage couples and middle-age couples and old-age couples. And there were some mixed-age couples—fathers dancing with daughters, grandmas dancing with grandsons. He tried to comprehend the dance steps, but he just got more and more confused. The swaying couples weren't dancing a polka—he could tell that much—but he didn't know what they were dancing. They seemed to move their feet very fast, the same way they had seemed to talk back before he learned to understand them. The dancers were beginning to kick up a good bit of dust, which the orange moon turned into gold dust. It gilded the swaying bodies and made them look like dancing statues. Jimmy thought the dancers looked so pretty that he longed to join them, but longing was as far as he got. Frightened by the strange dance steps, he soon returned to the horses.

Still, Jimmy's gaze kept reverting again and again to a brown-haired girl in a yellow calico dress which had some sort of design on it. He couldn't quite make out the pattern in the darkness. He had seen her at school, had seen her at services at the Hard-Shell Baptist Church, had nodded to her and even said hello to her a couple of times. Like most of the girls, she was a farmer's daughter, but he thought she was prettier than the others. He remembered that her name was Rachel.

"Should I ask her to dance?" he asked the horses in the "Human" tongue. "I mean if they ever play a polka." There wasn't a word for "polka" in the Human tongue so he said it in English. "What do you think?"

One of the horses flicked its tail and shifted its weight from one hind leg to the other.

"What's that supposed to mean?" he asked.

Jimmy told himself that he was not a "running-heart." He reminded himself that he had been on the warpath and so should not be afraid of something as harmless as a young girl at a dance.

The band moved from one tune to another. Listening closely, Jimmy thought he heard a polka. Watching closely, he thought he recognized polka steps being performed on the packed earth. He saw his cousin Jeff dancing what appeared to be a polka with a horse-faced girl. He hated the idea of Jeff being braver than he was, so he started walking.

As he made his way across the playground, Jimmy tripped again. He blamed his big boots. He blamed his unhappiness. Whatever was to blame, he was not graceful on his feet. He would have to be crazy to ask a pretty girl to dance. But then everybody already thought he was crazy, so what did he have to lose? He just hoped he wouldn't trip on the dance floor and fall on top of her. He reminded himself that he wasn't just awkward but also ugly. His hand went up and touched the patch over his ruined eye.

And then there was that damn birthmark that made him look even uglier. He touched it, too. The mark was just a series of small purple dots arranged much like the stars in the Big Dipper, only it had a couple of extra stars in its handle. The pointer stars of the Dipper's cup lined up not with the North Star but with his missing left eye, with his patch. The birthmark seemed to be pointing at the patch, making sure nobody missed it, not that many ever did. With his patch, with his birthmark, he would have to be crazy to think that any girl would–

"Scuse me," Jimmy mumbled. "Wanna dance?"

Rachel, the pretty girl in the yellow dress, didn't say anything. He couldn't tell whether she was shy or just hadn't heard.

"Wanna dance?" he asked louder.

She looked uncomfortable.

"No," she said at last. "I'm sorry."

Jimmy raced his running-heart back across the playground. He felt clumsier than ever and uglier than ever. And he even felt less white. He didn't belong here with these people.

Standing with the horses once again, Jimmy couldn't help thinking about Lifts Something. She hadn't refused to dance with him. She had been willing to love him. But she was–

No, stoppit, Jimmy scolded himself. Don't think her name. Don't think about the past at all. How many times did he have to remind himself? Wouldn't he ever learn?

Although he was discouraged, Jimmy felt he owed it to himself to pick out another girl, work up his courage, and ask her to dance. He wished he could see the girls better, not just whether they were pretty or not, but whether they looked sympathetic. He found his curiosity–or whatever it was–focusing more and more on a redhead with freckles. He really couldn't see her spots or even the color of her hair in the dim light, but he had seen her at school and church and knew what she looked like. He told himself that she was much prettier than the first girl he had asked. He should have started with her. What had he been thinking of? He didn't really know her, but everybody said she was nice. She wouldn't hurt his feelings. This girl's name was Sarah.

When the band played another polka, Jimmy gathered his courage and made another clumsy charge across the dusty dance floor. He didn't trip this time, which he took to be a good omen.

"Scuse me," he repeated the formula. "Wanna dance?"

Sarah looked embarrassed. Jimmy couldn't think of anything else to say and didn't know what to do. He just stood there.

"I'm sorry," Sarah said at last.

Jimmy shook his head. He couldn't believe it. What had happened to all her niceness? His expression asked: Why not?

"I cain't," she said.

"You cain't?" he asked. His face said: Why would you hurt me?

"My daddy told me not to," she whispered.

Jimmy turned and fled once again. So that was it. The girls' parents had told them not to dance with the savage. They believed he was unclean. They thought he was half-heathen. They knew he was crazy because he was always talking about the biggest canyon in the world, the prettiest place in the world, the best ranching country in the world–which they figured was about as real as the Seven Cities of Gold. They didn't want him touching their daughters. He would show them. Maybe.

Jimmy said goodbye to the horses and started walking home.

2

Fall was beautiful but hard. The leaves changed colors overhead, but on the ground the crops needed harvesting. The hay had to be mowed with hand scythes. Corn ears had to be gathered in. Worst of all, cotton, the cash crop, had to be picked, which was backbreaking work. And of course school started again. But at least the weather turned cooler in the fall and the fair came to town.

Jimmy, who had never been to a fair, wondered what it would be like. In his early years growing up in the family fort at the edge of the frontier, no fair dared to come around. Sideshow strongmen and two-headed ladies were as scared of Indians as anybody else. Of course, there hadn't been any country fairs in the big red canyon where the Humans lived. At fair time last year, the family hadn't taken him because they could see that he was still more Crying Coyote than Jimmy Goodnight. They hadn't known how he would respond to the crowds, or how the crowds would react to him. Maybe they had been a little ashamed of him. Anyway, everybody had gone to the fair but him. Back then, his aunt had stayed with him one day while his uncle took the rest of the family to the fair. The next day, his uncle guarded him while his aunt and the others went out for a good time. Crying Coyote hadn't really understood what he was missing, but he knew he was missing something. This year, Jimmy would be going to the fair.

After church, the family changed out of their Sunday-go-to-meeting clothes and then piled into the grey wagon. Even the old plow horses seemed to be excited about going to the fair. They tossed their heads and pulled with a sense of purpose. The road got rougher and more crowded as it neared the fairground.

When Jimmy finally saw the fair from afar, he was amazed; it looked like a Human village. As he drew closer, he could see the differences: these tents were made of canvas rather than buffalo hides. Also, these canvas shelters were larger than Human tepees. But in spite of all the differences, Jimmy still felt more and more at home as he rolled nearer and nearer the tent village.

The spirit of this village on the outskirts of Weatherford didn't seem so different from the spirit of the village in the deep canyon. This one, like that other one, was crowded with children and dogs, and rang with noisy good humor. This one, like that other one, churned up its own dust storm. Jimmy smelled the dust and the bodies of animals, the bodies of children, the bodies of adult men and women, and he smiled. Then he sneezed.

Jimmy's Uncle Isaac passed out nickels to the children, including his adopted nephew. Each one got one. Then the kids were on their own. Rhoda and Naomi ran off hand in hand. Jeff had too much teenage dignity to run, but he shuffled away rapidly. Jimmy just stood for a while staring down at his nickel, turning it over and over, studying the shield on one side, then the big number 5 on the other. He felt rich.

Looking around for someplace to spend his new wealth, Jimmy saw that the canvas tents were arranged in a large, imperfect circle. At the center of the circle, the hub of the wheel, a crowd had gathered. From time to time, a cheer would go up from this mob.

"What's that?" Jimmy asked, pointing.

"Come see," said Uncle Isaac.

Jimmy followed his uncle and aunt to the edge of the crowd at the center of the circle. Standing on tiptoe, he could see a blacksmith's anvil in the middle of the mob. He recognized a big farmer. Well, he had seen him before, but he couldn't remember his name. He recognized him by his size. He was a real giant. His back was bent. The muscles of his arms bulged out. His face turned red and then purple.

Jimmy heard what sounded like a gunshot, and he saw the giant stumble backward, lose his balance, and sit down hard on the ground, raising a great cloud of dust. He swore loudly, causing Aunt Orlena to put her fingers in her ears. Then Goliath started picking himself up off the ground. When he was upright, he swayed a little unsteadily on his feet and then hurled himself at the anvil again. He seemed to want to strangle the dead chunk of iron. But a skinny man wearing some sort of apron managed to get between the giant and the anvil.

"Hold your hosses," Jimmy heard the skinny man yell. "You'll git another turn. But first you gotta gimme another nickel. And then I gotta put in a new handle."

"I don't understand," Jimmy said.

"What?" asked Aunt Orlena, who still had her fingers in her ears.

"I don't understand," Jimmy said a little louder. "What's goin' on?"

"He's trying to pull the ax outa that there anvil," Uncle Isaac said.

"What?" asked Aunt Orlena.

"There's an ax stuck in that there anvil," his uncle explained.

"Really? I wanna see."

Jimmy worked his way through the crowd to get closer. Soon he saw the blade of an ax plunged into an anvil as if the chunk of iron were a wood stump. The ax's handle was splintered. Jimmy scratched his head and wondered. He looked around and found his aunt and uncle standing right behind him. Aunt Orlena had taken her fingers out of her ears, but she still appeared uneasy.

"How'd that happen?" Jimmy asked. "How'd that ax git in there? Is it some kinda trick?"

His uncle scratched his head. He was trying to figure out how to explain something complicated to somebody with limited English.

"A cyclone done that," Aunt Orlena said. "A twister. You know what I mean?" She spun her finger in a circle.

"Uh-huh," Jimmy said.

"Well, that old twister just picked up that there ax," she said, "and stuck it in that there anvil clean as a whistle. It was some kinda miracle. The kind of miracle that often turns up in cyclones. I heard tell of a hoe handle got stuck plum through a tree trunk. And another time a piece a straw–"

"Mama," Uncle Isaac said, "you're wanderin' off the subject."

"I just thought he'd be interested in all them there miracles," Aunt Orlena said. "Gawd works in mysterious ways."

"Anyhow," interrupted Uncle Isaac, "that there ax got stuck in the anvil durin' a twister way back. I don't recall just when. Anyhow nowadays it travels 'round the countryside, and bigguns try an' pull it out. But the most they ever do is bust the handle."

"Oh," said Jimmy.

He could see the skinny man with the apron replacing the splintered handle with a new one, pushing and hammering.

"How come they wanta pull it out?" Jimmy asked. "Won't that kinda ruin the whole thing? I mean there's lots a axes. And there's lots a anvils. But there's only about mebbe one anvil with an ax stuck in it. Only about one in the whole world. So why bust 'em up? I don't git it."

Uncle Isaac scratched his head and took a deep breath. Answering all these questions was turning into work.

"It's vainglory," said Aunt Orlena. "All vainglory. They just wanna show how big and strong they think they are. They don't care about miracles."

"That and the thousand dollars," said Uncle Isaac.

"What thousand dollars?" asked Jimmy.

"The thousand you git if'n you pull the ax out," said his uncle.

Jimmy took a moment to do some figuring. He hadn't learned much math yet in the one-room schoolhouse, but he was pretty sure this proposition was mathematically unsound.

"I still don't git it," he said. "That guy ain't never gonna take in enough nickels to make a thousand dollars. Where's he gonna git the prize money at?"

"He don't need no prize money," Uncle Isaac explained, "because nobody ain't never gonna pull that damn ax outa that goddamn anvil."

"Don't blaspheme," said Aunt Orlena. "Besides, them nickels add up."

When a new handle was firmly in place, Goliath paid another nickel and stepped up to the anvil again. He spit on his huge hands and rubbed them together. Then he grasped the handle and pulled up with all his might. His back bowed as if he had hooked a whale and was having trouble landing it. His eyes bugged out. His veins were thick vines climbing up his bare arms and across his face. This time the wooden handle remained whole, but something broke inside Goliath. He let go the single-bladed ax and grabbed his stomach. He was in so much pain he couldn't even stand up straight. Jimmy turned away from the suffering. He had seen enough hurting in his life, too much, and was anxious to move on.

"Let's–" he began.

But then he realized Aunt Orlena and Uncle Isaac were no longer behind him. He had been so engrossed in the giant's struggle to rob the anvil of its ax that he hadn't noticed them go. The boy was on his own at the fair.

Not knowing which way to turn, Jimmy sniffed the air searching for an aroma worth pursuing. He smelled cow manure to the west, pig shit to the south, horse droppings to the east, and sugar to the north. Following the sweet scent, Jimmy approached a tent that looked like all the others but smelled like a house in a fairy tale.

Peeking into the gingerbread tent, Jimmy saw not only fragrant ginger loaves but also pies and cakes and cookies on parade. Walking down a procession of pies, Jimmy noticed a blue ribbon beside one of them (apple) and a red ribbon brightening another (lemon meringue) and a white ribbon decorating a third (mince). Moving on, he reviewed whole brigades of cookies, some wearing more red, white, and blue bunting. Unable to resist, Jimmy bent down so his nose almost touched a plate of brownies and sniffed loudly. When he saw people scowling at him, he turned away self-consciously and hurried out of the fairy-tale tent.

Hearing shouts and laughter, Jimmy glanced back in the direction of the miraculous anvil. Another giant was attempting to separate what had been joined together by the cyclone, or the god of cyclones, or the Great Mystery, or maybe even Aunt Orlena's grumpy Jehovah. Who could say? The ax and the anvil were obviously great crowd-pleasers. Jimmy considered paying his nickel and taking a turn, but five cents was a lot of money. Besides, if fully grown giants couldn't budge the ax, what chance had a tall but skinny boy who had just turned eighteen? He decided to be smart and save his one and only nickel and spare his back.

Continuing to explore, Jimmy entered a large tent on the west side of the circle and saw a herd of cattle. He was surprised because the Human Beings never allowed animals inside their tepees. This race of "Writers" continued to puzzle him.

Jimmy admired the biggest, fattest, handsomest bulls he had ever seen in his life. They were wonderful to look at but horrible to smell. The tent locked in and intensified the odor of dung. He could hardly bear to breathe, but nobody else seemed to notice anything unusual or unpleasant. Making a hurried tour of the cattle tent, he saw more blue, red, and white ribbons. Curiously examining a blue one, he discovered that it had writing on it: FIRST PLACE. A red ribbon proclaimed: SECOND PLACE. And a white one said: THIRD PLACE. So Jimmy finally worked out that he was observing some sort of contest. Writers were so competitive. Unable to stand the stink any longer–

cattle dung smelled much worse than buffalo chips–Jimmy made his way back out into the open air.

When he heard yells and laughter, Jimmy knew where to look for the source. He soon found himself heading back in the direction of the anvil and the ax. He hated the thought of parting with his newly acquired nickel fortune, but he was nonetheless drawn to the blade in the block of iron. He realized he wasn't as strong as the big farmers who had failed one after the other, but he had begun to wonder if maybe the giants weren't relying too much on brute force. He had begun to hope there might be another way to coax the ax from the anvil.

When he reached the center of the circle, Jimmy found a crowd of big old farm boys daring each other to try their luck. He walked up to the skinny man in the apron and took out his nickel, but the seller of chances didn't notice him. He wasn't being rude. He just had no idea that such a beanstalk would attempt to outpull giants.

"Excuse me, mister," Jimmy said, "I'd like to give it a try."

The seller of chances was caught off guard and laughed before he could stop himself. His laughter proved contagious. Soon all the big men and strapping boys were laughing, too. The merriment grew and grew as the news spread outward from the center of the crowd. Jimmy overheard them telling each other that the half-wit didn't know any better . . . that he had a weak mind and weaker back . . . that he had gone savage and thought he was better than white folks . . . that the white savage was gonna fall on his damn ass and they were all gonna enjoy it. He saw them pointing as if he were some animal on display. Now he wished he had never seen that anvil, that he had never coveted that ax, that he had never come to the fair. He wanted to run, but he didn't want to give them the satisfaction.

"Here's my nickel," said Jimmy, handing over his riches with a wince. "Git outa the way."

"Okay, Chief," the apron man said. "Go to it."

Hearing the laughter and the jeers, Jimmy stepped up to the anvil, dropped to his knees out of respect, and then addressed the mass of iron in the Human tongue.

"Excuse me, O Great Anvil," he began, speaking the way the Sun Chief had taught him to speak. "I've got something to say to you. Uh. Something important. Uh. I have great respect for your strength. Uh. I hope you also have respect for my weakness. I couldn't possibly take your ax away from you, so I won't try, but I hope you will give it to me willingly. You see, I need it a lot worse than you do. I need your ax so people will stop laughing at me . . ."

Meanwhile, the crowd continued to laugh and mock. "Look, he's prayin' to it!" "He looks like he wants to hump it!" "He's makin' love to it!" On and on . . .

"I need your ax so they will respect me," Jimmy droned on. "I could also use the thousand dollars. Let's be honest. O Anvil, Great Anvil, Mighty Brother, please release your grip of steel. I will take good care of your ax. I will oil it and sharpen it. I will keep it with me always. So what do you say?"

Jimmy got up off his knees, rose to his feet, placed his hands on the wooden handle, and pulled gently as if helping up a girl who had fallen down. Realizing full well that he couldn't overpower the ax or the anvil, he didn't try. He didn't strain. He was tender to the ax, kind to the anvil. He thought he felt a slight relaxing of the metal grip, but he wasn't sure.

"You will never leave my side," Jimmy said in the Human tongue. "You will be my constant companion. If you help me, I will help you. You will no longer be a spectacle. You will no longer be pawed by strangers. My home will be your home. What do you say?"

He pulled a little harder, but it didn't feel right, so he tugged even more gently. He imagined that he had asked a young girl to dance, and she said yes for a change, and so he took her by the hand and was leading her to the dance floor.

"Come with me," he said softly to the iron. "Come dance with me."

Jimmy felt the anvil loosening its iron grip, felt the ax surrendering itself to him. He wanted to hurry, but he told himself to be patient. Slowly, easy now, gently. He gave the slightest tug and drew the ax from the anvil.

The crowd swallowed its mean laughter and seemed to choke on it. It couldn't get its breath. It gasped. Jimmy smiled and raised the ax high over his head. The crowd fell utterly quiet and everybody started backing up to give him room. Somebody at the back of the crowd cheered. Then other voices took up the hurrah. The cheering was as contagious as the laughter had been. The cheers became a mighty yell.

Horses whinnied. Roosters crowed. Bulls snorted and kicked up red dirt. A donkey brayed. A red-tailed hawk screamed high overhead. Mice squeaked, grasshoppers leapt high in the air, spiders stopped their weaving and looked around. Prairie dogs came up out of their burrows to see what had disturbed the universe. A turtle hurried. A baby cried in its mother's arms. An old diamondback rattled its tail. A single drop of rain fell out of the pale blue sky and hit Jimmy right between his good eye and his bad one.

Blinking, Jimmy stared up at the ax in his hand, at the sky, at the sun. He let out a scream that began as a war cry but ended in laughter. He shook his new weapon at the heavens, and bees buzzed loud about his head.

They started coming early the next morning. The first one, the town blacksmith, was waiting in the yard when Jimmy emerged from the house to do the milking. The smith approached the boy–who carried a pail in one hand, his new ax in the other–and said: "Mawnin', Jimmy. If'n you're willin', I'd sure be proud to go see that there red canyon."

By the time Jimmy had finished his milking, two others, big farm brothers, had joined the blacksmith. They too wanted to see the biggest canyon in the world. He hurried inside, a timid leader of men.

While he was eating breakfast in the kitchen, Jimmy watched the yard fill up with men of all sizes and ages. They talked among themselves and waited patiently. They were in a good humor, smiling and laughing. Jimmy was already beginning to think of them as his men.

Still shy, still hesitant, Jimmy finally worked up the courage to venture outside. His new volunteers crowded around him. He was puzzled, intimidated, even frightened by what he saw written on their faces. They saw him as a leader while he saw himself as a follower. But that would have to change because he couldn't disappoint these faces. He had to pretend that he was the man–the leader–he saw reflected in their believing eyes. He desperately wanted to be the man they saw, but how did you become a leader?

He thought about the shaman. Should he take off all his clothes and paint himself yellow? That would certainly get their attention, but it might just compromise his dignity. Did you need dignity to lead? Maybe he should ask the tallest tree he could find. Or the fastest horse. Or the meanest bull. Or try to talk an eagle out of the sky. Hey, come on down here and give me some good advice. Or maybe, like Moses, he should just strike up a conversation with a lowly bush.

Should he change his walk? Could he deepen his voice? What

about his posture? Certainly that could be improved. Head up, shoulders back, gaze on the horizon? He tried it but soon slumped again. Should he speak faster or slower? Louder or softer? Should he say more or say less?

How had Sam Houston done it? How had Lincoln? Or Robert E. Lee? Or Jesse James? What was their secret? And was it always the same secret? Were there as many secrets as there were leaders?

What was he going to do? Or not do? How was he going to make sure he didn't disappoint people? Didn't let anybody down?

At long last, he more or less persuaded himself–although he still harbored doubts–that he did have one advantage: He knew where he wanted to go and what he wanted to do when he got there. He was fortunate to have a dream.

3

On a fine April morning, Jimmy Goodnight and his outfit perched on the rim of the canyon that stretched beneath them as deep and measureless as time. He felt his good eye trying to stretch itself to take in such a vast and gorgeous panorama. He had begun to worry that he had lost his ability to see beauty, but now he was blind to it no more. He had gotten his eye back.

Turning his attention from the canyon to his men—Coffee, Too Short, Simon, Black Dub, Tin Soldier, and Suckerod—the boss watched their faces as they stared down into the abyss. He hoped he had chosen his cowboys wisely. Three times as many had wanted to come, but he had limited the size of his crew to the bare minimum he felt he couldn't do without. On the brink of the abyss, the boys' wisecracking and ribbing had suddenly stopped. The outbursts of laughter had died away. Jimmy Goodnight thought his bunch looked almost reverent. They were behaving as if they had ridden into the biggest church in the world rather than to the edge of the biggest canyon on earth. Well, anyway the biggest one Jimmy had ever seen or heard tell of in Texas. The sight of the canyon confirmed his prophecy and him as the prophet. He had not parted the Red Sea but rather the red earth itself. Now his men were once again looking at him with that look: the look that said they trusted him. The look that made him all the more determined not to let them down. He had to live up to their look, and he had to live up to the canyon. He couldn't disappoint any of them.

"Take a good look," Jimmy Goodnight shouted. "Ain't this the purdiest sight"—he reveled in the superlative—"you ever seen in your life?"

But his boys had been struck dumb by the void before them and didn't answer. They looked so solemn, they were funny. He wondered if they were more reverent or more afraid? They stood perched on the rim of the known world. They had come to the boundary that separated the everyday from the extraordinary. They were acting as if they had reached the edge of the earth and were worried they were going to fall off.

Then the cook did go over the edge: the four mules that pulled his chuck wagon spooked, stampeded, and charged right out into the void. Poor Bob Wanger, better known as Coffee, started screaming, which didn't help to calm down the mules any. The pots and pans in the chuck wagon were banging and clanging away, sounding like a blacksmith gone insane, which didn't help the mules' nerves any either. Jimmy Goodnight started laughing so hard he couldn't breathe. Poor Coffee was speaking some primeval language that didn't have any words in it but expressed fear eloquently.

"Let 'em run!" Jimmy Goodnight yelled when he got his breath. "You never seen a purdier place for a drive!"

Coffee tried to curse, but he was too scared for the words to come out right. Jimmy thought: He's screaming so loud he's liable to hurt hisself, and I'm laughing so hard I'm gonna hurt myself. He wondered who would get hurt first. It seemed like some kind of race.

Jimmy Goodnight laughed even harder when the bedrolls started bouncing out. This chuck wagon was just a regular wagon with a kitchen cabinet built on the back of it. Pots and pans and coffee and beans and flour rode in the cabinet. And all the cowboys' bedrolls traveled in the bed of the wagon. But now the wagon was bouncing so high and so hard that everything that could get out did get out. The cowboys were so pleased to be revenged on Coffee–who somehow made red beans taste like coffee and coffee taste like red beans–that they didn't even mind seeing their bedding scattered all over the side of the canyon. The freed bedrolls were racing each other down the steep inclines, hopping, jumping, having a good old time.

Then the chuck wagon door, the cabinet door, banged open, spilling out the coffee pot and the bean pot and pans and metal plates and tin cups. The plates raced the bedrolls to see who could get to the bottom of the canyon first.

Jimmy Goodnight didn't think he could howl any harder, but then he did. All the cowboys were laughing except Coffee–until they saw a big bag of coffee bounce out of the back of the chuck wagon. The cloth bag burst open and scattered coffee across the canyon cliffs. Then a bag of flour followed, exploded on impact, and left a white scar on the red face of the canyon wall. Now that was carrying the joke too far.

The mules seemed to agree, for they tried to call a halt to their reckless race down the cliff. They put on the brakes so fast that the chuck wagon almost ran over them. Their hooves skidded on the loose canyon scree. But eventually the wagon did start slowing down.

Jimmy Goodnight kicked his horse–Mister Goddog by name–and hurried forward to see if his cook was alive and his wagon still in one piece. They both appeared to be in better shape than they had any right to be.

"Nice drivin'," drawled Jimmy Goodnight.

"It ain't funny," Coffee said, his chest still heaving.

"You okay?"

"I bith my tongue."

"Sorry. We better take the wagon apart and pack it down in pieces. It's almost apart already, huh?"

The cowboys got busy rounding up the bedrolls that hadn't rolled too far. They would pick up the others as they made their way on down into the canyon. The cowboy named Too Short Johnson roped a maverick coffee pot so he didn't even have to get off his horse to pick it up. Too Short was small and wiry, with black hair and a drooping black mustache. It was too long just as he was too short. But on a horse he was tall enough and could outrope most men. He tossed the coffeepot to the cook, who accidentally dropped it and watched it roll on down the canyon. Too Short started the laughter and the other cowboys joined in.

"I'm gonna poison all you sons-a-bitches," Coffee threatened. "I'm warnin' you sons-a-bitches."

"We ain't the ones that run away," Too Short pointed out. "Poison them damn mules."

"Naw, but you laughed."

"You wouldn't kill a man just for laughin' when somethin's funny."

"Naw? Well, I'd sure watch what chew eat if'n I was you."

Jimmy Goodnight decided it was time to make peace. If he was going to live up to that look in their eyes, maybe he should try starting now. He decided to give an order and see what happened.

"Okay, boys," said the boy boss, "git busy and pick up that spilled coffee 'n' flour." He straightened up taller in his saddle. He spoke slower. He was trying to copy how the shaman would have done it–short of taking off all his clothes and painting himself yellow.

"Pick it up?" protested Coffee. "It'll be full a dirt!"

"Prob'ly taste better," said Too Short.

"Don't worry," said Jimmy Goodnight. "We'll strain out the biggest rocks. Now git to it. You, too, Coffee."

Strangely enough, the cowboys–Coffee too–obeyed his order. They climbed down off their horses, balancing on the steep canyon side, and started picking up coffee and flour. Since the sacks had exploded, they collected these staples in pots and pans. Seeing his men respond to his order, Jimmy Goodnight felt he had passed another test. He didn't bother to tell them that he was who he was, the boss he was, because of what he saw in their eyes. It was as if the mirror made the man, rather than the man making the reflection.

"Pick it up a grain at a time if'n you have to," chimed in Simon Shapiro, who had the biggest hat. "They ain't another store like my daddy's for a month a Saturdays, so we gotta make this here grub last."

"You mean a month a Sundays," said Coffee.

"No, I don't neither. I'm Jewish and mighty damn proud of it. Month a Saturdays. Trouble with you, Coffee, is you don't take no pride in nothin'. You drive too fast and cook too slow. Course your cookin' slow's a mercy, come to think on it."

Coffee picked up a rock and cocked his arm.

"Take it easy," said Jimmy Goodnight. "You know Simon don't insult you less'n he likes you. It's kinda a compliment."

"Hate to have the son-of-a-bitch in love with me," Coffee said.

"Don't worry," said Simon. "Chances are real slim you're gonna cook your way into my heart. You dunno matzo balls from calf balls."

"That's enough fun," Jimmy Goodnight said. "Git back to work, both a ya."

Then once again he waited to see if "his" men would obey him. He was pretty sure he could handle Coffee, but he wasn't too sure about Simon. For Simon came from a different class. He was richer and better educated than the rest of the boys, but he didn't talk like it because he wanted to fit in. Perhaps for the same reason, he got right down to work picking food up off the ground.

Simon's father, a successful merchant in Weatherford, had substantially outfitted this expedition. Of course, some money had changed hands, but not much. The flour and coffee and other staples scattered all to creation had been more or less his gift. It had been the father's way of supporting his son's participation in a venture that he didn't entirely approve of. The merchant had said he hoped his boy would get cowboying out of his system and come back to the store one day. But if he didn't return–if this wild red-canyon scheme worked out–then his son would probably have a more interesting life than he himself had had. Jimmy Goodnight hoped that if he ever had a son, he would be as understanding. But, well, he wouldn't count on it.

Simon's participation had meant that Goodnight could save most of the $900 he had won at the county fair for future expenses. Of course, he had supposedly "won" $1,000, but he had been forced to take $100 on account, which probably meant he would never get it. The fair had claimed the $900 was all the ready money it had on hand. Jimmy's uncle told him he was lucky to get that much.

When they finished picking up all the coffee and flour they could find, the cowboys attacked the chuck wagon with hammer and crow bar. Black Dub Martin, who had been a slave as a boy, did most of the heavy lifting because he was the biggest and the strongest. He had been one of the strongmen who broke an ax handle trying to pull the blade from the anvil that memorable day at the fair. Black Dub single-handedly lifted the cabinet off the back of the wagon and tied it to the back of a mule. They didn't have to jack the wagon up to take its wheels off. Black Dub just picked it up, one end at a time.

"Hey, we don't need no mules," said Tin Soldier Jones. "We got Black Dub. He could pack this sucker down all by hisself. And he'd think it was fun."

Tin Soldier, the very first volunteer, who had been a blacksmith back home in Weatherford, owed his name to the steel helmet he had made for himself at his anvil. It looked sort of like an upside-down pot, but it had a spearhead on top. If worse came to worse, he could butt his enemies to death.

They pulled apart the wagon and attached the pieces to the mules as best they could. So, instead of *pulling* the chuck wagon, the poor mules had to carry it down on their backs. It was going to take several trips. Served them right for running away.

"We better start workin' the cattle down," Jimmy Goodnight said. "Don't rush 'em. Take it nice 'n' easy."

Soon his cowboys began feeding the 1,600 longhorns down single file. This herd had cost nothing except the effort it had taken to round it up. Which was considerable. During the Civil War, when the men in Texas marched off to fight the Yankees, their cattle ran off. Now the state was full of wild longhorns–owned by nobody–hiding out in the brush-and-breaks country. So Jimmy Goodnight and his bunch had just helped themselves to a herd.

The longhorns followed a narrow, four-mile Comanche trail that Jimmy Crying Coyote remembered from his life among the Human Beings. Jimmy Goodnight wondered where the Humans were now. He had expected a few curious braves to make an appearance by now. He was looking forward to a reunion with old friends and relatives. He hoped he might even see the Sun Chief again. He felt sure that the vast red canyon was big enough for both Writers and Humans, for both his cattle and their shaggy, heavy-headed, hump-backed "Human-cattle." He planned to suggest that the boundary line be the bloodred river that ran down the middle of the canyon. He would ranch the land south of the river and leave the territory north of the river for the Humans. Or the other way around. It didn't make any difference to him. He looked forward to proving to the world–or at least to Texas–that red men and white men could live in peace and friendship together. And who was better prepared to lead such an experiment than he was?

Goodnight supposed that his cattle represented the first domesticated cloven hooves ever to leave their tracks on this wild path, this trace. They seemed nervous but not badly frightened as they wound their way down toward the center of the earth. It was slow work. The cattle trickled down into the canyon all morning, then all afternoon and on into the evening. As the light began to fail, Jimmy Goodnight knew that he would soon have to call a halt to this single-file cattle drive. The Comanche trail was dangerous enough in broad daylight but would be impossible in the dark.

"Hold 'em up!" Jimmy Goodnight yelled. "Bring them that's started down on down, but don't start no more. Pass the word up." He felt he was beginning to get the hang of this leadership thing. He sure hoped so.

So that night the herd was divided, half on the rim above, half on the canyon floor below. Jimmy Goodnight assigned Tin Soldier and Black Dub to stay on top and look after the cattle up there. The rest of the cowboys would spend their first night in their new home, the red canyon.

4

The next morning while his men continued working the cattle down, Jimmy Goodnight began reexploring the canyon, reacquainting himself with its network of narrow interlocking gorges and washes. The design reminded him of the pattern of lines on the palm of his hand. He looked at his palm, which he cupped slightly, then back at the canyon, then back down at his hand. He smiled to himself. And he wondered: Was this canyon the palm of the Great Mystery's hand? He spit in his right palm. Had he just created a flood? He rubbed his hands together and put such nonsense out of his head. But he half-expected it to rain. All day long, the cattle kept coming down.

By nightfall, the entire herd had reached the floor of the canyon, where the cattle feasted on tall clumps of buffalo grass. They drank from the river that divided the canyon. And they were fenced in by the high walls of the canyon. Goodnight's herd was as secure as if he held it in the palm of his hand.

The next day, Jimmy Goodnight and his men began pushing the herd along the floor of the red canyon, which grew wider and wider. Crying Coyote had been happy in this place, and Jimmy Goodnight felt he would be happy here once again. He believed this red canyon had a benevolent spirit.

His reveries were interrupted by Suckerod Lawrence, who had been riding point, but who was now approaching at a gallop. Suckerod shook all the time because of an accident he had had as a boy. He had fallen off a windmill, had broken many bones, and had been expected to die. When he lived, folks started calling him Suckerod because of his connection to windmills and because he was so tall and skinny. The windmill's sucker rod was the slender rod that went up and down, up and down, sucking water from deep in the earth. The first time Jimmy Goodnight met Suckerod, he thought he was a nervous wreck, maybe even a coward, but he soon learned that this cowboy was one of his steadiest and bravest men. He just shook.

"We got company," Suckerod said when he got close enough. "Buffalo up ahead."

"They in our way?" asked Jimmy Goodnight.

"'Fraid so. Mebbe we better hold up the herd. Huh?"

"Ya think so?"

"Well, last thing we need's for somethin' to spook them woolly heads, then for them woollies to spook our cows."

Jimmy Goodnight knew there was plenty to be concerned about. He and his men could easily be caught in a double stampede of cattle and buffalo. The canyon walls would funnel and intensify the fury of this living flash flood of animal flesh. The walls would also cut off any route of escape. He imagined his whole outfit being swept away on a fleshy flood tide.

"I better go take a look," Jimmy Goodnight said.

He, Suckerod, and Too Short rode up ahead of the herd to see about the buffalo. They found ten thousand shaggy animals stretched from one side of the canyon to the other like a majestic army barring their way. Somehow this formation would have to be breached if the longhorns were to reach the lower valley where the best grazing was.

"Less go, Mister Goddog," Jimmy Goodnight said. "Giddyup, ol' boy."

Tightening his legs around his horse, he rode ahead of the others. He studied the great beasts carefully, not as a herd but as individuals. He was looking for a particular buffalo. No, not this one. Not that one either. Telling himself not to hurry, he rode slowly along the fringe of the herd looking, looking, looking. While he studied the animals, he could feel his men studying him. He knew he puzzled them, but he couldn't worry about that now because he had just found what he had been searching for: the chief of the herd.

Turning Mister Goddog, Jimmy Goodnight, the chief of his outfit, rode out to meet the Chief of the Buffalo. The lesser animals scattered before him, turning and running, kicking up their heels, bucking, but the old chief just turned to face him, lowered his heavy head, and waited. Jimmy Goodnight rode at a slow walk, not wanting to alarm the herd, not wanting to show disrespect for the chief. When he was about twenty yards from the old bull, Goodnight reined in Mister Goddog and stopped.

"Excuse me, O Chief of the Buffalo," he began in the Human tongue. "I have something to say to you. We do not need your meat because we have brought our own meat. So we will not harm you or yours. I come simply to ask a favor."

Jimmy Goodnight wondered if the buffalo chief was listening to him. He couldn't tell whether he had made any impression on the old bull or not.

"O Chief of the Buffalo, hear me," he said. "There is enough grass for your herd and my herd. There is enough water for your herd and my herd. There is enough room for your herd and my herd. I ask only that you allow my cattle safe passage through your herd of Human-cattle. We wish to reach the lower canyon. And you are in our way. So please move. How about it? What do you say?"

The Chief of the Buffalo just stood there and stared. Jimmy Goodnight stared back. Glancing over his shoulder, he saw the cloud of red dust that signaled the approach of his herd of cattle. He felt nervous, but he tried not to show his uneasiness either to the buffalo chief or to his men. Still, he wondered if he had made a mistake in not halting the cattle before they got this close. Why hadn't he? Did he want to show off? Well, it was too late to change his mind now.

"Excuse me, O Chief," Jimmy Goodnight said. "I hope you will stay calm. I hope your followers will stay calm. We don't need a lot of running here. You don't need it, and we don't need it. All we ask is that you remain quiet and let us pass. What do you say?"

He felt Too Short and Suckerod edging up to him. He knew they had expected him to do more than have a chat with the buffalo herd. They had figured he would yell and shoot in the air and get the woollies the hell out of the way before the longhorns got too near. But he hadn't. Now he and his men were trapped between the two herds, and it was too late to make a lot of noise because it might set off a living avalanche. Normally, a cattle herd moved at the slow, steady pace of the seasons, but this one seemed to be hurrying toward him. He could already hear them mooing and smell their bodies and their shit. The great cloud churned up by their hooves looked like a red cyclone.

"We better git outa here," said Too Short.

"No place to git to," said Suckerod.

"Excuse me, O Great Chief of the Buffalo," Jimmy Goodnight

tried one last time in the Human tongue. "Please move out of my way. I don't mean to hurry you, but it's time to go. I'm telling you this for your own good as well as my own. What do you say?"

The buffalo chief turned slowly and walked back through the great sprawling mass of his woolly subjects. And as he moved among them, the herd of buffalo parted. They moved to the left and to the right, leaving an open path in the middle.

Not even Jimmy Goodnight was sure–really sure–why the buffalo herd had parted. Maybe they saw the approaching cattle herd and just decided to get out of the way. Maybe they didn't like the way cattle smelled. Maybe they were worried about all those long horns. But he didn't think so. Jimmy silently thanked the Sun Chief for all he had taught him.

Jimmy Goodnight, Too Short, and Suckerod rode at the head of their cattle herd, which passed right through the middle of the herd of buffalo. A river of long horns flowed through an ocean of short horns and woolly shoulders.

"Just like the Red Sea," said Suckerod. "Gawddamn!"

"This ain't no time to cuss," said Jimmy Goodnight. "Don't press our luck."

"I take it back," said Suckerod.

5

Jimmy Goodnight, former Human Being, decided to go looking for the Humans. They normally pitched their tepees on the banks of the river that had carved this canyon, so he planned to follow the red water until he found their village. He rode alone because he didn't imagine any of his cowboys would be anxious to accompany him in search of what they would think of as trouble. Besides, he thought the Humans would be less nervous if they saw a lone rider approaching.

He wished his *Tuhuya* would go faster, but he didn't want to wear him out because he didn't know how far they had to go . . . *Tuhuya* . . . "Goddog" . . . Yes, he had thought "horse" in the language of the Humans. He was thinking in the Human tongue again as he made his way toward them. His iron-shod Goddog made deep, well-sculpted tracks in the soft, deep, red-clay riverbank.

The longer Jimmy Goodnight rode, the stranger it seemed that he saw no trace of the Human Beings. The red canyon felt eerily empty, like a deserted house. Where could they be? Lots of answers occurred to him. They might be out on the High Plains following the Human-cattle. But the humpbacks were here. He had seen them, thousands of them. So why weren't the Humans here, too? Of course, if they were nervous and hiding out, they could have taken refuge in one of the many arms of the labyrinthine canyon. That seemed the most logical explanation. But then how would he ever find them?

Maybe he had better just count on them finding him. He figured they would locate him faster if he made a little noise. Jimmy Crying Coyote let out a loud Human cry that echoed down the red canyon, and then he laughed at himself. He laughed again when he wondered how hearing that cry was affecting his cowboys. They were probably all reaching for their guns and trying to keep from peeing in their pants. He let out another cry to scare his boys and to alert his relatives to his homecoming.

But the red canyon was still an empty house. Jimmy Crying Coyote's questions were turning into concerns. Now he urged Mister into a trot. He was in a hurry to get some place, but he wasn't sure where.

He scanned the ground as he passed over it, looking for shoeless Goddog tracks, searching for any trace of the Humans. He saw lots of Human-cattle spoor. He found the place where a herd of deer had come down to the river to drink, carving beautiful tracks with their chisel hooves. He paused where raccoons had visited the stream to wash their food before they ate it. They left miniature hand prints in the clay. He even saw the tracks of a couple of bears and one mountain lion. But he did not see any Goddog tracks or any other sign of the Humans. He was beginning to get frightened.

Jimmy Crying Coyote took his cap-and-ball revolver out of his holster and raised it over his head. Its grip felt strangely like a plow handle in his hand. He thumbed back the heavy hammer and shot a hole in the bright heavens. The reverberation seemed to shake the red walls that appeared to hold up the blue ceiling. The Humans *must* hear such an explosion. They were either very frightened, pulling deeper into their holes, or they weren't in their favorite canyon at all. He stood up in his stirrups as if a few inches more would help him to find what was lost in this vast place. He fired two more shots. He stood in his saddle again. Still nothing. He emptied his gun at the sky as if the single cloud up there were his enemy. He didn't rise in his stirrups this time because he didn't think it would do any good. He rode on in silence, sinking lower in the saddle with every mile, but he kept going.

The sun was sinking and the heavens reddening to match the canyon when he saw the two buzzards circling, black specks in a red world. He shivered either because of the cool of the evening or because of the specters overhead. Turning Mister Goddog, he left the river and tried to follow the buzzards. He wanted to see what they saw. Or rather he didn't want to see it, but he had to find out. He rode into an arm of the canyon that was a small canyon itself. Kicking Mister, he galloped, stirring up a red cloud.

When he saw the bones, Jimmy Crying Coyote let out another cry. It was not a war cry. It was not a hailing cry, for he no longer had any hope of the Humans hearing him. It was a cry of mourning. For he believed he had found the Human Beings at last. The bones completely filled the little canyon. The canyon was a vast open grave.

Jimmy Goodnight pulled Mister Goddog to a halt. He didn't want to see any more, but he urged his horse forward once again and headed deeper into the canyon. He continued to stare at the ground, not because he was looking for tracks, but because he had found the place where all tracks ended. He walked his mount, then trotted, then galloped. He had to see and be sure.

Reaching the mountain of bones, Jimmy Crying Coyote jumped from his horse. He swayed on his feet as if he were drunk. Picking up a large bone, he wondered how such a giant could ever have lost a battle. Then he reminded himself that guns killed giants and dwarfs alike. But then he picked up a skull that was too big to be a Human skull, too large even to be the skull of the largest giant. It was the unmistakable skull of a Goddog. Climbing the mountain of bones, Jimmy Crying Coyote found more huge skulls, more great leg bones. He examined enormous bone chains that were the spinal columns of Goddogs. There weren't any horseshoes, so he knew who these animals had once belonged to. Climbing the white mountain, his boots slipped and skidded on bones. He fell on bones. He rolled in bones.

The former Human Being kept looking for Human bones mixed in with the bones of their Goddogs, but thankfully he found none. All he saw were the bones of their mounts. He could not imagine what had happened, but he knew that it must have been a terrible disaster for the Humans. Their wealth had been destroyed. They must now be a poor people. They were probably also hungry since they would not be able to hunt the Human-cattle without their Goddogs.

Examining the bones more closely, he found round holes in many of the skulls. They had been shot. They had been systematically murdered by an enemy with an endless supply of bullets and cruelty. He thought it over carefully: the only people with access to that many bullets had to be the United States Army. He tried to count the skulls, but it was impossible, there were so many of them. He figured maybe a thousand, maybe fifteen hundred, maybe as many as two thousand dead Goddogs. The greatest riders in the history of the world would now have to hunt their food and face their enemies on foot.

Jimmy Crying Coyote, Human Being, sat on the mountain of bones and sang a death song for his people: "O Sun, you live forever, but we must die. O Earth, you remain forever, but we must die."

6

Goodnight felt two ways about the cowboys who smoked. He disapproved of the use of tobacco, but he still felt sorry for his boys who were addicted to it because they had long since run out. Every morning, Goodnight watched with amusement what had become a regular ritual. One by one, the cowboys would shamble over to the large stump of an old cedar tree where they would get down on their knees. Were they praying? No, they were picking up old, dry, ugly coffee grounds. Every morning after breakfast, Coffee the cook would bang his old, dented coffee pot against the cedar stump to knock out the dregs. And every afternoon, the cowboys would drop by the stump, pick up the dry grounds, roll them inside cigarette papers, and smoke them. Too Short rolled, lit up, and then made a face. Goodnight smiled.

Tobacco wasn't the only thing the Home Ranch was out of. They didn't have any flour or cornmeal. They didn't even have any beans. They ate meat three meals a day. Wild turkey for breakfast. Bear meat in the middle of the day. And buffalo at night. For variety, they would switch the meats around.

And then they ran out of coffee, too.

Goodnight was especially fond of buffalo meat, which he had come to love during his life as a Human Being, but his cowboys didn't like it much. They thought it was too tough. Most white men would shoot a buffalo and skin it and cut out its tongue and leave the rest for the flies and buzzards. But Goodnight insisted on using the entire buffalo. The steaks were broiled. The marrow bones were roasted and then cracked open. The tongue was buried in coals overnight. Goodnight loved buffalo, but even he would not have minded having a biscuit to go along with it. The shortages led inevitably to short tempers. Flare-ups were most likely to happen at mealtimes when the boys were most reminded of what they didn't have.

"Hey, Too Short," Simon said one night at supper, "I heard some disappointed lady was the one give you your nickname. Any truth to that there rumor?"

"Goddamn you!" growled Too Short.

He threw his dinner–buffalo steak again–at Simon and then dove on top of him. Tin plates and tin cups went every which way. Food landed in the dirt. The two brawlers rolled into the campfire and hurriedly out again.

"Black Dub, you wanna break that up?" Goodnight asked.

Black Dub got unhurriedly to his feet, walked over to the cowboys wrestling on the ground, grabbed both of them by the hair, and lifted them off the ground. He wouldn't put them down until they both promised to be good.

Finally, Goodnight knew something really *had* to be done when he started dreaming about beans every night. He normally considered beans the bane of the cowboy's existence. Now he missed them, longed for them, had visions of them. It was time to go get some supplies. High time.

Goodnight took Too Short, Suckerod, and Coffee with him. The cook drove the chuck wagon, which would be used to haul the provisions back to the Home Ranch. They headed north toward Tascosa, a brand-new town, which was a little over 150 miles away. Goodnight led them up yet another Comanche trail that climbed the steep red walls. Zigzagging slowly, they climbed out of the sheltered canyon, bound for the harsh plains. Heaven and hell had somehow gotten mixed up, turned upside down: for you descended into this cattleman's paradise, but you climbed up to the constant winds and baking sun of Hades. Goodnight thought: How about that?

The hardest part was getting the damn chuck wagon from heaven up to hell. Goodnight had picked a trail that wasn't quite as steep this time, and the wagon was empty, so they didn't have to take it apart. But it kept getting stuck. Goodnight, Too Short, and Suckerod all had to get down off their horses and push. Their boots slipped and skidded on the scree. Sometimes it seemed that the wagon was going to run away backward, dragging the poor mules behind it, and running over the cowboys. They wedged rocks behind the wheels to try to prevent such a calamity. And then they pushed harder.

When all that work finally got them up on top, Goodnight wondered why anybody would go to so much trouble to reach such a depressing panorama. The land was as flat as a flapjack and about the same color. The sun was doing its best to melt the riders as if they were pats of butter. Goodnight remembered how much he liked flapjacks, how much he missed them, how much he would love to bite into a stack of them right now, even the way Coffee made them. He dreamed his dream of pancakes as he rode wearily across the pancake earth.

After they had gone fifty yards, they could no longer see any trace of the great red canyon. It disappeared as if it had never existed. Had it been just an illusion? Could it be a hole in the mind rather than a hole in the earth?

On all sides, Goodnight saw nothing but the bleak Staked Plain, what the Mexicans called the Llano Estacado. Some said the name was supposed to refer to stakes placed across the featureless face of the plain to mark a trail. Others said the markers weren't stakes but rather piles of rocks arranged to show the way. Which made more sense because there wasn't any wood to make stakes out of on this treeless tabletop. Who left these markers? Some said it was Old Coronado playing Hansel and Gretel, but his stakes–or piles of rocks–were long gone by now. There wasn't anything at all to navigate by except, of course, the punishing sun.

When the lazy sun finally began to descend and shadows stretched out forever on the tableland, Goodnight called a halt. There was no obvious place to make camp because one corner of the table was no more inviting than another part. So Goodnight did what he knew a leader had to do: he made an arbitrary decision, but he did it convincingly, so it didn't seem arbitrary. He wondered if he might actually be learning to lead men.

There was no wood to burn. They picked up dried buffalo chips to make their campfire. They all chewed on dried bear meat. Then they rolled up in their smelly saddle blankets and went to sleep.

7

On the third day, Jimmy Goodnight heard Tascosa before he saw it. The sound of gunfire carried a long way in the dry air across the flatland. There were no mountains or trees to absorb it. Goodnight wondered if the town could be under attack by the Human Beings. If so, he wasn't sure whose side he would be on. And so he hoped for some other sort of trouble.

Goodnight urged his horse to go faster and the others followed his lead. Even the chuck wagon's wheels turned over a little more rapidly, but the animals weren't yet running full tilt. The town was still invisible, but the shooting grew louder.

When the roofs of Tascosa finally rose up over the flat horizon like the sails of advancing ships, Jimmy Goodnight spurred his horse into a gallop. Suckerod and Too Short stayed right behind him. Coffee and the chuck wagon couldn't keep up. Goodnight looked but couldn't see any Humans harassing the town. He was thankful. But if not the Humans, then who? Then what? Then why? Reaching down to the rifle scabbard that was tied to his saddle, he felt not the stock of a long gun but the head of a single-bladed ax. Now he began to wonder if he had made the right choice, bringing along his lucky blade instead of firepower. Well, it was too late to change his mind now.

Goodnight pulled back slightly on the reins and slowed Mister Goddog. He had been in a hurry to find out what was wrong, but now he didn't want to gallop blindly into trouble. Slowing to a walk, he drew his revolver from the holster buckled around his waist. Glancing to his left and right, having to turn his head farther one way than the other, he saw that both of his men had their rifles out now, carrying them across the pommels of their saddles. He noticed that Tascosa seemed to be constructed mainly of adobe, which made sense on a treeless plain where lumber was even scarcer than tobacco.

Leading the way, Goodnight advanced on Main Street at a slight angle, so he couldn't see down it. But he didn't really mind because whoever was shooting couldn't see him either. He cautiously approached the mud-brick blacksmith shop, which stood at the end of Main Street. When he finally reached it, he dismounted quietly and peeked around the corner.

Goodnight saw a tree stump in the foreground and in the background somebody getting hanged. He blinked his good eye anxiously, trying to see. The hanged man began to look like a hanged woman. Goodnight blinked again and refocused. She was a woman all right. She had on a light grey dress that blew in the gusting wind. She was hanging from a pole that extended from the second floor of an adobe hotel. It was probably a fence post that somebody had carried upstairs and poked through a second-floor window. It looked like a fishing pole with the woman dangling at the end of the line like a caught big-mouthed bass. And she was flopping like a fish. She was surrounded by cowboys who were laughing and whooping and shooting in the air. Goodnight felt his face heating up as he got angrier.

Then he noticed something strange about this hanging. The poor woman, whose feet were well off the ground, had both her hands up in the air, well over her head. She looked as if some robber had pulled a gun on her and ordered, "Hands up!" Goodnight stared harder.

"What's goin' on?" asked Suckerod, who had come up behind.

"Looks like they're hangin' some ol' gal," Goodnight said. "She's kickin' but won't die."

"Less see," said Too Short, who had also arrived.

He moved around Goodnight so he could take a look. Then he started shaking his head.

"What is it?" asked Goodnight, the one-eyed man.

"They're hanging her by her thumbs," Too Short said.

"No." Goodnight's face got hotter. "Who are they?"

"Dunno," said Too Short. "Could be the boys from Robbers' Roost. They say they're partial to havin' a good time."

Goodnight had heard a lot of stories about a place called Robbers' Roost that was located somewhere on the Canadian River, which ran parallel to the red canyon. They said it was ruled by an outlaw named Jack Gudanuf–of all things–who was rumored to have an extensive ear collection. He was supposed to be a tall, thin man with long blond hair who didn't look like a robber. In fact, he was said to be the best-looking man in West Texas. Of course, there wasn't much competition because there weren't many men, handsome or ugly, in this part of the state. Still, Goodnight felt slightly intimidated by the pretty robber. His hand reached up and touched his patch and then stroked the purple stars of the Big Dipper. He couldn't help it. Then he scratched his ear while he wondered if that business about a collection could possibly be true. Goodnight told himself that it was time to stop woolgathering and do something.

"Let's mount up," he said at last. "We'll ride in bold as brass like we don't know nothin's goin' on. When we see what's up, we'll make out like we think it's great. You know, whoop it up. Shoot in the air. And then git the drop on 'em. Leastwise try to. Okay?"

The other two nodded.

"I reckon we better play like we're drunk," Goodnight added. "Anybody know any good drinkin' songs?"

The other two looked puzzled, trying to think.

"All I know's cow songs," said Suckerod, his hands shaking.

"I think I can recollect some church songs," said Too Short.

"Bless you," Goodnight said with a grin, "but that ain't just the attitude we're tryin' to strike. Cows it is. Less go. Put your guns up for now."

Goodnight, Suckerod, and Too Short moved cautiously to their horses and tried not to make any noise as they mounted. In spite of their care, the saddle leathers seemed to make a terrible racket. Once they were all settled, Goodnight nodded and they all rode forward.

Rounding the corner of the blacksmith shop, Goodnight was still angry, but he also felt nervous and a little foolish. He knew he wasn't much good at pretending. He was sure he wouldn't be able to fool anybody. He was even afraid his own men would break up laughing at him and so give the game away. He took a deep breath between lips forming a counterfeit smile. When he saw the hell-raisers turn and look in his direction, he started swaying drunkenly in his saddle.

"Come on, Suckerod," Goodnight whispered, "sing."

The cowboy who knew cow songs shook more than ever.

"Come a tie-yie-yay," Suckerod sang softly. "Git along little dogies . . ."

"Louder," whispered Goodnight.

"You sing too," Suckerod whispered back. Then he raised his voice and sang: "Come a tie-yie-yay, git along little dogies, for it's your misfortune and none a my own . . ."

"Come a tie-yie-yie," Goodnight sang drunkenly, "giddiyup li'l' dogies, fur iss yo' mishfor–mishfor–bad luck and none a my own . . ."

Too Short was moving his lips, but no noise seemed to come out.

"Come a tie-yie-yay," Suckerod sang again.

"Sing the next verse," sang Goodnight.

"Thass all I know," sang Suckerod. "Git along little dogies. Sing, Too Short. For it's your misfortune . . ."

Too Short moved his lips faster, but still no music came out.

"Sing!" Goodnight ordered.

"Just give me that ol' time religion," Too Short sang. "Iss good enough for me . . ."

"Come a tie-yie-yay," sang Suckerod.

"Come a tie-yie-yie," sang Goodnight and then hiccupped loudly.

While he was playacting, he watched the outlaws talking among themselves. They were obviously trying to decide what to make of the newcomers.

"Come a tie-yie . . . old time religion . . . your misfortune and none a my own . . . good enough for me . . ."

Goodnight relaxed slightly when he saw smiles breaking out on the faces of the badmen. He swayed even more wildly in the saddle and almost fell off his horse. He told himself that he was playacting a little too much. Taking his revolver out of its holster, he fired it in the air and let out a yell. He watched to see how the outlaws would take it, but they didn't seem to mind. Maybe he was a better actor than he realized. Well, he just wished he had a bottle, just for show, a prop. He tried not to look at the suffering girl because he couldn't afford to let his fury show.

"Wasss goin' on?" Goodnight slurred.

His choir fell silent. He could hear his own breath, which seemed louder than usual. Not a good sign. He hiccupped again when he saw a tall, good-looking outlaw step forward.

"Just havin' a little fun," said Jack Gudanuf. "Who wants to know?"

Goodnight swayed again in his saddle and this time lost his balance completely and fell to the ground. He lay in a heap in the dust without moving. He had almost fallen on the leader of the outlaws and now huddled at his feet. When he had worked up the nerve, Goodnight started drunkenly climbing up Gudanuf's leg as if it were a tree.

"No," the outlaw protested, "stoppit."

Reacting instinctively, Gudanuf reached down to pull the drunk cowboy to his feet, not because he wanted to help, but because he wanted to get the soused slob off him.

"Come on, git up," Gudanuf said. "Git up."

Stumbling to his feet, Goodnight bear-hugged the outlaw as if clinging to keep from falling down. He knew the badman wouldn't be able to turn his gun on him as long as he hugged him tightly. Goodnight felt an urge to reach up and touch his patched eye, and the small constellation beneath it, but he had his hands full.

"Git off me," Gudanuf said.

Goodnight tightened his grip with his left hand but stopped hugging with his right hand, which still clutched his pistol. Still moving drunkenly, staggering, almost knocking the outlaw over, he placed the muzzle of his gun under Gudanuf's chin.

"Quit it," the outlaw demanded. "Stop pawin' me."

Goodnight jammed the gun into Gudanuf's throat so hard it hurt. The outlaw grunted.

"Drop your gun!" Goodnight ordered in a sober voice. "Drop it or I'll shoot your head off. Right now!"

He felt the outlaw trying to decide what to do, so he pressed the steel even harder. The badman coughed.

"Ouch!" he said like a little boy.

"Drop it!" Goodnight said again. "And tell your men to drop their guns, too."

Now Suckerod and Too Short had their revolvers out covering the other five bad men, who were caught by surprise. The outlaws had superior firepower, if they chose to use it, but the first one who tried to shoot was bound to get killed. And their leader would certainly die.

"Better do what he says," Too Short said. "He's the boss."

Gudanuf opened his hand and let his pistol fall to the ground. Then one of his men dropped his gun. Then another and another. The firearms fell and lay in the dust the way the "drunk" cowboy had fallen a short while before. Goodnight stopped hugging the chief of the outlaws and stepped back.

"Suckerod, git her down," Goodnight ordered.

The trembling cowboy rode over to the suspended woman and lifted her up onto his saddle with him. She sat sideways in front of him.

While keeping the outlaws covered, Goodnight moved to his

horse, pulled his lucky ax out of the rifle holster, and handed it to Suckerod's quaking hands. The cowboy used the sharp ax blade to cut the ropes that were tied to the young woman's blue thumbs. Then he lowered her to the ground where she collapsed and lay in a heap.

Goodnight knelt beside her. "Are you aw right?" he asked, knowing that she wasn't.

He wanted to touch her, to comfort her, but he was afraid touching would be too familiar. If she hadn't been quite so beautiful, he would have behaved naturally and reached out to her. But instead, he just knelt there in the dust feeling foolish.

Now that the outlaws were no longer dangerous, the townspeople poured back onto Main Street, most of them carrying weapons. There were buffalo guns and carbines and brooms and clubs and even a couple of muskets. An old man with white hair actually carried a sword. The mob milled about, crowding around the young victim of the hanging. Now that it was all over, she started crying.

A man wearing a suit and tie approached, knelt beside her, and touched her on the back. She looked up at him and tried to smile. Goodnight was surprised to feel a twitch of jealousy. When the man started unknotting the ropes still tied around the young woman's thumbs, Goodnight felt cheated. He had saved her and so he should have been allowed to minister to her. Citizens of the town were thanking him and congratulating him, but he hardly paid them any attention.

Goodnight studied the young woman being cared for by the other man. She appeared slightly taller than average. Her hair was either dark blond or light brown. Her figure was ample. Goodnight felt a little ashamed of himself for noticing. Was he being unfaithful to Lifts Something? Her legs were a little too thin. He was glad to find something wrong with her.

8

Telling himself he had better get back to business, Goodnight turned his attention once again to the outlaws. He was afraid they might attempt to make a break for it in all the confusion. Or they might try to retrieve their discarded firearms.

"Okay, you boys," Goodnight addressed them, "you better just line up in the middle a the street so I can keep an eye on you. Come on. Less go."

He herded them with his single-bladed ax in one hand and his revolver in the other. They moved slowly but eventually obeyed.

"Okay, that's purdy good," Goodnight said. "Now you better just kneel down like you was prayin'. Wouldn't hurt you none to really pray."

They knelt in the dust in the middle of the road. Now that the outlaws seemed utterly defeated and on their knees, the townspeople descended upon the gang's horses and started pulling money, jewelry, watches, and silverware out of the saddlebags.

"Where's the jail?" Goodnight asked.

"We don't got none," said a fat man with an apron tied around his waist. He probably ran the big store or tended bar. "Nobody wanted to pay for no jail. Hangin's a lot cheaper. I'll even throw in the rope free of charge." So he was the storekeeper.

The rest of the citizens murmured their approval: hanging was the best way, the cheapest, the fastest, the surest. The outlaws on their knees started praying in earnest.

"I dunno," said Goodnight. "Let's not be hasty."

He sensed all the good citizens looking at him as he pondered what to do. He just felt instinctively that it would be wrong to rush into a multiple hanging. He wished there were some judge or lawman to turn to for an answer.

"Where's the sheriff?" Goodnight asked. "Hadn't we better ask him?"

"We ain't got none," said the storekeeper. "Too expensive."

Goodnight told himself he should have known. No jail. No sheriff. This was sure some skinflint town. Too damn cheap to buy any law and order. Well, if law was too expensive, then there ought at least to be some rules. The Humans had rules that depended upon a just balance. A balance between man and nature. A balance between man and man. Goodnight figured the Writers of Tascosa could stand some balancing, too. How else could they ever work out what was right and what was wrong, what was just and unjust.

"Lemme ask you somethin'," Goodnight said.

"Fire away," said the storekeeper.

"Did these boys kill anybody here this afternoon?"

The outlaws kneeling in the middle of Main Street began to protest that they had not. Goodnight noticed that Gudanuf didn't look quite so handsome now that he was all dusty and humbled. That was a kind of justice in itself.

"Are they tellin' the truth?" asked Goodnight.

"Reckon so," said the storekeeper. Then he shouted, "Anybody lost anybody?" Nobody raised a voice. "Guess they ain't killt nobody. Far as we can tell. Not here anyway. Not today anyhow." He thought for a moment. "But they shot up the town purdy good. It was just a pure dee accident nobody got hisself killt."

"So they ain't killt nobody," Goodnight said. "Did they have knowledge of any a your women?"

"You mean–?" asked the merchant.

"That's right. Did they or didn't they?"

The men kneeling in the street once again protested their innocence. They might have pillaged, but they didn't rape.

"Not that I heard tell of," said the man in the apron, embarrassed. "You mind if I don't shout that question all over town?"

"Well, I'd like to know the answer."

"I'll ask around."

Goodnight watched the prudish storekeeper moving through the crowd, whispering to first one person, then another. And one after another shook his or her head.

"Reckon not," the apron reported at last. "No complaints of, well, what you said. But the way they handled Miss Revelie, they weren't doing her no good, you unnerstand."

Once more, the kneeling outlaws began to protest. Goodnight walked over and stood in front of Gudanuf to hear what he had to say.

"We didn't mean no disrespect to Miss Revelie," the outlaw chief stammered. "We was just after money. And we knowed her daddy was holdin' out on us. Knowed he had a whole passel a money hid somewheres. An' we was aimin' to find it. We thought about hangin' him up by his thumbs, but he's a purdy tough ol' bird. So we figured it'd be faster to work on his daughter. But the son-of-a-bitch still wouldn't spill. Look, he's worse 'n we are. Makin' her suffer an' all."

"Shut up!" ordered Goodnight. "You talk way too much."

He pondered again. His mood darkened when he noticed the well-groomed man kissing Miss Revelie's swollen, discolored thumbs. Angry at the fortunate man, he glowered at the unlucky badmen on their knees. Then he made up his mind.

"Well, here's how I see it," said Goodnight, and everybody listened. "Killin's a hangin' offense, I reckon, but they ain't killt nobody." He put his ax over his shoulder. "And foolin' with women ag'inst their will, now that's a hangin' crime, too, but they didn't." He rocked the ax on his shoulder. "So as far as I can figure out, they're guilty of robbin' and just plain meanness. That's bad. That's real bad. But that ain't enough to hang six grown men. Not in my book."

The citizens of the town groaned and protested. The reverent robbers looked relieved.

"Now wait a minute," the fat storekeeper raised his voice. "Who give you the right–?"

"I caught 'em," said Goodnight, "and I reckon that gives me the right. So as I was about to say, we oughtn't to hang 'em, and we cain't lock 'em up, but we cain't just let 'em go neither. So I figure we better just make the punishment fit the crime. Like it says in the Bible, an eye for an eye, and a tooth for a tooth." He paused a moment thinking it over. "A thumb for a thumb."

He could hear the townspeople and the outlaws all wondering out loud what he was talking about. He let them mull it over for a while.

"So here's the deal I'm offerin' these boys here," Goodnight announced at last. "They can either pay for their crimes with their necks or with their thumbs. It's up to them."

And he brandished his ax. Goodnight noticed some of the citizens starting to smile and the outlaws looking very hangdog.

"That's butchery!" cried Gudanuf, the talkative outlaw. "That's savagery. That's heathen. You're still a damn savage. You shouldn't oughta be allowed to mess with Gawd-fearin' white folks."

"So you've heard of me?" asked Goodnight.

"I heard a your damn ax."

"I see. And you'd rather these good Gawd-fearin' white folks stretched your necks than that a savage like me messed with your thumbs? Okay, fine by me. Boys, let's go."

Goodnight turned his back and started walking away.

"No, come back," begged Gudanuf. "You cain't let 'em hang us. It's like you said. We didn't kill nobody. You gotta be fair."

"My justice or theirs?" Goodnight said. "Necks or thumbs? Make up your minds. I hope I'm a fair man, but I ain't a patient one. So let's have it. Which'll it be?"

Gudanuf just knelt in the dust and looked like he was going to cry. He looked at his thumbs, first one, then the other, then looked up at the impatient Goodnight.

"Right now!" said the self-appointed judge.

Gudanuf bowed his head and put his hands over his face. Goodnight nudged him with the blade of his ax. The outlaw looked up.

"I don't wanta die," Gudanuf admitted at last, his voice choked. "I guess I'd rather lose my thumbs than lose my life. If that's the only choice you're givin' me. But it ain't fair."

"Good," said Goodnight. "Now how 'bout the rest a you? Necks or thumbs?"

He stared at them as they grumbled.

"Shut up! I'm tired of listening to you. You're aggravatin' me."

One at a time, they made up their minds, then held out their thumbs, as if giving happy thumbs-up signs, but all the lines on their faces turned down.

"You first, Gudanuf," Goodnight said.

"You've heard of me, too?" asked the outlaw.

"Less go. Git up. Come on."

When the boss of the badmen got to his feet, Goodnight took him by the arm, turned him, placed the muzzle of a revolver between his shoulder blades and marched him down the middle of Main Street.

He noticed smirks on the faces of the townspeople as they accompanied him and his prisoner. He knew that they were thinking that they would have preferred a hanging, but a good thumb-chopping might be fun, too, and more novel. Well, he couldn't help how they felt. He couldn't prevent their having a good time. He couldn't stop their enjoying what was going to happen to the outlaws. He tried to tell himself that a mob of Human Beings would have behaved differently, but he didn't convince himself. He figured Human nature and human nature were probably pretty similar in this respect. Goodnight didn't stop until he reached Henry Kimball's blacksmith shop.

"Okay, Gudanuf, step right on up to that there tree stump," Goodnight ordered.

"Looks sorta like a choppin' block, don't it?" said Too Short.

"Put your right thumb on top. Come on, don't be shy."

While Gudanuf hesitated, Goodnight stared at the tree stump, which had been sawed off flat. What was it doing here? This was a treeless plain. Where had it come from? It looked like an ancient mesquite. He wished he knew its story.

"You heard him," said Too Short, nudging the outlaw in the back with his gun. "Git!"

Reluctantly, Gudanuf did as ordered. The townspeople murmured and gaped and crowded in to make sure they got a good look.

"Move back," Goodnight said. "Give us some room."

Stepping around in front of the outlaw, Goodnight measured the stroke with his ax. He lowered the blade so it just kissed the thumb, then raised it, shifted his feet, got ready. He noticed the outlaw had his eyes closed. He didn't blame him. He started his swing–then at the last moment stopped. He wasn't sure he could do it.

Taking a deep breath, Goodnight gathered himself again. He had to do it, so he might just as well get it over with. But at the last moment, he stopped again. No, he couldn't do it. Yet surely he had to do something. He wondered if the pretty girl was watching his hesitation. Did she find it unmanly?

Goodnight shrugged and turned the ax on his shoulder. When he swung, the blunt end, not the blade, came down hard on the outlaw's outstretched thumb. There was a crunch as if somebody had stepped on a beetle with his boot.

Gudanuf screamed. Then he opened his eyes and looked down

and saw his thumb still attached to his hand and probably couldn't believe it. Tears rolled down his face, but he smiled. His thumb was much flatter than it had been before, but it wasn't twitching in the dust.

"Thank you," the outlaw said.

"Well, I figured you didn't spill no blood," Goodnight said, "so I reckoned I wouldn't neither. Now t'other thumb."

9

Goodnight was actually tired. He was surprised to find that busting a dozen thumbs had turned out to be hard work. He supposed that the emotional strain involved in causing so much pain must have made the chore all the more draining. The head of the ax rested on the ground as if it were tired, too. Goodnight leaned on the ax handle as if it were a cane. He rubbed the back of his arm across his sweating forehead. It was too hot for such manual labor.

He watched the outlaws mounting up. The citizens had wanted to keep the bad men's horses and make them walk out of town, but he felt they had suffered enough. Besides, he figured they would have died out there in the badlands if they had been on foot. And if he had wanted them dead, he would have just hanged them in the first place.

Goodnight couldn't help feeling sorry for the badmen, who looked so awkward as they tried to figure out how to ride with busted thumbs. They had trouble getting up because it hurt to grab the horn. They didn't know how to hold the reins without using their thumbs. They reminded Goodnight of children who didn't know what they were doing but were trying hard.

The army of townsmen—who were plenty brave now that the outlaws were not only disarmed but would have had trouble cocking guns if they had had any—escorted Gudanuf and his gang out of town. The citizens fired in the air the way the badmen had done earlier. And the white-haired old man hit the leader's horse in the ass with his sword. He turned it broadside and used it like a paddle.

"Excuse me, sir," said an unfamiliar voice.

Goodnight turned to see the well-groomed man who was the object of his jealousy approaching him. He wanted to turn away but prevented himself from doing so. The man had on a high, clip-on collar. Stuck in the short lapel of his suit coat was some sort of pin that looked like a medal for something. Goodnight now noticed a vest beneath the jacket and, most remarkable of all, velvet britches. He reached up and touched his patch and his stars.

"Hello, allow me to introduce myself," said the suit, waistcoat, and tie. His pronunciation sounded funny. "My name is H. B. Sanborn."

Then he stuck out his hand. Goodnight didn't want to shake it, but he told himself not to be childish. They clasped hands.

"My name's Jimmy Goodnight," he said.

"Glad to meet you, Mr. Goodnight," said Sanborn.

"Likewise," lied Goodnight.

When the handshake was over, he didn't know what to do with his hands. He wanted to touch his patch again, but he remembered that he had just done so.

"I would like to thank you," said Sanborn, "for what you did for my daughter."

Goodnight sensed his face stretching into a stupid grin, but he couldn't stop it. He felt silly, but he didn't really care. He even found that he liked the look of a good waistcoat and didn't even mind velvet britches.

"Why, you're right welcome," Goodnight said. "I'm just glad we could help."

The daughter, who still looked weak, came forward to stand beside her father. Her dad put his arm around her to steady her.

"Mr. Goodnight, m-m-my name is Revelie Sanborn," she introduced herself in a quavering, uncertain voice. "I would like to th-tha-thank you personally. I wish I could shake your hand, but I'm afraid it would h-h-hurt."

She moved the thumb on her right hand back and forth to see if it still worked. It was too bloated to move as well as it normally did. She studied it with a frown.

"Jimmy," he said. "Call me Jimmy."

"What those m-m-men said about my father wasn't true," she said. "He had already given them all the money he had. They just wouldn't believe there wasn't any more. That's why they did that to me."

Goodnight touched his patch. He noticed that her face was still wet from crying. He saw that her eyes were green and bloodshot.

"I cain't help myself," Goodnight said. "I've gotta just come right out and tell you. You're the purdiest sight I've ever seen in my life."

Then he saw that he was embarrassing her, and her embarrassment embarrassed him. He wished he hadn't been so open and frank, for he appreciated the position he had put her in. Obviously, she couldn't repay the compliment. She certainly couldn't tell him that he was the prettiest sight she had ever seen. She would be a bald-faced liar.

"Thank you again," Revelie said. She seemed to be trying to think of something else to say, but she was stumped. Then her face cleared. "Would you come to supper tonight?"

"Yes, do come," said her father.

"Sure," said Goodnight. "Sure thing."

Goodnight spent the rest of the day buying supplies and looking forward to and worrying about supper. He called on the storekeeper whose name turned out to be I. M. Wright, but who was generally referred to as I Am Wrong, which he didn't seem to mind. Goodnight purchased gallon cans of Arbuckle coffee. He added gallons of A&P sorghum to sweeten the coffee and life in general. He chose Calumet baking powder with a Human chief in full headdress pictured on the cans. He also bought sacks of flour and meal and many tins of tobacco of which he disapproved.

Before the invitation, he hadn't planned a bath or a shave or a haircut, but now he decided he had better put up with this waste of time and money. So he paid a visit to the barber, where he cleaned up all over.

Then Jimmy Goodnight took a walk down Main Street until he came to a rickety footbridge thrown across Tascosa Creek. The banker and his daughter lived in a single-story home built on the bank of the creek. He reached for his eye patch, touched it as if it were both talisman and curse. Then his fingertips trickled over the stars on his cheek. Now he was ready to knock on the door. Revelie, her thumbs bandaged, opened the door gingerly.

"This is the purdiest house I ever seen in my life," Goodnight said right away. "It sure is."

Then he saw once again that Revelie didn't quite know how to respond to his superlative.

"I'm glad you think so," she said at last.

"It's a shack," said a woman in a red dress. "Nothing but a shack."

"Mother, this is Mr. Goodnight," Revelie said.

She was a striking woman who wore a pinafore that made her look like a little girl–or a doll. It resembled a fancy apron with lace ruffles at the hem and more ruffles over the shoulders. It was spotless white, starched, and tied in the back with a bow. She also wore white gloves.

"Not Mr. Goodnight," he said. "Please just call me Jimmy."

"I don't know you well enough," said Mrs. Sanborn. "Are you a religious man, Mr. Goodnight?"

The guest wondered how it could be that this woman–who didn't know him well enough to call him by his given name–nonetheless felt she did know him well enough to question him about something as personal as religion.

"No," he stammered. "I'm a teetotaler but not religious."

Natural beauty always made him feel reverent, but churches didn't.

"Then you've never read the Bible?"

"Well, frankly, ma'am, it's the only book I own, so I read it some. So I won't fergit how to read. And because it's full a good tales. But it's a little too bloodthirsty for my taste, ma'am."

"I see."

But Goodnight hoped she didn't. He had been trying to confuse her. He didn't like being cross-examined about religion.

"Thank you again for what you did this afternoon," Revelie said.

"Yes, thank you," echoed Mrs. Sanborn, "for that."

She had not been on the scene to see the rescue, and Goodnight had the impression that her daughter and husband had downplayed the incident so as not to worry her. So her thanks were not particularly warm.

Soon they were all seated around a table with real china and actual silverware. The tablecloth was white and crocheted. Goodnight had never sat at such a table in his life. It was far fancier than anything his aunt Orlena had ever attempted. He found himself thinking of it as a real Writer's table.

Goodnight felt that Mrs. Sanborn did not believe he was good enough for her table. She obviously did not approve of his easy first-name manners, and yet she talked with her mouth full of food. The nourishment in her talkative mouth was chicken. She evidently felt that eating beef was somehow plebeian. After all, cows were so common in this country. Goodnight didn't particularly like chicken.

"Don't you like your dinner, Mr. Goodnight?" asked Mrs. Sanborn.

"It's delicious," he lied.

"Then try to show a little more enthusiasm, Mr. Goodnight," she instructed. "My chicken is famous all over Massachusetts."

"I thought I made the chicken," said Revelie.

"Yes, dear, but you made it from my recipe," said her mother.

Knowing who cooked the chicken, Goodnight tried to like it better. But he still preferred beef or buffalo or even roast prairie dog.

Mrs. Sanborn did most of the talking at the table. Much of what she said was not just to impress but to intimidate. From her ill-spirited chatter, Goodnight began to piece together something of a history of the Sanborn family. They were from Boston, where Mr. Sanborn had graduated from Harvard College. Mrs. Sanborn didn't say anything about her own education. Besides providing the town of Tascosa with a heavy safe in which to store its cash, Mr. Sanborn also represented several wealthy English speculators who were anxious to cash in on an anticipated "beef boom." The British Empire seemed intent on buying back a part of the America it had lost. Goodnight had come to supper because he was interested in the daughter, but now the father began to interest him as well. For the rancher knew he needed capital. The Sanborn family had evidently come west only about six weeks earlier, and had found their new hometown to be considerably rougher than they had expected.

The visitor formed an impression that Mrs. Sanborn had come from a relatively poor Boston family but had somehow managed to marry up. Now she appeared to be determined that her daughter would not marry down. She had no wish to get mixed up in a drama that might be entitled "The Cowboy and the Lady." Or so the cowboy thought.

Goodnight, of course, wanted to make a good impression on the mother and father if possible, but most of all upon the daughter. And yet in spite of all his desire to shine, he found himself saying little more than "Yes" and "No." And he didn't even manage to say yes or no very often.

Growing more and more nervous as he said less and less, Goodnight–who could talk to Goddogs–realized he simply couldn't talk to Revelie Sanborn. He loved beauty, but he was afraid of it. He longed to get out of that dining room where he didn't feel welcome, but he was reluctant to go before he had succeeded in saying something that would convince Miss Revelie that he wasn't a complete nitwit.

And yet he couldn't think of anything.

10

Jimmy Goodnight sat under a chinaberry tree trying to turn himself into a Writer. He could hardly believe it himself. He had long considered Writers to be his enemies. He had gone on the warpath to rape and murder Writers. And now he wanted to become one. Now he needed to be one. For he was trying to write a letter to Revelie Sanborn. But he had missed too many school years to be able to write easily. During his days as a Human Being, he had always considered Writers to be too soft. But now he was in the process of revising that opinion. Being a Writer was harder than he had imagined.

He wrote, "Dear–"

But then he stopped because he wasn't sure how to spell her name and he didn't know what to say next. He studied his pencil, wishing it were a pen, which would have been more fitting. But he didn't happen to have a pen.

Finally, he scribbled, "Dear Miss R–" Then he wrote, "Thank you for diner."

He stared at it for a long time because it didn't look right. He wished he had somebody to check his spelling and grammar, but he wasn't sure any of his men could spell any better than he could. Besides, he didn't want any of his cowboys to read this letter. It was bad enough that Revelie would be reading it. He was actually breathing hard and sweating as if the pencil weighed a hundred pounds.

He wrote, "Will you marry me?"

Having done the hardest part, he got up and went for a walk. Now that the heavy lifting was done, he felt he had earned a rest. As he strolled beneath the walls of his canyon, he continued to worry about his letter. It pursued him. He had a feeling that he hadn't said enough, but had also said too much. He wished he could think of a way to soften the blow, but he had no idea how to go about it. Well, walking wasn't getting him anywhere. So he went back and sat down beneath his tree and picked up his heavy pencil.

He wrote, "I am ernest."

Then he couldn't decide how to say goodbye. He knew he couldn't say "Love." But he didn't know what else to say.

So he just signed it: "Jimmy Goodnight."

Then he went looking for Too Short, who would be his mailman.

Goodnight didn't know what to do with himself while he waited for an answer. He was normally an active man, but now there was nothing more to do to advance his cause. All he could do was passively hope for the best. Still he *had* to do something. He knew it had to be something with sufficient intrinsic interest to take his mind off the answer he awaited. Novelty would help. A little danger would be even better.

So Goodnight decided to rope a buffalo. When he announced his intention, Suckerod said he would be proud to go along. They saddled up and went buffalo hunting with lassos instead of buffalo guns. Riding southeast, they watched the red canyon open out wider and wider like a horn of plenty. They knew the buffalo generally preferred the broader and flatter part of the canyon. They didn't expect the beasts to be hard to find, but they rode a long while without seeing any sign of them. The Human Beings had disappeared from the canyon, and the Human-cattle were beginning to vanish, too. They rode past the small tributary canyon where the Goddog bones lay bleaching whiter and whiter in the sun.

But today Goodnight was more concerned with passing a few hours as painlessly as possible than he was with the passage of an era. He kept looking for buffalo but seeing Revelie's face. He kept rewriting his letter in his head, finding phrases that would have been much better, but they all contained words he couldn't spell.

Eventually, Goodnight located a small herd of buffalo in the lower canyon. He stood up in his stirrups to look for the herd's chief. Locating the largest bull, he rode slowly toward him. The animal turned to face the rider, lowering his shaggy head, pawing the earth in ritual fashion. When Goodnight was a dozen yards from the buffalo, he reined in his horse. The two chiefs stared at one another.

"O, Great Chief of the Human-Cattle," he said in the Human tongue, "I have a favor to ask. I need to git my mind off something, so I am looking for a little fun. I need your help. I am asking your permission to rope you. I will do you no harm. What do you say?"

The big bull raised his head and sniffed the air, then lowered it again. Goodnight hoped the buffalo was nodding.

"Thank you," he said.

Then Goodnight lifted his lariat and shook out a large loop. He yelled and slapped the rope against his chaps to make a racket. The rest of the herd started to run, but the old bull stood his ground. Goodnight thought roping a standing target would be about as much fun as throwing a loop over a stump, so he yelled again even louder and slapped his rope over and over. The bull reluctantly turned and started to trot. Goodnight fired in the air with his revolver. The bull ran faster and the roper gave chase.

Once he finally got moving, the Chief of the Buffalo proved to be fast in spite of his bulk. He soon caught up with the others and led the mad charge. As Goodnight tried to catch up, he heard the sound of dozens of hooves beating the earth like a drum, their drumbeat echoed and amplified by the canyon walls. They sounded like a stampede of thousands and almost drowned out Goodnight's throbbing doubts about his letter. Now he was able momentarily to shift his worries from Revelie to the danger of prairie dog holes that could break his horse's leg and send them both crashing to the earth. Then horse and rider would both be trampled to death. And there were prairie dog towns all over this part of the canyon. Beginning to overtake the bull, Goodnight started swinging his lasso over his head. Now he had to concentrate on what he was doing, which meant that he didn't have time to think about what he had no control over. His mind was right here, right now, which was where he wanted it.

Now! Goodnight threw his lariat. The rope seemed to float in the dry air, appeared to have a life of its own, was transformed into a flying snake. The living lasso fell over the buffalo's huge head and horns. As the rope tightened around the bull's neck, Goodnight reined in his horse, which stiffened its front legs and sat down on its haunches as it bounced to a stop. One end of the rope was wrapped around the saddle horn; the other was tied to a runaway locomotive. When the buffalo hit the end of the rope, the horse staggered and almost fell. Then Goodnight realized he was being dragged along, horse and all, behind the bull. Mister Goddog tried valiantly to hold his ground, but he couldn't and so went skidding across the red earth. The buffalo seemed to have roped the horse and rider rather than the other way around.

Suddenly, the bull stopped in a storm of dust. That was more like it. But then the buffalo turned and charged. Now Goodnight was really living right here, right now. The onrushing bull drove any concerns about grammar and spelling from his mind. Mister Goddog wheeled to try to get out of the way, but only succeeded in offering a better target. The bull hit the horse broadside, driving in its short horns. Goodnight hung onto the saddle horn as his mount reared. The horse came down on top of the buffalo, which seemed to drive both animals insane. They both started bucking, the bull below, the horse above, as if they were two halves of one monster.

Goodnight felt himself losing his hold and his balance. He fought desperately to cling to his horse's back, but it was no use. As he felt himself falling, he tried to jump clear of the thrashing hooves. He landed on his back on a rock. Wanting to put as much distance as possible between himself and the monster he had created, he tried to get up and run, but he found he couldn't move his legs. He was paralyzed. So he started crawling, or trying to, using his hands to drag himself along while his dead legs trailed behind him.

Goodnight grew even more alarmed when he saw the buffalo and the horse finally fight free of one another. For the old bull charged right at him. The fallen man started rolling over and over to try to get out of the way, but he knew it was hopeless. The buffalo chief was on top of him . . .

Then Goodnight heard a shot. And another. And another. Three explosions coming as fast as a repeating rifle could be cocked and fired.

The bull collapsed with his head across Goodnight's useless legs. As soon as he realized he was safe–as soon as he knew Suckerod had saved him–Goodnight started worrying about his letter. Was the spelling all right? How about the grammar? Why had he written it anyway when he knew very well that he was no writer?

Then he asked himself: Why had the bull charged him? Had he lost his ability to talk to buffalo? What about other animals? He wondered: Had this loss of powers begun when he found he couldn't talk to a young female of his own species?

The fear of being paralyzed for life reared up and momentarily drove his fears about Revelie from his mind. He saw himself lying in bed, a helpless cripple, until the day he died. Then his fears of paralysis combined with his fears of never winning Revelie, for she certainly would have no use for a man paralyzed from the waist down. Losing her and his legs—and the use of his third leg—all at the same time was the worst disaster he could possibly imagine. But he didn't want Suckerod to see him unmanned. He had to pretend not to be terrified.

"I cain't move my legs," he said calmly. "Tie me on my horse." Then Goodnight wondered if Mister Goddog might be too badly injured to carry him. "Make sure he's up to it. Check his belly."

When Suckerod approached Mister, the badly shaken horse shied away. But the cowboy talked soothingly to the frightened animal and managed to calm him down. Holding the horse by the reins, he bent down and looked at the bloody belly.

"He's scratched up," Suckerod reported, "but there ain't no guts hangin' out."

"Figure he can carry me?" asked Goodnight.

Suckerod shrugged. "Figure we gotta chance it."

Goodnight felt foolish, like an overgrown baby, as he was hoisted onto Mister Goddog's back. He would have fallen right off again if Suckerod hadn't steadied him. Then the cowboy used his lasso to tie his boss's feet in the stirrups.

"How you doin'?" Suckerod asked.

"You shoulda shot me instead the buffalo," Goodnight growled.

They took it easy returning to the ranch, just walking the horses. Goodnight had plenty of time to worry over lots of interlocking questions. How could he marry anybody if he was paralyzed? But she was going to refuse him anyway, wasn't she? Under the circumstances, a refusal would be the best outcome, right? So why worry about it anymore? But if she didn't say no, he would have to, wouldn't he? So no was the answer to hope for, wasn't it? So why couldn't he force himself to hope for rejection? What was wrong with him?

The ride felt endless. Time seemed to have stopped in the ancient canyon. This giant hole in the earth was also a hole in time. It was no longer the prettiest place he had ever seen. It had lost its charm and possibilities. But time had not quite stopped, only slowed down. The endless ride did finally end.

"Untie me," Goodnight gasped, exhausted.

Suckerod released the knots that bound his boss in the saddle. Then Goodnight fell off the horse's back and dropped into the cowboy's arms. The boss again felt like a baby.

"Hitch up the chuck wagon," Goodnight said. "You gotta go git that buffalo. We cain't just leave him out there to rot. That's dishonorin' the dead. Besides, it was my own damn fault. Well, this is one damn mistake we can eat."

11

Day and night, night and day, Goodnight rode his bedroll. It was one of the worst rides of his life. With paralyzed legs, he had no choice but to be passive. All he could do was wait. Wait to see if any feeling would return to his limbs. Wait for an answer to his letter. Wait for confirmation of his worst fears.

Wait and watch as the Home Ranch slowly began to look a little more like a ranch. His cowboys finished a corral and started work on a barn. Of course, the ranch house remained a distant dream. What was wrong with sleeping in the open? Except when you couldn't sleep. Except when it rained and you couldn't even crawl to shelter.

Over and over, lying on his back, lying on his side, lying squirming on his stomach, Goodnight would calculate in his head when Too Short should return. His own round trip to Tascosa for supplies had taken a week, but they had been slowed down by the chuck wagon. A lone rider should make much better time. If he hurried, Too Short could be back in four days. But four days came and went bringing no sign of the postman cowboy. What had happened to him? Had his horse gone lame? Could Gudanuf and his gang have gotten him? Had he somehow lost his way? Was he lying somewhere with arrows in him? Had he just gone on a long drunk as soon as he reached the Jenkins & Dunn Saloon? Or had he taken his business to the Equity Saloon on the edge of town? What was a saloon doing being named Equity, anyhow? Goodnight didn't know whether to worry about Too Short or feel sorry for him or get angry at him.

Goodnight, his legs still paralyzed, lay on his saddle blanket with his head resting on his saddle. His only roof kept changing. Now it was high and pale blue and empty. Later it was streaked with white cloud rafters. Later still, a white lumpy ceiling descended. Were those rain clouds? He certainly hoped so. This country could use a good wetting.

Lowering his gaze, Goodnight saw another kind of cloud, a red one that boiled up from the earth. He couldn't see the rider yet, but he knew there must be one, and he must be coming fast to raise such a red storm. If he was in such a hurry, he must have news that was in a hurry to be told.

Goodnight told himself not to expect the worst, but he couldn't help it. He told himself that he was getting the hurt out of the way ahead of time, so the blow wouldn't be so painful when it actually landed. And yet he suspected he still wouldn't be able to bear the blow. He begged the oncoming horse to run slower. He told the cowboy that there was no hurry. His news would keep. Go slow. It's a big country. You'll wear yourself out.

Squinting into the sun, Goodnight saw–all too soon–the dark rider leading the red cloud. He wasn't slowing down. He ought to spare his horse at least. Didn't he have any respect for horseflesh? What was wrong with him? Goodnight would have to give Too Short a good talking to when he arrived on a lathered mount. That was no way to treat a–

But it wasn't Too Short. He was too tall. Squinting, Goodnight made out Suckerod galloping toward him. What was wrong? What had happened? Goodnight couldn't wait to find out. Why didn't the cowboy ride faster?

When Suckerod finally arrived on his lathered horse, Goodnight felt drained. Why couldn't the rider have been Too Short? The wrong cowboy swung down out of the saddle and stood over him.

"You're in an all-fired hurry," Goodnight said.

"The bulls," Suckerod wheezed out of breath.

He seemed to be shaking even worse than usual, but it was hard to tell.

"Now calm down," Goodnight said. "What about the bulls?"

"Somebody's been shootin' 'em!" Suckerod gasped. "Cuttin' off their damn ears! And brandin' 'em! Goddammit."

"Don't cuss. Now just tell me slowly what happened."

Suckerod took several deep breaths. Goodnight watched him trying to make his hands stop shaking, but of course he couldn't.

"We found three of 'em so far," Suckerod said slowly. "Shot dead. All of 'em shot the same way, oncet behind the foreleg and oncet more at close range between the eyes. And bloody stumps for ears."

"All bulls, right? That what you said? Our breedin' stock?"

"'Fraid so."

"You said somethin' about brandin'?"

"Uh-huh, they done took a damn runnin' iron to your brand. Turned your 'HR' into a damn 'RR.'"

Goodnight saw in his mind how easily it could be done. He branded his cattle with irons that spelled out "HR" for Home Ranch. The process was similar to the way printers used type to print letters on paper. But a running iron was like a writing pen. A very hot writing pen. It was just a rod with nothing on the end but a blunt point. When that point was heated red-hot, it could write whatever brand it wanted on cattle. More important, it could rewrite brands. It would have been a simple matter to change the Home Ranch's "HR" into "RR."

"Now they couldn't a branded them bulls till they was dead, right?" said Goodnight. "I mean a cow mebbe, but not a bull."

"Thass how I figure it," Suckerod agreed.

"How come anybody'd wanna brand dead bulls?" Goodnight asked, but he already knew the answer. "I guess they was purdy proud a what they done, huh? Signin' their work and all. Went to a buncha trouble, huh?"

"Uh-huh. Guess they figured it was worth it."

"Like as if cuttin' their ears off waddn't enough."

"Uh-huh."

Goodnight clenched his fists. He could feel his hand shaking, like Suckerod's.

"Ya know," Goodnight said, "I sorta figured that ear-collectin' stunt was just gossip and exaggeration."

"Me, too," said Suckerod. "And anyhow, waddn't it s'posed ta be just people ears?"

"Mebbe he's branchin' out. You find any tracks?"

"Some. Figured I'd git some a the boys and go after 'em. They cain't of got too far. Bulls ain't been dead long."

Goodnight wanted to tell Suckerod to go ahead. Ride down the outlaws. Get even. Don't spare the horses. But at the same time, he knew he couldn't give such an order.

"Cain't spare you right now," Goodnight said. "Better wait till Too Short gits back and I git back on my feet."

"Trail might be purdy cold by then," Suckerod said.

Goodnight nodded, but they would just have to wait. He wasn't about to miss the hunt for the ear collector, and he couldn't go now.

12

After three weeks, Too Short came riding back into camp. Goodnight managed to get to his feet to greet him. He had slowly regained the feeling in his legs and yesterday had walked for the first time. He was still weak and shaky on his legs, like a damned toddler, but he was already making plans to go after Gudanuf.

"Where's my letter?" Goodnight demanded.

"What letter?" asked Too Short.

"'What letter!'" (Goodnight could feel disappointment swelling into fury.) "I sent you off with a letter *from* me." (He was angry at Too Short and angrier at Revelie.) "And you was supposed to come back here with a letter *to* me." (She had simply ignored his proposal, thrown it away–oh, no!) "So where's my damn letter?"

"You didn't say nothin' about bringing you back no letter."

"Do I have to tell you ever'thing? Explain ever'thing? What's the matter with you? And where the blazes you been all this time anyhow?!"

"They wouldn't let me go," Too Short said.

"What the hell're you talkin' about? You ain't makin' no sense. Who wouldn't let you go?"

"Miss Revelie and her folks."

"You're talkin' plum crazy."

"They're crazy, you ask me."

"Shut up! She made you stay?"

"Her–and her folks."

"Why? Because you was too good-lookin' to let git away?"

They just stared at each other. Goodnight's was a jealous stare.

Too Short took a deep breath. "They made me stay," he began, "on account of they got a hankerin' to see this here ranch. Only they didn't know how to find it. Figured they'd git lost. Made me stay to guide 'em. Then they took a month a Sundays to git ready."

"Month a Saturdays," said Simon.

"Shut up," said Goodnight. "They wanna see my ranch?"

"Thass right. When we got close, I come ahead to warn you."

"No!"

"'Fraid so."

"Who's comin'?"

"Ever'body. Mom, Dad–and her."

Goodnight just shook his head. Now he figured Too Short had come back too soon. A couple of years too soon. The Home Ranch wasn't exactly equipped to look after visitors. Especially not these visitors. Goodnight limped over, sat down under the chinaberry tree where he had written his letter, and waited for doom. On top of everything else, he would have to put off hunting down that damn ear collector. Too Short came over and squatted down beside him.

"Well, what the blazes you want now?" asked Goodnight. "Ain't you done caused enough trouble already?"

"Sorry, but I gotta git back and show 'em the injun trail, or they'll break their necks tryin' to git down here."

"Then go on, git outa my sight."

Watching Too Short go, Goodnight thought about calling him back. The prospect of Mother Sanborn breaking her neck rather appealed to him.

Goodnight felt as if he were being invaded by a foreign army. U.S. Cavalry troops escorted the Sanborn family when they made their appearance at the Home Ranch. The Human side of his mind could not help seeing them as an enemy Writer army. He hated to welcome them here in what had long been a natural Human fortress. But actually, they were just ensuring the safety of a Sanborn family outing. Mr. Sanborn was obviously an important man in these parts.

Yes, Goodnight hated to see the Writer warriors, but he could not help feeling that the real invading enemy was Mrs. Sanborn. She and her daughter, neither of whom knew how to sit a horse, arrived riding in a U.S. Army ambulance. Goodnight noticed that it had springs, unlike most other vehicles in this part of the world. Of course, Mrs. Sanborn would insist on springs. Her husband helped her down from the ambulance while she complained about the horrors of the descent into the canyon. She did not seem to have noticed that she was descending into heaven, not hell.

"Where's your ranch, Mr. Goodnight?" demanded Mrs. Sanborn, who again wore white gloves and a frilly pinafore.

"You're lookin' at it, ma'am," he said.

"Where's the ranch house?" she asked. "Where's the bunkhouse? Don't ranches have bunkhouses? I've heard so much about this kind of house. But what is it? Some sort of a cowboy hotel?"

Goodnight noticed his cowboys trying to hide their smirks, but he found nothing amusing about the situation. He glanced over at Revelie with an expression that begged for help. She smiled at him, which pleased him, but she didn't come to his rescue. He thought she looked like a princess in a fairy tale who was guarded by a dragon.

"Well, ma'am," he said at last, "I'm afraid we don't have a regular bunkhouse or anything like that. We just live in an ol' dugout. Or sleep under God's own leaky ceilin'. Someday . . ."

He looked down and noticed that his boots were covered with red dust and animal shit. He felt dirty all over.

"A dugout?" she said. "I thought a dugout was a canoe. You don't live in a canoe, do you, Mr. Goodnight?"

"No, ma'am," he said.

"Then could you explain to me what you're talking about?" she asked. "I'm afraid I don't speak your language."

"Well, ma'am, mebbe I better just show ya," he said reluctantly. "It's right over here. Just follow me, ma'am."

Goodnight limped along slowly, in no hurry to get where he was going, but it was unfortunately a short trip. The dugout was located in a small grove of cedars. Goodnight had once been rather proud of this humble structure, for it was his first home in which he was the boss, but now it seemed to shrivel before his gaze. It also got dirtier and darker.

It was just a shack, half in the ground and half out of it. It was dug into the side of a small grassy mound and looked like a part of it. The back wall and the two side walls were made of stones piled on top of each other and mortared together by clay. The front wall, the face of the dugout, was made of cedar logs standing upright, placed side by side. The small black doorway cut in this wooden wall looked like a missing tooth. There weren't any windows. The peaked roof was made of lodge poles found in a devastated Human campground not far from where all the Goddogs had been shot down. These lodge-poles-turned-rafters were covered with sod, so the dugout's single room was like a large coffin with grass growing above it.

"Do I understand that you live in this so-called dugout, Mr. Goodnight?" asked Mrs. Sanborn.

"Yes, ma'am," he said. "I mean I sleep here sometimes. I mostly live outdoors."

"What about your cowboys?" she asked. "Do they have their own dugout things?"

"No, ma'am," he said. "There's just one dugout and we all sleep in it."

"Really. May I look inside, Mr. Goodnight?"

"Okay, if you want to."

She had to stoop to get through the small doorway, and she wasn't a tall woman. Goodnight stayed outside because there wasn't much room inside and he had no desire to be trapped in close quarters with this woman. He could only see her from the waist down as she paced back and forth over the dirt floor. He realized she was measuring the dugout's only room. It was about eight steps wide and twelve steps deep.

Mrs. Sanborn poked her head out of the little door. She was holding her nose. "Mr. Goodnight," she said in a nasal voice, "your home smells." She shook her head sorrowfully. "You and your poor men, you live like prairie dogs."

Staring at her hopelessly, Goodnight had the feeling that he had roped another buffalo. What was he going to do with this woman?

"Well, ma'am, prairie dogs have towns," Goodnight said. "We ain't quite that grand, I'm afraid."

"I see," said Mrs. Sanborn. "Or rather I don't see. I don't see where my daughter and I are to sleep. I don't see where we are to perform our toilets."

Goodnight was embarrassed. He wasn't accustomed to hearing words like "toilet" used in mixed company.

"Er, ma'am, we weren't exactly expectin' you," he said. "I'm sorry."

"Do you mean we aren't welcome?" she asked.

"No, ma'am, I didn't mean that atall," he said. "I just mean this is gonna take some figurin'."

Goodnight studied his dusty boots and tried to figure. The canyon seemed terribly quiet all around him. Even the birds, normally so noisy in the cedar and chinaberry trees, had nothing to say. Goodnight found himself wondering: What would the Sun Chief have done? And posing the question suggested a possible answer.

"Well, what about if we built you a tepee?" Goodnight said in a soft voice. He looked apprehensively at the mother, then beseechingly at the daughter, then nervously back at the mother again. "I reckon we could scratch one together purdy fast. How'd that be?"

He watched Mrs. Sanborn think over the proposal. He could see her turning it this way and that, looking for ways to criticize it. Well, at least she hadn't rejected it out of hand.

"You don't expect us to pee in our tepee, do you, Mr. Goodnight?" she asked.

Goodnight was shocked at Mrs. Sanborn's language. "Well, I wouldn't if I was you," he said.

When Mr. Sanborn laughed out loud, his wife gave him a withering look. He tried to swallow his laughter and ended up choking.

"Very funny, Mr. Goodnight," Mrs. Sanborn said. "But in all seriousness, where do you expect us to pee?"

"It's a big canyon," he said.

He hunched his shoulders because he expected a verbal attack, but it didn't come.

"Very well," Mrs. Sanborn said. "Beggars cannot be choosers. And under these peculiar circumstances, we find ourselves the beggars. We accept your offer of the tepee–and the canyon."

Goodnight was delighted to be able to escape into work: to give orders, to make decisions, to select a site. It felt good to be doing something he knew how to do, namely, building a tepee, rather than doing something he had no idea how to do, namely, talking to the dragon guarding the princess. He probably knew more about tepees than any other white man, but he was a helpless, ignorant child when facing a pretty girl's mother. He could feel himself relaxing, even showing off. Finding a level piece of ground beside the red river, Goodnight took a cedar stick and drew an almost perfect circle. Then he marked where the door flap would be, where it should be, facing east. For the skeleton of the tent, he chose cedar logs, which would perfume the air. The Humans would have covered this skeleton with Human-cattle skins, but Goodnight did not have enough of them so he used a combination of buffalo and longhorn hides. One of those skins had once belonged to the woolly old bull that he had roped and regretted, but he was now glad to have the hide. While he worked feverishly, he kept looking around to see if Revelie was paying attention to him doing something he knew how to do. Sometimes she was; other times she was talking to her mother. After a couple of hours, Goodnight and his boys had finished the job.

"Ah, well, Miz Sanborn, Miss Revelie," he began uncertainly, back to doing something he didn't know how to do, "would you like to take a look? Huh?"

"You sweat a lot, don't you, Mr. Goodnight?" said Mrs. Sanborn. "Well, thank you for your hard work. Come, Revelie, shall we inspect?"

Goodnight held the door flap open for the two women as they entered the tepee. He thought about following them inside. A part of him wanted to, the part that wanted to be with Revelie; but another part didn't, the part that was afraid of Mrs. Sanborn. He told himself that it wasn't really fear . . . It was a matter of taste . . . It was a conflict of personalities . . . But it sure felt a lot like fear, he had to admit. He waited outside and listened to them moving about inside. Soon they reappeared.

"Revelie says it will be fun," Mrs. Sanborn announced. "I'm not quite so easily won over. Frankly I have my doubts. My health is fragile, you know. But I don't see that we have much choice. And anyway, it's aboveground, so we won't be living like groundhogs."

13

Goodnight was happy to be on horseback and away from Miz Sanborn but unhappy about being separated from Revelie. He had suggested that she accompany them on their ride, but the father had pointed out that the young ranch had no sidesaddles.

"But even if you did," Velvet Pants said, "my daughter still couldn't join us because she doesn't ride. She fell from her horse when she was a little girl. Hit her head. She was unconscious for hours. Her mother has refused to let her ride ever since. And you know my wife."

Goodnight and Mr. Sanborn rode southeast following the canyon on an inspection tour. For Revelie's father was seriously considering investing some of his British clients' money in the Home Ranch. Goodnight needed investors because he did not actually own the land on which his herd was growing fat. The red canyon still belonged to the State of Texas. He hoped Mr. Sanborn liked what he was seeing.

The colors were growing brighter moment by moment in the early morning sun. Somber trees cheered up as the light spilled over the canyon rim and fell on them. Boulders emerged from the shadows and reasserted themselves. The river gleamed, and mockingbirds sang. Goodnight felt that nature was conspiring to help him with his sales pitch.

"Every morning I wake up," he said, "and I think this is the purdiest spot in the whole world."

"It is nice," said Mr. Sanborn.

Goodnight felt his guest's response was a little bit tepid, but he didn't press him. He wanted more from him than compliments.

"And it's more than just purdy," he said. "It's practical. It's got plenty of water thanks to the river and a passel of springs. It's got protection from blizzards and that sorta thing. It don't need no fences 'cause it's got walls."

"That is nice," said Sanborn.

• • •

That night, Goodnight didn't feel like sleeping in the stuffy, smelly dugout. With Mrs. Sanborn's arrival, he had taken refuge there, hoping to avoid her whenever possible. Her presence had literally driven him underground. But he wasn't a prairie dog, so why should he live like one? He rolled up in a blanket with a chinaberry tree for a roof. A cedar tree rose nearby and made the air fragrant. He loved his new bedroom, but he had a hard time getting to sleep in it. Over and over in his mind, Goodnight walked the red earth of his canyon with Revelie, and time after time he was as mute as the canyon walls. They had both seen a lot, he and the canyon, but neither could put what they had witnessed into words. The canyon made up for its vast silence with its beauty. Goodnight knew he wasn't that lucky.

When he finally fell asleep, Goodnight dreamed that he had been captured by Gudanuf and the Robbers' Roost gang. They tied him to a tree, forced his mouth open, and cut out his tongue. Then they rode off and left him there. When he tried to call for help, he sounded like a frightened horse neighing . . .

Goodnight felt somebody shaking him. Still lost in his dream, he tried to fight back, but he was tied too tightly. Then he opened his good eye and saw a steel helmet reflecting the early-morning sun. He was bound in a blanket that was wrapped around and around him. His attacker was Tin Soldier. When Goodnight finally managed to free his hands, he tried to wipe the sleep and the dream images out of his good eye.

"Bad news," Tin Soldier said in a hushed voice.

"What?" asked Goodnight, fearing that something terrible had happened to Revelie.

"They got Mister."

"What?"

"Kilt him."

"How? I didn't hear no shots."

"Cut his throat."

"No!"

Now Goodnight wished he hadn't trusted his favorite horse to run free at night. There was a makeshift corral where Mister Goddog could have spent the dark hours in the company of other horses, but Goodnight hated to think of him always penned up. He didn't even hobble the horse at night. Mister always came when he called him in the morning. But he wouldn't be coming anymore.

"That all?" Goodnight asked hopefully. "They just cut his throat and leave it at that?"

"No," said Tin Soldier. But he seemed reluctant to say more.

"Well, what? Tell me."

"They done took his ears."

"They brand him?"

"No."

"Well, thank God for that."

"Carved some initials."

"No."

"I'm sorry."

"RR?"

"Yeah."

Goodnight felt sick. Now he wished he were back asleep and dreaming that terrible dream.

"Don't tell Miss Revelie," Goodnight said. "Don't tell none of the Sanborns. I don't want 'em worried. Mum's the word for now. Unnerstand? We'll settle up with them RR devils later on."

Goodnight didn't want to frighten Revelie off. He didn't want to lose her, too. But it was hard to wait. The loss of Mister Goddog could not help but remind him of considerably more painful losses, but he told himself not to think about them. It hurt too much.

14

Miss Revelie and Goodnight took an afternoon walk along the river. Again, he tried not to think of his lost horse or all his other losses. He gave all of his mental energy over to trying to think of something to say, but his voice was trapped in his head. He was screaming inside but mute outside. Some villain had cut out his tongue.

"Too Short told me," Revelie began, "you can talk to animals."

"I used to could," Goodnight said.

"How do you do it?" she asked, ignoring his past tense.

"Well, I dunno."

"Please, I'm interested. How'd you learn to? Really."

Goodnight didn't want to talk about where his most important learning came from. It was too painful to revisit. Besides, she would probably misunderstand and think him a savage.

"I just learned."

"Nobody taught you?"

Goodnight wanted to lie to her about this, but at the same time he hated to lie to her about anything. Ever.

"Uh?"

"Please tell me. I'm really interested."

He hesitated. Not only would it hurt too much to recall those days, but worse, it would completely alter how she saw him forever. He had seen that reaction before. At school . . .

"Please."

"I, uh, I, uh–"

"Tell me!"

He felt he had no choice.

"I used to live with the Comanches. And they done told me. That's all I can tell you." He paused. "If I told you about it, I'd go crazy."

He searched for words. "It'd be like a stampede in my mind. I couldn't control it. I'd lose my mind and be a babblin' idiot."

"We wouldn't want that," Revelie said, taken aback. "I'm sorry. I didn't know it was so private. Please disregard the whole thing. I'm sorry I asked."

Now Goodnight felt doubly awkward. He felt her recoiling from him. And he sensed that an important opportunity was about to be lost.

"No, no," he said. "I can–I mean sometimes–I can talk to stuff. Animals, plants, other stuff. Er, well, I just talk to them like they was people. That's all. Nothin' much to it."

They walked along in silence once again. The shadows were deepening and gloom was descending.

"Well, then," Revelie disturbed the silence of the canyon, "maybe you could turn it around. Maybe you could talk to a person as if she were an animal. Think of me as a buffalo or something."

"I ain't had much luck with buffalos lately," he said.

"Well, then some other animal. I don't know. What was the first animal you ever talked to?"

"A bee."

"Well, make believe I'm a bee. What would you say to me?"

Goodnight looked up at the sky as if begging the Great Mystery to help him. He didn't think he could pretend Revelie was a bee. She didn't look like a bee. She didn't sound like a bee. She didn't smell like a bee. But she was staring at him expecting bee talk, so he figured he had better try.

"Er, well, I usually talk to them in Comanche," Goodnight said. "I don't reckon you know Comanche, do you?"

"No," Revelie said. "Don't any bees know English? What would you say to a bee who spoke English?"

"Er, well, I reckon I'd say somethin' like, uh," he began. "I guess I'd say that I'm not gonna hurt you. And I hope you're not gonna hurt me. Somethin' like that."

"I won't," she said. "Go on. Please."

Goodnight hoped he could count on her promise, but he had misgivings. She might not even know when she was hurting him. It would still hurt.

"Uh," he said, "I'd say I wanna gather some flowers. I need flowers."

"Why?"

"Oh, I dunno. Somethin' or other."

"Is that what you told the bees?"

"No."

"Well, what did you tell them?"

"Medicine. I needed some kinda medicine."

"What kind?"

Goodnight thought about lying to her. He had a choice: tell a lie or get embarrassed. But he didn't think he could tell stories to Revelie. He figured she would know.

"Well, medicine for coughin' and that sorta thing."

He watched her staring at him. He figured she knew he was holding something back. Well, here goes.

"For coughin' and for babies," he said.

"For babies' coughs?" she asked.

"No, not exactly," he said, and then lowered his gaze so he couldn't see her. "For makin' babies."

"You mean like the birds and the bees?" she asked.

"Well, sorta. The flowers make a medicine for women who cain't have no babies. They take it and then they can. See?"

"I think so. What kind of flowers?"

Goodnight looked up at the empty sky once again. No help there.

"Horehounds," he said.

"What?" she asked.

"I didn't name 'em."

"But what did you say?"

"Horehounds. I said horehounds. But I didn't name 'em. That's just their name. Their name in English, not Comanche. I'm sorry."

"Don't be sorry. I just didn't hear you. Or anyway I thought I didn't hear you right. But I guess I did. Horehounds, huh? The flowers out here have more colorful names than I realized."

"Yeah."

Neither of them knew quite what to say now. They looked at each other, and then they looked away.

"What other animals do you talk to?" she asked, evidently deciding that a slight change of subject was in order. "You said you talked to buffalos?"

"Not lately," he said.

Then silence descended again.

"What else do you talk to?" she asked at last. "Trees? Do you talk to trees?"

"Sometimes."

"Well, make believe I'm a tree. Talk tree talk to me. What about that? Do I remind you of a tree? I mean any particular tree?"

Goodnight studied Revelie, trying to see her as a tree. He tried to imagine her as a chinaberry tree because it had a long trunk and she had long legs. But somehow he couldn't quite picture her as a chinaberry. He attempted to see her as a cedar, but cedars were too chunky. Then he realized . . .

"You're not one tree," he told her. "You're lots of trees. You're a whole forest of trees."

"What do you mean?" she asked.

Goodnight noticed her green eyes. They were beautiful, but at the moment, they were something else, too. But he couldn't figure out what.

"Well, the Comanches figure," he said, and then took a deep breath for the hard work ahead, "that we're all a part a nature. Right? Thass on the one hand. But we're a reflection a nature, too. Thass on the other hand. See?"

"No, not really."

"The Comanches figure we've all got forests inside us. And rivers inside us. And springs inside us. And canyons inside us. And thunder and lightnin'. That sort a stuff. See?"

"I think so. Tell me what you see in me."

Goodnight studied her again. He was glad to have the license to stare at her.

"Well, I reckon I see a dark forest in you," he said, willing to play this game. "It's full of big ol' trees. Not mesquites or cedars or chinaberries like we got out here. But oaks. Live oaks. Like they got in East Texas where I used to live. So there's lots a shade in your forest. It feels cool. And it's kinda mysterious like."

"That's what you see?"

He nodded. He was no longer playing. He really saw a primeval forest.

"The forest in you is quiet and calm," he said. "It seems safe. But there are wild animals in it."

"What kind of animals?" she asked.

"Deer. Lots of deer."

"I like deer."

"But there are also wolves. Not coyotes like out here. But wolves."

"I don't like wolves."

He shrugged. "And mountain lions."

As they were walking "home"–back toward the dugout and the tepee–Goodnight felt better and better. More confident. He had talked to her. He had actually had a conversation with her in which he had done most of the talking. Somehow he had performed a miracle. He could hardly believe it, and yet he knew that believing was just what had made it possible. Somehow by sheer act of will–or desperation–he had forced himself to believe in himself enough to tiptoe back into the realm of enchantment. For he considered being able to talk to Revelie a much greater feat of magic than being able to talk to buffalo or anvils.

Seeing a small tribe of bright yellow sunflowers growing beside the red river, Goodnight decided to pick a bouquet of them to present to Revelie. He wanted her to carry back with her something beautiful to decorate the memory of their talk. He led the way and she followed. But when they reached the sunflowers, which all looked in the direction of the sun, they found them covered by bumblebees. Revelie stopped, but Goodnight stepped closer. He looked for the chief of the sunflowers, the one with the most magnificent headdress of yellow feathers, and soon located him at the center of his tribe. Goodnight dropped down on his knees.

"O, Great Sunflower Chief," he said, not in the Human tongue but in the tongue of the Writers.

He had never tried to talk to a flower in this alien language before, and he wondered why he did so now. He supposed he was probably showing off for the Writer woman. But he didn't suppose the Chief of the Sunflowers would much care which language got used. He figured flowers didn't understand the tongues of man but rather the spirit in which the languages were used. All he could do was hope like hell he was right on account of he sure wasn't anxious to look like a damn fool in front of Revelie. And he didn't want to get stung.

"O, Great Sunflower Chief, I wanta ask a favor of you. I'd sure like to gather some of your flowers. Not all, you unnerstand, just some. I need 'em to give to this here young lady whose name is Revelie. I want her to have 'em as a token of my feelin's for her. How about it?"

Goodnight couldn't be sure, but he had the feeling he was getting through. Two fists, one inside his head and the other in his chest, seemed to unclench and relax.

Now he turned his attention to the bumblebees. He knew none of them was the chief because the high-toned bees stayed home close to the honey: These were just the warrior-workers. So he could be more democratic and talk to all these workin'-stiff bees at the same time.

"O Bumblebees," he said, "I know some of your little cousin bees purdy well, but I don't know you, so let me introduce myself. My name's Jimmy Goodnight, or Crying Coyote, whichever. And I'm gonna ranch this here canyon, if you don't mind. It's gonna be the best ranch in Texas. And this is the purdiest spot in the whole world. And this young lady here's the purdiest girl in the world. And I'm hopin' with your help we can kinda get all these here things together. The best damn ranch. The purdiest damn spot. And the purdiest girl who'd make the purdiest wife in the whole damn world. Now you kin do your part by sorta movin' on back and lettin' me pick some of these here flowers for Miss Revelie. How about it?"

The bumblebees buzzed loudly as if they were angry, but they were just warming up for the collective move to the back of the patch of sunflowers. Goodnight looked around at Revelie to see if she was impressed.

"That's amazing," she said.

"Ain't it?" he said. "Look at 'em go."

"I don't mean the bees," she said. "I mean you. At first, I thought you were never going to start talking. And then when you finally got going, I began to wonder if you were ever going to stop."

15

Goodnight kept expecting her to mention his letter. He didn't want to be the one who brought up the subject because he knew he hadn't written elegantly. Because he was in no hurry to get bad news. Because the whole matter now embarrassed him. Because he didn't want to seem to be putting pressure on her. But he figured she would bring it up. Day after day, he waited for the blow to fall.

Every day, Goodnight and Mr. Sanborn rode up and down the valley. From time to time, the rancher would point out a spring or some other valuable feature, and Velvet Pants would make a note of it in a little leather book that he carried with him. He wrote a small neat hand. Goodnight envied Mr. Sanborn his handwriting. Velvet Pants was all business. If he was aware of a proposal of marriage, made formally if somewhat crudely, he didn't let on. He acted like a potential partner but not a possible father-in-law.

Day after day, Mrs. Sanborn remained in her tepee, which was all right with her host. She stayed inside because she was sick. Anyway, she said she was sick. Goodnight wondered how sick she really was. He had never met anybody like her and hadn't figured her out. All he knew was he felt more secure outdoors with her indoors.

Goodnight began to wonder if the whole Sanborn family–father, mother, and daughter–might one day ride away without the subject of marriage ever coming up. He had always supposed that if you asked a young woman to marry you, she would at least answer you. She might say yes. She might say no. She might say she wanted time to think it over. But it had never occurred to him that she might never say anything about it at all. Was she so far above him socially that she didn't even deign to notice that any proposal had been made? He didn't quite know whether to be insulted or not. He felt he just had to find out what she thought of his terrible letter and his sincere offer. He was still in earnest.

• • •

One morning, Mr. Sanborn came to breakfast with a big smile on his face. Goodnight thought maybe Mrs. Sanborn was well, but that wasn't it.

"Mr. Goodnight, I say, why don't we make a holiday today," Velvet Pants proposed. "Let's cease our search for springs and go after bigger game."

"Like what?" Goodnight asked.

"Buffalo."

"Well, I dunno. There's too much work for me to do around here to take off and go buffalo huntin'."

"But it will be great sport. A real Western experience. I wouldn't miss it."

Goodnight felt as if he were trapped in some sort of dead-end box canyon. He didn't want to say no to his prospective partner and possible father-in-law, but he didn't like the idea of senseless buffalo-killing either.

"Less git some grub," Goodnight said, stalling, "before Coffee throws it out."

He moved toward the chuck wagon and Mr. Sanborn followed. They held out tin plates and the cook forked griddle cakes onto them. Then they poured a thick layer of sorghum over the top. Goodnight squatted down to eat, and Velvet Pants hunkered down beside him.

"I'm in earnest about this hunt," Mr. Sanborn said.

Goodnight remembered a similar phrase in his proposal letter. He wondered if Revelie's father was making fun of him. He was a little irritated, but he wasn't sure he had a right to be.

"Well, I don't hold much with shootin' buffalo just for sport," Goodnight said a little too sharply. "Now it would be different if we was hungry and needed the meat, but we're drowning in meat all around us. So I don't see much sense to it."

Mr. Sanborn looked at his host sternly. Goodnight wondered if he had said too much. Well, there was no unsaying it now. Besides, he believed what he had said.

"Mr. Goodnight, I wasn't asking your permission," Mr. Sanborn said. "I don't need your permission to hunt buffalo. I mean, they aren't your buffalo. They don't belong to anybody."

Goodnight thought he knew who they belonged to, but he didn't say so.

"I didn't say they were mine," he said.

"They belong to whoever shoots them," Mr. Sanborn said. "That's all. If you don't choose to accompany me, that's your affair. Just as going is my affair."

"Well, I cain't stop you. That's true. But I still don't hold with it."

Goodnight suddenly felt that he was tired of this Sanborn family pestering him all the time. The father wanted to murder a buffalo for the fun of it. The mother was always complaining. The daughter wouldn't even get on a horse, which meant you had to walk around on your two legs like some damn chicken if you wanted to talk to her. And then when she talked, she wanted to talk about everything in the world except what he most wanted to talk about, but which he was afraid to bring up. Well, why didn't they just all get on their horses and ambulances and get the hell out of his canyon and leave him alone? Who had asked them to stay anyway? Who needed them, anyhow? That was what he wanted to know.

Velvet Pants did get on his horse and ride away. He was accompanied by a couple of the soldiers from Fort Elliott, who seemed to have nothing better to do with their time. Goodnight grumbled to himself about the waste of tax dollars, but they might at least keep the great hunter from getting lost. That way, Goodnight wouldn't have to go looking for him.

"If you're not going with my father today," Revelie said, "would you like to take a walk?"

Goodnight jumped because he hadn't seen her come up. He thought she was still in the tepee ministering to her ailing mother. Seeing her appear so near him, almost as if by magic, he studied her to see if she were some kind of mirage. She looked real all right.

"I dunno," he said. "Lot to do around here."

Goodnight told himself that he was tired of these silly people and all their silly games. But she didn't look silly or sound silly. She looked like a young woman whose soul was a dark forest. Her voice was the wind through those trees.

"I hadn't thought of that," she said. "Could I help?"

"Most of it's horseback work," he said.

"Then you go ahead. I understand."

"No, less walk. Ain't nothing I gotta do right this minute."

"You're sure?"

They walked a long time without talking, but this time Goodnight did not find the silence oppressive. He watched her growing admiration for his canyon, for its plants and animals, for its lofty promontories and its dark caves, for its flowers but also for its thorns. He thought the valley had a kind of fierce beauty. He thought she had it, too.

"It's still the purdiest place I ever seen," Goodnight said. "Could be the purdiest place in the whole wide world."

"It's lovely," Revelie said.

Goodnight was a little disappointed. Lovely? That was like saying the face of God, the face of the Great Mystery, was lovely. If it was lovely at all, it was the loveliest. If it was beautiful at all, it was the most beautiful. If it was moving at all, it was the most moving. If it was like God's face at all, then it was one of the holiest places on this earth. Didn't these Writers know how to speak their own language? Didn't they appreciate the distinctions it could make? Or was it just this one particular Writer who didn't understand? Who got a letter but didn't know how to read it . . . who saw God's work and didn't know how to praise it . . . who was going to miss life because she didn't notice it passing by . . . who made him so angry . . .

"I hate to be the one to bring this up," Goodnight said, exasperated, "but I wrote you a letter. I know it waddn't a very good letter as letters go. But it was about something and not all letters are, I reckon. Couldn't you read my handwritin'? Mebbe that's the trouble."

He could see that he had flustered her. Well, at least that was some reaction. She might be a dark forest on the inside, but on the outside she was pretty much still water. Now he had stirred up a little ripple, which pleased him and worried him at the same time.

"I didn't say anything," Revelie said, "because I didn't know what to say. I know I owe you a lot. You saved me from those men. But . . ." She evidently couldn't think of the words to go on.

"Then why'd you come out here?" Goodnight asked.

"My father wanted to come," she said, "to look at your ranch. He thinks it might be a good investment for his clients. And so I asked to come along, too."

"Did you tell him about the letter?" he asked.

"No, but I told my mother. I made her promise to keep it a secret. She said if I was coming, she was coming. It was really very brave of her. She hates everything about this canyon. How big it is. How wild it is. How much of it is outdoors."

Goodnight coughed and laughed at the same time. "She's a piece of work, I'll give her that."

"And she returns the compliment," Revelie said. "I came because I wanted to get to know you better. And now I do know you better. And you know me better." She paused. "But I still don't know. It's such a big step and I still feel so small. This canyon is so big. It might swallow me forever. It's such a wild place. It's lovely but it frightens me."

"Loveliest spot I ever seen," Goodnight said, giving her a hint, showing her how to talk.

"Yes, it's very nice to look at," she said, not taking the hint. "But do I belong here? I don't even know how to ride a horse."

"I been thinking about that," he said. "I got a proposition for you. I figure I know a little about somethin' that you don't know, and you know a lot about somethin' I don't know. So I figured mebbe we could up and swap. Trade like. If we got–uh–well–if you was to come live here, see, I figure I could teach you to ride. And you could teach me to read 'n' write. I mean I know my alphabet and stuff, but I could sure stand some brushin' up."

"You want a teacher?"

"Well, you'd be my teacher, but then again I'd be yours. Fair trade like."

"Why, Mr. Goodnight, didn't anybody ever tell you that you don't have to marry somebody to get them to teach you to read and write. I'm sure you could find–"

"That's not why I want to. That ain't it atall." He decided it was time to give up being a coward, for a little while at least. "I want to marry you, Miss Revelie, because my mind cries for you."

"What?"

"That's what the Comanches say. Only they don't call themselves Comanches. They just say Human Bein's, see? And they don't call it 'love' like white folks. They say, 'My mind cries for you.' I like that part about the mind fallin' in love insteada the heart. Makes more sense, really. Anyhow to me. So that's it. My mind cries for you. I know I'm ramblin', but . . ."

Goodnight stopped talking because he saw that she was crying. He was just stepping forward to take her in his arms–if she would let him–and comfort her when he saw something that stayed his step. Two horsemen were approaching at a trot. Then as they drew closer, the two riders turned into three. One horse carried a double load. Squinting, he recognized Mr. Sanborn mounted behind one of the Fort Elliott soldiers. The father seemed to have dropped from heaven at just this moment in order to thwart Goodnight's attempt to embrace Revelie. God damn your eyes, Velvet Pants.

"Your daddy's comin'," he said, pointing.

Revelie looked and started trying to dry her eyes. She obviously did not want her father to catch her crying. Goodnight could sympathize because he didn't want Mr. Sanborn to think he was in the habit of making Revelie cry.

When the horses were a dozen yards away, they stopped. Nobody said anything. On the one hand, Goodnight was put out with Velvet Pants for going on a buffalo hunt, but on the other hand, he figured the father had every right to be put out with him for driving his daughter to tears. The rancher decided just to call it a draw and not say any more than he had to. Revelie wasn't anxious to talk either, maybe because her voice might sound funny. And the soldiers never said much anyhow. Who knew why Mr. Sanborn kept quiet? It wasn't his nature.

"Daddy, you're hurt," Revelie broke the spell. "What happened to your leg?"

Now Goodnight noticed that Velvet Pants's left velvet leg was torn and dirty and stained by blood. A bandage was tied around his knee. Goodnight wondered why he hadn't noticed sooner. Well, his mind had been on other things.

"I was a damned fool," Mr. Sanborn said. "That's what. I'd read somewhere that it was great sport to shoot a buffalo with a Colt revolver. The idea was to ride alongside your target, matching him stride for stride, and fire at him from the saddle. I could see the picture so clearly in my mind. I really could. But it wasn't quite as simple as I had imagined, suffice it to say." Then he fell silent.

"Please, Daddy," Revelie begged, "tell me what happened to you. I want to know."

Her father shrugged. "Well, it turned out to be harder to shoot from a galloping horse than I had realized. The revolver was bouncing all over the place. It's difficult to see what you're doing or where you're aiming. I just kept shooting and shooting. I don't know if any of my bullets hit the buffalo I was chasing. But I do know one shot hit my horse in the back of the head. Poor animal. I had a nasty fall."

"Oh, Daddy."

"I'm sure Mr. Goodnight is thinking that it served me right, and I suppose it did. Don't tell your mother. She'll worry."

16

"I think we'd better have a little talk," Mr. Sanborn said after breakfast the next morning. His eyes flashed, but the rest of his bruised body was moving stiffly. "Just the two of us."

Goodnight shivered. Had Revelie at last unburdened herself to her father about his proposal? Was Velvet Pants–who had on a brand-new pair today–going to tell him to leave his daughter alone?

"Fine," Goodnight said uneasily.

The two of them withdrew into a grove of hackberry trees. The limbs were so interwoven that they formed an almost impenetrable wall around a small clearing at the center of the thicket. This thorny dell was as private as any oak-paneled den.

"What can I do for you?" asked Goodnight nervously.

"Well, it's quite a place you've got here," said Mr. Sanborn. "Or anyway it will be."

"Uh-huh."

"I believe in your canyon, Mr. Goodnight."

"Thank you." He wished this man's daughter had said those same words. "I appreciate that."

"I am prepared to advise my clients to invest in your enterprise–provided we can come to some sort of agreement on what form that investment would take."

"Come again."

"Terms, Mr. Goodnight, terms. We must agree upon the terms of our partnership. I must know what I am buying. We must put our relationship on a sound business footing."

"Well, I ain't never had much truck with business."

"Ranching is a business, Mr. Goodnight, pure and simple. There's no getting around it. You must learn business, and I will be your teacher, if you will allow me. I have had some considerable experience."

"Teach away, Mr. Sanborn."

Velvet Pants took a sheet of creamy white paper out of his coat pocket and carefully unfolded it. The page was covered with small, neat words and numbers. He did the race of Writers right proud. Goodnight looked down at the paper with considerable misgivings, for he knew that writing gave Writers an advantage that he didn't know how to counter. Writing was Writer magic. Writing was Writer medicine.

"I have taken the liberty to draw up some terms that I consider to be fair," Mr. Sanborn said. "May I read them to you?"

"Of course," said Goodnight, but he already dreaded the words. Seeing them in black and white made them seem so final. The majority of the written words he had ever seen were in the Bible, and they didn't have much give-and-take in them. You were just stuck with them and no arguments. Goodnight knew this agreement wasn't in any Bible, but he was nonetheless intimidated by it. He didn't figure there would be much give-and-take in its commandments either.

"The agreement will run for five years," Mr. Sanborn read from the written page. "I will undertake to finance this enterprise in full. That will include paying you a salary of twenty-five hundred dollars per annum–"

"Excuse me," Goodnight interrupted. "I don't git much outa them four-bit words."

"Per annum," Velvet Pants taught, "means 'every year.'" He found his place with his finger and started reading again. "In addition, I agree to fund the purchase of one hundred thousand acres of land from the State of Texas at a price not to exceed twenty-five cents per acre for a total price not to exceed twenty-five thousand dollars." He looked up. "Am I going too fast?"

Goodnight shrugged and shook his head at the same time.

"Good," Mr. Sanborn said. "That's what I promise to do. Now we come to your part of the bargain. Let's see, where was I? Oh, yes, you will furnish the foundation for the herd and direct the enterprise. You will also repay my investment in full plus a ten percent charge for interest."

"Interest? I'm not sure I–"

"We'll come back to that. When our agreement expires in five years' time, we will divide the residual properties, one-third going to you, two-thirds to me."

"Rewhat?"

"Residual properties. That means whatever property is left after five years. What remains. We'll split that up according to the terms of our agreement. See, business isn't so hard, is it?"

Goodnight shrugged again. He didn't know what to make of the proposed agreement. He didn't much like the idea of paying Mr. Sanborn back all the money he had invested, plus interest, whatever that was, and then turning around and giving him two-thirds of the ranch. Two-thirds of the land. Two-thirds of the cattle. Two-thirds of the whole shootin' match. He hadn't gotten very far in math in school, but he knew two-thirds was over half. It wasn't a matter of even-Steven. The more he thought about it, the more he didn't much like it, but it was all written down in black and white. Not in pencil that you could erase but in ink that was indelible. You could change pencil-writing. You could fiddle with it until you got it like you wanted it–or try to. But ink was another matter entirely. Ink was once and forever. If Mr. Sanborn had chiseled the contract on a stone tablet, it would have been a little more intimidating, but not much.

"I see," Goodnight said at last.

"Good," said Mr. Sanborn. "If you'll just sign this agreement, I'll sign it, too, and we'll be in business. Congratulations. I predict a very bright future for you, for this canyon, for us all."

Goodnight studied Velvet Pants's broad smile and wondered why he was wary of it. Mr. Sanborn was a soft man, a foolish man who shot his own horse, a man who couldn't do much of anything except write, but writing was evidently enough.

"I dunno," Goodnight said.

"What don't you know?" Velvet Pants asked. "Here, look it over."

He handed the written agreement to Goodnight, who stared down at it dumbly. It seemed to have cast a spell over him. The words blurred before his good eye and bumped into each other. He felt a little dizzy.

"Is anything wrong?" asked Mr. Sanborn.

"No, I'm all right," said Goodnight.

"I was referring to the agreement."

"Oh, yeah, right. Course."

Goodnight stared at the document with a Human eye. The handwriting looked beautiful from a distance, but up close the letters were hard to make out. He squinted. He caught himself wondering if he would have been able to read better if he had had two eyes. He could have just admitted that he wasn't a very good reader and was befuddled by the written agreement, but he was ashamed. He didn't want his potential partner–and possible future father-in-law–to think he was a dumb hick. He couldn't stand that.

"It looks okay to me," Goodnight said at last.

"Very good," said Mr. Sanborn. "Splendid. Allow me to offer you the use of my fountain pen."

Velvet Pants withdrew the newfangled contraption from his inside coat pocket and handed it to Goodnight. The rancher wasn't exactly sure how to use it. He didn't even know how to open it, much less write with it. He had of course seen Mr. Sanborn use it day after day, but he hadn't watched closely. He paid about as much attention to how Velvet Pants used a mechanical pen as he did to how wrens wove nests. He never figured he'd need to know how to do either one. What did such a writing machine have to do with somebody like him? He felt as if he were about to lose another war to the Writers.

"No, please," Goodnight said. "You better go first. It's more fittin'."

The rancher held out the fountain pen as if it were some dangerous weapon that he was anxious to get rid of. Mr. Sanborn took it from him.

"Very well, if you insist," he said. "I will be happy to do the honors. Turn around. I'll use your back as my desk."

"What?" asked Goodnight. "Excuse me."

"I need to press against something when I write. Since we don't have a desk or a table, I propose to use your back, if you will be so kind as to turn around."

Oh, no! Turn around! Then he wouldn't be able to see a thing. Then it would be his turn and he still wouldn't know how to use a fountain pen. He had to stall until he could think of something.

"Oh, no," Goodnight said. "Somethin' thass this important, you gotta do it right. Cain't afford not to. We'll sign it on the chuck wagon."

Not giving Velvet Pants a chance to raise objections, Goodnight rushed out of the hackberry grove as if somebody were chasing him. He didn't stop until he reached the chuck wagon, where he found Coffee mixing up some hotcake batter for Revelie's breakfast. She had not gotten up quite as early as her father or her suitor.

"Outa the way, Coffee," Goodnight said. "Mr. Sanborn wants to borrow your table there."

He was referring to the door of the chuck wagon's cabinet that was hinged not on the side but at the bottom, like those round-topped tin mailboxes stuck on top of posts back in civilization. The mailboxes opened that way, from top to bottom rather than from side to side, just because they did. But a chuck wagon opened that way for a reason, because when it did, its door formed a kind of kitchen table where the cook prepared the meals. Coffee picked up his tin bowl full of batter and retreated a few steps. Goodnight started blowing stray flour off the chuck wagon door so the agreement wouldn't get soiled.

"There you go, Mr. Sanborn," he said. "Have at it."

"Thank you, Mr. Goodnight," said Velvet Pants. "You are too gracious."

"What's going on?" asked Revelie.

"Come over here," said her father. "You can witness our signatures. That is, if Mr. Goodnight has no objections."

Mr. Goodnight objected all right but silently. He had been worried about making a fool of himself with that fountain pen in front of Velvet Pants. Now he had to worry about looking like an idiot in front of Revelie, too, which was infinitely worse.

"No objection," Goodnight said. "Witness away."

"Thank you," said Revelie with what seemed mock courtesy. "I would be delighted. What are you signing?"

"Partnership papers," said her father.

"Are congratulations in order?" she asked.

"Certainly," the father said.

Goodnight just shrugged. He wasn't so sure.

"Well done," she said.

Velvet Pants placed the written agreement on the door of the chuck wagon. Then he began unscrewing the top of the fountain pen with Goodnight watching closely. He had to rise up a little on his tiptoes and crane his neck to see over the businessman's shoulders. So that was how you did it! Before beginning to write, Mr. Sanborn reached for some sort of metal lever on the side of the pen and pulled it out a little way, which had the effect of forcing ink into the tip of the pen. Then he released the lever and bent to his work.

"Now it's your turn," said Velvet Pants, holding out the fountain pen. "Be my guest."

Goodnight was relieved to see that Mr. Sanborn had not replaced the top on the fountain pen, so he wouldn't have to fuss with that.

Visualizing what his new partner had done, Goodnight reached for the little lever on the side of the pen and gave it a good yank. Ink spurted out of the tip of the pen and hit Velvet Pants just below the belt.

"Oh, no!" Goodnight moaned. "I'm sorry. I'm real sorry."

"Think nothing of it, my good man," Mr. Sanborn said in a tight voice. "Really, I don't mind. An accident. Couldn't be helped."

Revelie was in danger of hurting herself from laughing so hard. Goodnight wanted to cry. He was more embarrassed at having shot Mr. Sanborn in his velvet pants than Velvet Pants was at having shot his own horse in the head while riding it.

17

Late in the afternoon, Goodnight and Revelie went for a last walk together to say goodbye. The Sanborn family with its escort of troops would be pulling out in the morning. They had been there only a week, but now Goodnight couldn't imagine the red canyon without them. As they left their tracks side by side on the bank of the river, he found himself wishing that these footprints would not wash away. He caught himself wondering if his memory of this moment would erode also. If this parting turned out to be goodbye forever, then he hoped his memory of Revelie would remain as indelible as writing on paper, for it would be all he had left of her. And yet if he lost her, maybe he would want to forget her, because remembering would drive him crazy. Wouldn't it? Goodnight knew a bit about how memory worked, how you tended to remember what was painful and forget what had been pleasant. He already feared that his memories of Revelie were going to hurt him, which was both good and bad. Good for the memory but not so good for the heart. Of course, if the memory was *too* painful, you could just block it out of your mind completely. He knew something about that, too.

Glancing in Revelie's direction, Goodnight was startled once again to find her looking at him. This time, he didn't look away so quickly because he wanted to see if she would look away. She didn't. She just kept studying him, measuring him, finding fault with him, or whatever it was she was doing. He couldn't stand it any longer.

"You're looking at me," Goodnight said nervously.

"Yes," Revelie said.

Well, he had really managed to clear that up. "Why?" he asked.

"You're so big," she said. "You take up so much room. You need all this room. You belong here in this big place. I can't decide if you were made for the canyon, or if the canyon was made for you. And you make other people big. You make them big enough to have forests inside them. That's pretty big."

She looked at him now as if she expected him to say something.

"I don't know what to say," he said.

"I don't either," she said.

Goodnight realized that he had never considered the possibility that she might run out of words. He liked her better if such were possible.

"I suppose all this bigness frightens me," Revelie said at last. "The canyon. The sky. Back home the sky is much smaller. You're big and you can stand up to this place. I'm little."

"Not so little," Goodnight said, concerned about the drift of the conversation.

"This place makes *you* bigger," she said, "but it makes *me* feel small. I can't help it."

They fell silent again. Their walk carried them to the very edge of the shadow cast by the western wall of the canyon. They were still in the bright sunlight, but soon the beginning of darkness would touch them. Goodnight felt a chill as if in anticipation of that moment.

"I've really enjoyed my visit," Revelie said a little stiffly, a little formally. "I've seen a world I never knew existed. Thank you."

"You're welcome, ma'am," Goodnight said, a little formal himself. "Right welcome."

"I'll miss it," she said.

"We'll miss you," he said. "I will. The canyon will, too. And the bees and all."

Their feet were in shadow now. The world was growing colder.

"I'm glad I came," she said.

"Me, too," he said. "I hope you'll come back."

"Maybe. You never know."

"I was hoping you'd promise to come back."

They walked in silence while the shadow of the canyon crawled up their bodies. They seemed to be sinking into darkness.

"Won't you promise?" he asked.

"Promise what?" she asked.

"To come back."

"But I don't know."

"What don't you know?"

"If I'll come back. If it'll work out."

"Please promise."

"I can't."

"You're sure?"

"I just can't. I don't know. I'm sorry."

Walking in the gloom of the canyon, Goodnight felt his mind crying. It cried for her because it loved her. It wept for her because it couldn't have her.

He knew he had closed his deal with the wrong Sanborn.

18

Goodnight and Black Dub rode through a dark, rain-soaked night. Now and then, big lightning would flash in the distance, and then small lightning would crackle between their horses' wet ears. Actually, Black Dub forked a mule rather than a horse. He claimed none of the horses were strong enough to carry him. The riders were cold, miserable, and sleepy—but there was no point in stopping because they wouldn't be able to sleep anyway with this storm blowing. Unless they could find shelter.

"How're you doin'?" asked Goodnight.

"I'm okay, but I'm worried about this here mule," said Black Dub. "He's gittin' pretty tired. Pretty soon I'm gonna have to git off and start carryin' him."

Goodnight found himself wondering if the strongman was serious. "You're not serious, are you?"

"Bossman, has this here rainstorm done washed away your sense a humor?"

Goodnight laughed self-consciously.

The horse and mule's jobs were made more difficult by the incline up which they trudged. Goodnight and his traveling companion were climbing higher and higher into the Rocky Mountains in search of Robbers' Roost, which was supposed to be somewhere up ahead in southeastern Colorado. That much everybody in this crowded corner of state boundaries seemed to know. But now they needed better directions and a place to spend the cold, rainy night.

Two weeks ago, Goodnight had gathered his hands together to tell them what he wanted them to do in his absence. They were of course to care for the herd and the horses—but they were also to begin constructing a ranch house. In Goodnight's mind, the house was a part of the courtship of Revelie. He doubted that she would consent to marry him if it meant living in a dugout or a tepee. He drew the plans in the red dust of the canyon floor and warned his boys not to step on its lines. Keep the animals away from his diagram, too.

And he knew where he wanted his new home. Goodnight had crisscrossed the canyon on horseback, imagining his house in different places. He looked out of imaginary windows and admired different views. He tried to see with her eyes because he wanted to please her.

The site Goodnight finally chose was between an impressive peak and a beautiful mesa. The peak was topped by a large stone that looked a little like a face. It wasn't exactly a human face. So what was it? Squinting up at the frowning rock, Goodnight decided it looked like a monkey. Or rather it resembled pictures of monkeys in his schoolbooks. His Writers' schoolbooks. But this rock monkey looked sadder than all those book monkeys. He figured maybe he would call it Sad Monkey Mountain. Turning his attention to the mesa, he noticed that it flared from top to bottom like a woman's skirt. This skirt was decorated with horizontal bands of color. A pink band, then a white band, then a red band, then another white band, then a purple band, another pink, then violet, white again, red again, then maroon . . . This skirt was more colorful than the ones Revelie usually wore. It reminded him of the skirts he had seen in Weatherford worn by the Mexican women. Maybe he would call it Mexican Skirt Mesa. Yeah, he liked the name. He liked the place. He would build Revelie a house between Sad Monkey Mountain and Mexican Skirt Mesa. It would be the prettiest house in the world in the prettiest canyon on earth. He just hoped the prettiest girl in the world would make up her mind to live there.

Having given his cowboys their instructions, Goodnight had picked one of them, Black Dub Martin, and had ridden away on a search for vengeance. He was determined to find Gudanuf and his gang and make them pay in blood and ears. Goodnight and his chosen partner would be outnumbered if they ever caught what they were chasing, but they would worry about that later. Black Dub was as strong as three men, which would help in a fistfight, but in a gunfight he was just a bigger target. It had been a hard trip, either too hot and too dry, or too cold and too wet. This mountain country was beautiful but treacherous. Black Dub's mule was more surefooted than Goodnight's Red. The rancher missed his good horse Mister Goddog more and more, which just made him want to catch Gudanuf all the more.

He debated whether to cut the outlaw's ears off before or after he hanged him.

"Look yonder," said Black Dub.

Goodnight squinted in the direction the big man was pointing, but he couldn't see anything but rain and darkness. He wasn't surprised that Black Dub could see what he couldn't. The giant's eyes were as strong as his back.

"What?" asked Goodnight.

"I swan," said Black Dub, "but there's a light up there. See, right there. Lookit."

"I'll take your word for it. What does it look like?"

"Hard to say. Mebbe a campfire. Cabin. Forest fire. We gonna have to git closer."

"Nice spottin'."

"Aw, I just looked up and saw it. Nothin' special."

They rode on in silence watching the little lightning sparking between their mounts' ears. The little thunder was a barely audible crackle. It was ten minutes later that one-eyed Goodnight finally saw the light. He noticed that it flickered but not much, which suggested a cabin rather than a campfire. That held out the possibility of shelter. Shelter and food. Ever since their pack mule drowned crossing the Red River they had been existing on extremely short rations. (Goodnight had managed to shoot a skunk, but its meat was definitely a mixed blessing.) Now he tightened his legs around Red to nudge him faster. He could feel saliva in his mouth.

"Yeah, I see it," Goodnight said.

"It's a dugout," Black Dub said. "Door's open. There's a candle on a table. Fire in the fireplace."

"What's for dinner?"

"Don't kid me now. My eyes ain't that good. But, ya know, it could be stew. There's a pot hangin' in the fireplace."

Goodnight wanted to kick Red in the sides and race toward the light, but he was afraid he would end up at the bottom of a cliff. Still, Red sensed his mood and started to trot. Goodnight eased back on the reins to restrain his horse's enthusiasm. He wanted to make sure he actually got to the light in one package.

They rode down a long incline, then up another, then down, then up. Goodnight still couldn't see the pot bubbling over the fire in the fireplace, but he had no trouble imagining its savory contents.

• • •

Rain-drenched, Goodnight and Black Dub rode into a small clearing commanded by a dugout. Now the one-eyed man could see the bubbling pot, and he could feel his mouth go watery. The two riders swung down from their mounts and a dark figure appeared in the open doorway of the dugout. He blotted out the light.

"Who the hell are you?" shouted the dugout dweller. "And whaddaya want?"

"Shelter if you've got any to spare," Goodnight replied, "on a cold and rainy night."

"And I s'pose you're hungry, too," grumbled the dark figure. "Never met a stranger who waddn't hungry."

"Something does smell good," Goodnight said, attempting a light tone.

"You're a grasshopper, aincha?"

"What? No, my name's Jimmy Goodnight."

"Yeah, but you're still a damn grasshopper. You got no food, and you come lookin' for some poor ant to mooch off of. Well, this here ant's damn tired a feedin' you hippitty hops."

"Please, mister," said Black Dub. "Cain't we just sleep under your roof. It's powerful wet out chere. We don't hafta eat nothin' if you don't want."

The industrious ant smiled for the first time, showing yellow teeth. "Who're you?"

"His name's Black Dub Martin. And like I say, I'm Goodnight. Glad to know ya."

"I can see he's black. Mebbe I just got one eye left, but I can tell black from white."

"You've just got one eye?" Squinting in the darkness, Goodnight made out an eye patch. "Me, too. I just got one eye. I been lookin' at the world through a knothole ever since I was knee-high to a–uhm, grasshopper."

"That don't exactly make us brothers," said the one-eyed ant, "no matter what you think."

"I s'pose not."

The ant was using his good eye to study the giant black man, looking him up and down, impressed. It was almost as if he were trying to decide whether to buy him.

"Well, come on in," the hardworking ant said to Goodnight. "I like your friend or else I'd leave you out in the rain. No skin off my ass."

"Thanks."

The dark figure turned and burrowed back into his dugout. Goodnight and Black Dub followed him inside.

By the light of the fireplace, Goodnight got his first good look at his host. He was extremely short without being a midget or a leprechaun. He stood less than five feet, but his barrel body looked strong. He had a full beard that had gone white, and his still-brown hair was thinning on top. And now Goodnight could plainly see the eye patch that he had missed in the dark.

"We live in a dugout, too," Goodnight said, "but it's not as nice as yours." He was trying to ingratiate himself. "Thanks for takin' us in."

"We told you our names," said Black Dub. "Who're you?"

"Well, behind my back, folks calls me the Ole One-Eyed King," said their host. "To my face, they calls me Abbo King. That's short fer Albert. Satisfied?"

"Uh-huh," said the black giant, looking down at the short man in front of him.

"Well, siddown, I'll git the grub," said the Ole One-Eyed King. "Thass what you come fer, ain't it?"

"We come for shelter, but we'll gladly accept a meal," said Goodnight. "Thank you."

"Thass what I thought."

Goodnight and Black Dub took seats on a split-log bench. They pulled it up close to a split-log table. Using a rag, the One-Eyed King lifted a boiling pot out of the fireplace. He carried it steaming to the splintery table and set it in front of Goodnight and Black Dub.

"I don't got no dishes," said the One-Eyed King. "Hope you don't mind if we all pick outa the same pot."

"Course not," said Goodnight.

Black Dub shook his head.

"Dig in," said the One-Eyed King.

The host speared a square morsel of meat with his big-bladed bowie knife. Goodnight followed suit by thrusting his pocket knife into the brew and coming out with a pyramid-shaped piece of flesh. Then Black Dub stabbed a trapezoid with his long skinning knife. They all chewed.

"It's good," said Goodnight, "but I don't recognize the flavor. What is it?"

The One-Eyed King hesitated and then said: "It's badger meat. How you like it?"

"You eat badgers?" asked Black Dub. "That ain't–"

"I'm glad you like it," said the One-Eyed King. "Sometime you git tired a deer meat or bear meat or even squirrel meat. You want change. Like now."

"Don't taste much like how I figured badger would," said Black Dub.

"You callin' me a liar?"

"Course he ain't," said Goodnight.

"Good badger," said Black Dub.

They ate in silence for a while.

"What brung you to these parts?" asked the One-Eyed King. "Less I'm bein' too nosey."

"We're trailin' some men," Goodnight said.

"Who's that?"

"Man named Gudanuf. Him and some boys that call theirselves the Robbers' Roost gang. Ever heard of 'em?"

"Course. I ain't ignorant."

"You wouldn't know how to find 'em, would you?"

"I hear tell they hold up at Robbers' Roost."

"I know, but where's that?"

"I dunno. They's bad folks to git mixed up with."

They returned to eating in silence.

"Whass this?" asked Black Dub. He held a curved piece of meat on the end of his skinning knife. It looked like a link of sausage, but it had bones inside it.

"Looks sorta like a finger?" Goodnight said.

"Thass what I thought," said Black Dub.

"It's the badger's tail," said the One-Eyed King. "They ain't got much of a tail, but it's worth eatin'. Sweet."

"Mebbe you'd like it," said the giant. "Here."

He pointed his knife at the powerfully built little man, who plucked the morsel off the sharp point with his fingers. Then he popped it into his mouth.

"Mmmm, thanks."

Then he spit out the linked bones. He smiled at his guests. Black Dub's generosity seemed to have warmed his personality.

Goodnight speared something in the stew pot and held it up. "I got another one! How many tails has this badger got?"

"I killed two of 'em. They was married or somethin'. Try it, you'll like it a lot."

19

Goodnight tried not to close his eye all night: a one-eyed man trying to keep an eye on another one-eyed man. He wasn't particularly satisfied with the tale of two badger tails, but he wasn't sure what to think. Those tails did look a lot like fingers, but he couldn't make himself believe that they really were. It was impossible.

Goodnight and Black Dub lay rolled in their bedrolls in front of the hearth, where embers still glowed. The One-Eyed King slept on a mattress of corn husks nearby. Every time he turned over, the husks rattled. The racket they made helped Goodnight stay awake.

But sometime between two and three in the morning, Goodnight's eye closed and didn't open again. He dreamed of cannibals. They tied him to a spit and were about to roast him alive when he woke up wet all over. He looked around and found everything peaceful. Black Dub was snoring softly. The One-Eyed King turned on his corn husks, *rattle, rattle.*

Goodnight renewed his promise to himself to stay awake, but Black Dub momentarily stopped snoring and the One-Eyed King stopped rolling. In this silence, he fell asleep again.

Rattle, rattle, rattle.

The louder-than-usual corn-husk–rattling roused Goodnight briefly. He half-opened his eye, silently swore at his host for disturbing his sleep, turned over and closed his eye again. He dozed.

Then Goodnight's good eye fluttered open again. He wasn't sure what had roused him, but he saw the One-Eyed King kneeling over Black Dub with his broad-bladed bowie knife in his hand. He seemed to be looking for the best place to plunge it in.

Rolling, Goodnight unwound himself from his bedroll, and in the same motion he grabbed his ax, which was never far from him. He rolled up onto his feet like a lynx.

"Git back!" Goodnight shouted.

The One-Eyed King looked up startled. He saw an ax poised to decapitate him.

"What?" said the King.

"Git away from him!" ordered Goodnight.

"What?" asked Black Dub, rousing. "Whass goin' on?"

"He's got a knife."

Black Dub reached up, grasped King's wrist, and, *crack,* broke it. The bowie knife fell to the packed-earth floor.

"Owww!" screamed the little man.

"What you want I should do with him?" asked the giant.

"Hold him," said Goodnight. "I'll git a rope."

"Don't hang me! I took you in. I give you a roof over your head."

"I didn't say nothin' about hangin'. We're just gonna tie you up for now. Keep you outa mischief."

"Aw, thanks."

"We'll wait'll mornin' to hang you."

"Now, why you wanna do that?"

"'Cause I think you eat people. Them wasn't badger tails in the stew pot. Them was fingers."

"No, that ain't so."

"I didn't wanna believe it. Fact is, I didn't believe it till I saw you ready to butcher us in our sleep. Were you gonna skin us and hang us up by our heels?"

"Not you! I'd never eat a white man."

"Shut up!"

"Really, I just eats darkies and Meskins and Injuns. Swear to God."

Goodnight hit the Ole One-Eyed King in the mouth with the blunt side of his ax. Broken teeth fell from his face like hail from the sky.

"You mean that badger meat was man meat?" asked Black Dub.

"'Fraid so," said Goodnight.

The black giant retched and then threw up on his prisoner. Then he looked embarrassed.

"Awww," complained the Cannibal King.

"Less kill him right now," said Black Dub, taking hold of the maneater's neck.

"No, we better wait for daylight," Goodnight said. "I still cain't git over thinkin' there's somethin' wrong with killin' somebody when it's dark."

"How come?" asked Black Dub.

"It's a Human taboo. I mean Comanche. It's a Comanche taboo."

"Oh."

They rolled the Ole One-Eyed King in his bearskin cover so only his head stuck out. Goodnight fetched rope from his saddle, and they bound him like a sausage in this casing. Leaving him on the dirt floor, the victors crawled onto his corn-husk mattress, which complained vociferously at the weight. Soon they were both asleep again.

The Ole One-Eyed King continued to roll this way and that in the night, but his restlessness did not disturb the sleepers. The packed earth did not let out a single crackle.

20

Early the next morning, as the light was just reaching this mountain valley, they placed the Ole One-Eyed King on the back of Black Dub's mule. Then they maneuvered mule and rider beneath a pine tree. Goodnight took his time tying an almost perfect hangman's noose. He fitted it around the King's neck.

"Got anything to say before you go?" asked Goodnight.

Black Dub raised his hand to slap his mule's ass.

"Wait!" yelled the One-Eyed King. "I kin take you to that there Robbers' Roost. Really, I kin. I sell 'em meat in the winter. They're grasshoppers like you two. Never think about tomorrow. Never. So if'n you really wanta catch up with them guys? I mean, if'n you kills me, what–"

"Shut up!" said Goodnight. "You done said yore last words on this here earth."

Black Dub slapped his mule's ass. It bolted forward, leaving the One-Eyed King dancing in the air to fast music.

"Grab him!" yelled Goodnight.

Black Dub grabbed the Ole One-Eyed King and held him up so he wouldn't choke to death.

"You sure?" asked Black Dub.

"Less see what he really knows."

Black Dub lifted the choking man high enough to relieve the pressure on his throat. The Cannibal King coughed.

"Don't kill me," he sputtered. "I kin guide you. I'll show ya! Lemme."

"You better," said Goodnight. "How far is it?"

"Three days' ride. Mebbe four."

"I'll give you two days to find it. If we ain't there by then, you ain't gonna be King no more. Your name's gonna be Nobody. Nobody Atall. You hear?"

• • •

They rode in an ascending row, as if they had been arranged by height. Riding bareback, King was first in line on his own emaciated donkey. Then came Goodnight on Red and Black Dub on his mule named Abraham Lincoln. The cannibal still had the noose around his neck. Goodnight held the other end of the rope.

"How'd you git into the people-eatin' bizness anyhow?" Black Dub called out.

"Don't bother me," King mumbled through broken teeth.

"You better answer him," Goodnight advised, "less'n you want the other wrist broke and maybe an ankle besides."

"Both ankles," said Black Dub.

They rode in a hostile silence.

"Started the first winter we was up here," King said at last. "We didn't know what to expect. My partner and me. Man by the name of Prince. Funny, huh. Anyhow, we was starvin' in the middle of a big snow blow. Really starvin'. You ain't got no idea how hungry a man can git. I figured just one of us was gonna make it to spring, so I decided it was gonna be me. Nothin' personal. Just math. I lived on him for weeks. Just a little at a time. After a while, you kinda git to like the taste, you know."

"What color was he?" yelled Black Dub.

"White, whaddaya think? I wouldn't partner up with no–"

"But you said you don't eat no white folks."

"He was the last one. I knowed it was wrong. I really suffered over it. So's I up and promised God from now on I'd only eat them there black and brown races."

Goodnight pulled on the noose rope so hard that it jerked King backward off the donkey's back.

"Don't kill him before we gits there," said Black Dub. "Calm down."

That night, they camped in a small clearing surrounded by pointed trees. They didn't make a fire because they didn't have anything to cook. Besides, they didn't want to advertise their presence in these mountains. All they had to eat were dried strips of venison that they had confiscated from the dugout. They made sure it was venison. Supper didn't take long. Then Goodnight and Black Dub rolled King in his bearskin again and tied him like a sausage. The noose was still around his neck. They left the prisoner on hard ground while they heaped up pine needles for their own beds. King didn't have a pillow. His captors used their saddles.

Goodnight again dreamed of cannibals. He tossed and turned during the dream, but the pine needles were quiet beneath his restlessness. He always woke up just before they started to cook him.

The next morning, Goodnight missed the coffee that had drowned along with the pack mule. He rolled up his bedding, brushing off pine needles as he went. He wondered what kind of coffee could be made out of ground pine nuts.

"Mornin', Bossman," said Black Dub. "Mornin', Piece a Shit."

"Mornin'," Goodnight said.

"Untie me," King said. "The rope's too tight. I couldn't sleep atall all night."

"Good," Goodnight said. "Remember, you only got one more day to find what we're alookin' for. If we ain't found nothin' by sundown, you ain't gonna have no trouble sleepin' 'cause that's all you're gonna be doin' from now on out."

"Then loosen this damn rope and less git goin'."

"When we git around to it."

"Besides, I gotta pee."

"Pee in your bed for all I care."

Goodnight and Black Dub took their time saddling their mounts. They tied their bedrolls on behind the saddles. Then they untied and unrolled the prisoner, and they smelled urine.

"Nice work," said Goodnight.

"I done told you I had to go," said King. "Do I hafta keep wearin' this here necktie?"

"Yes, ma'am."

Goodnight thought a moment and then tied a knot in the rope just above the noose. Now it would be much harder to remove. Then he tied a second knot.

"Thanks," said King.

"You're welcome," said Goodnight.

They all climbed on their mounts–the horse named Red, the mule named Abraham Lincoln, the donkey named Prince–and set off in search of Robbers' Roost. They wound up and they wound down. They rode through dense forests and they picked their way across rocky slopes. They didn't stop at noon for lunch, but Goodnight distributed dried venison as they rode.

"We gittin' closer?" asked Goodnight.

"It ain't much more," said King.

"How much longer?"

"I ain't sure."

How much longer?"

"Not far."

"You said that miles back."

"Not far atall. Honest."

"Yeah, sure. Can you feel your neck already gittin' longer?"

"Why you gotta talk like that?"

"Shut up."

Winding down a steep canyon, they came to a river. It wasn't too wide, but it was swift. It looked cold and deep. Goodnight shivered involuntarily in anticipation.

"I s'pose we gotta cross that thing."

"Yeah, sorry, it's not far after that. Honest."

"Lead the way."

"That ain't gonna work. Prince here always balks at water. He won't lead off 'cause he's ascared."

"What?"

"If'n y'all go first, you kin lead him behind."

"Okay, I'll lead, then you, then Black Dub."

"No, if we ain't last, Prince just ain't gonna go atall. You'll see. Honest."

"That don't make no sense."

"It's the only way he'll cross, I'm tellin' you. I knows him real well. Whut he'll do and whut he won't. We kin sit here jawin' till the cows come home, but it ain't gonna change nothin', and I'm in a hurry. I gotta git you to Robbers' Roost by dark or you're gonna hang me."

"That's for damn sure. Okay, you're prob'ly lyin', but we gotta git movin'. Black Dub, you go first, then me, then this son-of-a-bitch. I'll lead him and his balky Prince."

"Cain't you take off this noose while we cross?"

"No, ma'am."

Black Dub and Abraham Lincoln splashed into the river and the mule was soon swimming. Goodnight and Red followed them into swift water. The cold bit through the denim trousers and produced a shudder. Goodnight yanked on Prince's reins and he jumped unhesitatingly into the frigid river. The donkey didn't seem balky.

"Be careful," Goodnight called to Black Dub. "I don't like the looks of this."

"I's careful," the giant called back.

Goodnight glanced back over his shoulder at King, who was smiling. Why was he amused? What did he have to grin about? The cannibal's eye gleamed brightly in the late afternoon sun. Looking ahead, Goodnight glimpsed the danger.

"Come back!" he yelled. "Black Dub–!"

But he had called too late.

"Owww!!" screamed Black Dub.

The whirlpool had him. The giant was caught in a watery twister, a liquid tornado. Abraham Lincoln fought the swirling current but was no match for it. Mule and rider were swallowed by the freezing water.

Reacting instinctively, Goodnight spurred his horse toward the whirlpool to save Black Dub. Then the whirling water took him, too. Now, of course, he knew the river crossing was a trap. King had methodically guided them into danger in the hope of winning his life back. Pulling the reins hard to the right, upriver, upstream, Goodnight prayed that Red could save both their lives. He not only didn't want to die, but he didn't want King to live, to win.

Red fought the circling water. The horse kicked up foam fore and aft. He struggled to turn upstream against the current. Goodnight knew that his life depended upon his Goddog and asked the Human gods to save him from the spinning death force. Red pulled away from the cyclone, good, uh, then was drawn back into it.

"Revelie!" Goodnight screamed and then felt foolish. Save your breath, he told himself, you may need it. "Revelie! Revelie! Revelie! Revelie!"

21

Red responded to "Revelie" or to his own will to live. He rode the water harder, legs churning, froth all around.

"Go!" Goodnight yelled into Red's ear, speaking the Human tongue. "Fight! Fight!"

Then Goodnight felt a jerk. Looking back, he saw King trying to break away, pulling back on Prince's mane. Goodnight clung tighter than ever to the donkey's reins and the noose. If he drowned, he intended to take the cannibal to the bottom with him. He owed it to the world. He promised the world that he would never let go, but the pressure got heavier and heavier. He couldn't hang on any longer. He had to let go. No! But he had to. No! No! But he had no choice. He was being pulled inexorably into the vortex. He felt the wet reins slipping through his clenched fist. No!

Goodnight raised his spurred heels and then brought them down again, kicking Red in the sides. The kick was in slow motion because it happened underwater, but it literally spurred Red to a renewed effort. The horse's legs churned wildly like a windmill in a storm. The froth and foam were storm clouds. Red raced against death and slowly, a little, a little, he pulled away upstream.

Looking back, Goodnight saw Prince and King disappear into the whirling maelstrom. He felt the donkey's reins pulled forcefully from his hands, but he clung desperately to the noose rope. He was determined not to be outwitted by a cannibal. At the end of the noose rope, King flopped about like a big fish on a line.

Slowly, the far bank came closer. The fish continued to struggle, pulling this way and that against the line. Now Red had his feet on the bottom and was climbing up a steep slope to dry land. Goodnight didn't care if his fish was drowned or not, so long as he didn't wash away downstream. In his mind, King and Gudanuf were all mixed up—and he hated them both with a fury so hot that it was painful.

Goodnight looked around wildly. Where was Black Dub? Dead? Were fish now eating the meal that King had once hoped to enjoy?

Red burst up out of the freezing water into the freezing air. The horse shook himself and the rider shivered. Red climbed up the bank and thought his horse thoughts about saving himself and his master.

Once on the far bank, Goodnight began pulling in the rope, reeling in a big one. That fish was King, it was Gudanuf, it was all the hurts, all the pain the fisherman had suffered in his life. Goodnight wanted to wreak his vengeance upon this fish for what had happened to his good horse Mister Goddog, what happened to his sister long ago, what happened to the Humans, and what happened to Black Dub.

When he came out of the water, King looked dead. He lay motionless on the bank. Goodnight saw that he had lost his eyepatch and his empty socket was a gaping wound.

"Hello!"

Goodnight looked up and saw Black Dub riding toward him along the bank of the swift river. Suddenly, he was as happy as he had been angry. Then he noticed that the giant's right foot was pointing in the wrong direction. He felt as if his stomach were filled with man meat and he had to throw it all up.

Dismounting, Goodnight ran to Black Dub and tried to help him down from the saddle. When the giant's weight descended on him, Goodnight staggered. Then he half-lowered, half-dropped the big man. Goodnight ended up on the ground with the giant sitting in his lap.

"Thanks," said Black Dub.

"You're welcome," said Goodnight.

Then they both laughed in spite of their hurts.

Remembering his Human training, he set the break: an agonizing realignment of throbbing bones. He wrapped the leg in his bedroll and tied it up like a sausage. Finally, he added two of the straightest tree limbs he could find–one on either side of the leg–and bound them in place.

"He's movin'," said Black Dub.

Looking around, Goodnight saw King get awkwardly to his feet and start running. The cannibal staggered drunkenly up the bank.

Rising from his knees, Goodnight ran, too. He caught King before he reached the trees and tackled him. Then he twisted the cannibal's right arm behind him and marched him back down the bank.

"Less hang him," said Black Dub.

"Maybe hangin's too good for him," said Goodnight.

Forcing King to the ground, Goodnight sat on top of him, pinning his arms at his side.

"Whut you got in mind?" asked Black Dub.

Goodnight produced his pocket knife, opened a long blade, and plunged it into King's one good eye.

The hunt for Gudanuf was over for now. It was time to take Black Dub home.

The No-Eyed King would just have to get along the best he could. They left him on foot on the far side of the swift river. Surely something would be eating him before too long.

22

Descending into his home canyon, Goodnight looked for two landmarks: Sad Monkey Mountain and Mexican Skirt Mesa. There they were. His eye searched the swale between Monkey and the Skirt. He could make out a light-colored speck, but that was all. Was that speck a house under construction? He couldn't tell.

"How you doin'?" Goodnight called over his shoulder to his companion.

"Just fine," said Black Dub, but his voice was stretched tight.

The giant had ridden out of the mountains astride Abraham Lincoln because there was no other way. Then he had insisted on riding the rest of the way because he was stubborn.

When they finally reached the flat floor of the big canyon, Goodnight asked again if Black Dub was okay. The giant reassured him again that he was all right. Was he sure? Of course. Was he dizzy? No. Light-headed? No! Want me to shut up? Yes.

Then they emerged from a grove of cottonwoods and there it was, glowing a pale pink in the late afternoon light: Revelie's house. Of course, she didn't know it was hers, didn't know what was being prepared for her–and probably cared less. Would she ever see her new home? Could she ever admire it as much as he did? The structure looked like a couple of log cabins built about ten feet apart with a single peaked roof connecting them. The space between the cabins–a breezeway–was called a dog run.

After sleeping a single night in his new home, Goodnight was ready to travel again. Early in the morning, he saddled Red and rode off to ask Revelie to come and live with him in his new two-room log palace.

23

When Goodnight rode into Tascosa again, his heart was pounding like outlaw guns being fired in the air. He rode past Henry Kimball's blacksmith shop, where he smiled down at the tree stump as if it were an old friend. He slowed his horse as he approached the office of W. S. Mabry, Surveyor. He was in no hurry to get where he was headed. But he kept on going past McMasters' Store and the Post Office, past the Wright & Farnsworth General Store, past the North Star Restaurant. He stopped when he got to the Jenkins & Dunn Saloon. He swung down from his horse and tied the reins to the saloon's hitching rail, but he didn't go in. He continued on down Main Street on foot until he came to Tascosa Creek. The shaky footbridge matched his mood. Feeling weak, he attempted to knock firmly at a well-remembered door.

Then Goodnight waited and listened. He found himself hoping Revelie wouldn't open the door herself. His sudden appearance at her home might shock her. Or more likely seeing her in the doorway could stop his heart. It would be better to ease into this reunion. Take it slowly . . .

But then he had a frightening thought: If Revelie didn't open the door, her mother would! No, Goodnight would rather have Revelie greet him. That would be much better. Get it over with. Don't prolong the agony. Grab the bull by the horns. No, that wasn't how to put it.

Then Goodnight began to wonder if he had knocked loudly enough. He had been so nervous that he might not have struck firmly. He raised his right fist and knocked again. This time he really hammered the door. And he went on hammering until it suddenly occurred to him that he was making a fool of himself with all this racket. He felt like a mule kicking at the barn door. Now he dreaded the opening of the door because it could only lead to embarrassment.

But eventually nervousness and fear and embarrassment gave way to impatience. Goodnight went from being afraid somebody would open the door to feeling irritated at being kept waiting. Why didn't they answer the door? He had waited for weeks to see Revelie again, but he didn't intend to wait many more minutes on this doorstep. Were they being deliberately rude to him? Who did they think they were? Who did they think he was? Wasn't he good enough to cross their threshold? Hell!

This time he really pounded on the door. He was trying to hurt it. He made it jump on its hinges. Then he got afraid he might break it and stopped. He couldn't believe how he was behaving. He felt like the Big Bad Wolf outside the pigs' house. He dimly remembered his mother telling him that story.

Suddenly, he had to get out of there. He didn't want anybody to come to the door. If they did, they would see how crazed he had become. He would slink away and come back and try again later. He hurried shakily back across the shaky bridge.

Once he was back on Main Street, Goodnight started to calm down. He wondered what he should do now. He eventually decided to pay a call on the bank to see if Velvet Pants was in. He could talk to the father about his daughter before seeing her himself. He was back to his old idea of easing into the long-wished-for reunion.

Entering the bank, Goodnight saw a single teller behind bars in a kind of cage. He didn't see anybody else. He kept looking around wondering how this place worked and where Mr. Sanborn was.

"Can I help you?" asked the teller.

"I dunno," said Goodnight, ambling forward. "I was kinda lookin' for Mr. Sanborn."

"He's in the office," said the young man, who was wearing a white shirt and a black tie. "Just knock on the door."

Goodnight looked around. Seeing only one door, he walked up to it and knocked on it, but this time he restrained himself. He didn't make the door do any dances.

When the door opened promptly, Goodnight saw Mr. Sanborn smiling at him. He tried to smile back, but he wasn't sure he was doing a good job of it. He felt nervous again.

"Well, hello, stranger," said Mr. Sanborn. "How did you know?"

"Know what?" asked Goodnight.

"That your money just got here. It came yesterday. I was a little worried how I was going to get in touch with you. And now here you are. Johnny on the spot."

"My money?" said Goodnight in something of a daze.

"The money to buy our ranch, of course. It took it a while to get here. I had to write to London for it. These immense distances. It seemed to take forever. But it finally got here. And you're here. Let's go right over to the surveyor's office and get down to business."

Mr. Sanborn started toward the bank's front door, but Goodnight just stood where he was. At the moment, he was much more concerned about the partnership deal he wanted to make than the one he had already signed up for. His mind just wasn't on business, even though he was in a bank.

"Come on," ordered Mr. Sanborn.

Goodnight followed. Mr. Sanborn held the door open for him. They both passed out into Main Street.

"It's not far," said Mr. Sanborn.

"I hope your wife and daughter are well," Goodnight said.

"Oh, yes, they're very well, thank you. They went back to Boston. My wife wasn't happy here. It's not the country for her."

24

Goodnight was lost. He no longer recognized the earth over which he rode. It had changed. Or he had changed. Anyhow, he saw no familiar landmarks. Not that there were many landmarks out here on the stakeless Staked Plain. He wondered if he would ever find his way home again.

The land looked to him like a piece of paper on which God or the Great Mystery or Whoever had not yet written. Which was perhaps why this part of America was the last part conquered by the Writers. When rain fell on this land, it didn't run away in babbling sentences. It just disappeared into the earth. Trees punctuated most landscapes, but there wasn't any punctuation here. None! Nothing had been scratched out or erased by erosion. Goodnight couldn't read this unmarked land. Not now. Not anymore. He wondered if he had lost the ability to read with a Human eye. Now he could only read what Writers read. And Writers could only read what they could see.

Then he saw an armadillo and was glad for the company. He decided to discuss his plight with this armored possum who seemed to know very well where it was going.

"O Armadillo," Goodnight called out in the Writer's tongue, "I've got a favor to ask you. Hope you don't mind. I got myself lost. I cain't find a big, red canyon. You know the one? I was hopin' mebbe you could sorta point me in the right direction. How about it?"

The armadillo suddenly disappeared into the earth, the ground swallowing it in one gulp. Riding closer, Goodnight found the hole down which the armor-plated rodent had run, but from a few feet away it had been completely invisible. It might just as well have been in another state, in another country, on the moon. Goodnight was devastated by the experience. Not only did it prove to him how hard it was to find holes on this plain, even a hole as big as the red canyon, but it also suggested something even more disturbing: he had lost his ability to talk to nature.

That armadillo had not listened to him at all. It hadn't helped him. It hadn't cared about him. He could no longer close the gap between himself and other manifestations of the Great Mystery. Now he really felt alone. Now he was truly lost.

Goodnight was feeling particularly sorry for himself when he noticed an imperfection on the horizon. As God or the Great Mystery or Whoever had drawn the line separating earth and heaven, It had accidentally let fall a drop of ink. As this black spot drew closer, it was transformed into a buffalo. And as the buffalo came nearer, it turned into a horse and the hump on its back changed into a rider. Goodnight squinted into the heat waves at his salvation.

Tightening his legs around his horse to urge it to go faster, Goodnight started waving at the distant rider. But the rider did not wave back. The lost man took off his hat and swung it back and forth over his head, but the other man did not seem to notice. Goodnight was not a man who liked to raise his voice, but he started yelling. No voice answered his cry.

Goodnight became terrified that the other rider wouldn't see him, would go off and leave him, would abandon him in this desert. Staring into the heat waves, he became convinced that the other horseman was growing smaller rather than larger, was moving away from him rather than toward him. Oh, how he wished he had two eyes now, which would have made him better able to judge distances. The one-eyed man felt he had to get the other man's attention or perish here in this wasteland, so he yelled louder and waved his hat harder. But it didn't do any good. He had the feeling of coming so very close to salvation but missing it nevertheless. He had to do something! But what could he do?

Then he knew. Goodnight took out his revolver, cocked it, and started firing in the air. The other rider would have to hear these shots. Now he would ride to the rescue.

But he didn't. He didn't wave. He didn't yell a greeting. He didn't fire in the air. He didn't respond in any way.

Goodnight had to reload his cap-and-ball pistol. It was hard work on horseback, especially with only one eye. He even managed to drop some ammunition on the ground, but he finally got his gun loaded again. Raising it over his head, he started firing at God in His heaven.

And then suddenly his prayers seemed to have been answered. Goodnight saw a puff of white smoke rise from the other rider, which meant that he had fired an answering shot. The lost had been found. His plea had been heard. Goodnight was flooded with a sense of unconditional happiness . . .

Then an ax hit him in the chest. Anyway, it felt like an ax. The blade seemed to strike him right in his breastbone, right where his ribs joined in front, right where his heart was. He was already falling when he heard the sound of the shot. It sounded like a rifle. Goodnight hit the ground and felt himself die. He saw himself fall into an ocean of water and go down and down. And then he didn't see anything. His world was black . . .

When he opened his good eye, not knowing if he was in heaven or hell or lost in the Great Mystery, he saw a good-looking stranger standing over him. He had blue eyes and arched black eyebrows. Goodnight rebelled at the idea of having been killed by a handsome cowboy. It was so unfair. The good-looking should pick on the good-looking, not somebody like him with one eye.

"Hell, why'd you shoot me?" Goodnight asked.

"Because you was shooting at me," said Blue Eyes.

"No, I waddn't. I was just trying to git your attention. I'm lost."

"Where you tryin' to git to?"

"There's a big red canyon around here somewheres. I sorta misplaced it."

"The red canyon. That's where I'm goin', too."

"You got business there?" Goodnight asked suspiciously.

"Don't know as how that's any a your business."

"Dammit, you shot me, so humor me, okay?"

"Well, I'm lookin' for a fella named Goodnight, if'n you gotta know."

"Hell, I'm Goodnight."

"No?"

"Yeah."

"Damn, I heard a lot about you. I'm on my way to work for you, if'n you'll have me."

25

I'm sorry," said the cowboy. "I surely am sorry."

"Oh, shut up!" Getting shot made Goodnight cranky. "What's your name, anyhow? I reckon I oughta know the name a the man who killt me."

"Jack."

"You got a last name."

"Loving. But I ain't too partial to it."

"Jack Loving, huh? Well, I cain't say I'm glad to know ya. But I gotta admit, you're a purdy fair shot. Damn, it hurts."

"I'm sorry."

"Stop bein' sorry. You're wearin' me out."

Loving dropped to his knees in the buffalo grass. Goodnight could see the good-looking killer trying to figure out how to help his victim, but he clearly didn't know much about doctoring.

"Mebbe you better roll me over on my side," Goodnight said. "See if your damn bullet went clear through or not."

Goodnight could see that Loving was reluctant to touch him, as reluctant as an inexperienced lover, wanting to do it right but not knowing exactly how.

"Just do it," hissed Goodnight. "Git it over with. Hurry."

Loving obeyed. He put his hands gently under Goodnight's left shoulder and hip and rolled him over onto his right side.

"Damn, that smarts," grimaced Goodnight. "How's it look? Any blood back there?"

"Yes, sir," said Loving.

"Bleedin' bad?"

"Yes, sir."

"Don't sir me."

"I'm sorry."

"Don't sorry me either."

"No, sir."

Goodnight could feel himself losing touch. The world was slipping from his grasp. He slipped back into the black water and sank deeper and deeper . . .

When he woke up again, Goodnight was surprised still to be alive. He hurt in his body and his mind. He wondered how many times he would have to die to be dead. All this dying and coming back to life again was so damn tiring. He was plum tuckered out. He had never figured dying would be such hard work. He just wanted to sleep . . .

When he came back to the surface once more, Goodnight was burning up. *Burning.* He couldn't stand being this hot. *Burning, burning, burning.* It was somehow worse than the pain in his chest. He found himself wishing he had the strength to locate a devil's pincushion. That's what he needed. That's what would suck the poison out of him. That's what would bring the fever down. But he couldn't move, so a devil's pincushion remained as unattainable as Revelie in Boston.

"How you doin'?" a strange voice asked.

Then Goodnight remembered that Loving was there with him. Maybe the man who had tried to kill him would be willing to run an errand for him. But first the burning man would have to summon all his strength, open his mouth, and talk. He didn't know if he could. It was going to be the hardest thing he had ever tried to do in his life.

"Duh-duh-devil's pincushion," Goodnight managed to whisper.

"What?" asked Loving.

"Cactus. Small." He stopped to catch his breath. "Looks like fishhooks on top. Med'cine."

"Save your strength. Just nod if'n I'm right. You want this here cactus 'cause you figure it'll do you some good."

Goodnight nodded.

"I reckon the fishhooks're thorns, huh?"

Goodnight nodded.

"You figure there's some 'round here somewheres?"

Goodnight nodded.

"Be right back."

Goodnight could feel that Loving was glad to have an excuse to leave him. Of course he would want to get away. Who wanted to sit around with a dying man? Stop rambling. Try to think. Concentrate. You forgot something. Something important.

"Loving!" Goodnight shouted. He was surprised he had that much voice left in his dying body. "Loving, come back!"

He heard his killer hurrying back to him. He heard his boots in the dry grass. He heard him breathing hard from anxiety. He realized this murderer-turned-Good-Samaritan thought he was dying right now.

"What's wrong?" asked Loving, his distorted face blocking out the sky.

What's wrong? Everything was wrong. He had been shot. He was in pain. Fever was burning him up. He was dying. What wasn't wrong!

"Ask," whispered Goodnight.

"Ask what?" Loving said.

"Ask permission."

"Ask who?"

"Ask the devil's pincushion's permission. Say you need it to make med'cine. Git down on your knees."

Loving looked at Goodnight strangely. The wounded man knew the good-looking cowboy thought he was raving.

"Okay."

He was humoring him.

"I mean it. Promise me. Promise you'll do just like I say. Just promise, okay?"

"Yeah, right, I promise."

"Cross your heart!" Goodnight demanded.

What had come over him? Was he getting younger and younger as he got closer to death? Was he living his life in reverse? Where did he think he was? In the damn school playground at recess?

"Cross my heart," said Loving. And he made an *X* over his heart with his trigger finger.

26

Goodnight felt somebody bothering him, and he got angry. Why would anybody wake him up when he so wanted to sleep? How inconsiderate! How downright mean! When he was a boy, he had hated to go to sleep because it was too much like death. He was actually afraid of sleep. So he well understood why the Humans referred to sleep as "blanket-death." But now he was in so much pain . . . he was so hot . . . he felt so miserable all over that he longed for death because it was so much like sleep. Death would be so comfortable. Death would be so soothing. And now somebody was trying to wake him up from this sweet lullaby of death. Damn his soul!

"Stoppit," Goodnight grumbled. "Git away. Lemme alone."

"I'm sorry," said a strange voice. "I surely am."

"Quit it."

"I said I'm sorry."

Goodnight opened his eye and saw a vaguely familiar face. He studied it, trying hard to recognize it. The eyebrows were black. The eyes were brown. No, they were supposed to be blue. They ought to be blue. What was wrong? What was happening?

"Who are you?" asked Goodnight.

"Jack Loving," said the brown-eyed cowboy.

"What's wrong with your eyes?"

"Nothin'. Be still."

As his head cleared somewhat, Goodnight remembered that this was the man who had shot him. But he had had blue eyes back then, and now they were brown. This cowboy must have "much medicine." Was it some kind of robber's trick? Was it some sort of disguise?

Studying the eyes, Goodnight once again noticed the black eyebrows. They were so dark that they looked as if they had been drawn. Which made the face look slightly effeminate. Loving was almost pretty.

"You're too damn good-lookin'," Goodnight said.

"I said I'm sorry," Loving said.

"Stop sayin' that."

"I'm sorry."

"What're you doin' to me?"

"I got that there devil's pincushion you wanted. Had a devil of a time findin' it, as a matter a fact."

"Stop complainin'."

"I'm sorry. I'm almost finished. Just hold on."

Goodnight remembered now. He hoped the devil's pincushion would suck out the infection and bring down his fever. With just one eye, he had to crane his neck to see what was happening to him. He saw Loving chewing pieces of devil's pincushion to pulverize it. Then he spat it out and stuffed it under bandages, front and back, next to the wounds. Loving was doing it right, doing what had to be done, even though it hurt like hell and all.

"There, that's got it," said the blue-eyed, brown-eyed cowboy. "That's the last of it."

Then he set about trying to clean stray cactus pulp out of his mouth with his trigger finger.

"Thanks," said Goodnight.

"Least I could do," said Loving. "Kin I do anythin' else for you?"

"Yeah."

"What?"

"Tell me. What color are your eyes?"

"First one thing and then another."

"Damnedest thing. Now shut up. I wanna sleep."

When Goodnight woke up again, he thought Revelie was with him. He told "her" how glad he was to see "her." He said his mind cried for "her" now more than ever. He told "her" how disappointed he had been when "her" father had told him that "she" had gone back East. But now "she" had come back to him, and he was so grateful. He thanked "her" over and over again for coming.

"I'm sorry," said a strange, masculine voice, "but I ain't her whoever she is. Hate to disappoint you."

When Goodnight heard the stranger say "sorry," he remembered Jack Loving. He realized his mistake. This cowboy had a girl's eyebrows, but he wasn't Revelie. Not by a long shot. The disappointment seemed to press down on Goodnight's painful chest, and he found it hard to breathe. Now he didn't have the breath to sing his death song. So he just gave up and let go.

Waking once more, Goodnight thought maybe he was dead because he couldn't see anything. He was sorry he wouldn't ever see Revelie again. Then he saw a single star in the blackness of death and realized it was night. Just night.

He drifted in and out of consciousness. Sometimes it was night. Other times it was day. Sometimes he thought he was awake when he was really dreaming, dreaming the dead had come back to life, dreaming his sister Becky was alive again, dreaming Wekeah had come back to him. Dreams were tough. You couldn't block the dead out of your dreams the way you could from your waking thoughts. Even their names crept in. Other times he thought he was dreaming when he was really awake. Sometimes he was afraid of death. Other times he wanted to die and join the dead, his dead.

On the fourth day, Goodnight felt well enough to be irritable and bossy. He told Loving that he could travel now but, no, he didn't want to go back to Tascosa to see some sawbones. He wanted to go home to the Home Ranch.

"You ain't goin' nowhere," Loving said. "You cain't fork a horse, and I ain't got no wagon to haul you in, mebbe you didn't notice. So you're stayin' put. I'm sorry."

Goodnight flinched at the apology. He wondered how he was ever goin' to break Loving of the habit.

"You kin be as sorry as you want," he said irritably. "But I'm goin' home. You kin haul me in a Comanche wagon. That's plenty good 'nough for me."

Goodnight watched the cowboy's blue-brown eyes go slightly out of focus as he tried to figure out what he was hearing.

"We don't have no injun wagon neither," Loving said. He looked behind him as if he were afraid one might be sneaking up on him.

"You're gonna build one," Goodnight bossed. "Get two long poles–"

"Oh, you mean a travois."

"Right."

Loving just squatted beside Goodnight, glancing first to the left, then to the right. He was trying to decide just how to put whatever it was he was trying to say.

"I know you don't want me to say I'm sorry," Loving said, "so I won't. But I swear I don't see no long poles around cheer. You know they ain't enough wood on this here Staked Plain to make a little bitty campfire, much less a damn travois."

"I'm sorry," Goodnight said. "Look now, you got me sayin' it. I guess I forgot where we was at. Mebbe I'm still a little weak in the head. But we cain't just stay here. We gotta do somethin'."

The two men were silent for a moment while they tried to figure out what to do. Goodnight caught himself playing with his eye patch. Loving pursed his lips.

"You better go on to the ranch," Goodnight said. "Git the chuck wagon and come git me. Whaddaya say?"

"I ain't leavin' you," Loving said. "Just fergit it. I'm—never mind."

They thought some more.

"Well, I dunno," Goodnight said at last, "but mebbe you could look around for a dead buffalo. They're scattered all over this here country. Mebbe we could fiddle around and make somethin' outa buffalo bones."

"I dunno," said Loving.

"You got a better idea?"

"Nope."

"Then you better git goin'."

Goodnight watched Loving shrug, get slowly to his feet, and start saddling his horse. The cowboy moved with an easy grace and an economy of motion. He didn't seem to hurry, but he was soon mounted and ready to go.

"So long," Loving said. "Be back as soon as I kin."

"Don't shoot nobody else," Goodnight said, "less'n you got to."

The mounted man spurred his horse with small rowels and galloped off in a hurry. As he moved farther and farther away, he seemed to sink into the flat land.

Goodnight felt relieved. He no longer had to listen to Loving say how sorry he was. What was more, he didn't have to try to entertain the cowboy when he didn't really feel up to being entertaining. Then just as he was beginning to feel real good about being alone for a change, Goodnight realized that he missed Loving. He felt abandoned even though he had sent the strange-eyed cowboy away. He was lonely. He almost longed to hear Loving say how sorry he was.

He had a long, lonely wait. The sun sank toward the flat land, like a big, fat egg falling slowly toward a flat griddle. The light softened on the plain. Goodnight generally enjoyed this time of day, but today it made him worry. Where was Loving? What kind of trouble could he have gone and gotten himself into? He worried for the sake of the cowboy. He also worried for his own sake. Maybe Loving had run into a Human hunting party and hadn't known how to behave. What if they mistook him for a buffalo hunter? Or maybe he had bumped into Gudanuf's gang. While he was preoccupied with these waking nightmares, Goodnight drifted off to sleep.

Much later, Goodnight was awakened by a strange racket. Looking about for its source, he saw a moonlit rider approaching, pulling some strange contraption behind him. He soon recognized the man as Loving, but he couldn't figure out just what he was dragging. As it drew closer, the contraption began to look more and more like a sled. Not a little sled for kids, but something considerably bigger. A sleigh. The kind of sleigh you sang "Jingle Bells" about. But it wasn't Christmastime. The first snow was still weeks away. What was a sleigh doing out here jingling across the Staked Plain? Goodnight figured it must be a mirage. Or he was dreaming. Or he was having a spell again and didn't know what was real and what were fever pictures.

"Howdy," Loving called from afar. "How you gittin' along?"

"Fair to middlin'," Goodnight called back. "What's that there thing followin' you?"

"I built you a wagon."

"Looks more like a sleigh."

"Yeah, it does, don't it. Seems like it's holdin' together so far. Knock on wood. But we both know there ain't no wood nowheres around here. Whaddaya think?"

Goodnight stared at a Staked Plain sleigh made entirely of buffalo bones. The rib cage of the buffalo formed the body of the sleigh. Two long thighbones were tied on underneath to do the job of the sled's runners. Loving had woven his lariat in and out of the ribs and around the backbone to help reinforce the buffalo's skeleton. With any luck, it might hang together for a few miles. Goodnight just kept staring at the chariot Loving had built for him. He finally decided it was the most beautiful wagon he had ever seen, and he was ready to ride it home to the most beautiful canyon he had ever seen, the prettiest spot in the whole wide world.

27

Riding in the belly of a buffalo, Goodnight bumped and jarred his way across the face of the Staked Plain. He imagined himself an unborn calf in his mother's womb. He would be the new hope of his doomed race. He and his woolly descendants would rule over the Great Plains forever and ever. He was the Prince of Calves. He felt great until he figured out that he was delirious again.

The buffalo-bones sleigh ran fairly well on its bone runners–requiring only a few stops for repairs–so long as their path lay across a table-flat plain. Unlike the one-horse open sleigh, this one was pulled by two horses: Loving's and Goodnight's own Red. Lying on his saddle blanket inside the rib cage, the wounded man felt every pebble and bounce, but he could stand it. He was going home.

Then the bone sleigh came to the brink of the red canyon. At first, Goodnight didn't know why the horses had stopped. He raised up to complain and then saw over the edge of the abyss. What were they going to do now? It wasn't the first time this question had crossed his mind. It had plagued him like a low-grade fever for miles, but he had never been able to come up with a solution. He wondered if he would have to camp out on the lip of the canyon until he could sit on a horse. His spirits had been soaring, and now they plummeted. He wanted to sink into the earth.

"Damn," said Goodnight. "Damn, damn, damn."

"Hold your horses," Loving said, turning in the saddle. "Don't go damnin' nobody yet."

"Don't tell me this here chariot's gonna fly," said Goodnight. "I'd like to see that."

"That's a good idea," said the handsome cowboy. "I hadn't thought a that."

"This here contraption'll bust up goin' down that there trail. You dunno how rough it is. I do."

"I'll take your word for it. I never figured on taking a sleigh ride down that slope, much fun as it looks like it'd be."

Watching Loving swing gracefully down off his horse, Goodnight was surprised to discover that he was physically afraid. He feared this gentle cowboy was going to hurt him without intending to. He didn't want to suffer any more. He told himself he should be ashamed of himself, but he remained tense and felt brittle.

"Whachew gonna do to me?" Goodnight asked.

"Carry you," said Loving.

"What?"

"Don't worry. I won't hurt you."

"You cain't. It's too steep and I'm too heavy."

"My mom was a mule."

"I won't have nobody talkin' ag'in' their mama."

"That was a compliment."

Despite Goodnight's muttered protests and complaints, Loving scooped him up and carried him to the brink of the yawning canyon. They both looked into the red void. Then Loving started down. He carried Goodnight like a baby. The baby was surprised at the slender cowboy's strength and his surefootedness. Goodnight began to relax, the tension trickling out of him . . .

Then Loving's boots slipped on the loose scree and he started dancing on the brink of the abyss trying to regain his balance. Goodnight sucked in a breath and held it as if he expected to be plunged underwater, even though no water was in sight. At the same time, he hugged Loving more tightly, which did not help the dancer, who needed all his dexterity to keep from falling. But somehow he succeeded in regaining his balance.

"Scared you, didn't I?" Loving laughed.

"No," Goodnight lied.

"No?"

"Okay, yeah."

"Scared myself a little, too."

"You better put me down."

Loving didn't say anything, but he started walking again, carrying Goodnight on down the treacherous trail. Soon he slipped on the scree again, but he regained his balance again.

"It's kinda like walkin' on marbles, ain't it?" Loving said. "Ticklish business."

"Be careful," said Goodnight.

"Good idea."

Loving's breathing became more and more labored. His burden was getting heavier and heavier.

"You sound like a cow havin' a calf," Goodnight said.

"Thanks," said Loving.

"Didn't mean no disrespect."

Loving eventually gave in and took a rest stop. He set his baby down carefully on the sheer side of the void and then collapsed on the wall of marbles. The trail was only a little over a mile long, but Loving needed half a dozen rest stops. Then at long last, after two hours of hard labor, he dropped to his knees as if praying and deposited his child on the red canyon floor.

After a rest, Loving climbed back up the canyon wall to get the horses. He tied the bone sleigh on the back of Goodnight's horse, which was a tricky arrangement, but somehow it worked. Then he got on his own horse and led the way back down the Comanche trail. When he reached the bottom of the canyon, he found Goodnight fast asleep.

Goodnight returned to the Home Ranch riding a dead buffalo. His cowboys welcomed him back warmly even though they were surprised to see him come home with a new gunslinger instead of a bride. He hadn't told any of them why he had wanted to go to Tascosa, but they all knew anyway. They all eyed Loving warily, trying to size him up, guessing at his skills. They wondered where he stood with Goodnight, whom he had almost killed and then saved.

28

"I just wisht I'd ever loved somebody that much," Loving said. "I surely do."

They were alone in the north room of the two-room house. All the cowboys were out doing their appointed chores. Loving's only job was to continue to nurse the man he had shot.

"Well, didn't do me much good," Goodnight said a little irritably, "did it?"

"Not yet," Loving said.

"She's gone."

"She ain't dead, is she? If'n she's dead, I figure she's gone. Otherwise, well, she's just misplaced."

"Don't try to be funny. I don't feel much like laughin' right now."

Goodnight watched Loving pacing up and down the cedar room.

"I'm jealous," Loving said at last.

"Nothin' to be jealous of," Goodnight said. "I ain't got nothin', leastwise not what I wanted. Now kin we drop the subject. I'm tired."

"You don't seem like no quitter. I didn't come all this way to work for no quitter. Quittin' didn't git these cows here."

"Shut up! Who asked you to come look me up, anyhow? Git outa here!"

Loving obeyed. He walked out the door into the sunshine. Goodnight wondered if he would ever see him again. Good riddance.

Coffee brought Goodnight his supper. Beans and beef and biscuits. Then the cook went back to the chuck wagon to feed the hands, and the boss was left alone and lonely. He didn't have Revelie to live with him in his new house, and he didn't have Loving either. He had managed to drive them both away.

"Whose chow you like best," asked a familiar voice, "mine or Coffee's?"

Looking up, the wounded man saw his nurse coming through the door.

"Coffee's," said Goodnight.

"Me, too," said Loving. "But that ain't sayin' much."

The cowboy with the tricky eyes squatted down–there wasn't any furniture in this palace–and dug into his own plate of beans, beef, and biscuits. He ate in silence as the cedar room got dark and darker. When he was finished with his supper, Loving got up and lit a coal-oil lantern.

"I got somethin' to show you," Loving said. "It's a new-fangled contraption."

He unbuckled a saddlebag that was lying on the floor and rummaged around inside looking for something. When he found it, he hid it in his hand. He extended the closed hand until it was only a few inches from the wounded man's face. Then he opened his fingers and revealed a fountain pen. Goodnight recoiled as if somebody had just thrust a rattlesnake under his nose. He made an inarticulate noise like an animal.

"What's the matter?" asked Loving.

"Git that damned thing away from me!" Goodnight yelled.

"I'm glad to see you're in a better mood."

"Never mind my mood."

"It's just a fountain pen."

"I know good 'n' well what it is. I don't much like fountain pens."

"How come?"

"Why won't you just leave me alone?"

Goodnight closed his good eye and pretended to be trying to go to sleep. He could feel Loving watching him.

"How come you got one of them damned things?" Goodnight asked, opening his eye a crack.

"I got a mother somewheres," Loving said. "I don't want her to fergit my name or my handwritin'."

"Oh."

"What's wrong with that?"

"Nothin'."

Loving took a deep breath and began: "See, you don't have to go traipsin' to Boston after that there girl. Your words can do all the damn traipsin' for you. Just write her a letter. Tell her how you feel about her. Like what you was sayin' when you was out of your head. Maybe she'll up and come back. Never know."

Goodnight studied Loving carefully. He was trying to figure him out. He wondered what he wanted.

"How come you're so interested in all this?" Goodnight asked.

"I like you," Loving said. "I shot you. I want to make it up to you. You're about the last person in the world I'da wanted to hurt."

"We're square. You shot me, but then you turned around and saved my damn life. That's the end a that. Let it be."

Loving started pacing again, measuring the cedar room again. Goodnight just stared at him.

"I cain't let it be," Loving said.

"Why not?" asked Goodnight.

"Because I heard how much you love her. Just write her a damn letter. Do it for me."

"I ain't no Writer."

"You don't hafta be much of a writer to write a damn letter. It don't even hafta be that long." He paused. "Less'n you mean you never learnt how atall."

"I cain't spell too good."

"I kin spell more or less. You kin ask me how to spell the hard words. I'll help."

Goodnight braced himself. He was about to admit something he surely hated to own up to. But making a hard admission would be easier than writing a goddamned letter.

"I cain't write," Goodnight said. "I mean, I cain't do no script. I just print. Looks like a first-grader. And I hate fountain pens."

He watched Loving think over his confession. The cowboy pursed his lips and his black eyebrows arched.

"You tell me what you wanna say," Loving said at last. "I'll write it down. My writin' ain't much to write home about, but I reckon it'll do in a pinch."

"I don't know what to say," Goodnight said.

"Tell her what you done told me about her."

"What did I tell you? I was crazy."

"Lotta stuff."

"You remember it?"

"Sure."

"Well, I don't. Just write down what you remember I done said. That'll do fer a letter, maybe. Okay?"

Goodnight watched Loving think over this proposition. The lips pursed. The eyebrows arched. Then the mouth frowned.

"I cain't put it the way you put it," Loving said. "I kin hand-write, but I cain't put the words together. You gotta do that part." He scrounged around in his saddlebag for paper. Then he unscrewed the top of the fountain pen. "Just pretend you're outa your head ag'in and start talkin'."

Goodnight lay back on his pallet, stared at the ceiling with his one good eye, then closed it in order to better see an interior landscape. He wasn't sure he wanted to share his feelings about Revelie with this writing cowboy, but evidently he already had, so he wouldn't really be giving anything away. He didn't know if he was up to talking a letter, but he didn't want to lose her.

"Dear Revelie," Goodnight began uncertainly, and then stopped. He stared up at the peaked cedar ceiling. Then he began to speak in tongues.

Loving just stared at him because he was making no sense at all.

"That's Comanche talk," Goodnight explained. "I can say some things better in Comanche. Now all I gotta do is try an' translate 'em into English." He paused again. "Write this down: 'My mind cries for you.'" Pause. "'My mind weeps for you. My mind mourns for you.'" Long pause. "'The forest inside me is dying. The trees fall one by one.' That's it, I reckon. Think it'll do any good?"

"You never know. Better'n nothin'."

"I'm gonna rest now." Writing was such hard work.

Goodnight lay with his eye closed, hoping he would fall asleep, but he found he couldn't stop thinking about the letter. Phrases occurred to him. Whole sentences marched through his cluttered mind. He couldn't sleep with all this racket going on inside his head.

"Now don't laugh," Goodnight said, opening his good eye.

"I won't," Loving said.

"Promise."

"Cross my heart." He drew an *X* over his heart with the fountain pen. "Shoot."

"Well, here goes," Goodnight sighed. "Write: 'Revelie, my mind cries for the dark forest in you. I was hopin' to keep on explorin' that damn forest all my damn life.' Only don't say 'damn.' 'An' I'd always be afindin' new places an' new animals. An' some a them critters'd be gentle fawns, and some'd be killers that eat them fawns. An'–"

"How come you say 'and' so often?" Loving asked.

Goodnight felt a flash of anger. This job was hard enough already without this interference. But he soon calmed down.

"You don't hafta write down the 'ands,'" Goodnight said, "but I gotta say 'em. I cain't talk no other way. That all right with you?"

"Fine."

"Fine. Now where was I?"

" 'Killers that eat fawns.' "

"Oh, yeah. 'An' there'd be warm sunny days.' Only you don't hafta say 'and,' okay? 'An' there'd be terr'ble storms. An' lightnin' an' thunder–'"

"I thought this here was supposed to be a love letter."

"That's just what it is."

"Suit yourself."

"'An' I'd find whole tribes in your soul. Tribes of damn pines. Tribes of big ol' oaks. Tribes of cottonwoods and tribes of aspens. Tribes of, I dunno, poison ivy.'"

"Poison ivy? Some love letter."

"Well, I don't wanta sound sappy. I mean I figure when I say somethin' nice, then I gotta say somethin' to sorta take it back. Right? See? Like poison ivy."

"Yeah, I guess so."

"Less see. 'An' tribes of gods. Forest gods. Water gods. Wild gods. Real ol' gods. Your gods and my gods. An' I'd worship all them there gods.'"

Goodnight fell silent. He saw Loving staring at him with his eyebrows arched like horizontal question marks.

"Well?" Loving said.

"Well what?"

"Well, whatcha gonna say to sorta take that back?"

"Take what back?"

"You know, the sappy stuff about all them gods."

Goodnight thought for a moment. Maybe Loving had a good point. Perhaps he should stick in some poison oak or grass burs or thistles to sort of even things out. But he somehow didn't feel like it.

"Leave it," Goodnight said at last. "Mebbe girls like that sorta stuff."

"Suit yourself."

29

Coffee took the letter into Tascosa the next time he went for supplies. Then Goodnight waited for an answer. While he waited, the hole in the middle of his chest healed. He got back on his feet, back on a horse, and went back to work. While he waited to hear from Revelie, Goodnight and his cowboys built a barn. While he waited, he and his boys put up a cook shack. While he waited, they clapped together a blacksmith shop where Tin Soldier went to work forging horseshoes and other iron gadgets. While Goodnight waited on and on, corrals sprang up on the floor of the red canyon. While he waited, the snow fell and turned the red canyon into a white canyon.

Then one afternoon in the early spring when the chinaberries were just putting out tentative leaves–peeking green noses outside to see if it was still too cold–a rider came hurrying down the north wall of the red canyon. Goodnight pulled his field glasses out of a saddlebag and aimed them at the rider. Focusing, he didn't recognize the horse or the man, which he took as a good sign. This stranger in the canyon might well be a messenger. Goodnight's answer could even now be winding its way down into the red earth. But why was this messenger in such a hurry now–after waiting all these lazy months?

Well, Goodnight was in a hurry now, too. He suddenly couldn't wait for Revelie's answer. He dug his spurs into Red's ribs and galloped toward the yes or no that would brighten or blight his life. Two red dust storms rode toward each other. But why the hurry? Goodnight knew why he was in a hurry, but he still couldn't imagine why the strange rider was. Could Revelie really be *that* anxious to marry him? Or to break his heart?

When he reached the steep north wall of the red canyon, Goodnight rode right up it. He met the stranger on the sheer face of the cliff.

"How do," said Goodnight.

"Howdy, Goodnight," said the stranger.

"You got the advantage a me. We know each other?"

"I'm Gibson. They call me Gibby. I was there when you busted them there thumbs. You do nice work."

"Thanks. Well, what can I do for ya, Gibby? Any chance you got a message for me, I hope."

"You hope?"

"Yeah, I been waitin' some time. Hope it ain't bad news."

Goodnight could feel his shoulders hunch as if he expected a sharp blow. And his heart was beating too fast, the way it used to back in his school days, when the teacher would call on him to read.

"I don't reckon I unnerstand," said Gibby Gibson, "but it's bad news all right. How come you been waitin' for it? How'd you know?"

"Know what?"

"About the girl-stealin'."

Goodnight was suddenly frightened in a new way. Had somebody harmed the woman who had kept him waiting so long for an answer? She was supposed to be safe back home in Boston, but who knew how safe those Eastern cities really were. Or maybe she had come back—only to be carried off to Robbers' Roost.

"Revelie," Goodnight whispered hoarsely. "They done got Revelie?"

"That's who they was after, all right," Gibson drawled. "But they didn't know she went back East. So they done carried off the hotel keep's daughter instead."

Good, thought Goodnight.

"What happened was," Gibson explained, "they busted into Sanborn's house lookin' for Miss Revelie. But all they found was Miss Katie. Ya know, the Russell girl."

"Who?"

"Her folks run the Exchange Hotel. Evenin's she carries supper over to Mr. Sanborn at his house. That's where she was when they busted in. Pore girl."

"Who busted in?"

"Most likely the Robbers' Roost boys. They wore han'kerchiefs over their faces. And gloves, too, mebbe to hide a bunch a flat thumbs, huh? That's accordin' to Mr. Sanborn. Mebbe you shoulda hung 'em when you had the chance, huh?"

"Mebbe."

"They come bustin' in. And they grabbed ahold a Miss Katie, but they was callin' her 'Miss Revelie' or just 'Revelie' 'cause they figured that's who she was. See?"

"Uh-huh."

"An' while they was still callin' her by the wrong name, see, they done tol' Mr. Sanborn to be sure an' tell you that this here was all yore fault. Payin' you back or somethin'."

"Damn," Goodnight said. He felt an angry burning in his chest.

"Shore 'nough mean boys," said Gibson. "Anyhow, Miss Katie was yellin' an' screamin' that she waddn't Miss Revelie. That she was Miss Katie. That they was makin' a bad mistake. But they just said, aw hell, an' took her anyhow. If they couldn't git their hands on Miss Revelie, then Miss Katie'd hafta do."

"Damn," said Goodnight again.

He spat on the ground and watched the earth change color. He felt a sharp pain behind his sightless eye. All the air in the deep canyon had been breathed up. His hands grew larger and they shook. They had dared to come after his woman. Except she wasn't his. That was the rub. She wouldn't even write to him.

"One of 'em kept on rantin' an' ravin' about how he was gonna nail yore ears to the saloon's swingin' doors. Mr. Sanborn tol' me to run out cheer and tell you what was goin' on."

"That's the only message you've got for me?" asked Goodnight.

"Thass all. Ain't that enough?"

30

Goodnight led his cowboys in search of the stolen woman. Loving rode beside him. The other boys were scattered out behind. All except Coffee and Suckerod who had been left behind to look after the ranch and the stock. If they kept on at this rate, their horses would all be dead before they got halfway to Tascosa.

Eventually, Goodnight slowed the pace. He was in a hurry to catch the kidnappers, but he was more concerned with sure than fast. He had promised himself that the outcome of this chase was as certain as death. Saving the horses would doom the outlaws.

As he rode along, Goodnight got angrier and angrier. He kept imagining what the gang was probably doing to the daughter of the hotelkeeper. And he knew they had intended to perform those same actions on Revelie. It was almost as if they really were raping and torturing the woman whom he loved. He would never forgive them not only for what they were doing but for what they had intended to do. He channeled all the frustration of his weeks of waiting into a lust for revenge. He would make them suffer as they had planned to make Revelie suffer. Maybe it would be fun–well, not exactly fun, but satisfying–to cut off their ears before he hanged them. Nail *their* ears to swinging doors. They would have enough ears to ornament the doors of both of the saloons in Tascosa.

But first he would have to find them.

When they finally reached Tascosa, Goodnight, Loving, and the cowboys rode down Main Street and stopped in front of the bank. They tied their horses to a crowded hitching rail. The cowboys lounged about outside while Goodnight and Loving went inside to see Sanborn. He was wearing brown tweeds instead of his velvet pants. Goodnight introduced Loving to the banker.

"Good of you to come," said Sanborn. "We're very worried about Katie. She's been gone for three days. We don't know what to do."

"Ketch 'em," said Loving.

"That's right," said Goodnight.

"Do you believe you will be able to do so?" asked the banker.

"We're gonna," said Goodnight.

"When I think it could have been Revelie–"

"How's she doin'?"

"Oh, she's well. Thank God."

"She write you reg'lar?"

"Why, yes, she does."

Goodnight wanted to ask if Revelie ever said anything in her letters about him, but he couldn't quite work up the nerve. Still, he couldn't let the subject completely alone.

"Writes a good letter, huh, does she?" Goodnight asked.

"Why, yes, as a matter of fact, she does," her father answered.

"That's good. I been hopin' ta git one myself. But so far, no such luck."

"I'm sorry."

Goodnight couldn't tell whether this banker was really sorry or not.

"Any thoughts," Loving said, "on where we might oughta start lookin'."

"Look for Robbers' Roost," said the banker.

"We kinda figured that much," said the handsome cowboy.

"We'll ask around town," Goodnight said. "See what we turn up. Maybe somebody's got a notion."

Tin Soldier was the first cowboy to bring any news. His source was the bartender at the Jenkins & Dunn Saloon, who remembered a cowboy who had bellied up to the bar last month wearing gloves. This cowpuncher kept his gloves on while he drank his whiskey. But when he went to pay for his pleasure, he took a glove off to reach for coins in his pocket. The bartender got a glimpse of a busted thumb. Later on, he noticed that Busted Thumbs left with some riders who worked for the Milliron Ranch. That was a hard-luck spread that lay a couple of horseback days southeast of Tascosa.

"When was that?" asked Goodnight.

"Barkeep wasn't too sure," replied Tin Soldier. "A month ago mebbe. Mebbe more."

"Not exactly a fresh trail."

"Sorry."

"But we cain't hardly ignore it. I mean it's the only trail we got."

Goodnight got all the boys together and they saddled up. They rode until dark and didn't stop then. Remembering his Human days, the former Crying Coyote decided to keep his men moving the way a Human war party would move. They rode deeper and deeper into the night. They weren't favored with a full Human moon, just a half-moon, but it was enough to help light the way. Goodnight hated to admit to himself that he was enjoying himself. It was like old times. He was hunting Writers. They didn't make a waterless camp until after midnight.

The next day, the Goodnight-Loving gang came to the ragged edge of the plains. They left the high tableland and descended into breaks country. The landscape resembled the red canyon, but all the features were smaller, less magnificent, messier. Rather than one great canyon, there were many little canyons running into each other. It was a puzzle, a labyrinth. Goodnight thought of it as good rustling country, where stolen herds could easily be hidden among the geological riddles and mysteries.

Loving had been to the Milliron Ranch before, so he pointed the way, but he did it unobtrusively. Goodnight never felt his authority undermined. And even if he had, he wasn't sure he would have minded. He liked Loving's company too much.

They rode on down the dangerous maze. The horses reared and snorted when they saw or heard or smelled rattlesnakes. When his mount jumped, Tin Soldier lost his steel hat, which rolled all the way to the bottom of a tricky little canyon. He dismounted and went after his helmet on foot. When he finally retrieved it, he couldn't climb back out of the gorge. He was trapped. Goodnight had to throw him a rope and pull him out.

The riders watched carefully for holes that could break a horse's leg. Burrs caught in the horses' hair and had to be pulled or cut free. These breaks had everything that was bad about the red canyon and none of what was good. Goodnight pitied the ranchers who had bet on this part of Texas. Well, they hadn't had his upbringing, so they didn't know any better.

Goodnight followed Loving up the steep side of a small plateau. When they reached the tabletop, they scanned the horizon. Black Dub was the first to see the small feather of smoke fluttering above a distant hill. He pointed it out.

"That oughta be Milliron headquarters," said Loving. "Mebbe git there before dark."

31

The Goodnight-Loving posse rode down a rugged bluff toward a ramshackle collection of buildings. The disordered structures seemed to reflect the broken, chaotic nature of the landscape. As the newcomers clattered closer, an old man emerged from the cabin with the smoking chimney. He stood on the front porch and shaded his eyes to see better. He wore overalls like a farmer. His head was bald. He was skinny. This hard land seemed to have used him up. Goodnight raised his hand in the Human fashion long before he was close enough to holler. The old man waved back.

"How do," Goodnight said when he was near enough to be heard.

"Howdy," said the old man, who didn't have any teeth. "What kin I do for ya?"

Still sitting in his saddle, Goodnight leaned forward until his forearms rested on the pommel. He stared down at the old man, trying to decide how honest he was, how much trouble he might be.

"Well, we're looking for a rider," Goodnight said. "A boy with a coupla busted thumbs. Sometimes wears gloves to hide 'em. Sound familiar?"

"Well, I cain't exactly say yes, an' I cain't exactly say no. Less'n I know who wants 'im and what they wants 'im for."

"Fair enough. My name's Goodnight."

"Mine's Milliron."

"Glad to know you, Milliron."

"I'd be glad to know yore business, Goodnight."

"Well, I'm lookin' for some men with busted thumbs that carried off a girl. I mean to git her back."

"That so? How long ago this here happen?"

"'Bout a week."

"Where?"

"Tascosa. They rode right into town and grabbed her."

Old Man Milliron took a while to digest all this new information. His mouth moved as if he were talking, but no sound came out. Goodnight figured he must be talking to himself. He decided not to interrupt the conversation.

"Well, how I figure it is, if'n I had any busted thumbs 'round here, they ain't gone missin' lately. Been doin' their chores day in an' day out for a month er so. Right cheer. Couldn't hardly be yore man. Thanks for stoppin' by."

Goodnight lifted his sweaty hat and scratched under it. Then he set it back in place.

"Well, how I figure is, mebbe he waddn't in on the girl stealin'. Mebbe he quit that there busted-thumb gang. Mebbe he's reformed an' all."

"Mebbe," said Milliron.

"But mebbe he still knows wheresomever that there gang likes to hide out. Mebbe he knows where they'd most likely take this here girl for funnin' with her. So mebbe we'd like to talk to him if'n you don't mind."

Old Man Milliron thought for a moment, chewing his cud.

"Tell me, Goodnight," said Milliron, "be you the man with that funny ax I heared tell of."

"Depends on what you call a funny ax," Goodnight said. "I got mine off'n an anvil." He patted the scabbard on the side of his saddle that held his ax.

"Yeah, that's the one. Must be. You figure I might could take a look at it? Be much obliged to you."

Goodnight didn't particularly like being parted from his ax. He counted on it to give him luck. You didn't readily hand your luck into the hands of another. Much less a stranger. Besides, he had promised the ax–on that day at the fair–that he would always keep it with him. But on the other hand, he wanted the old man's help, so a favor might be in order. And he didn't plan to let the ax out of his sight.

"Sure thing," Goodnight said.

He pulled his ax out of its scabbard and handed it down handle foremost to Milliron. He watched closely as the old man accepted it respectfully. Watched as he brushed the blade with the side of a wrinkled old thumb. Watched him pucker his lips as if he meant to kiss the steel, but he pulled back just in time. Watched as the old man's eyes glittered and got younger.

"Like it?" asked Goodnight.

"Love it," said Milliron. "I oncet give it a pull myself. I was a big strappin' fellow then. Didn't budge. You mind tellin' me how you done it?"

"I reckon you loosened it up for me."

"Thanks, but thass not what I heared. I heared you talked it out. Wha'd you say?"

"Don't 'member right off hand. Not exactly. Less just say I'm a real persuasive fellow."

"Must be. I reckon I'm persuaded. The boys'll be comin' in for chow anytime now. An' last I looked, one of 'em had busted thumbs. But he may be a little harder to persuade than me, most likely. Git down and stay to supper."

"Thanks."

Goodnight swung down off his horse and Loving and the other cowboys followed his example. They tied their mounts to the posts of a nearby corral. Old Man Milliron went back to his cooking inside the log cabin. The Home Ranch cowboys squatted on their heels and leaned back against the cabin and waited. Goodnight's good eye was always busy, watching for the return of the riders. Every so often, he would glance over at Loving, whose eyes were intently watching, too. The other boys were half-dozing.

Soon a couple of riders appeared over the top of a western hill just as a big red sun was going down behind it. Goodnight didn't like the idea of anybody with busted thumbs coming at him right out of the sun. He squinted but still couldn't see very well. Knowing he was at a disadvantage, Goodnight got slowly to his feet. Loving stood up, too. Goodnight let his hand rest on the butt of his revolver. Loving didn't bother.

Hearing a sound behind him, Goodnight looked around quickly. He saw the old man putting tin plates on a table. When he had finished, Milliron came forward, squinted, shaded his eyes, and grunted.

"Hold yore hosses," the old man said. "That ain't him."

Loving sat back down, but Goodnight remained standing. He kept watching. The sky was getting dark fast. He wished Busted Thumbs would hurry. He was getting impatient. Unfortunately, impatience often led to mistakes. Goodnight looked down at Loving, who appeared to be completely relaxed. He hardly seemed to notice that the black riders coming out of the sun were getting bigger and bigger.

"There he be," said Milliron. "Yonder."

Goodnight looked to see where the old man was pointing. His finger was aiming at a clump of brush in the distance. Goodnight didn't see anything.

"Where?"

"There."

Finally, Goodnight saw three miniature riders emerge from the brush. They didn't seem to be in any hurry. Goodnight decided to ride out to meet them. But before he reached his horse, he felt Loving's grip on his elbow. The grip said: "Be patient, wait."

The two riders coming out of the sun arrived first. They rode their horses into the corral, dismounted, and removed their saddles, which they pitched on the top rail of the fence. Then they sauntered toward grub.

"Company come," Milliron said to his men. "Stayin' to supper."

"Ev'nin'," said one of the Milliron cowboys.

The other one mumbled the same. They introduced themselves all around in a casual way.

"Nice hat," said one of the Milliron hands.

"Thanks," said Tin Soldier, nodding.

Goodnight studied the newcomers. They had ridden in on poor horses with sway backs. Their threadbare clothes barely seemed to cling to them. These weren't outlaws unless they were very bad at their trade.

Soon Goodnight returned his attention to the three riders approaching from the brush. As they drew nearer, he could see that their horses were as poor as the others. He decided to wait until they dismounted and unsaddled. Then there would be less chance of the man he wanted getting away. Wait, wait.

As the three cowboys approached the cabin on foot, hungry for supper, Goodnight recognized one of them. He didn't even need to look at the man's hands. He recalled his face. He remembered watching from across a stump as those features distorted.

"Company come," Milliron sang out again.

The gloved cowboy looked wary. Goodnight smiled warmly and pulled out his gun. Loving's revolver cleared its holster, too. All the Milliron cowboys altered their poses–their shoulders straightened, their heads turned, their chins came down–but none of them drew.

"Hey, Busted Thumbs, hold on there," Goodnight called. "I got a coupla questions to ask ya."

"What?" asked the gloved cowboy.

"Remember me?"

"No, why should I?"

"Lemme see your thumbs?"

"What for?"

"I'm in kind of a hurry. You an' your buddies stole a girl outa Tascosa a week back. I want her back."

"I was right here last week. And the week before that, too. I don't know nothin' about no stole girl."

"I won't argue the point. Don't have time to. Less say we do you a favor: we believe you. Then less say in return you do us a favor: you lead us to this here famous Robbers' Roost that ain't exactly on no maps. How about it?"

The gloved cowboy looked down at the dry ground, carefully examined the dust on his well-worn boots, then started shaking his head as he slowly looked up.

"No, I don't reckon," he said softly. "I got too much work to do 'round here. Don't expect I could git off just now."

"I say you can git off," Goodnight said, his voice soft, too.

"Wisht I could," said the cowboy in gloves, "but I cain't. Fact is, I never been there. Sorry you boys made all this trip for nothin'."

"Less see how things stand. I reckon your old friend Gudanuf promised he'd kill you if'n you ever told. But I'm promisin' I'll kill you if'n you don't tell. An' it just so happens that I'm here an' he ain't. See? So who you gonna listen to?"

The cowboy just shrugged.

Goodnight was so angry he wanted to strangle Busted Thumbs where he stood. Or hang him. Looking around for a tree, Goodnight didn't see any, naturally, but he did see something else that gave him an idea. It was a cart.

"Black Dub, why don't you sorta tie this fella's hands behind his back?" Goodnight said, his voice still soft. "An' while he's doin' that, Tin Soldier, I got a little job for you. Why don't you go 'round an' collect any firearms you come acrosst? Now nice an' easy. I don't want nobody gittin' excited." He was using the same voice he used when he wanted to calm cattle.

Evidently, none of the cowboys working this hard-luck ranch considered himself much of a gunman. At any rate, Tin Soldier had no trouble collecting their guns and a couple of bowie knives besides.

The cowboy with the gloves didn't put up any fight either. Black Dub had no trouble tying him up.

"This country's poor in good hangin' trees," Goodnight said, "but less wander over to that there two-wheeled contraption. It oughta do in a pinch."

Now the bound cowboy looked as if he wished he had put up more of a fight. When Black Dub took him by the arm and attempted to lead him to the cart, he resisted. He tried to dig in his heels. Black Dub just picked him up, threw him over his shoulder, and carried him to the hanging cart.

Loving quickly and neatly fashioned a hangman's noose at the end of his lariat. He was smiling warmly as he slipped the loop over the unfortunate cowboy's head and pulled it tight around his throat.

"I'm Jack Loving, by the way," he said. "What's your name? It ain't polite to hang somebody without even bein' introduced."

"Roy," stammered the cowboy.

"Roy what?"

"Just Roy."

"You sure are a closed-mouth fella, ain't chew? Not no genius neither. You know this ain't gonna be no purdy way to die. No chance a breakin' your neck. You're just gonna hang there an' choke to death."

"Tie your rope to the wagon tongue," Goodnight said. "You know, clear out on the end. Don't give it much slack."

"Come on, Just Roy," said Loving.

Pulling on the rope, he led the condemned man to the end of the wagon tongue.

"You ain't really gonna do this," Roy said in an uncertain voice. "You wouldn't. I ain't never done nothin' to you. Don't know nothin' about no girl."

"Bend over," Loving said.

"No."

"Have it your way."

Loving passed the rope beneath the wagon tongue and pulled hard. Roy's head went down and at the same time the tongue came up. Then Loving tied the rope so there was about six inches of play between the noose and the knot, which was a double half hitch. It was tied very neatly and at the same time very securely. Goodnight admired the workmanship.

"Okay, Too Short, you and Black Dub, here's what I want you to do," Goodnight said. "Both a you step on the back a this here cart." He turned to face his prisoner. "An' then here's what's gonna happen. The back a this contraption's gonna go down just like a seesaw. An' that means the front's gonna go up like a seesaw. An' I figure that's gonna lift our friend here's feet right off the ground. Right? Come on, hurry up, less try it and see if'n it works." He paused for a moment. "Less'n old Roy here's got somethin' he wants to say."

The cowboy remained silent.

"Okay, good, less go."

Black Dub and Too Short both stepped on the back of the two-wheeled cart. The back end went down. The front end went up. And Roy started dancing with his boots about a foot off the ground.

Goodnight counted to himself: one thousand one, one thousand two, one thousand three, one thousand four, one thousand five.

"Okay, let him down," he said. "See if'n he's had a change a heart."

Too Short and Black Dub jumped off the back of the cart. The back end went up. The front end came crashing down. And Roy collapsed in the dust.

"Loosen up that rope a little," Goodnight said. "Give him a breath of air in case he's got somethin' to tell us."

Loving stepped forward, bent over, and gave Roy a little neck slack.

"Changed your mind?" asked Goodnight, standing over the cowboy.

Roy coughed but didn't say anything else.

"Okay, ready to go up again?"

Another cough.

"Good. Do the honors, boys."

Black Dub and Too Short, one too big and the other too small, climbed onto the back of the cart once again. Once more Roy tried to walk on air. And Goodnight counted to himself. One thousand one. He wasn't as angry at the cowboy as he had been. One thousand two. The heat had gone out of his chest. One thousand three. But he was still determined. One thousand four, one thousand five, one thousand six, one thousand seven. Roy's face was turning purple. Goodnight was afraid the cowboy might die before he got a chance to give up and talk.

"Let him down."

Roy came crashing to earth.

"Give him some air. Better hurry up. He ain't gonna last too much longer."

Loving moved quickly without seeming to. Roy gasped. His chest started to heave. Goodnight walked over and knelt beside him on the ground. He looked into the cowboy's eyes, which were glassy and unfocused. The hanged man was unconscious.

"He'll come around," said Loving.

"Spect so," said Goodnight.

"Spit in his face," suggested Simon. "That'll bring him around."

Goodnight considered spitting, but eventually decided not to. He didn't think it would work. Besides, he was feeling pretty cottonmouthed at the moment.

Then Tin Soldier appeared with his tin hat full of water. He dumped it on the unconscious cowboy.

"Don't drown him," said Goodnight. "Or me neither." He started brushing off water that had splashed on him.

Roy sputtered and woke up. He shook his head back and forth. He blinked his dead eyes and they came back to life.

"How much more a this you figure you can take?" asked Goodnight. "Huh?"

"Okay, you win," Roy said hoarsely. "I'll show you where it's at."

"Good," said Goodnight. "I'm beginnin' to like you better already."

32

Goodnight, his men, and their prisoner rode northwest. The journey jarred loose old, unwelcome memories, for he had once made a similar journey when he was the prisoner. Now he was the boss in control of everything but his own emotions. And he was working on controlling even them.

The posse jingled as it rode. The cowboys' spurs made a cheerful sound. The prisoner's chain added a more melancholy note. Before leaving the Milliron Ranch, Tin Soldier had fashioned a pair of handcuffs for Roy. These cuffs were different from most in that no key could unlock them. After all, Tin Soldier was a blacksmith, not a locksmith. The chain, which was only about six inches long, was heavier than the type normally used because it was all they could find. The iron cuffs chafed, according to the prisoner.

Black Dub led Roy's horse. To further limit the captive's chance of escaping, his boots and filthy socks had been taken from him. Simon kept telling him how much fun it would be to step on a snake barefooted. Your whole foot would swell up the size of a pumpkin before you died. And according to Simon, there were snakes everywhere.

Following Roy's directions, the posse was aiming for a spot where Oklahoma, New Mexico, and Colorado all came together. Robbers' Roost was supposed to be on the Cimarron River in the southeast corner of Colorado. Goodnight had explained carefully to Roy that he had better not be lying or he would get hanged without any reprieve or any ears.

When they reached the Cimarron, Goodnight and his riders followed it upstream. Now they were no longer in danger of dying of thirst on a waterless plain. Cottonwoods lined the riverbank, reminding Goodnight of home.

He almost wished Revelie had been the one carried off by Gudanuf because then he might well be seeing her soon. He told himself not to think such crazy thoughts. He felt as if he were being disloyal to Revelie even to entertain such a daydream.

Think about a plan. Try to make a plan. Decide what to do. Roy said the gang felt so secure in their hideout that they usually didn't even post a watch. So these outlaw Writers felt about their Roost the way the Humans had felt about their red-canyon home. Somehow all thoughts seemed to lead back to tragedies of one kind or another.

Early one morning, Goodnight decided to ride ahead of his men. He knew he could approach more quietly alone than at the head of his posse. After giving orders to the others to slow down, he speeded up. Once he had put some distance between himself and his men, he slowed again. Slower was quieter.

As he moved steadily forward, Goodnight kept trying to come up with a strategy that would affect a quick rescue without endangering the life of the young woman being rescued. But every idea seemed to have its drawbacks. He felt frustrated. Why couldn't he think clearly and plan well? He was angry at himself. He knew he was trying too hard. Goodnight told himself to relax and see what happened. Don't try to figure out everything in advance. Just see what unfolds and try to make the most of it. That was when he saw the buffalo.

He smiled in spite of his grim mission. He was always happy to see these woolly heads. The Human-cattle cheered him up just by being there. The old ways were dying, but they weren't completely dead yet. There were about three hundred, which would have been considered a small herd in the old days, but it was a large one now. Lost in his admiration for the buffalo, Goodnight forgot all about needing a plan, which was when one popped into his mind.

Leaving the buffalo behind, Goodnight kept them very much in mind. He would need their help. He was still smiling. He wasn't sure the plan would work, but he no longer worried. He would just see what happened. The buffalo had made him believe in his luck again.

About half an hour after he parted from the herd, Goodnight came upon Robbers' Roost. It was just as Roy had described it, a one-story stone house, built on the bank of the Cimarron River. It was actually a handsome place. Goodnight didn't see anybody moving around outside. The outlaws were probably all inside playing cards–or with their captive. The place wasn't deserted because there were horses in a cottonwood corral. Goodnight admired the rock house–jealously–for a long moment.

Then he turned back to look for his boys, to tell them his plan.

33

In midafternoon, Goodnight and his cowboys smiled down on the buffalo herd that was grazing peacefully in a shallow swale. They had ridden in downwind from the nearsighted animals who hadn't scented them yet.

For his plan to work, Goodnight was counting on his knowledge of the nature of Writers. Specifically, he was depending upon the white man's love of the senseless slaughter of buffalo. Not that he actually intended to let them kill any–not if he could help it–but he knew he might not be able to protect them all. Which saddened him. He would just do the best he could and see what happened.

"Stay here," Goodnight told his cowboys in a low voice. "I'll be back in a minute."

Goodnight surveyed the herd, looking for its chief. He saw several impressive bulls, but they really didn't have the bearing of chiefs. He kept looking, scanning the herd from right to left, then left to right. Maybe the chief had been killed. Perhaps another leader had not yet emerged. When Goodnight finally saw the chief, he couldn't believe he hadn't noticed him right away. The old bull held his massive head up and stared right at the oncoming rider. He was in charge, all right. The other animals began warily retreating, but not the old chief. He stood his ground and waited. He had surely survived many dangers. Goodnight hoped that the old bull had enough luck, enough medicine, to survive a few more.

"O, Great Chief of the Buffalo," Goodnight called from about two hundred feet away, "I have a big favor to ask."

Then he paused to let the bull absorb what he had said. He had spoken in the Writer tongue rather than the Human tongue because it was so much easier now. Pretty soon he wouldn't be able to talk Human at all.

"It's a real big favor," Goodnight began again. "See, there's some outlaws stole this here girl. And I gotta git her back. Them outlaws' hideout is just right over there in that damn rock house. Excuse the 'damn.' Anyhow they call the place Robbers' Roost. So what I figured was this here: If'n you and your herd was to run past in fronta that there house, well, them outlaws just couldn't resist. They'd grab their guns and come runnin' out to kill themselves some buffalo. Writers is like that. Well, you know that."

Goodnight had been afraid that when he said "kill," the old bull might react. Paw the earth. Bellow. Perhaps even start a stampede. But this old bull just tossed his head as if mildly annoyed. Was he telling Goodnight to get the hell out of there? Or was he just chasing flies away?

"Good, now we've got over the roughest part," Goodnight told the buffalo chief. "See, the idea is that when they come runnin' out wavin' their guns, well, we're gonna be waitin' for 'em. We'll ambush 'em and that'll be that."

Goodnight let the woolly chief think the matter over. He didn't want to hurry him.

"I sure hope my plan's okay with you, see, 'cause I cain't think a no other way to git them outlaws outa their rock hideout. That there place is some kinda fortress. So we really do need your help. Might even be a chance for you to git some revenge if'n you ever think a that sorta thing. Well, now, how about it? Whaddaya say?"

The old bull nodded, or maybe just shooed a pesky fly. It was hard to tell.

"Thanks."

Goodnight turned around in the saddle and motioned his men to come forward. As he did so, his heart came alive in his chest. He noticed he was smiling again. He just couldn't help it with so many buffalo around. When the cowboys reached him, Goodnight quickly explained his plan. Then he issued brief orders.

"Okay, Loving, you and Too Short go on ahead. Keep your heads down. Good luck."

Too Short and Loving would attempt to close in on the rock house unobserved. They would take cover and wait for the action to begin. Goodnight had picked Loving for this assignment because he knew from personal experience that this cowboy could shoot straight. He chose Too Short because he was also a pretty good shot and was generally level-headed. Also it didn't take much cover to hide him. Goodnight hadn't picked Tin Soldier because he was afraid the sun might glint off his tin hat and warn the outlaws.

Loving spurred his horse and set off in the direction of Robbers' Roost. Too Short trailed a horse length behind. They were moving fast now, but they would slow down as they neared the house.

"Okay," Goodnight said, "let's start workin' 'em on down. Don't spook 'em. We don't want 'em runnin' just yet."

Goodnight, Simon, Black Dub, and Tin Soldier spread out to form a sort of semicircle. Then they advanced on the herd. The buffalo were as usual–even after all the slaughter–too trusting for their own good. Goodnight wished they had sense enough to run in all different directions as soon as they saw a white man, but they didn't. His plan wouldn't have worked if they had. As the riders approached, the buffalo began an orderly retreat, moving slowly in the direction of the rock house.

Riding along at an easy walk, Goodnight kept listening for sounds of trouble up ahead. He figured outlaws probably didn't do too many chores, but they must do some, and what if they picked now to do them? They might well spot Loving and Too Short creeping up on them. Goodnight hoped the outlaws liked to take afternoon naps. That's what lazy, good-for-nothing people did, wasn't it? Of course, they could be in bed for another reason, taking turns.

Goodnight noticed that the old bull hung back behind the rest of the herd. He was the rear guard, ready in case these ominous Writers tried anything funny. The woolly chief seemed to feel about his subjects the way the rancher felt about his cowboys, and yet neither leader could always keep others from harm. Goodnight couldn't help worrying even though he knew it didn't do any good. He was especially worried about Loving, even though he knew that Loving was good at taking care of himself.

Up ahead, Goodnight saw a slight rise that he had noticed earlier and made a point of remembering. He knew that behind this elevated ground lay the rock house.

It was time to start the buffalo moving faster. He lifted his hat, which was the prearranged signal. Then he spurred Red and charged the buffalo. The other cowboys followed his lead. Goodnight beat his hat against his chaps to make noise. Tin Soldier banged his tin hat on the pommel of his saddle to make even more noise, *clang, clang, clang.* Black Dub shouted and whirled his lariat over his head. And Simon cracked an impressive bullwhip that his father had given him. Hearing the whip, Goodnight hoped it didn't sound too much like gunfire to the outlaws behind their rock walls.

The buffalo acted as he had hoped. They started running toward the still unseen hideout. The river, which lay to the animals' left, helped to funnel them in the right direction. Soon flight had become a full stampede.

Now Goodnight started worrying about Loving and Too Short for another reason. He hoped they wouldn't get trampled. Goodnight knew that if he were responsible for killing Loving, who had once almost killed him, he would never forgive himself. He didn't want Too Short to get hurt either.

The riders were no longer driving the buffalo but chasing them. As he neared the crest of the rise, Goodnight reined in Red and looked to make sure that Simon, Black Dub, and Tin Soldier did the same. They all dismounted in a hurry. They dropped their reins to the ground, which would ground-hitch the horses to a spot as if they were tied to hitching posts. Then the four men crouched and ran after the buffalo. Goodnight, breathing dust and coughing, noticed that the others carried rifles. He had only a pistol because he didn't travel with a rifle. He preferred an ax in his saddle scabbard, but he didn't figure a blade was going to do him much good right now.

Reaching the crest of the rise, Goodnight still couldn't see the rock house because the buffalo screened it from him. Which also meant, he hoped, that the outlaws couldn't see him. His chest was burning from the effort and from all the dust he had sucked down into his lungs. He wanted to stop running–or at least slow down–but he wouldn't let himself. The dirt in his one good eye nearly blinded him. He stumbled, falling, falling, but he caught himself. Then he tripped again and fell. But he quickly rolled back up again.

When he saw a glimpse of Robbers' Roost over the bouncing backs of the woollies, Goodnight crouched lower and started looking around for cover. Noticing a rock over to his left, he headed for it. Somehow the stone had looked larger at a distance than it did close up. It was only about the size of a washtub, but there didn't seem to be any better alternatives. He dropped down behind the rock and waited to see what would happen.

From behind this cover, Goodnight looked to see if his boys had managed to hide themselves. Simon and Tin Soldier had found rocks of their own, but Black Dub, the biggest, was still running. Get down! Come on, get down! Black Dub dove behind a small mesquite bush. It wouldn't stop any bullets, but at least would conceal the big man for the time being.

Peeking over his rock, Goodnight saw that Robbers' Roost was about thirty yards away. Now he really wished he had a rifle because he wasn't sure he could hit anything with a pistol from this range.

Watching the buffalo herd bearing down on the outlaws' hideout, Goodnight still didn't detect any activity in or around this fortress. He couldn't even see Loving or Too Short. He was still worried about them. In spite of his concern, Goodnight's chest was beginning to feel better. He took off his hat, which had been jammed down hard on his head, so it wouldn't stick up above his rock.

Now Goodnight had a moment to admire the buffalo as they ran. He marveled at the grace of these animals who–lovely as they were–looked as if they should be rather clumsy. Somehow their big heads, big shoulders, and slender hindquarters all moved well together. They were much too wonderful to die at the hands of girl-stealing outlaws. He would blame himself if any of them were harmed.

When the leaders reached the rock house, they separated like a river dividing around a stone. Then they joined up again after they had passed the hideout. Robbers' Roost was now an island in a flood of buffalo–well, a small flood anyway.

Goodnight could imagine what was going through the outlaws' minds as the woollies raced past them. When they first heard the hoofbeats, they must have been startled. They would have wondered what was making all the racket. Was a posse thundering down on them? No, there was too much noise for a posse. Maybe a whole damn regiment of cavalry? Surely they had run for their weapons in alarm. But then they would have looked out their narrow windows and seen the buffalo. Their alarm would have changed to amusement. This was going to be fun. Now they would be anxious to rush out and murder them some buffalo. But if they dashed out too soon, they would get trampled. So they would just have to be patient until the stampede passed. They might try taking a few pop shots from inside, but their cramped windows would give them trouble. They were mere slits–built for safety like the windows of a damn castle–and so were hardly ideal for shooting at fast-moving targets. Or so Goodnight hoped.

Goodnight heard a shot, but he didn't see any of the animals go down. Then there were two more shots in quick succession. But again no woolly fell. So far so good. Of course, some might have been wounded. Goodnight told himself again not to worry about what he couldn't control or even influence. He tried to concentrate on and prepare for what he could do.

When the last of the buffalo passed the stone house, Goodnight ducked a little lower behind his rock and felt his heart thumping the ground. Just as he had expected, the door of the hideout banged open and heavily armed outlaws came tumbling out. They ran in the direction of the corral that penned their horses. They were in too big a hurry to look to the right or the left. The buffalo were getting away.

Goodnight kept looking for Loving and Too Short, but he still didn't see them. Where could they be? He worried all over again that they might have been trampled. He couldn't stand it if he lost Loving and . . .

The crack of a rifle and a puff of smoke–then another–told Goodnight where his lost cowboys were. They were inside the horse corral firing from behind posts. One outlaw fell and didn't move while another writhed on the ground. Good, Loving was all right. And Too Short, too. So far.

The firing from the corral continued as fast as Too Short and Loving could cock their repeating rifles. The outlaws raced, dove, and rolled to get out of the way of the bullets. And they started returning fire.

Goodnight could smell the acrid smoke from the gunfight. The horses in the corral reared and screamed in their way. A handsome bay tried to climb the air and then fell sideways. Crashing to the earth, it threw up a great cloud of dust. Goodnight felt responsible for the animal's death.

Two outlaws crouched behind a watering trough. Two others had taken cover behind a small pile of rocks–which were probably left over from building the rock house. Another man crouched behind a fallen body. Still another had managed to run behind a corner of the stone house. Six outlaws were now concentrating their firepower on the two men in the corral. The bullets made the corral railings tremble and shiver.

From his angle, Goodnight could see about a third of Loving's body. He watched the smooth, rhythmic motions as his friend cocked and fired, cocked and fired. All the movements economical. No evidence of haste. And yet the shots followed rapidly one upon the other. Goodnight almost felt hypnotized as he watched his friend work. Or was he paralyzed by fear? Not for himself. For Loving.

When Loving spun around and dropped to his knees, Goodnight bit the inside of his cheek and tasted blood.

Goodnight was on his feet and running before he was aware of having made any sort of decision. He couldn't just lie there while bad men killed his best friend. He knew he couldn't be of much help from thirty yards away with a pistol in his hand, so he had to get closer.

The outlaws, who were shooting the other way, didn't see him coming up behind them. Hearing other footsteps, Goodnight looked back over his shoulder and saw Simon, Black Dub, and Tin Soldier all racing after him. He wanted to tell them to go back. They had rifles. They could kill outlaws from far away and from behind cover. But he was their leader and they had followed his lead. He just hoped he didn't get them all killed. Well, that's what they got for looking at him as if he were a leader all those months ago. He had gone and become one–and now he was leading them into slaughter.

34

Goodnight bore down on the outlaws twenty-five yards away. He couldn't believe they didn't hear him coming because he was breathing so hard. Twenty yards away. His own breath was screaming in his ears. Fifteen yards away. Now they heard him.

They were turning around. He looked for cover, but he didn't see anywhere to hide. So he thumbed the hammer back and pointed the barrel at the horse trough. He doubted he could hit anything while he was running and his chest was heaving, but maybe he could scare them into not hitting him. The report of his revolver drowned out the roar of his breath. He saw the water in the trough splash. Nice shooting. He had killed some muddy water.

But then Goodnight was surprised to see an outlaw rise up from behind the trough, and start walking toward him. Coming out to meet him. Welcoming him to Robbers' Roost. He had a puzzled look on his face. He was still trying to figure out what this death business was all about. How did it work? He had never died before and didn't know how to do it. He fell on his face, but his legs were still trying to walk. A part of him still thought he was alive.

Good. Another one of them down. But was it too late? Was Loving already dead? Had he gotten his best friend killed? He would never forgive himself if . . .

Thumbing back his hammer again, Goodnight pointed his barrel, pretending it was just a finger, at a second man who rose from behind the horse trough. He looked scared and confused. Where could he hide? Goodnight was surprised to see the outlaw jump into the trough and disappear under the dirty water.

Now Goodnight heard gunfire coming from behind him. He glanced back and saw Simon and Tin Soldier sprawled on the ground, their rifles to their shoulders, shooting at the bad men. Black Dub, the biggest target, stood straight up and fired. With his peripheral vision, Goodnight saw an outlaw go down by the corner of the house.

Ouch! A bee stung Goodnight's ear. He had always been afraid of bees–and with good reason. Damn, it hurt! He could feel blood running down the side of his face. The pain made him madder than ever. He hated these girl-stealers, these bull-killers, these horse-murderers. These damned best-friend shooters! He was going to get even. Count on it. The problem was he was almost too angry to aim.

Goodnight wasn't sure who had shot him, so he just picked out one at random. He pointed at the outlaw who had chosen a body as his cover. He tried to control his anger so he wouldn't shake. When he pulled the trigger, the outlaw dropped his rifle and grabbed his neck. But Goodnight wasn't sure whose bullet had hit the man. He hoped it had been his, but he wasn't convinced. Then he was surprised to find that he was taking the battle so personally. What did it matter who had shot the outlaw? Well, maybe it didn't matter, but he still hoped he was the one.

Now Goodnight pointed his Colt at one of the outlaws who had taken cover behind the rock pile. He aimed at the man's head. He wanted to see brains on the ground soaking up dust. This one's for Loving!

"Don't shoot!" shouted the outlaw. "Don't shoot! I'm outa bullets. I give up."

The man threw down his empty rifle and held up his hands. Goodnight decided to shoot him anyway. Damn him to hell. Served him right. But his trigger finger, with a mind of its own, hesitated.

"Stop!" cried another voice. "Don't shoot me! I surrender."

The second outlaw at the rock pile dropped his rifle and raised his hands.

"Hold your fire!" Goodnight shouted the order. "That's enough!"

The shooting stopped. Goodnight had forgotten about the outlaw in the trough, so he was surprised to see him rise up out of the water dripping. He had his wet hands raised over his wet head.

Now the moment had come that Goodnight dreaded.

35

As he ran, Goodnight could feel the tears running down his face. He could taste them. It had been so long since he had cried. He should have cried more, but he hadn't. Now he couldn't stop.

Not even when he saw Loving stand up in the corral and wave. He waved with his left hand. His bloody right arm hung at his side. But he was smiling.

Goodnight told himself that he would never forgive himself if that arm had to be taken off. Damn sawbones. But in spite of his worry, in spite of blaming himself for the injury, he still smiled. Then laughed. Trying to wipe the tears from his good eye, he managed to smear it with blood.

"I was afraid you was dead," Goodnight choked.

"Me dead?" Loving said. "You're the one looks dead. All covered with blood from head to toe."

"It's just my ear."

"Funny, you wouldn't think an ear'd have that much blood in it, now wouldja?"

"How bad're you hurt?"

"Just shot through the arm's all, so's I couldn't shoot. Never learned how left-handed. Didn't seem to matter till now. Just kept my head down. Sorry I waddn't more help."

Goodnight started to tell Loving not to say he was sorry, but then he changed his mind. He was too happy to find his friend alive to lecture at the moment. He just wanted to celebrate.

"You did great," Goodnight said. "You're alive, ain't you? What could be greater'n that?"

Looking around, Goodnight saw that his other cowboys were busy tying up the outlaws who were still alive. It turned out that only two of them were actually dead. The first to fall was never going to get up again. And the man whom Goodnight had shot through the water trough was also beyond help. The outlaw who had tried to hide behind a dead body was bleeding badly from his throat. And the one who had taken cover behind a corner of the rock house had been shot through the knee, which surely hurt. Three other outlaws weren't hurt at all or just nicked: the two at the rock pile and the one in the trough. All the living, even the wounded, soon had their hands tied behind them and their feet tied to their hands. They weren't going to run away or even roll away. They were caught good.

But Goodnight was disappointed. Gudanuf was missing. The rancher had only seen the outlaw chief that one time, but he was sure he remembered him well enough to know that he was not among the dead or the prisoners. None of them were good-looking enough. He reached up and touched his eye patch and brushed the Big Dipper.

"Where's Gudanuf!" Goodnight shouted, and he was not a man to shout.

None of the outlaws answered him. He walked up to one of the bound but uninjured men.

"Open your mouth," Goodnight ordered.

The man obeyed. Goodnight shoved the barrel of the gun inside the outlaw's mouth.

"Now answer my question," he demanded.

"He left," the outlaw mumbled, his mouth full of gun.

"Where'd he go?"

"Kansas."

"Where in Kansas?"

"I dunno."

"You're lyin', but I ain't got time to fool with you right now. I'll tend to you later."

Goodnight turned and slowly approached the front door of the handsome rock house. He retarded his steps because he was worried about what he might find inside. There could still be outlaws in there just waiting for him to step inside, but more badmen were not what he feared most. He was worried about the girl. What condition would she be in? Had they gotten there too late? Would she be there at all? Was she still alive?

By the time Goodnight finally reached the door, his cowboys had finished their tying-up chores and had hurried to join him. Even the wounded Loving. They didn't want Goodnight going through that door alone. Now they all had their handguns out for close work inside a closed room. Even Loving held a pistol unconvincingly in his left hand.

The door stood partially ajar. Staring at the crack, Goodnight couldn't see anything but darkness within. That was the problem with those little castle windows. They wouldn't let in many bullets, but they wouldn't admit much light either.

"Be careful," Goodnight said. "I reckon it's time to look alive. Here goes."

Turning slightly, he charged the door and hit it a sound blow with his right shoulder. He was surprised at how heavy it turned out to be. The wood must have been four or five inches thick. His shoulder hurt. This rock house really was a fortress. But thick and heavy as it was, the door moved. It swung slowly back and open. He stepped forward onto the square of light admitted by the door.

Looking around the room, Goodnight didn't see anybody inside. He was glad not to find any outlaws, but he was brokenhearted not to discover the girl. They had come all this way for nothing. She was probably buried someplace out there on the trackless Staked Plain, a small mound of earth rising ever so slightly above the general flatness. Nobody would ever find her grave if they had even bothered to dig one. They could have just left her for the animals to dispose of. Goodnight was profoundly sad. He was infinitely weary of not being able to protect people, not being able to save them, not being able to keep them from dying.

Then *she* rescued him from his flash flood of misery. In his excited state, Goodnight thought he saw his sister moving in a dark corner of the room. She seemed to have come back to him now as she had so many times before in dreams. Fortunately–or unfortunately–it was a dream he dreamed less and less often. But here she was back at last, back for good, a light figure moving in the darkness.

36

Then as his eye slowly accustomed itself to the gloom of the room, Goodnight saw that she wasn't his sister, and his heart screamed, just as it always did when he woke up from one of those dreams. The girl in the corner was a complete stranger to him, but at least she was alive. Goodnight hurried toward her. The place smelled the way the old dugout smelled, like the bodies of unwashed men. Sweaty men. And he was pretty sure he knew how they had worked up some of those sweats. He already wanted to get out of there, but he couldn't go yet.

The girl knelt and squeezed herself as tightly as she could into the corner. Goodnight realized that since she was a stranger to him, then he was certainly a stranger to her. She hadn't seen the battle because the windows were too small. She probably thought all the shooting was just another buffalo slaughter. Now she must be imagining that he and his men planned to treat her as other strange men had. He stopped about six feet from her.

"Don't worry," Goodnight said in the tone of voice he usually reserved for animals and plants. "I won't hurt you. You're safe. I promise."

She peeked up at him but didn't say anything. She still wasn't sure she could trust him. Or the others either. Maybe they did look a little like outlaws. A pretty scruffy bunch. He didn't blame her for having her doubts about them.

"Really, it's all right," Goodnight said softly. "We come to git you back."

"Where are they?" she asked.

"Dead or tied up," Goodnight said.

"You ain't foolin' me, huh?"

"No, ma'am."

"He crosses his heart," said Loving, "an' hopes to die."

The other cowboys laughed softly. The captive just looked blank. Goodnight knew how she felt. He had been there himself. He wasn't surprised that her expression did not change. She was beyond smiles and frowns.

"Can I come closer?" Goodnight asked. "I don't mean you no harm."

The girl on the floor took a long time making up her mind. She must have been trying to figure out what was happening–trying to decide who to trust–but none of her thoughts showed on her face. Hers was dead.

"By the way, my name's Goodnight," he said. "These here are my boys. We're from the Home Ranch down in the red canyon. Maybe you heard tell of it?"

She still didn't say anything. Goodnight was a little disappointed. He had counted on her knowing who he was. Maybe the Home Ranch wasn't as impressive to others as it was to him.

"I reckon you're Katie Russell, huh?" Goodnight said. "From the Exchange Hotel?"

At last, she nodded slightly. "Come on," she said.

As he stepped forward, Goodnight saw the chain. One end of it was wrapped around her neck and fastened with a heavy lock. The other end was secured by a second lock to a ring built into the fireplace. The heavy chain appeared to be about twelve feet long. Goodnight's stomach hurt as he knelt in front of the Russells' daughter. He reached out to touch the chain to see if it was real, as if touching was believing, but she misinterpreted his move and recoiled.

"I won't hurt you," Goodnight said again. Withdrawing his hand, he looked back over his shoulder. "Tin Soldier, can you git this here thing unlocked?"

The cowboy with the tin hat stepped forward and knelt beside his boss. He stared at the lock and chain for what seemed to be a long time.

"No," Tin Soldier said at last, "I don't do locks."

"Too Short, git my ax," Goodnight said, "if'n you don't mind."

Hearing the cowboy heading for the door, Goodnight walked on his knees over to the fireplace. He wanted to study how securely the ring was attached. A cleat, which held the ring, fitted between two large stones. It was mortared in place. He tried to move the cleat, but it wouldn't wiggle at all. He ran his finger along the seam between the rocks. The mortar didn't flake. This wasn't going to be easy. He kept wondering what was taking Too Short so long to fetch his ax. Then he remembered that his horse and ax weren't just outside the door–as he had been imagining–but rather were over the crest of a nearby hill.

"Just be patient," Goodnight said to the young woman but also to himself. "We'll git you loose in a minute."

Then he heard hoofbeats outside. Too Short must have run all the way to Red and then ridden him back to the rock house. He came in still breathing hard.

"Here y'are," Too Short said.

Goodnight raised up and took the ax. Then he stood like a baseball player ready to bat. He took a couple of practice swings measuring the distance to the cleat.

"Better close your eyes, Miss Katie," Goodnight said.

He waited until she did so. Then, using the blunt end of the ax, he took a good swing at the ring and cleat. Pieces of mortar flew, but the cleat didn't seem to budge. The ring just jingled a merry tune as if mocking him. He swung again. A mortar fragment stung his cheek just below his good eye, which made him a little nervous. He would feel like a big idiot if he ended up blinding himself. He would have liked to close his eye when he swung the ax again, but he was afraid he would miss the "ball" and look ridiculous in front of his men.

Goodnight decided to change sides. He moved over and took a couple more practice swings. He felt somewhat awkward working from this side of the ring. He hoped his men wouldn't laugh if he swung like a girl. They didn't. And this time the cleat moved slightly. He could see that he was making progress. He swung again and the cleat moved again. He struck again. Then he bent down and tried to pull out the loosened cleat with his hand. Now it wiggled, but it wouldn't let go.

Goodnight changed sides again. Now he felt like a more coordinated batter. Larger chunks of mortar flew. The floor was now littered with grey dust and shards. He struck again. The cleat moved more than ever. He cocked his ax and swung as hard as he could. The mighty blow reverberated up the ax handle to his hands. He dropped the ax. He couldn't help it.

Bending over to pick it up, Goodnight reached out and gave the ring another yank. It gave up and came out. It had suffered enough. He smiled at finally succeeding and still having one good eye.

"You can open your eyes now, miss," Goodnight said. "Less git outa this damn gloomy place."

Katie stood up slowly, still pressing herself into the corner. Goodnight held the other end of her chain. He felt as if he had her on a leash. Hurriedly, he coiled the chain as if it had been a lariat and handed it to her. She took it with a frown.

"Come on," Goodnight said. "Less git some fresh air."

He led the way and the cowboys followed, but she remained where she was. It felt good to be outside in the light, but it made him squint. He didn't mind.

"It's a lot nicer out here, ma'am," Goodnight called. "Honest."

He waited but she didn't appear.

"They're out there," she called at last.

"They won't hurt you no more," he promised. "They cain't. Their hurtin' days is about over."

"But they're still out there. I don't wanta see 'em."

Goodnight shrugged and walked back into the smelly darkness. He was momentarily blinded, but his eye soon adjusted. Katie hadn't moved. She remained by the fireplace as if she were still chained.

"You're safe, miss," Goodnight said. "You really are. You don't wanta stay in this stinkin' place no longer. Do you?"

"I cain't come out," she said softly.

"Why not? You ain't chained up no longer."

"It ain't that."

"What is it then?"

"I don't wanta be looked at."

"Why not? I don't understand."

"I don't wanta say."

"Oh."

He wondered what they had done to her. Well, he was pretty sure he knew what games they had practiced on her, but he didn't suppose what they had done would show. Surely she was changed inside but not outside.

"Okay, take your time," Goodnight said. "We got a few chores to do outside anyhow. Come on out when you're good and ready. Okay?"

He turned to go. He had to get out of there.

"Wait," she said in a small voice.

He stopped and turned back around. He waited. She seemed to be on the verge of saying something, but she was in no hurry.

"I don't wanta go out," she finally said in the smallest of voices, "because, well, you'll see through my dress."

"What's wrong with your dress?" he asked.

"It ain't the dress." She hesitated. "It's what ain't under the dress."

Goodnight didn't know what to say. He was a little embarrassed. He just waited for her to explain if she was of a mind to. He tried to make his face look sympathetic.

"They done took away my underwear. This here's a summer dress. It ain't thick. You'll see right through me."

Goodnight started to promise her that they wouldn't look, but he didn't want to lie to the girl. They might not exactly mean to, but they would eventually glance her way. He looked around the gloom for some solution to her problem. He noticed a bed near her which he hadn't paid much attention to before. It was the only bed in the room. The gang slept somewhere else in the house. This was her bed which was within reach of her chain. Staring at the bed, he imagined what had happened to her on it.

"Well, wrap up in a blanket," Goodnight said, gesturing toward a pile of twisted bedding.

"No!" she cried. "I ain't never gonna touch them things ag'in."

"That's all right. You don't hafta. We'll think a somethin' else."

But what? He didn't have any idea. He searched the room again, but he didn't see anything useful. So he pretended that he was outside looking around. Now he "saw" something.

"How about one a ours?" Goodnight said. "I mean, we got bedrolls. Would that be all right, huh?"

She considered the proposal carefully.

"I guess that's all right," she said. Then after a moment's pause, she added, "Thanks."

Goodnight was happy to have an excuse to get out of the dark room where he had found his sister and lost her all over again. The cowboys looked at him curiously, but he offered no explanation. He just went up to Red, untied his bedroll from the back of the saddle, and carried it inside. The cowboys' looks were more curious than ever.

Entering the mean room once again, Goodnight saw Katie exactly where he had left her in the corner. She was free and yet a prisoner still. He unrolled his bedroll as he walked up to her. It was a single patchwork quilt that his Aunt Orlena had given him as he was leaving her home for good. He handed it to Katie, who took it with her right hand while her left still held the coiled chain.

"Here," she said handing him the chain.

Then she used both hands to wrap the blanket around her shoulders. The movement reminded Goodnight of the way the Humans loved to wrap themselves in buffalo robes. He smiled seeing the woolly animals in his imagination.

"Less go," Goodnight said.

"Just a minute," said Katie.

He had the feeling that she was never going to leave this terrible place. And if she wouldn't, he couldn't. What was wrong now?

"I wanta tell you somethin'," she said. "I couldn't say it in fronta all them other men. But mebbe I kin tell you."

Goodnight nodded.

"Then we'll go out," she said.

He nodded and tried to smile sympathetically in the dark. He just hoped it wasn't going to be a long story.

"They done branded me."

Goodnight felt a pain throb behind his empty eye socket. Again he noticed that his hands felt strange, as if they didn't belong to him, as if they were a giant's hands. And they were shaking. He hated the outlaws because of what they had done to their poor captive. He hated them even more because he knew they would have done the same to Revelie if they had had a chance.

"I'm sorry," Goodnight said, sounding like Loving.

"I'm glad I told," Katie said. "I didn't know if'n I ever would. Just have this secret thing." She thought a moment. "I feel better now."

"Good," he said because he didn't know what else to say.

"It's right here." She pointed to her right buttock. "It says 'RR.'" She started crying. "I was afraid mebbe it'd show through my dress." She cried harder. "I feel like ever'body kin see it even when I know they cain't."

37

Goodnight sniffed the air and smelled the rusty-nail odor of a branding iron getting hotter and hotter. The scent brought back pleasant memories of calf-branding at the Home Ranch. He recalled that the male calves not only got branded but also castrated. These outlaws deserved such treatment much more than those little longhorns. This notion appealed to him. It wasn't quite as simple as an eye for an eye, but it was similar. It had a balance to it.

The five surviving outlaws, sprawled helplessly on the ground, smelled the heating iron, too. He hadn't told them that he meant to brand them all, but they had guessed his intentions. They had protested, begged, and wheedled, but he hadn't changed his mind, and eventually they had shut up. The branding iron in the fire was their own, which had been found in the rock house. This one wasn't a running iron but had the two large *R*s spelled out in metal at the end of a three-foot-long rod. Wait until he told them that branding wasn't all he was going to do. Then they would really have something to cry and moan about.

Goodnight glanced over at Katie, who sat by herself on the rock pile behind which outlaws had taken cover not long ago. The cowboys seemed to sense that she didn't need crowding at the moment. They allowed her her privacy. She was toying with her chain that was still locked around her neck. She had been freed from her captivity, but its horrors still had a grip on her. Goodnight knew a thing or two about not being able to free yourself from the past no matter how hard you tried.

"Reckon it's hot enough?" asked Tin Soldier, who knew something about working with hot metal.

Goodnight walked over and stared down into the fire. The "RR" glowed bright red. Then he realized his face was hot, but was it from the heat of the flames or from the anger that still burned within him?

With a gloved hand, he reached down and pulled the branding iron out of the fire. Carrying the "RR" over to the nearest outlaw, he held it an inch from the prisoner's distorted face. The man had a white scar on his cheek that seemed to whiten as his face reddened with fear.

"That hot enough for you?" Goodnight asked.

"You're a savage!" cried the outlaw.

"Pull down his pants," Goodnight said as he returned the branding iron to the fire to keep it warm. "We'll brand his butt. Then we're gonna turn this here bull into a damn steer. See how he likes that. Huh?"

"No, no, please, no!" the outlaw begged. "Don't!" He squirmed on the ground as if in pain. "You cain't! No! No! No!"

Goodnight saw his cowboys staring at him. He hadn't told them about the branding of Katie, not wanting to embarrass her, so his men were surprised at the viciousness of his anger. It wasn't like him.

"You heard me," Goodnight said. "Go on."

Now his men moved, all but Loving, who just stood there holding his wounded arm. The boys might be surprised, but they were nonetheless willing. They set upon the scar-faced outlaw as if he were a roped calf. Too Short, Simon, and Tin Soldier held him while Black Dub, the strongest, went to work shucking him out of his trousers. It was an awkward job because the outlaw's hands were still tied to his feet behind his back. In spite of being hog-tied, the outlaw put up a surprisingly good fight. He bucked worse than a calf, perhaps because he understood more clearly than a calf what was about to happen to him, but Black Dub eventually won the tug-of-war. The pants didn't come off–they couldn't, thanks to the ropes–but they were pulled down below the outlaw's knees.

"No! Stop!" he kept screaming. "Don't!"

"Turn him on his stomach," Goodnight ordered. "I'm gonna brand his hindquarters."

The boys rolled him onto his belly and held him there. He continued to buck and blubber. Goodnight retrieved the branding iron from the fire. The handle felt hot even through his glove. He enjoyed this small discomfort.

"This is gonna be fun," he said. As he carried the hot iron to the outlaw, Goodnight felt a smile stretch his face. He was looking forward to the man's pain. "Now if'n I was you," Goodnight said, "I wouldn't squirm too much. You hear? 'Cause if'n you do, this here poker's just gonna slip and slide all over your butt. And instead a havin' a nice neat brand, it's just gonna be a big smear."

The outlaw made sounds that weren't really words. He even sounded a little like a frightened calf.

"Hold him tight," Goodnight said.

Raising the red-hot iron over the exposed ass, Goodnight took careful aim. Then in one quick motion he rammed it down onto the white flesh and held it there. He heard a hiss and saw smoke rise.

"Now be still," he said.

Then Goodnight saw the fire and smelled flesh burning. The hairs on the outlaw's ass had burst into flames. The rancher had seen calf fur blaze up during branding, so perhaps he shouldn't have been surprised, but he was. It had never occurred to him that a man could have enough hair on his ass to catch fire. The sight and the smell made him feel sick. He dropped the branding iron–which fell sideways, blurring the brand–and staggered backward. The fire burned itself out. Goodnight turned away and threw up.

"Just hang 'em," Goodnight said. "Go on. Take 'em all down to the river and hang 'em from a cottonwood tree." He fought back nausea. "Hurry up."

It seemed to him that his cowboys looked relieved. Black Dub grabbed two outlaws by their ankles and started carrying them like a couple of buckets down to the cottonwoods that grew by the river. Simon and Tin Soldier picked up another between them and followed after Black Dub. Too Short tied a lariat to the knees of one badman, then moved over and tied it to the knees of another. Then he jumped on Red and started dragging the two to their doom. After resting for a moment, Goodnight followed them. Then he remembered something, stopped, and turned.

"You wanta come?" he asked.

"No," she said, and rattled the chain in her hands.

Goodnight nodded and then resumed his journey to the riverbank. As he walked along, he felt ashamed of himself for what he had intended to do. He never wanted to feel this feeling again. He promised himself that he wouldn't. But he knew that if he was going to keep this promise to himself, then this country was going to have to change. And if it was to change, he was probably going to have to be the one to change it. He wanted something beyond an eye for an eye, a brand for a brand, a wound for a wound, blood for blood. He wanted rules.

He wanted boundaries. He wanted justice if that wasn't too much to ask. He wanted it almost as much as he wanted Revelie. Actually, his two wants were connected because he couldn't expect her to live in such a wild and savage land.

They hanged the five outlaws from a single sturdy branch of a crooked cottonwood tree. Black Dub pulled them up until their dancing feet were at about eye level.

38

Goodnight would have liked to camp out beside the rock house and wait for Gudanuf to return. But he was afraid to. He wasn't afraid of the outlaw. He was afraid for his best friend. He wanted to get Loving to a doctor as soon as possible. Goodnight considered leaving a couple of his cowboys behind to lie in wait for Gudanuf, but he finally decided not to. Who knew what kind of force the outlaw leader would return with? He might overwhelm a couple of honest men. They would either all stay or they would all go. Since they couldn't all stay, they all rode away from Robbers' Roost together.

Looking back, Goodnight admired the thick smoke rising high into the air, but the rock walls would still remain after the fire burned itself out. Goodnight again felt the frustration of a job left half-finished. After all his effort, the walls and Gudanuf himself would be left standing. He clenched his fists into tight knots–his mind felt knotted, too–as he rode along.

When they reached the tree where Roy was still tied upside down, they cut him down. The outlaw was furious because they had given him the worst headache of his life, but relieved because he had been afraid they would leave him there to die. He was also scared because they might be planning to hang him right side up this time.

"Lemme go," Roy begged. "Ain't you done enough to me already. My head's killin' me."

Goodnight thought the outlaw had a point. He hadn't taken part in the stealing and raping of Katie. He had been working at the down-and-out ranch when all that took place. He probably had committed similar crimes in the past, but there wasn't any proof. Goodnight didn't believe in hanging a man on suspicion. Maybe Roy was what he claimed to be: a retired outlaw. Of course, he would probably backslide one of these days, but Goodnight didn't believe in preventative hanging either. There was too much random violence in this country. He didn't want to add to it.

"Let him go," Goodnight said.

"What?" asked Too Short.

"Give him his horse and turn him loose."

"If you say so."

Goodnight nodded. Too Short shrugged. The other cowboys were surprised, but they didn't protest.

"What about these?" asked Roy, holding up his improvised handcuffs.

"I dunno," said Goodnight. "Tin Soldier, can you do somethin' about them chains?"

"Not without some tools," Tin Soldier replied.

"Sorry," Goodnight said. "Well, Roy, you're welcome to ride along with us far as Tascosa. Course, I don't know how popular you're gonna be there. It's up to you."

"Thanks but no thanks," said Roy.

"Well, we're in kind of a hurry," Goodnight said, "so I guess we'll cut the goodbyes short."

The rancher put out his hand. The outlaw took it. They shook. Then they all mounted up. Goodnight and his posse rode almost due south. Roy headed east with his chain jingling.

Katie's chain jingled, too. She rode a horse that had once belonged to one of the dead outlaws. She wrapped the chain around the saddle horn so she wouldn't have to carry it. She still looked like a prisoner, and perhaps felt like one, too. Freedom would take a while to get used to. Maybe forever.

As they rode along, Goodnight tried to focus on the future so he wouldn't remember the past. The future did require some careful planning. For he was no longer willing to accept the present state of chaos.

After careful thought, Goodnight decided that he would offer one of his cowboys to Tascosa as acting sheriff. But which one? He considered each of his men in turn, and settled on Black Dub. He believed that Black Dub's physical strength would allow him to solve many problems with his muscles rather than with his gun. He hoped there would be less bloodletting. Of course, Black Dub's strength would be missed around the ranch. Who would pick up the back of a wagon stuck in the mud and set it on dry land? But Tascosa probably needed Black Dub's strength more than the Home Ranch did, at least at the moment. Goodnight planned to continue to pay Black Dub until the town got organized enough to collect some taxes. When he told the giant about his plan, the black man smiled. He had been a slave and now he was going to be a sheriff. And if any of the white folk didn't like it, well, they could take it up with the bossman. Or they could wrestle. Take their pick.

Naturally, a sheriff would need a jail. Until Tascosa had some kind of lockup, the town would just go on hanging outlaws, or suspected outlaws, without the benefit of law or trials. Goodnight had just presided over the lynching of five men, and he had planned to do worse. A whole lot worse. He hoped that law and some semblance of order would protect him from his own worst instincts. And protect the country from its. He wanted to make this country a fit place for a woman to live in. All women. And a particular woman.

In his mind, he walked the streets of Tascosa looking for a structure that could be quickly converted into a jail. He "walked" down Main Street past the Equity Saloon, past John King's drugstore, past the Cattle Exchange Saloon, past the Exchange Hotel, which was run by Katie's parents, past the Wright & Farnsworth General Store, and past W. S. Mabry's surveyor's office, which brought him to the end of the street. So far he hadn't noticed any likely prison. Turning left down McMasters Street, he "strolled" past an adobe home. He wasn't sure who lived there. Moving on, he studied a large square corral on his right. Next to the corral stood a barn. It wasn't very large, but it looked sturdy. That barn might do. Of course, a few iron bars would have to be added, but such fixtures shouldn't be a problem. After all, Tascosa had a blacksmith, and Tin Soldier would be happy to lend a hand. Goodnight felt almost certain that he had found his jail.

39

Back in the red canyon now, Goodnight was more or less satisfied with what he had been able to accomplish. Old Man McMasters, for whom McMasters Street was named, had agreed to donate his barn as a temporary jail. And the town had eventually agreed to accept Black Dub as its new sheriff. Better still, the doctor in Tascosa had been able to treat Loving's arm without sawing it off. It had even rained recently. So all seemed to be going well in the red canyon, except Goodnight missed Black Dub. And of course he missed Revelie, too. Even more.

"You asleep?" Goodnight asked one night. Now it was his turn to nurse Loving.

"No, just restin' my eyes," Loving said.

The two of them shared half the house with Suckerod and Tin Soldier, who were doing chores elsewhere.

"I was thinkin' a writin' another letter," Goodnight said. "You ain't lost your ol' fountain pen, have you?"

"I reckon I can put my hand on it."

"Figure you can write?"

"We'll see. Arm gets better ever' day."

With his left hand, Loving rustled about in his saddlebag and eventually located pen and paper. He took a seat on an unpainted cedar chair that had been carved since the writing of the first letter. Goodnight sat on a second chair facing Loving. They would be more comfortable this time around.

"Shoot," said Loving, shifting the pen gingerly to his right hand, ready to write.

"'Dear Revelie,'" Goodnight began, and the pen scratched. "Less see . . . Don't write that. I'm just wool-gatherin' . . . Uh . . . 'I hope you got my last letter. You should see the place now. We've been makin' a lotta changes around here. The ranch is actually startin' to look like a ranch.'"

"Hold your horses. Lemme catch up. I ain't as fast as I used to be."

Goodnight leaned back in his new chair. He waited until the pen stopped scratching.

"'This is just the beginnin','" he started up again. "'I've been thinkin' a lot about what we're gonna do here in this here canyon.'"

He paused to let the pen catch up.

"'It's mebbe somethin' like what your ancestors got to do when they was first settin' up Boston. They got to start all over and make this brand-new country as close to perfect as they could figure out how to.'"

He paused to think out what he wanted to say.

"'An' that's just the chance we've got in this here canyon. We can start all over, too. We can build up a world like we want it. We can leave out all the ol' mistakes. Anyhow, we can try. I already got Black Dub set up as sheriff in Tascosa. Imagine that.'"

"Wait." Loving scribbled. "Okay."

"'I figure mebbe we need somethin' wrote down. Rules or somethin'. Laws and what to do if'n folks break them laws. We gotta cut out lynchin' an' all that sorta carryin' on.'"

Goodnight paused again to let Loving catch up.

"'But we need more'n just that. We need rules not just for what you cain't do. We need 'em for what you're supposed to do, too. Stuff like bein' trustworthy an' loyal. An', less see, brave. An' self-reliant, right? Somethin' about standin' on yore own two feet.' Hummm."

Goodnight scratched his head and listened to the pen scratch. The itch wasn't actually on his scalp but below it. He itched to put into words what he felt about this special land and the special qualities it required of those who lived on it.

"'Somethin' about fair. Somethin' about ever'body bein' worth the same. A white man ain't worth more'n an Injun. Or a black man like Black Dub or whatever. A cow ain't worth more'n a buffalo. Dog ain't worth more'n a wolf ain't worth more'n a coyote. Rose ain't worth more'n a horehound and the other way 'round. Man ain't worth more'n a woman.'"

"Hold on." Loving's pen raced. "Okay, shoot."

"Maybe we kin invent the world all over ag'in in this here wild place."

40

In the spring, Coffee came back from Tascosa with tobacco, baking soda, bags of flour and meal, a bucket of sorghum, and a telegram from Boston:

> MY PAPA WROTE ME THAT YOU ARE GOOD AT RESCUING STOP PLEASE RESCUE ME STOP I MEAN IT STOP WARMEST REGARDS REVELIE

BOOK TWO

CODE

41

When the newlyweds came home to the red canyon, they were in love.

Revelie carefully studied her new home. Her blue eyes filled with tears that magnified them. She sniffed. She wiped her eyes with fingers that had red dust on them, so her face was streaked with red. She looked so miserable that Goodnight stopped being in a good mood. He felt like a guilty criminal for having brought this unfortunate girl to this lonely place that was a hundred miles from any other woman. And he had expected her to live in this rude log cabin after she had grown up in a Boston mansion.

"Forgive me," Goodnight said. "What'd I do?"

"What have you done?" Revelie said. "You're building a new world. Just like you wrote in your letter. None of this was here before."

"You like it?"

"I love it. I really love it. It's magic."

"But it ain't what you're used to."

"I'm tired of what I'm used to."

Goodnight smiled broadly, his good mood restored. He looked around to see what impression his new wife was making on his outfit. He was pleased to see that they were all smiling. He studied Loving especially, since he was the only one who had never met her before. He was glad to see that his foreman was staring with open admiration at Mrs. Goodnight.

"Let's go inside the house," Revelie said. "I want to see it from the inside out."

"Less go," said Goodnight.

He led the way, then opened the door of the north room, where he and Revelie would live together as man and wife. The rest of the cowboys, all six of them, would have to make do with the south room. Revelie entered and Goodnight followed. The space seemed smaller to him than it had ever seemed before. Once again, he could not help making comparisons with Boston.

"Ain't hardly room to turn around in," Goodnight said, "huh?"

"Stop apologizing," Revelie said. "I love it. And you're not going to change my mind no matter how hard you try. So you might just as well give up. We don't need a big house because our real home is your red canyon. Don't you know that?"

"I know," he said. "I just didn't know that you knew."

They smiled at each other.

42

After supper that evening, the cowboys threw a wedding dance for the newlyweds. The ballroom was the dog run—the breezeway—between the north room and the south room. The dance floor was packed earth. Unfortunately, there weren't quite enough women to go around. Revelie was, after all, the only Eve in an Eden full of Adams, so measures had to be taken if the ball was to be a success. They agreed to draw straws to see which cowboys would be girls and which ones could remain boys. Those who got the short straws would be the females, the long straws, the males. The short straws would tie white handkerchiefs around their left arms to indicate that they were the weaker and fairer sex.

Goodnight was looking forward to the fun, but he knew this dance would be a far cry from their wedding ball in Boston. He hoped Revelie wouldn't mind the difference too much. He almost wished the boys hadn't come up with this idea. He was afraid they might embarrass him by acting like hicks. He was equally worried that his wife might look down on the cowboys and their antics.

"Miss Revelie," Coffee said, "would you hold these here straws?"

"I'd be honored," said the bride. "But what if Mr. Goodnight draws one of the short straws. Does that mean I can't dance with my own husband at my own wedding ball?"

"Oh, no," said Too Short. "He don't hafta draw. It'll just be us run-a-the-mill heroes."

"Very well," said Revelie.

She held out her hand and Coffee placed the straws across her palm. Then she turned her back and took her time mixing them up so nobody would know which was which. Turning back around, she held out her right hand, which was closed in a fist. Just the tops of the straws peeked out above her curled index finger.

"All right, Coffee," Revelie said, "you draw first."

"No, ma'am," said the cook, "I don't git to dance on account a I'm the orchestra."

"All right, you're excused," she said. "What about you, Simon? Will you do the honors?"

Goodnight was proud of how his new wife was throwing herself into this game. He could tell that Simon was nervous as he approached Revelie. The groom smiled when he saw the great pains the cowboy took not to touch the feminine hand as he plucked the straw. It was a short one.

"Aw, no," Simon moaned.

All the other cowboys laughed.

"What are you laughing at?" asked Revelie. "What's wrong with being a woman?"

"Well, it's okay for a woman," Simon mumbled.

"All right, Suckerod, it's your turn," she said.

Goodnight felt sorry for the poor cowboy, whose hand shook even more than usual as he reached for a straw. He got a long one.

"Whew," Suckerod said.

"Black Dub, it's your turn," Revelie said.

Black Dub, the sheriff of Tascosa, was visiting the Home Ranch. It turned out that he missed them as much as they missed him, so he rode out fairly often. He got a long straw.

"Tin Soldier, now you," called Revelie.

He got a short straw and got laughed at.

"Welcome to the sewing circle," Revelie said. "Let's see, we've got one long straw and one short straw left. Who'll be the next to try his or her luck? How about you, Jack?"

"I don't dance much," Loving said. "I figure I better just pass."

"But you can't," Revelie said. "We need you to have an equal number. If you drop out, some poor woman–or it could be some poor man–won't have a partner. Come now, be a good sport."

"Then I reckon I cain't say no, huh?" Loving said.

He stepped forward, shrugged his shoulders, pursed his lips, arched his eyebrows, and picked a long straw. He smiled a little sheepishly.

"Too bad, Too Short," Loving said. "May I have the first dance?"

"*Dee*lighted, Mr. Loving," Too Short said. "I thought you'd never ask."

Soon Coffee was tuning up his fiddle. *Screech. Squawk. Screech.* The journey west had not been kind to the instrument, but before long the cook had it making sounds that passed for music.

"Hey, Coffee," Too Short taunted, "you're a better fiddler than you are a cook. Mebbe we better start callin' you Fiddle."

"Okay, I'm about ready," Coffee said. "Choose your pardners."

"No," said Simon. "The bride an' groom hafta dance the first dance all by theirselves."

"Okay, bride and groom, whaddle I play?" asked Fiddle.

Goodnight and Revelie looked at each other. They both shrugged.

"It's gotta be a waltz," said Too Short.

"Whichun?" asked Fiddle.

The bride and groom shrugged again.

"The one about Froggy the Frog," said Too Short.

"That okay by you folks?" asked Fiddle.

The bride and groom looked at each other.

"Sure," said Revelie. "'The Blue Danube Waltz' would be lovely."

"Shore," said Goodnight. "Play Ole Froggy."

The fiddler started fiddling and the groom took the bride in his arms.

"No, wait," said Revelie. "This isn't right. I have to change clothes. I'm underdressed for my wedding reception."

"It's just us," Goodnight said. "You look great."

"No, I want to."

Revelie disappeared into the ranch "house." Goodnight looked at his men and thought he could read their minds. They were all thinking: Well, that's a woman for you. She had managed to bleed all the energy out of the enterprise over a little matter of vanity.

The groom paced up and down between the cook shack and the house, getting more red dust on his boots. He couldn't imagine what could be taking his bride so long. Pretty soon it would be too late to dance. It would be time to go to bed because they all had work to do in the morning. No dressing up could be worth this amount of waiting around doing nothing.

When Revelie reappeared, Goodnight realized that he–and all his men, if they were thinking what he thought they were thinking–had been wrong. She was wearing her white bridal gown, knowing it would get dirty because of all the red dust, not caring, wanting to look like a bride at her cowboy wedding ball. All the cowboys started nodding their heads, knowing she had been right, realizing this was really a special evening, made more special by her.

"You're the purdiest thing I've ever seen in my life," Goodnight said. "I swear." He scratched his chin. "Mebbe I should change clothes."

"No," Revelie said. "You look fine the way you are. Besides, it's getting late. These boys have work to do in the morning."

Besides, Goodnight couldn't have changed into his groom clothes because he hadn't brought them out West with him. He had left them behind in the East because they didn't belong to him. He had gotten married in a borrowed morning coat.

"May I have this here dance?" Goodnight asked.

"My pleasure," said Revelie. "Let there be music."

Fiddle put his instrument under his chin and pretty soon Froggy the Frog was jumping over a log. The groom took the bride in his arms and whirled her around the dirt dance floor. Actually, he realized that "whirled" was a bit of an overstatement, for he didn't dance very well, not the Writer dances anyhow. He had grown up war-dancing rather than ballroom-dancing. But he tried to remember what his bride had taught him back in Boston, and he didn't think he was doing too bad. Anyhow, nobody was laughing. But the main thing was that he was happy, really very happy, and he believed she was happy, too. He told himself that this was the happiest moment of his life.

To help him keep time to the music, Goodnight sang softly in Revelie's ear: "Froggy the frog, hop-hop, hop-hop, jumped over a log, hop-hop, hop-hop . . ."

When the music finally ended, all the cowboys actually clapped. Goodnight knew he hadn't been *that* good, but he appreciated the applause anyhow.

"Now ever'body join in," he said. "Choose your pardners and don't be shy."

Suckerod made an elaborate bow and asked Simon for the pleasure of this dance. Simon thought it over a moment and then coyly accepted. Black Dub asked the lovely Tin Soldier to dance. Loving had already asked Too Short. And Revelie was pledged to Goodnight.

"Now you boys feel free ta sing along," said Fiddle.

Then he started fiddling.

"Put yore liddle foot," sang Black Dub, who had the prettiest singing voice, "put yore liddle foot, put yore liddle foot right cheer."

The "couples" danced side by side, hip-to-hip.

"Your little foot ain't so little," Suckerod grumbled to Simon. "I thought ladies was supposed to have charmin' little ol' feet."

"Just don't put your big foot on my little foot," said Simon.

Soon less gifted voices joined Black Dub's, and they all sang together.

"Take a step to the left."

They all stepped to the left, kicking up a storm of red dust.

"Take a step to the rear."

When they stepped to the rear, some of the couples collided with other couples who didn't step quite quickly enough, but that was part of the fun.

"Take a step to the right."

They all lumbered to the right.

"And forever stay near."

When the music stopped, the cowboys and cowgirls milled about on the dance floor. Soon the fiddle played a polka.

"Change pardners," Goodnight said.

Before long, Black Dub was dancing with Too Short. Loving whirled Tin Soldier around the dance floor. Goodnight tried to keep up with Simon, who loved to polka. And Suckerod danced with the bride in her wedding dress. They kicked up more red dust than ever dancing this spirited dance. The groom noticed that the bottom of his bride's gown was almost blood red.

"Nice sawin'," said Simon, out of breath, when the music finally stopped.

Fiddle played the schottische and the boys and girls danced side by side again. Goodnight paired off with Too Short. Suckerod selected Tin Soldier as his partner. Loving chose Simon. And Black Dub danced with Revelie. The groom loved this particular dance because the motion was much the same as riding. He imagined that they were all riding a circle in pairs. He was a better dancer when he danced this dance. All the cowboys now seemed more graceful. They were back on familiar ground. Goodnight wished he could have danced this dance with Revelie, but it hadn't worked out. Oh, well, he would have other chances.

The fiddle fell silent. Then the cook spent a few minutes tuning it. He plucked and tightened. When he was ready to start again, he played "After the Ball Was Over."

Goodnight asked Tin Soldier for the pleasure. Black Dub took Simon in his arms. Suckerod asked Too Short. And Loving danced with the bride in her flowing white and red gown.

As he watched the man who had become his best friend dance with his wife, Goodnight thought what a handsome couple they made. She was beautiful and he was not only handsome but unmarked. Nobody had robbed Loving of an eye or scarred him in any other way. Goodnight was proud of them, proud of their looks, proud of their grace, proud of being so intimately attached to them both. But he wondered fleetingly why Loving had said that he had never danced very much. He had certainly left the impression that he couldn't dance very well, and yet Loving now guided Revelie around the dance floor with skill and assurance. He danced the way he rode, the way he did everything, with an economy of motion that had a special charm. And Revelie in his arms mirrored his economy and matched his charm. They seemed made to dance together. Goodnight figured he could watch them all night. They were so lovely.

When Goodnight and Tin Soldier danced close to Revelie and Loving, the groom smiled at them warmly. The bride smiled back, but Loving looked in another direction. He either didn't care to return the smile, or else he hadn't seen it. Probably the latter. Goodnight felt all the clumsier on the dance floor as he watched Loving's easy elegance. He asked himself if he was jealous, but he found that he wasn't. He didn't particularly mind that Loving could dance so much better than he could. Goodnight's self-esteem did not lean heavily on dance steps. He was just happy for his friend and happy for his wife to have found such a partner. He was sorry when the fiddle played the last notes of "After the Ball Was Over."

"Thanks for the dance, Miz Goodnight," Loving said. "I reckon I'll be turnin' in now."

"Why so early?" asked Goodnight.

"I gotta work tomorrow," said Loving.

He turned and headed for his half of the log house.

43

That night Goodnight made love to his new wife on a mattress stuffed with the feathers of wild geese, wild turkeys, quail, and a few doves. He was surprised once again that Revelie made no objection to taking off all her clothes. He had imagined that a Boston girl would want to remain as well covered as possible even when making love.

Goodnight was also surprised at Revelie's passion. He had known passion before with Wekeah, but she had been a wild, uncivilized, untamed Human. He had supposed that a Writer woman, especially a Writer woman from Boston, especially a Writer woman from Boston who had such a mother, would be different. But she wasn't. This was a wild Writer woman. He could scarcely believe his luck.

Suddenly, Goodnight realized that Revelie was screaming. Well, it wasn't actually a scream. It was more of a moan, but it was a loud moan. Very loud. The cedar-log walls were thick, but not thick enough to be soundproof. What in the world were his cowboys thinking? That he was killing her? That they should ride to her rescue?

"Shhh," Goodnight whispered. "They'll hear us."

"I don't care," Revelie almost shouted. "I'm loud. I don't care who hears."

Goodnight couldn't believe what he was hearing. She didn't care who heard. She didn't mind that the whole outfit was listening to them while they made love. Even Wekeah, the wild Human, had been wild in a modest and discreet sort of way. But this Writer woman from Boston wanted everybody to know exactly what was going on. He wondered if he had misjudged Writers or just Revelie. Would she behave this way if her fancy mother and father were next door? He wasn't sure. Maybe. He couldn't believe that so much noise could come out of such a delicate female. And the racket seemed to be getting louder rather than softer. He imagined her grunts echoing up and down the canyon for miles and miles, frightening buffalo, stampeding cattle, causing landslides. She made more noise than that train that had carried him back to Boston–and then back West again–and she seemed as tireless.

Goodnight was especially worried about what Loving would think. He was different from the other men, made out of a rarer and more expensive fabric. He even had good-looking handwriting. He wouldn't be accustomed to hearing such immodest sounds. He would think less of the lovers after this night. Goodnight realized he didn't want to lose stature in Loving's eyes.

Then Goodnight felt as if he were falling. The sensation was similar to what happened when you were climbing down a steep trail and lost your footing and at first you thought you could save yourself but you kept falling faster and faster and couldn't stop. So you reached a point where you didn't even try to stop and just went with the fall. Falling, he heard himself scream. He screamed louder than she had ever moaned. He knew Loving and all the others heard his scream, but he didn't care. He bellowed his happiness to the whole echoing canyon. He was normally such a soft-spoken man that he surprised himself.

Then Revelie screamed and screamed again and again. Her screams burst out as his huge scream was dying away. Their screams mingled for a moment and then parted. He wasn't falling anymore. He had come to rest.

44

The next morning, the whole outfit gathered around the cook shack the way they had once gathered around the chuck wagon. The shack itself was just big enough for Coffee's supplies and a wood-burning stove, which Tin Soldier had built out of scrap metal. The boys were seated outside on rocks and logs.

Alone, Goodnight emerged from his side of the double cabin and headed for some breakfast. He had decided to let Revelie sleep late. When he reached his cowboys, the bridegroom felt quite shy, even sheepish, which was a hard thing for a cattleman to admit to himself. He hoped his men didn't think that–by making so much damn racket last night–he was flaunting his good fortune. Scanning their faces, he couldn't read them, which did not make him feel any easier. He seemed to be separated from them now by the high wall of marriage.

Goodnight was especially puzzled by the expression on Loving's face. His lips were pursed. His black eyebrows arched. His forehead was lined. But what did it all mean? Was he embarrassed? Was he disapproving? Was he disgusted? Was he envious? Goodnight, who the day before had been a big man with a small voice, felt smaller today because he had raised his voice. As he stared at Loving, and Loving stared right back, he felt himself shrinking. And yet he did not wish he could go back, relive last night, and make it different. But he was beginning to realize that even out here in his own canyon–cut off from the snares of citified civilization–it was still a complicated world. Well, he would just have to learn to live in it.

Goodnight saw all his cowboys turn their heads to look past him, over his shoulder, so he turned, too. Revelie had just emerged from her bridal chamber and was now making her way toward the circle of men. Goodnight was proud of her and anxious for her at the same time. He hoped she wasn't feeling too self-conscious. In the clear morning light, she must be embarrassed about all the racket last night.

When Revelie reached the circle, Suckerod was the first to get to his feet, his whole body shaking, almost spilling his coffee. Then the others got up, too. After a moment of indecision, Simon took off his hat and then the others followed suit, doing circus acts to balance their food and drink. Tin Soldier dropped his tin hat.

"Please don't get up," Revelie said after it was already too late.

"Mawnin', ma'am," said Tin Soldier. "Sleep well?" When he heard the others laugh, he realized his blunder. "No, I didn't mean. I mean—"

"Good morning, Tin Soldier," Revelie said. "I slept very well. Thank you for asking."

Goodnight was surprised at how well she pulled it off. He was beginning to think she was going to fit in pretty well around here. He smiled a still-self-conscious smile.

"Good morning, Black Dub," she said. "How did you sleep?"

"Mawnin', Miss Revelie," Black Dub said nervously. "Good. I did good."

"Black Dub," she said, "I'm not a miss anymore."

She didn't say but only implied that he must have heard the proof of that fact last night. All the men smiled except Black Dub, who coughed.

"No, ma'am," Black Dub said.

"Good morning, Suckerod," Revelie said. "How was your night?"

"Mawnin', ma'am," Suckerod said. "I done okay."

"Good morning, Too Short," she said. "How are you this morning?"

"Mawnin', ma'am," said Too Short. "Purdy good, I reckon. How're you?"

"Very well, thank you," she said. "Good morning, Simon."

"Mawnin', ma'am," Simon said. "*Mazel tov.*"

"Thank you and *shalom,*" she said. "Good morning, Jack. Did you sleep well?"

"Good mawnin', Miz Goodnight," Loving said. "Truth is, I had a restless night."

"I'm sorry to hear that," Revelie said with genuine concern in her voice. "What disturbed you?"

Goodnight thought she might be overdoing it. He didn't like the idea of her confronting the disturbance issue in quite so forthright a manner.

"I was turning somethin' over in my mind," Loving said. "I figured I'd wait around till after breakfast to bring it up. But mebbe I better just spit it out and git it over with."

"Please do," Revelie said.

"Well, I reckon I'm more of a drifter than I reckoned on. See, I been here in this here canyon for the whole winter. It's a purdy canyon, all right. 'Specially when it fills up with snow. But it's spring now an' I reckon I best be movin' on."

"No," Goodnight said, alarmed.

He felt as if he had been punched. Then he found himself wondering if all that immodest carrying on last night was driving Loving away. He had been worried that the noise might have made him uncomfortable–might even have offended him–but he had never imagined it would lead to such a breach. Goodnight told himself he was being silly. After all, Loving was a grown-up. He knew what husbands and wives did in bed. Maybe he had something else on his mind. Perhaps he just wanted to be asked to stay.

"Don't go," Goodnight said. "We need you here. If you think the canyon was purdy in the snow, wait'll all the wild flowers come out. You cain't go now."

"I got to," Loving said. "I promised myself I'd stay put till you got back. Sorta take keer a the place while you was gone. But you ain't gone no more. So the time's come to turn it back over to you and be on my way."

"Stay another month. Wait till brandin's over."

"That'd just be puttin' off."

"But why?"

"Like I said, I'm a drifter. Drifters drift. It's my nature."

"That ain't no reason. You cain't go for no reason atall. I won't let you."

Loving looked down at the red earth. He shrugged his shoulders. He shifted his weight from one boot to the other, then back again. He took off his hat, ran his fingers through his dark auburn hair, and put the hat back on again.

"Revelie, tell him he cain't go," said Goodnight.

She didn't say anything.

"Go on, tell him."

Revelie took a step forward. "Please don't go, Mr. Loving," she said. "Mr. Goodnight has told me so much about you. I've been looking forward to getting to know you. And now you're leaving just when I arrive. I almost feel I'm driving you away."

"See," Goodnight said, "she don't want you to go neither. If'n you won't stay for me, stay for her."

"I cain't."

"I been lookin' forward to all of us bein' here together. You. Me. Revelie. The boys. Buildin' somethin' new together. I was countin' on it."

"Sorry."

"Well, there's gotta be more to it. Somethin' you ain't sayin'. I just don't understand."

Loving just stood there. He rocked back and forth. He seemed to be about to say something, but then he stopped himself. He looked up and then down and then up again.

"You'll laugh," Loving said.

"No, I won't," Goodnight said. "Just tell me."

"How do you know you won't laugh? You ain't heard it yet. Huh?"

"I promise."

"Well, I heard an old girl I usta know done turned up in Tucson. You found yours. You give me a good example. Now I gotta find mine."

"How romantic," said Revelie, "the quest for love."

"Revelie, please, don't go talkin' no Eastern double-talk," said Goodnight. "Just convince him to stay."

"Please stay, Mr. Loving. You see how much it means to my husband."

"And you too."

"And to me as well."

"I'm real sorry, but I gotta be goin'. Git an early start."

Then Loving disappeared into the south room of the two-room house. Goodnight followed, then stood in the open doorway and watched in pain as his friend packed what few possessions he had into saddlebags. What wouldn't fit in the bags, he rolled up inside his bedding and tied the bundle with a short piece of rope. While he worked, Loving glanced up from time to time at Goodnight. Their faces were pinched, but neither one of them spoke. It didn't take long. Finished packing, the drifter picked up his saddlebags and bedroll and headed for the door. Goodnight got out of the way and let him pass.

Loving headed for the corral made of chinaberry trunks stacked in a zigzag pattern. Again, Goodnight followed behind, saying nothing, just watching. The pen held the outfit's remuda. Loving caught his horse, bridled it, then put on the saddle, moving as always with a graceful economy of motion, which Goodnight admired. Then the good-looking cowboy led his horse out of the corral and tied on his saddlebags and bedroll.

"Thanks," Loving said.

"For what?" Goodnight asked.

"Ever'thin'."

"You're welcome. Thank you."

"For what? For shootin' you? I'm sorry about that."

"Don't say you're–oh, never mind."

"So long."

"See ya."

Loving swung gracefully into the saddle and rode away. Watching him go, Goodnight was in pain. He was losing a loved one all over again. He "felt-missing" his lost loved ones with an agony that made him lose his balance and stagger. Revelie's soul might have been a dark forest, but Goodnight's felt like a waterless plain that was now burning with searing grass fires.

45

Goodnight and Revelie walked along the river while Coffee finished cooking supper. The cowboys were already lounging around the cook shack waiting to be fed. She wore a brown skirt and white blouse, which were spotless. He wore his old canvas pants and faded red shirt. He was peppered all over with red dust while she remained unsoiled. He seemed to live in a dirty place while she lived in a clean one. He wondered how she did it. This Writer woman had strong medicine. She was ready for afternoon high tea while he was ready for grub.

The sun was getting larger and cooler. A wild turkey emerged from a hackberry thicket and walked along the stream ahead of them. Goodnight pointed and Revelie did too, both at the same time. Each one wanted to be sure the other saw the remarkable bird that had come along to grace their walk.

"Where's the other one?" Goodnight whispered.

"Which other one?" Revelie asked.

"Whenever you see one, you usually see another."

The second turkey emerged from the thicket and followed its mate.

"I like that," Revelie said.

"Uh-huh," Goodnight agreed.

Reaching over, the cowboy took the lady's hand. She squeezed back. He expected her to release the pressure after a moment, but she didn't. She continued to hang on tight. He studied her to see if anything was wrong.

"Let's go home," she said.

"We are home," he said.

"Let's go to the house."

"Sure. Somethin' wrong?"

"No. Let's hurry."

"What's the matter?"

Goodnight felt himself being tugged along by his bride, who was walking faster than he was. He hoped she wasn't sick. He figured it was probably some female problem, so he decided not to press her too closely. He would just go along for the ride.

"Let's run," she said.

"What's wrong?" he asked again.

Revelie started running and he ran to keep up. They were still holding hands. Her skirts rustled as she ran, which attracted the attention of the hungry cowboys assembled at the cook shack. Goodnight read curiosity and concern on their faces.

"Faster," she said.

They picked up their speed and kicked up plenty of red dust. The cowboys started moving slowly toward them to see what was wrong.

"Tell them nothin's wrong," Revelie said.

"Nothin's wrong," Goodnight called.

They were getting near the house now, but she didn't slow down. He wondered if she would be able to stop in time to keep from running right into a closed door. Somehow she managed to skid to a halt just before she got hurt. He had more trouble putting on the brakes and ran into her from behind.

"Excuse me," he said.

Revelie was already opening the door to their bedroom. Goodnight followed her inside. They were both perspiring and breathing hard from their run.

"What's the matter?" Goodnight asked again.

"Take your clothes off," Revelie said.

He just stared at her as she began to undress.

"Come on, I'm serious," she said. "Hurry up."

Goodnight hurriedly started unbuttoning his dusty red shirt. She struggled out of her blouse and started on her skirt. He reached for his belt. She went to work unlacing her whalebone corset.

Goodnight was startled by a knock at the door.

"Anything wrong?" Simon's voice called.

"No, nothin'," Goodnight gasped, out of breath.

His wife took hold of her husband and pulled him down onto the bed. They kissed hard and rolled on the wild feathers. Now they were breathing even harder than they had been when they were running. She was soon moaning, but it didn't bother him because nobody was next door and because he just didn't mind.

Coffee rang the loud dinner bell at just the right moment. It was almost as if he were spying on them and so knew just when to ring it. To mark the moment. They laughed and hung onto each other–and decided to skip dinner.

Goodnight lay next to Revelie, hovering happily near sleep. He wanted to stay half-awake to savor the feeling, but at the same time dreams beckoned. He told himself that dreams couldn't possibly measure up to this reality, but his mind wasn't listening to him. Deeper, darker, calmer . . .

"Tell me your secrets," Revelie said.

"What?" asked a dazed Goodnight, coming up from strata of consciousness far below.

"Tell me your secrets," she repeated in a soft, happy, intimate voice. "That's what married couples do. No secrets anymore. We're one person."

Goodnight was groggy, flustered–and afraid. He had secrets he couldn't talk about, or so he believed. He didn't know what to do. He needed time to think.

"You tell me your secrets," he said defensively.

"I asked first," she said.

"Whass that got to do with it?"

"That's one of the rules. You've got to learn about rules, Mr. Goodnight. So I say again: Tell me your secrets."

"I don't have no secrets." His heart was a rabbit. "I'm just a simple man."

"Liar." Her accusation was serious, but her tone was playful. "Coward."

"I'm sorry. Not now. I'm tired. Later."

"I'll hold you to that," the bride said with a laugh.

46

Goodnight had worked on it all day long. He had expected to be finished by now, but he wasn't. It still wasn't right, still not quite good enough for her. So he worked on it a second day. By afternoon, he was ready to give it to her.

"Close your eyes," Goodnight said.

"Okay," Revelie said, "they're closed."

His wife sat on the corral fence with her hands over her eyes. She was wearing a pale blue skirt. Her husband led a horse out of the barn.

"Okay, you can open them now," he said.

She opened her eyes and studied the horse, but even though she squinted, she couldn't quite see what was so unusual about this particular animal.

"What is it?" Revelie asked at last.

"A present," said Goodnight.

"You're giving me a horse?"

"No. I mean, well, yes, you can have the horse if'n you want it, but that ain't the point."

"What's the point?"

"The saddle. I built you a new saddle. Not just new but a new kind. Ain't ever been a saddle quite like this here one before."

"Really?"

Revelie studied her new saddle, but she evidently didn't see anything particularly revolutionary about it. He was a little disappointed.

"Don't you see?" Goodnight asked.

"See what?" Revelie asked. "It's a sidesaddle, isn't it? All the horsewomen in Boston ride sidesaddle in the park."

"Look closely," he said. "It's a sidesaddle, but it ain't a sidesaddle like you ever seen before."

"If you say so." She shrugged. "I'm afraid I don't know much about any sort of saddle."

"See, most sidesaddles, they just got one post for a lady to hook her leg over. Now that's okay for back East. But for rougher ground, well, a lady needs more to wrap her legs around."

"And you know how much I love to wrap my legs."

"That ain't the point. The point is that this here saddle's got two posts. One pointin' up. T'other pointin' down. Now your legs'll have somethin' to hang on to. See?"

The top post looked like a big thumb giving a thumbs-up sign while the bottom one looked like a thumb giving thumbs-down.

"I'm not sure."

"Come closer. I'll show you."

Moving uncertainly, Revelie got down off the fence and walked to the horse. She stood beside her bridegroom.

"Look, you hook your right leg over this here top post," he said, touching the thumb pointing up. "And then you just put your left foot in this here left stirrup like some reg'lar rider. See?"

"You mean like a man?" she said.

"Well, uh, yeah, somethin' like that. Uh, like I was sayin', you put your left foot in this here stirrup, see? But if'n it gets rough, you can just lift up your left knee under this here bottom post." He touched the big thumb pointing down. "That way, with your right knee over the top post an' your left knee under the bottom post, you can squeeze them posts like a vise. See? Ain't no way you're fallin' off. Right? Git the idea? I wouldn't be surprised none if this here thing caught on."

Revelie studied the saddle, creasing her forehead, wiggling her nose.

"I think so," she said without conviction.

"Good," he said. "I'll help ya up."

"But I don't know how to ride," she said.

"I'm fixin' to teach ya."

Goodnight saw her shudder. Then she just stood there staring at the sidesaddle.

"It won't bite ya," he promised.

"What about the horse?" she asked.

"She won't bite ya neither, most likely."

"She's a she?"

"Yessum."

"Well, that's good. Anyway, I think it's good. A girl wouldn't hurt a girl, would she? Now that I think about it, that's a dumb question."

"Don't worry. The saddle'll do all the work. Then we can go ridin' around the canyon together. Gimme your left foot."

Goodnight made what looked like a stirrup with his hands, his fingers knitted together. She put her left foot in it, and he gave her a boost. But she didn't turn as she was going up, so she ended up lying on her stomach across the saddle rather than sitting on it.

"I did something wrong," she said, out of breath.

"I reckon so," he said. "Just slide down. I'll catch you."

Revelie let go of the saddle and slid backward on her stomach. Goodnight caught her around the waist and set her softly on the ground.

"I'll show you," he said.

Goodnight put his left foot in the left stirrup, stepped up, and half-turned, but rather than throwing his right foot over the horse's back, he simply hooked it over the top post. So both his feet were on the left side of the horse.

"You look real purdy!" Too Short yelled from across the corral. "I think I'm in love."

"You're too short for me," Goodnight shouted back. Then he turned his attention to Revelie and said, "See how it goes?"

"We'll see," she said.

Goodnight dismounted, gave the horse a pat, and then turned to his new wife.

"You'll git it this time," he said.

Once again, Goodnight made a stirrup with his hands. Once more, Revelie stepped into this stirrup and he gave her a lift up. She turned awkwardly but nonetheless managed to hook her right knee over the top post.

"Great!" Goodnight cheered. "You look great."

"Thanks," Revelie said. "Now what do I do?"

"Sit up straighter in the saddle. You'll be better balanced."

Goodnight watched Revelie obey. She straightened her back as if she were sitting in a cane-backed chair.

"That's purdy good," he said. "Now exaggerate it. Be a little sway-backed. Be a little pregnant."

"Be a little pregnant?" she gasped. "First, I'm grabbing these posts between my legs as if I were in love with them. And then I'm a little pregnant. What are you really trying to teach me, Mr. Goodnight?" She laughed.

He looked around quickly to see if any of his cowboys happened to be within hearing distance. They were all off doing ranch chores except . . .

"Thass right, Mr. Goodnight!" called Too Short. "What kinda place is this, anyhow?"

"Just a figure a speech," Goodnight yelled back. Then he lowered his voice and said, "Now do like I say or you'll fall off."

Revelie swayed her back, her stomach stuck out in front, and she looked quite pregnant.

"Thass the right idea," Goodnight said, "but you're overdoin' it just a smidgin."

Revelie relaxed a little.

"Thass good," he said. "Thass perfect."

"Now what does the pregnant lady do?" she asked.

"Now you give a little kick with your left heel."

"I've got a better idea."

"What?"

"The pregnant lady wants to go try to get more pregnant."

Without warning, Revelie suddenly jumped from the back of the horse. Stunned, Goodnight was momentarily paralyzed. Then he came back to life, rushed forward, and barely caught her. They smiled at each other.

"See," Revelie said, "I trusted you. I knew you'd catch me. Now you have to trust me. Tell me what you've been hiding?" She laughed. "It'll be all right. I promise. I know you lived with the savages."

Goodnight wanted to tell her about his lost years, his Human years, his years as a warrior. But he couldn't bear to mention the names of the dead. Couldn't bear to revisit their graves, even in his mind.

"Later," Goodnight promised again.

47

That afternoon, Goodnight and Revelie rode side by side along the red river that wound through the red canyon. He could tell that she was still nervous–and of course the horse could tell it too–but she was making progress. Her slightly pregnant posture on horseback was good, although she sat a little too stiffly. She held the reins a little too tightly in her left hand, leaving her right hand free for roping, which she wasn't really likely to try anytime soon. When her horse decided to stop, lower its head, and chomp some grass, Revelie did nothing to discourage it.

"Hold her head up," Goodnight said.

"I can't," Revelie said. "I'm not as strong as a horse."

"But you gotta make her think you're not just as strong but stronger."

"How am I going to do that?"

"Just act like you're stronger. If you believe it yourself, she'll believe it."

"But I don't believe it."

Goodnight stared at her with what he was afraid was an exasperated expression on his face. She looked back at him with a hostile expression. He decided to try to make up before a fight started.

"Well, this is as good a place as any for a rest stop," Goodnight said. "We ain't in no hurry. Less git down and sit a spell, huh?"

"Good idea," Revelie said.

He dismounted and then helped her down. They sat side by side on a large, flat-topped sandstone rock.

"You're doin' real good," Goodnight said.

"Thank you," Revelie said. "But I just don't feel comfortable yet."

"That'll come."

The newlyweds sat and watched the horses eat the new spring grass. They had noisy teeth.

"This grass'll git tough later on," Goodnight said, "but right now it's nice an' tender."

"Oh, yes," Revelie said, not particularly interested.

"The thing is a person could lie down on it now," he said. "While it's tender like this."

He got up from the rock and lay down in the soft grass. He stretched out and smiled. He rolled over and smiled again.

"How is it?" Revelie asked.

"Good," Goodnight said. "Wanta try it."

Revelie moved tentatively from the rock to the grass. She lay beside her husband. He rolled closer to her, placed his face over hers, and kissed her. His right hand reached for her left breast.

"Wait," she protested. "What do you think you're doing?"

He pulled his hand away. He was surprised, confused, and a little angry. She had led him to believe that she was always eager to make love, but now she rejected him. Was she only interesting in lovemaking when it was her idea? Was she trying to dominate him? To rule him? He had so looked forward to lying with her outdoors in his red canyon, and now she had ruined it.

"What's the matter?" he asked in a choked voice.

"This isn't a bedroom," she said.

"It's a great bedroom. The best bedroom in the whole damn world."

"What if somebody comes along? One of the cowboys?"

"They won't. I sent 'em all to work t'other end a the canyon."

"You did?" Revelie grinned. "You really did?"

"Uh-huh."

Goodnight reached for his wife's breast once again.

"Wait," she said. "No, it still doesn't seem right. I don't know. Out here, God can see us."

"God won't mind."

"You don't know. How do you know?"

"Because he made Adam and Eve."

"And you're telling me this is Eden?"

"Purdy near."

"So you think it would be all right?"

"Uh-huh."

When he reached for her breast this time, she didn't stop him. Soon they were making love in God's own vast bedroom. This time he was the wild one. The wild man in him led the wild woman in her to greater and greater heights–and lower and lower depths–of ecstasy. He danced a war dance on top of her and let out war cries.

"Shhh," she said, "they'll hear you."

"Who cares?"

Soon she was screaming her own war cries.

That was the best," Revelie said as she lay in his arms. "Why didn't you ever tell me about making love out-of-doors before?"

"I was waitin' for you to learn how to ride," Goodnight said.

"Why doesn't everybody make love out-of-doors all the time? Why does anybody ever make love inside?"

"I dunno."

The clouds overhead looked to him like huge feather beds chasing each other around the heavens.

"How did you know it would be so great out-of-doors?" she asked.

"Lucky guess," he said.

"Did you ever make love out-of-doors before?"

The question frightened him. He was sure she felt him jump. He didn't want to answer her question. He didn't even want to think about answering it. He knew he couldn't lie to her.

"Uh-huh," he said in a thick voice.

"You did! No! I wanted to be the first. I wanted to be the only."

"It was before I met you. I didn't know nothin' like you existed. I mean nothin' as great as you."

"Who was she?"

He knew she would ask. He couldn't keep her from asking. It was a big canyon, but now there was no place to hide.

"I don't wanta talk about it."

"Why not? I have a right to know," she said, no longer as exuberant but still smiling. "I'm your wife. I should know everything about you, just as you should know everything about me. There shouldn't be any walls, any locked attics, any secret dark places."

"Mebbe some day but not now. I'm serious about this here. I just cain't and that's all. Don't ask no more."

"Mr. Goodnight, you are selfish." The smile was gone now. "I haven't withheld myself from you, and that's not always easy for a woman, especially at first. But now you are withholding yourself from me. It isn't fair."

She got up, put on her clothes, and headed for the house. On foot.

48

At roundup time, Goodnight missed Loving. Actually, he missed him all the time, but particularly now that an extra hand would have come in real handy. He wondered why his friend would have gone off just before roundup when he must have known how short-handed they would be.

Coffee loaded up the chuck wagon again for the roundup. They would be gone from ranch headquarters for a good many days. By this time, the ranch also had a second wagon that they called the "hoodlum wagon," or just the "hood." It was for carrying whatever wouldn't fit in the chuck wagon. Extra bedding. Branding irons. Other tools. Whatever.

Revelie had decided she wanted to come along on the roundup. Not that a roundup was really the place for a lady like her, but she didn't want to be left all alone in the middle of the void. Her husband could understand her feeling. Besides, he was happy to have her along. Otherwise he would have been missing both Loving and her. Goodnight didn't miss Black Dub because he had ridden down from Tascosa to help out with the ranch's biggest job.

As always, this roundup persuaded Goodnight all over again of the wisdom of starting his ranch in this canyon. The steep walls kept the cattle fenced in so they didn't scatter too far and wide. Over time, the herd had grown larger and larger, or rather longer and longer, for it was stretched out up and down the banks of the shallow red river.

"Ain't they purdy?" Goodnight asked Revelie. "They must be the purdiest sight I ever seen in my whole life. Present company excepted."

"Thanks," Revelie said. "They do look rather pretty."

"'Rather purdy'?" he said. "You can do better'n that. Does it hurt you to say 'purdiest'? Purdiest in the whole world?"

"All right," she said. "They're what you said."

"I give up," he said, but he smiled warmly.

Rounding up was a simple chore compared to what followed. Once all the cattle had been collected in the middle of the canyon, the real work began. The cowboys started separating the calves from their mamas, which wasn't easy. Then the branding irons were unloaded from the hoodlum wagon. While they were heating to a red-hot glow, the cowboys sat around on their haunches sharpening their knives.

"Too bad Loving took off," Goodnight said, giving voice at last to thoughts that had been pecking at him for days. "With him we coulda had two teams. But I figure we'll git it done one way or another without him. So less go. I'll rope. Too Short, why don't you rope, too?"

"Sure, boss," the short cowboy said.

"You take the head," said the boss. "I'll do heels."

"Fair enough."

"Suckerod, you burn 'em."

"Fine."

"Black Dub, you hold 'em."

"Uh-huh."

"Coffee, you help him, awright?"

"Yep."

"Tin Soldier, you tend the fires. You're good at fires, ain't chew? Be just like back home."

"You bet."

"An', Simon, you cut 'em."

"My pleasure. Be sorta like a *bris* but different."

Goodnight started limbering up his rope. Too Short did, too. All the others dismounted to play their assigned roles.

"What will I do?" asked Revelie.

"Uh, why don't you go for a ride," Goodnight said, "or sumpun."

"No, I want to help."

"You ever seen a brandin'?"

"No."

"Well, it ain't just brandin'. There's a little more to it than that. See?"

"No, I don't see."

"See, they're gonna cut them there calves. It's gonna git kinda bloody."

"Why? The poor things."

"Well, we gotta."

"It sounds like some sort of pagan ritual?"

"No. It's how steers git made. You don't wanna see that."

Goodnight could see understanding move across Revelie's face, but she didn't back up, didn't retreat, just sat her sidesaddle and waited for . . . what?

"Please," he said.

"No," she said.

"Your funeral," he said. "Less git started."

Goodnight watched with pride as Too Short whirled his rope over his head and then tossed it in the direction of a mottled calf. The loop settled over the calf's head and the cowboy pulled it tight.

Now it was Goodnight's turn to see if he could do as well. He reminded himself that roping the heels was harder, so perhaps the cowboys would give him some slack if he missed. But would his wife? He twirled his rope and cast low. The calf stepped into his noose and he pulled it tight. Thank God. Or thank the Great Mystery. As a smile brightened his face, he turned to Revelie to see if she was watching. Of course, she was.

Goodnight's horse, trained in the art of calf-roping, began to back up. Too Short's mount backed up, too. With a rope around its throat pulling one way and a rope around its heels pulling another, the poor calf was stretched taut. Black Dub rushed in and flipped it over on its back and held it there like a wrestler pinning his opponent. Coffee sat on it. Suckerod came running with a red-hot branding iron trailing white smoke. He pressed the glowing iron against the flank of the calf. There was a hissing sound and a burning smell. When he removed the iron, flames flared from the wound, the calf's fur on fire.

"Help!" yelled Revelie. "Water! Do something."

"It'll go out on its own," Goodnight said, fighting down queasiness as he remembered the outlaw he had branded. He said a little too curtly, "I told you not to watch. Go for a ride. Go for a walk."

Goodnight found himself staring directly into her eyes. He saw defiance. She shook her head. Then she edged closer to the struggling, bawling calf.

Simon knelt beside the baby bull, took hold of its miniature scrotum, and pulled it up empty. Then with a sawing motion, he cut it off and tossed it away on the ground. The blood mingled with the red dust. Reaching inside the bloody hole, Simon pulled out one of the calf's balls. It was the size of a hen's egg and had a long, tangled string attached. Using his knife, Simon clipped the string and tossed the ball into a cooking pot. Then he reached in after the other ball . . .

Reliving his own brush with the knife long ago, Goodnight's whole middle was racked by nausea. He leaned crookedly forward and threw up on the ground.

Then he was afraid the cowboys–or even worse, Revelie–would make fun of him. After all, he had implied that she couldn't take such a scene when in fact he was the one who couldn't take it. It would serve him right. He had it coming. When he opened his eyes and looked sheepishly around, he saw that Revelie was throwing up, too. Thank God! Oh, thank the Great Mystery!

Then Goodnight noticed the ground beneath her. There was nothing there. His vomit stained the red earth, but hers had not left a trace. Oh, poor thing, she is having dry heaves. Those are the worst of all. Then he realized: she wasn't sick at all but just pretending to be to make him feel better. He had never loved her as much as at that moment.

Releasing his hold on the calf, Simon stood up. Too Short nudged his horse forward and his rope went slack. Black Dub hurried to remove the noose from around the animal's neck. Remembering his part in this drama, Goodnight edged his horse forward. Coffee removed the rope from the calf's heels. Then the baby longhorn struggled to its feet and hurried away crying for its mother, crying for its lost balls, crying because its life and destiny had been arbitrarily changed forever. And its brand still hurt.

Too Short picked out another calf, swung his rope, and lassoed the head. Praying he could pull himself together and act like a "man," Goodnight flipped his noose at the calf's heels. He missed. Then he reeled in the rope, which looked like a snake recoiling after a strike. He could feel everybody staring at him, waiting to see if he would be all right. The snake struck again and this time tripped up the calf, which flopped on the ground. Goodnight was relieved to see miniature tits. It was only later that he realized that Too Short had picked out a heifer on purpose. Suckerod rushed forward and branded the calf. This time there was no fire.

The third calf had tits, too. The fourth calf had balls, but Goodnight somehow suffered through the castration without vomiting. Perhaps because he had nothing left in his stomach. Soon the team had settled into a rhythm. Rope the head. Rope the heels. Flip. Brand. Cut or don't cut depending on the sex. Rope again. Flip again. Brand again. Cut again. It seemed to Goodnight that there were more males than females, more castrations than tits, but he knew there probably weren't.

"Wait a minute," Revelie yelled.

Goodnight and all the cowboys looked in her direction. Her husband wondered if all the cruelty had finally gotten to her. The effect on him had been immediate, but on her it had been accumulative. Now she had finally had enough. He wondered what in the world they were going to do with her, but nonetheless he was glad to see her more sensitive side.

"This is going to take forever," Revelie said.

It wasn't exactly the outburst her husband had expected. So, she was bored. He could understand that. He was sorry. But a cure did not occur to him immediately. Oh, well, maybe she could go pick hackberries.

"Well, it's a big job all right," Goodnight allowed.

"And twice as big as it should be," Revelie said. "The way I see it, you've got eight able-bodied workers, but you're only using seven. That throws the whole system off. You can just moan and groan about how much you miss Loving. Or you can let me take his place. I suggest the latter course. That way we would have two teams and finish twice as fast."

"You?" asked her husband.

"Yes, me," said his wife.

"What could you do?"

"Well, I can't rope. I'll give you that. And I might not be strong enough to flip. I'll give you that, too. But I could brand or cut."

"Are you serious?"

"Of course I'm serious!"

Goodnight thought a moment, took off his hat, scratched his moist scalp, put his hat back on, scratched his chin.

"Why don't you brand," he said. "If it's all the same to you."

She gave him a big smile.

Getting down from her sidesaddle, Revelie walked over to the fire where the branding irons were heating. She borrowed a pair of too-big gloves and looked to be ready to go to work.

"Okay," Goodnight said, "we'll work two teams. Second-team ropers: Tin Soldier and Suckerod, okay? Simon, you'll still cut, and Black Dub'll still throw. An' we'll have two burners, Revelie and Coffee. See how that works out." He didn't seem too sure that it would.

Too Short roped the front end of another calf and Goodnight lassoed the back end. Black Dub grabbed a front foot and flipped the calf on its back.

Goodnight wondered if his bride would be able to go through with her part of the deal. He couldn't imagine her inflicting pain on any of God's creatures. And of course there was always the possibility that a calf would inflict some pain on her with a well-placed kick. Her husband wished he had forbidden his wife to take part in what was clearly man's work, but he knew why he hadn't. He had been afraid it would harm his relationship with his wife. Her getting a few bumps and bruises would be better than their relationship getting roughed up. He watched her withdraw a red-hot branding iron from the fire, watched her run toward the struggling calf, watched her look down at her victim, watched her hesitate.

He was right: She couldn't go through with it. Good. No harm done.

Revelie slapped the glowing branding iron on the calf's rump and set its fur on fire. When he saw the flames flare up, the husband expected his wife to drop the iron and run, but she stood her ground undeterred by the fire and the sizzle.

Goodnight was in for one more surprise: a feeling of deep pride.

49

Goodnight watched his wife move about the cedar room. The windows now had curtains, which were made from flour sacks but didn't look it. They were white and ruffled. The rough split-rail floor was partially obscured by a rug woven from rags. It was a rug of many colors like the coat of many colors in the Bible. The bed was covered by a patchwork quilt of many colors. Revelie's womanly instincts did not seem to have been damaged by branding a few thousand calves. Then Goodnight became aware that she was giving him curious looks.

"What's the matter?" Goodnight asked.

"Well, I was just thinking," Revelie said, "maybe it's time."

"Time for what?" he asked.

"Time to write out your code," she said.

"What?"

"Don't you remember? Back when you were courting me by mail, you wrote to me that you were planning to write down some rules for life in this country. And you implied that you could use my help. Well, was that just something you said to get me to fall in love with you. Or were you serious?"

"Uh, well, both to tell you the truth. I wanted you to love me *and* I wanted help to write this stuff down. Wha'd you call it?"

"A code."

He scratched his chin. "Reg'lar writin's tough enough for me. I don't need no codes. Why'd I wanna write it in code, anyhow? I don't git it."

She smiled. "I'm not talking about that kind of code. I don't mean secret writing. I mean a code of laws. A code of rules. A code of conduct. A code to live by."

Goodnight was embarrassed at having misunderstood. He wasn't sure he had ever heard of that kind of code, but he tried not to let on.

"Oh," he said. "Sure."

"I think it's a good idea," she said. "I liked it when you wrote about it, and I like it now. I've been waiting for you to bring it up, but you never did, so I thought I might mention it. You still want to, don't you?"

"Sure," he said nervously.

"Good, so do I," she said.

She went to her store-bought chest of drawers, which he had bought for her in Tascosa and hauled home in the hoodlum wagon. She opened the top drawer and took out a paper and pen and ink. At least it wasn't a damn fountain pen. Nonetheless, as she approached him, he grew more and more nervous. He felt trapped.

"Uh, well, ya see," Goodnight stammered, "I don't write none too good. That's how come I ain't brung up that there code. I was sorta scared a you seein' how bad I write."

"But your letters were beautifully written," Revelie said. "What are you talking about?"

"Loving wrote them letters," he said.

"Are you telling me I fell in love with Loving," she asked, "not you?"

"No, no, thass not what I'm sayin'. Not less you just fell in love with how them letters looked 'stead of what they said. See, I said them words. I thought them thoughts. But I waddn't up to writin' 'em down. So he give me a hand. You might say the writin' was mine but the handwritin' was his. Are you mad?"

"No, that's what I thought."

"You did?"

"Sure. I'd seen your handwriting. Remember?"

"Uh-huh."

"But I had also heard you talk. I thought I knew something about how your mind worked. So I took the words to be yours but the penmanship to be somebody else's. I didn't know whose. But when I arrived here and saw how close you two were, I guessed he was the one."

"No kiddin'?"

"No kidding. What I loved about those letters wasn't the penmanship."

"It waddn't?" He chuckled.

"No."

Revelie sat down on a store-bought chair that her husband thought looked rather puny. It had spindly legs. She unscrewed the top of a small bottle of ink.

"I know I can't really take Loving's place," she said, "but my handwriting isn't too bad. It may be a trifle feminine for your taste, but I can't help that. We'll just have to live with that. What I am trying to say is that I would be happy to transcribe your code for you."

"That sounds good to me," Goodnight said. "Mebbe we could write this here thing together at that. You'll do more'n just spellin', won't you? You'll help me fix up the right words, the right ever'thing, won't you? We'll puzzle it out together."

"Of course."

Revelie dipped the tip of her pen in the bottle of ink. Then she wrote something at the top of a piece of paper. Goodnight tried to read it upside down, but he couldn't quite make it out. He wasn't even all that good at right-side-up reading.

"I reckon it oughta be some kinda contract," Goodnight said, "like the one I signed with your daddy. But this here contract won't be about bizness. It'll be about how you're s'posed to act."

"A social contract," Revelie said.

"Sumpun like that."

"How do you want to start?"

"I dunno. Mebbe we oughta start with number one."

"That sounds good to me."

Goodnight watched Revelie write "1" near the top of the page. He could evidently read numbers upside down.

"Less see," Goodnight said, "put down how you gotta be trustworthy. That's number one. Now you do number two."

"All right," said Revelie, "shall we make two bravery? How shall we put it? 'I promise always to strive to be brave.' How's that?"

"Real purdy. Now it's my turn. I reckon three oughta be 'self-reliant.' Is that okay?"

"That's fine. Now four." She wrote the numeral. "Maybe four could be 'fair,' always striving to be fair. Fair and impartial."

"Yeah, fair, and like you said because ever'body's worth the same amount."

"Equal?"

"That's it."

Her pen scratched across the paper.

"Read it to me," Goodnight said. "Read me what you wrote."

"All right," Revelie said. "'In all my dealings, I promise to be fair and impartial and to treat all people as equals.'"

"You ever think a writin' poetry?"

"As a matter of fact, I did–when I was a girl. Thank you for the implied compliment."

"Now whose turn is it?"

"Yours, I believe."

"What number?"

"Five."

"Okay, five, well mebbe five oughta be loyalty? Loyalty's a good one."

"How shall we put it: 'I promise to be loyal, loyal to my wife or my husband, loyal to my leader . . .' That's you. Who else?"

"Loyal to your family. Your mama and papa. Your brother and sister." He could hear the change in his voice, which seemed to thicken. His tongue felt swollen and worked awkwardly. "Yeah, right. An' loyal to your friends. An' loyal to the other hands on the ranch. An' loyal to the ranch, to the canyon, to this here country. Loyal to the animals, the buffalo, the wolves, the cows, the dogs. Loyal to the damn bees. Loyal to the plants. To horehounds that are some use. To mesquites that ain't. Loyal to this here red land."

"Wait," Revelie said. "Is this a code for the ranch or a code for the whole territory?"

Goodnight was stumped. He didn't know. He wanted to do so much but had the power to do so little. Or so it seemed to him.

"We will start with here," Revelie said, "and then we will expand."

"Good," said Goodnight. "So first off we'll ask our cowboys to sign this here code. Thass a start, huh? Then whatsomever."

She raised her hand and he watched her write. He loved the idea of her turning his thinking into words. Fancy words. Impressive words. Real writing. He realized he had a big, dumb smile on his face. He considered changing his expression but decided against it. He just left the big, dumb smile right where it was.

"Okay, I'm caught up," Revelie said.

"Well, uh, I've about run dry on ol' number five. Now it's your turn."

"Perhaps we should put in a few 'Thou shalt nots.'"

"Like what?"

"I don't know. Maybe we should put in something about not drinking."

"Thass kinda strict."

"All right, maybe something about not drinking too much. Not getting drunk and treeing towns."

"You mean like what happened to you that time? Good. Thass good. An' say sumpun about not disrespectin' women. Good. Good. Anything else?"

"It's your turn, darling."

"Well, the main 'don't' as far as I'm concerned is 'Don't kill nobody.'" His voice felt thick again. "An' if'n you do, you gotta promise to let the other boys be the jury. And I'll be the judge. And if'n you do it, you gotta pay. Thass about it. You got anything else you wanta add?"

"No. I can't think of anything."

"Good. We'll have all the boys sign this here contract just like I signed that paper with your dad. An' we'll sign it, too. We'll all sign it or make our marks."

"Right."

"Can I see it. I wanta look at it."

She handed it to him.

"That's real purdy," Goodnight said. "Real purdy. It's the purdiest piece a writin' I ever seen in my life."

Now he could finally read the words that his wife had written at the top of the page: "Code of the West."

50

Goodnight was dreaming a familiar dream in which Loving returned to the Home Ranch. In his sleep, he often corrected what had gone wrong, fixed what was broken, even raised the dead. Now he dreamed a dream of Loving, who had grown tired of wandering, and who came riding back into the red valley kicking up red dust. Dreaming was one of the ways in which he mourned—or perhaps avoided mourning.

Goodnight woke up wanting to sneeze and realized that his nose was being tickled by something other than a cloud of red dust. He sniffed the air and identified the smell.

"Revelie," Goodnight said in a low but urgent voice, "wake up." He shook her shoulder. "Revelie, you gotta wake up."

"What's wrong?" she asked in a sleep-thick voice.

"I think I smell smoke," he said.

He could hear her sniffing the air.

"You're right," she said.

"Yeah," he said. "We better check on the boys."

Grabbing clothes but not wasting time dressing, Goodnight and Revelie both ran naked and coughing into the fresh air of the dog run. Rubbing their eyes, they could see that the south room—the cowboys' room—was on fire. Through the windows, they beheld dancing flames. Goodnight was suddenly desperate. His fear turning him back into a little boy, he was terrified that he was once again going to lose somebody very close to him.

Then the door of the burning room burst open and cowboys came pouring and choking out. Goodnight strained to focus his good eye to penetrate the dark and the smoke. He managed to recognize Coffee, yes, good, and then Simon, crawling on his hands and knees, then Tin Soldier without his tin hat. But that was all. Where was Too Short? Where was Suckerod?

In spite of his fear, or rather because of it, Goodnight dropped the clothes in his hands and lunged at the open door. He sensed Revelie's moment of indecision, as she was torn between modesty and wanting to help, but thankfully she lingered. Why should she risk her life? Inside, Goodnight stared into a fiery chamber of horrors and wondered for a moment if anything could be done. Then he felt his wife's cool touch on his bare shoulder, and he knew he had to try.

"Get back!" he shouted at her.

Plunging into the furnace, Goodnight was blinded by the smoke. Unseeing, he rushed headlong at the flames as if they were some bully. Then he tripped and sprawled headfirst. His hands reached out to try to break his fall and the hot floor burned his fingers. Still smoke-blind, he angrily kicked out with his bare feet at whatever had tripped him. And then he realized that he was kicking a man. He had found one of his boys, still wrapped in his bedroll. While the married couple slept on a feather mattress, the cowboys still slept on the floor. But was this cowboy asleep, unconscious, or dead?

Rising to his knees on the griddle-hot floor, Goodnight grabbed the bedroll with both hands and started pulling in the direction of the open door, which let in the wind that fanned the flames. He could feel the body begin to slide toward him. Good. Backing up, still on his knees, he pulled again. His burden, which was heavier than he had expected, caught on something and wouldn't move. He jerked, but it didn't help.

Then Goodnight felt Revelie beside him. Her bare shoulder touched his, the way it did so often in the night, and her hands grasped the reluctant bedding and pulled. They pulled together. The burden released its grip on whatever it clung to and slid once more across the burning floor.

Coughing and gasping, Goodnight and Revelie pulled the unconscious cowboy through the doorway. Since he was baby-helpless, it was as if they were assisting at his birth—or rebirth. The husband and wife had delivered their first manchild, but would it be a stillbirth? Revelie started slapping his smoke-darkened face in a desperate effort to make him wake up and take a breath.

Recognizing Too Short, Goodnight realized that Suckerod must still be trapped inside. He hated the idea of charging back into the flames where he knew his skin would feel as if it were on fire and might be at that. Where every breath would scald his lungs. But he had no choice, so he lowered his head and attacked.

"No!" yelled Revelie. "Stop!"

Wanting to stop, Goodnight kept going. He had to save Suckerod. But just as he reached the burning threshold, he somehow lost his balance and fell sideways. He thought the house must have given way and fallen on him. Then he opened his good eye and saw that the house was Coffee. Goodnight tried to get up, but Coffee wrestled with him to keep him down, to keep him from plunging back into the fire, to keep him from throwing away his life. Soon Coffee had help when Simon joined his side of the fight. Goodnight finally gave up and slumped back in Coffee's arms.

"Everybody, close your eyes," Revelie said, "except you, Mr. Goodnight."

Then her husband remembered that his wife was naked. He looked in her direction and saw her still bending over Too Short, whose chest was now heaving. Goodnight figured that Too Short had probably opened his eyes, seen this vision of naked beauty, and been startled back into breathing. He was lucky he didn't have a heart attack or a stroke. Revelie turned to her husband with an ivory smile that made her sooty face beautiful. She was actually sooty all over.

Then she got up and gathered up the clothes she had dropped on the ground. Her husband wondered if any of the cowboys had closed their eyes very tight. He doubted it. He figured she doubted it, too, but she didn't seem to mind. He wondered if all the Boston girls were like her. Soon she disappeared into the hackberry thicket.

"You may open your eyes now," Revelie called, and then laughed raucously.

Getting gingerly to his blistered feet, Goodnight started looking around for his own dropped clothes. While he got dressed, he tried to piece together in his mind what must have happened. He wondered if Suckerod had been smoking in bed, something he had been warned repeatedly not to do. Well, maybe, but Goodnight told himself not to blame the dead.

Sensing an uneasiness in his men, Goodnight turned and saw Revelie emerging from the hackberry thicket only half-dressed. She had on her shoes and skirt, but she had evidently failed to pick up her blouse in her haste. Revelie stood before them with her whalebone corset fully exposed to their view, which brought back painful memories . . .

Telling himself to concentrate on the here and now, Goodnight fell to wondering whether the Robbers' Roost gang might have started that fire. He had burned their house, so maybe they had decided to pay him back by burning his. Then he saw the "RR" scratched in the red earth.

BOOK THREE

QUEST FOR LOVING

51

Late 1870s

Goodnight felt bad.

He still lived in the enchanted canyon but was no longer quite so enchanted by it. His life seemed to him to be as flat and changeless as the Staked Plain that surrounded his canyon. His soul was dying of thirst. Looking within himself, Goodnight found all his buffalo dead, all his mustangs broken, all his wolves trapped and skinned. All the wild Humanity in him had been rounded up and confined to a reservation. His spirit was fenced in with barbed wire.

In his unhappiness, Goodnight dreamed of Loving. It was that old dream again, the one about Loving returning from his wanderings, but this time he dreamed the dream wide awake. He hadn't seen the cowboy with changeable eyes for ten years, but he seemed to miss him more than ever. Whenever something went wrong in the red canyon, Goodnight always found himself wondering what Loving would have done. If he had been around, he might have prevented that long-ago fire. And even if the fire had happened, surely Loving would have been able to save the poor burned cowboy. Right? When Goodnight shared these thoughts with Revelie, she always reminded him that Loving might well have died along with Suckerod since they both slept in the same room. But Goodnight felt sure Loving would have smelled the smoke and put out the fire before it got out of hand.

And what was more, Loving could have talked Tin Soldier out of leaving the Home Ranch. Goodnight missed Tin Soldier every day. As he missed, even more acutely, Loving. Why had they gone? Goodnight really couldn't understand how anybody could voluntarily leave the prettiest spot in the whole wide world–even though he himself was not very happy there at the moment. Nor could Goodnight imagine any man willingly forsaking the circle of Revelie's charm. He felt that if he could just bring Loving back, then the circle would be whole again, and he could shake off his discontent.

The rancher thought these thoughts as he lay on a spotted-cowhide couch in the smallest room in a very large house. After the fire, he and his wife had decided to rebuild using materials that wouldn't burn. They told each other that they couldn't stand another night like the one that had killed one of their cowboys. The answer was stone. Now a red-sandstone house sprawled in the red-sandstone canyon. The home at the Home Ranch appeared to have risen on its own right out of the red earth. The couple now lived *in* the canyon in a different way, in a more complete sense, surrounded by canyon walls and also by walls made from stones cut from those walls. In a way, the big red house reminded Goodnight of his early days in the dugout: the mansion seemed a descendant of that old shack that had been dug directly into the canyon floor. Over the years, they had added to the big house, making it bigger and bigger.

The stone house was good, but Goodnight missed the days when they had all been happy living together in the cedar house: the new wife and the new husband, all the cowboys, all under one roof. Now the Home Ranch had a sandstone bunkhouse that stood apart from the big red ranch house. Now the rancher and his wife seemed to live on a different plane from the cowboys. Hierarchy had come to the ranch.

Lying on his couch, chewing his "cud," Goodnight had to admit that Revelie had a point when she named this cell his "brooding room." (He, of course, called it his office.) He kept the curtains pulled all the time, so the room was always dimly lit. Dim places were the best places for thinking. Revelie said the closed curtains just made his dark moods darker.

"Hello."

Revelie's voice startled Goodnight. "What?"

"I didn't intend to frighten you," she said. "I'm just doing some cleaning. As you know, we've got company coming. Very neat company. White-gloved."

"Don't remind me," he said, sitting up on the couch. "But she won't be coming in here, will she? This is *my* room. Don't clean up."

It was surely a mess, he had to confess, but he liked it that way. He loved the yellowing pieces of paper, random articles of clothing, spurs, hats . . .

"Sorry," she said. "I can't stand this mess, and my mother will like it even less, believe me."

"Then the both of you are invited to kindly keep outa here."

It was a fight they had often had before, but this time there was a new urgency, because Mrs. Sanborn was on her way. Velvet Pants wouldn't be accompanying her because he had died suddenly of a heart attack several months ago at age fifty-five. He left his estate divided equally between his wife and daughter, which meant the Home Ranch was now owned by three people: the rancher, his wife, Revelie, and Mrs. Sanborn. They were equal partners–one-third, one-third, one-third. So Goodnight was now in business with his mother-in-law, and she was on her way to inspect her new property.

"How can you stand it in here with the curtains closed and the window shut?" Revelie asked. "It isn't healthy."

She pulled the curtains back and opened the window. He wanted to get up, go over, close the window, and pull the curtains, but he managed to restrain himself. He knew from experience that this was a bad idea. He didn't want to start a wildfire that he might not be able to control.

"Can I throw this out?" Revelie asked, holding up an Austin newspaper that was almost a year old.

"No!" said Goodnight.

"Why not?" she asked.

"I wanna read it again," he lied. He just hated throwing things away. Even more, he hated *her* throwing *his* things away. "Please, just let everything alone."

"Okay, read it now." Revelie tossed the paper at him. "You've got plenty of light for a change."

He caught the newspaper but didn't read it.

"What about this?" Revelie asked, holding up a briar pipe. "Surely I may throw it out. As far as I know, you don't smoke."

"No, it's a gift."

She tossed it at him. He dropped the newspaper and caught the pipe.

"These are worn out." She held up ratty slippers. "They've got to go."

"They're just gittin' comfortable."

Revelie threw the slippers at Goodnight. They hit him in the chest and throat.

"Ouch," he coughed.

"Serves you right. You're a packrat. And packrats are just as bad as any other member of the rat family. Now come on, we've got to throw out some of this junk."

"No, we don't."

"Yes, we do." Revelie picked up a tattered page with numbers scrawled haphazardly on it. "You couldn't possibly have any use for this."

"Git your hands off that!" Goodnight commanded.

"Why?"

"Just don't touch it! I mean it! Put it down!"

"What's so special about this piece of paper?"

"Just leave it alone."

"If you don't tell me, I'm going to tear it up."

"No, you ain't. You may think you are, but you ain't."

Goodnight struggled up off the low couch, staggered momentarily, and then lunged at his wife. But he was too slow, or she was too fast. Before he could reach her, she tore the piece of paper in half. Goodnight screamed in agony. He tackled Revelie. The blow caused her to drop the two halves of the page, which fluttered down. She went down much faster and harder. The floor knocked the breath out of her, and then her husband landed heavily on top of her. She tried to scream, but there was no air inside of her. Panicking, Revelie started scratching Goodnight's face. He scrambled to his feet, grabbed her by her heels, and dragged her out of his sanctuary.

"Don't you ever come in this here office ag'in!" he bellowed. "Your mama neither."

"Go to hell," she screamed. "I'll go anywhere I like in my own home, and you can't stop me."

Leaving his wife in the hallway, Goodnight stepped back into his office and slammed the door. He wished the door had a lock, but it didn't. Well, maybe he would have one put on. He went to the window and closed the curtains. Then he picked up the torn page and placed it on a low table, fitting the two jagged halves back together. Maybe he could glue them. Returning to his cowhide couch, he lay down and tried to calm down.

52

The door swung open with a loud crack. Goodnight jumped. He saw his wife standing in the doorway. She didn't cross the threshold, didn't actually enter the office, so technically she wasn't defying him, but he was still irritated. Then Goodnight realized that Revelie held a basket in her left hand. What was she up to? He saw her reach into the basket with her right hand and pull out an egg. Why on earth? She cocked her arm and threw the egg at his head. It hit him on the chin and yellow goo splashed up into his nose. He sneezed and struggled to get up off the couch. He managed to raise himself into a sitting position just as she threw the second egg. When he ducked, it hit him right on top of the head, soaking, matting his hair. Goodnight told himself: Thank God she's throwin' eggs instead of bullets, because she's a damn good shot. Well, eggs would be a woman's weapon, wouldn't they?

"What the hell?" yelled Goodnight.

"You always keep me out," Revelie screamed. "Out of your office. Out of your secrets. Out of your mind. Out of everything except your bed."

As Goodnight lurched to his feet, Revelie threw another egg. It missed him and splattered on the wall behind him. Charging, his one good eye saw an egg zooming right at it. Oh, no. He tried to dodge but too late. Now his working eye saw nothing but yellow. Temporarily blinded, Goodnight just stood there paralyzed, an easy target. Then he felt an egg hit him in the crotch. Wiping the yolk from his eye, he saw a yellow Revelie, a yellow office, a yellow world.

Goodnight charged again. An egg broke on his belt buckle. Reaching Revelie, he put his shoulder into her stomach and lifted her off the ground. She dropped the basket and more eggs broke on the floor. Carrying her like a sack of flour, he could feel her fists beating on his back.

"Stoppit!" he yelled.

She didn't stop.

"You sure got some funny ideas about cleanin' up a place. Egg all over ever'where. Your mama ain't gonna like that. And it's gonna stay right there till she gits here."

He carried her out of the office, down the hall, across the big living room, past the big stone mantelpiece, past the two deer heads with their horns still locked in mortal combat, out the front door, across the wide porch, through the front yard to the sprouting garden. There he threw her to the ground. Then he grabbed the garden hose, which was attached to the windmill's high tank. He started hosing her down. She screamed, she shivered, she screamed louder.

Goodnight looked up and saw his cowboys standing all around him watching. Oh, no. Dropping the hose, he stalked back into the red stone house.

Back in his office, Goodnight tried to make sense of what had happened. Had he been wrong? Unfair? No, he told himself emphatically. But a small thought whispered that he could have at least told Revelie why the paper was so important to him. He could have explained that it was a rare relic of his dead sister, a long-ago arithmetic lesson. But he hadn't–because saying even that much would be too painful. Or so he told himself lying flat on his back in the dark, dripping egg.

53

That evening, Goodnight went looking for Revelie, wanting to make up. He found her in what was supposed to be the nursery but had been turned into her sewing room. She sat with sewing in her lap, but her hands were idle. Her face was neither happy nor sad. It didn't change when he approached her. He wondered: Was that good news or bad?

"What do you want?" Revelie asked in a flat voice.

"I'm sorry I turned the hose on you," Goodnight said.

Then he waited. She didn't say anything. She looked at him, but then she looked away.

"I said I'm sorry," he said. He waited. "Ain't you gonna say you're sorry, too?"

He waited again. She still didn't say a word.

"What do you want from me?" he asked.

"I want to know who you are," she said simply.

"You know who I am. We been married for years, for Christ's sake. Whaddaya mean, you don't know who I am?"

"You're so closed. You won't let me in."

"I'm the one," he laughed, "that's supposed to git in."

"That is low humor. I don't appreciate low humor. You know that."

"I don't know what I know anymore."

"I don't know you. There's a secret part of you hidden away. I thought marriage was supposed to be for better or worse, for richer for poorer, for no secrets between husband and wife. And as we all know, you've got secrets."

"I'll tell you someday."

"You've been saying that for years. Let me tell you: Mental walls can become physical walls. I know you won't believe me, but I know I'm right. That's why we've never made a baby."

"Let me tell you: I know somethin' about breedin'. So listen up: A cow don't have to know a bull's secrets to have a calf. That I'm sure of."

"So you think I'm a cow."

"No, I don't."

"You must have done something so terrible, so unforgivable, that you're afraid to tell me."

"No, that ain't it."

"I don't want to have a baby with you unless I know what you've done. Why do you feel so guilty? I don't want to pass this terrible defect on to my children."

"There ain't no whatever you called it. What are you talkin' about?"

"You tell me."

He didn't say anything.

"You make me feel barren. Dried up." She paused and stared at him. "You say your brooding room is your room. Well, this is my room. Please leave."

Goodnight got up and left the room.

54

Goodnight slept in his office that night, and got out of the house early the next morning. He figured he had better stay out of Revelie's way for a while. The boss and his cowboys spent the day checking the herd, looking for sick or injured cattle, bringing in strays. But the rancher found it hard to concentrate on his work. He kept thinking of his wife, trying to come up with the words that would quench her anger. He tried many lines of approach, but none seemed very promising. Self-consciously, he reached up and touched the new scratches on his face.

When he wasn't thinking of his wife, Goodnight thought about her mother. What a hell of a time for her to be expected! He and his mother-in-law had been corresponding for months, which hadn't made him like her any better. She was proving to be a very different kind of partner from what her husband had been. When the original five years were up, having earned $500,000 above expenses, Goodnight and Velvet Pants had renewed their deal on the same terms, except for a reduced interest rate, 8 percent instead of 10. The continuing partnership had been good for both parties, growing in value at 70 percent per annum, as Velvet Pants would have said. Their extraordinary profits made it possible for them to keep buying more land. Now the Home Ranch stretched over a million acres with 100,000 cattle. As long as business was good, Velvet Pants had left Goodnight alone, but Mrs. Sanborn didn't see it that way. She wanted an accurate <u>count</u> of <u>all</u> the cattle. (She loved to underline.) She also wanted <u>itemized</u> expenses. She acted as if she didn't trust him. And now she was coming out on a personal <u>inspection</u> tour.

"Hey, boss, company's comin'," announced Too Short.

Goodnight glanced up at the north wall of the canyon. Then he fished his field glasses out of his saddlebag. Focusing, he saw some sort of vehicle flanked by cavalrymen beginning a long and rough descent. She would be here all too soon. Goodnight considered making a courteous gesture, riding to meet her, greet her, and escort her to the house, but he just couldn't bring himself to do so. He would see her at the end of the workday. She would never know that he had seen her crawling down that wall. Besides, work was work, wasn't it? It had to be done, didn't it? His new partner wouldn't want him to leave a job half-done, would she?

He went back to not concentrating on his work.

As he rode home in the evening, Goodnight saw an ambulance, parked at his front door, grow larger and larger. Of course, she would have come in an ambulance, just like last time, with a cavalry escort, like last time. Two cavalrymen were seated on his front steps. He tugged back on Red's reins. His thirteen-year-old horse–already walking slowly–walked even slower. When he finally arrived at the stable, he took his time unsaddling and brushing his mount.

Goodnight stopped to say hello to the soldiers camped on his steps. Then he walked apprehensively into his living room, where he found Revelie seated in a big easy chair, which had been covered with an Indian blanket.

"My mother's here," she said.

"I kinda figured that," he said. "Where is your mama now?"

"She's napping. The journey was exhausting, and she's ill."

"What's the matter with her?"

"She simply cannot stop burping." Revelie paused. "She blames Texas."

They both laughed. And in the laughter, they were old friends again. But when it stopped, there was still a strain between them.

"Well, I think I'll take a nap myself," Goodnight said. "Your mom's got a good idea there."

55

Mr. Goodnight, wake up," Mrs. Sanborn demanded. "I understand, *burp*–excuse me–that you've been brutalizing my daughter. I might have known." She stood in the middle of his office, wearing white gloves, challenging him on his own ground. He really should have gotten a lock for his door. "This place is a pigsty," she added. "What are those yellow stains?"

"If you don't like it in here," he said, too groggy to be diplomatic, "you don't hafta stay."

"You're insolent, Mr. Goodnight, *burp*. I beg your pardon. But if I refuse to go, what are you going to do? Knock me down? Drag me out of your office by my heels?"

He just shrugged. She didn't look much older, showed very few grey hairs, but she appeared smaller. Had she shrunk, or had he grown? He wasn't sure. Maybe neither.

"Perhaps I should be the one asking you to vacate this room, *burp*." This time she just shrugged rather than apologize. "Let me remind you that my daughter and I now own two-thirds of your unholy hideaway. It is no longer yours; it is ours. Would you like for me to summon the sheriff and ask him to evict you?"

"Good luck," said her son-in-law, who knew the sheriff.

"Still insolent. I warned my daughter about you."

"I'm sure you did."

"Mr. Goodnight, I might as well tell you directly: I've come to rescue my daughter. I know she's not happy here. I've read her letters. We're going to sell this ranch and go home."

"You cain't sell it."

Goodnight got up and walked out of his office. His sanctuary had become a cage. But his mother-in-law pursued him. She was worse than barbed wire: you couldn't get around her or over her or through her. They faced each other on the spacious front porch.

"On the contrary, I assure you: we can and we will sell." She choked down a burp. "We own a majority interest in this ranch. That means you are a helpless minority. We can do whatever we want to, thank you very much."

The next morning, after another night spent in his office, Goodnight was packing his saddlebags on the front porch. Revelie appeared and stood over him. She didn't say anything, just waited for an explanation.

"I heard a rumor Loving was workin' on a spread in New Mexico," he tried to explain. "S'posed to be someplace outside a Hot Springs. Figure I better take a look before he drifts ag'in."

"You just want to get away from me and my mother," Revelie said. "I know you."

"I don't wanta git away from you."

He smiled and waited for it to be returned, but it wasn't.

"It's good you're leaving," Revelie said, "because really you've been gone for a long time already–if you were ever here. You prefer Loving because he doesn't ask any questions."

"Don't say that."

"Why didn't you come to bed last night?" she accused.

"I didn't think you wanted me."

"I want you, the whole you, not just a part of you. I'm tired of your shooting your mess into me but holding back your seed."

"That's crazy, Revelie," he protested.

"Maybe, but I don't think so. You won't share your thoughts. You won't share your feelings. You won't tell me what happened to you during those lost years. Since you're so bad at sharing, it makes sense that you won't give me a baby because you know you'd *have* to share it with me."

"Revelie, you're wrong. I want a baby just as bad as you do. I'd love to share it with you."

"Then why haven't you given me one?"

"I've tried."

"No, you haven't. You want the pleasure, but you don't want to give a piece of yourself. You make me so angry."

Goodnight didn't know what to say, so he said: "I figure this is a good time to go because you won't be lonely. Not with your mama to keep you company."

"I'm lonely when you're here."

"Don't say that."

"It's the truth."

Her tone made him feel guilty, but it also irritated him. He wouldn't mind being a hundred miles from his wife's moods. Or from his mother-in-law's personality. But he knew Revelie's complaints weren't entirely unjust. He *had* held back a lot from her. He told himself he couldn't help it. Told himself that for the thousandth time. But he certainly hadn't held back his seed. That was crazy. But if she really believed it . . . ? Who knew what havoc believing something could cause?

"Well, I guess I'll be goin'," Goodnight said, not in his most loving voice. He stood up, slung his saddlebags over his shoulder.

"Goodbye," said Revelie.

"Just like that?"

"Yes, sure, go on your quest. I don't give a damn. I won't miss you. You aren't here when you're here anyway. Go have fun on your Quest for Loving."

"What?"

"Your Quest for Loving."

"What's that supposed to mean?"

"Just go. Go play quest."

"I hope you'll be here when I git back. With Loving."

56

Goodnight beheld a magic landscape: snow in the summertime. He had been riding a long time and wondered if he had dozed off. He shook his head to see if he was awake. He seemed to be. And yet the snow didn't go away, didn't melt into an optical illusion, just stayed put right there in the middle of the desert. The lone rider felt as if he had let his mind wander and somehow lost track of time, even lost track of the seasons, maybe lost track of the years. That would teach him to daydream. But the wind was hot on his cheek. His shirt was sweat-soaked on his back. It was summer, not winter, wasn't it? He began to worry that he had been on a solitary journey too long. Been gone from Texas too long? Been too long in the emptiness of these New Mexico badlands. Was he going crazy? He reached down and touched the handle of his ax; he needed something real to hang on to. He would have preferred to take hold of Revelie's hand, but . . .

The snow shimmered in the distance as if it couldn't make up its mind whether it wanted to be solid or liquid. As he drew closer, Goodnight thought he could make out waves. He beheld a vast snow-white ocean. It reminded him of the blue ocean where he had once been so happy so briefly. He waded in the ocean of memory that flowed into the ocean of dream. He was getting his oceans all mixed up, just like his seasons. The ground shifted beneath him as if the whole earth were melting into liquid. No, that was just his horse stumbling. He told himself not to let his imagination get the bit between its teeth and run away with him.

Goodnight kept expecting the snow to change color, to tarnish, to fade, to muddy, but it never did. The closer he drew, the whiter and brighter it seemed to become. But the snow did alter, did change in character, did become heavier and coarser. The crystals were transmuted into grains.

But Goodnight was as amazed by the vast desert of pure white sand as he had been by the illusion of snow in the summertime. It couldn't be real and yet it stretched for uncounted miles. He rode into these white sands and entered a world that was unlike any he had ever known. His senses seemed to be playing tricks on him. He wasn't sure he could trust them. And yet he wasn't frightened. He felt exhilarated, enchanted. The landscape made him feel like a boy again, and he soon fell to wondering if perhaps he had discovered a child's paradise, a world made of sugar. He even got down off his horse and tasted the whiteness. It wasn't sweet. He spit it out because it tasted like dirt, but it didn't look like dirt. Or rather it was gorgeous dirt, dirt transformed, magnificent dirt.

Goodnight loved the rolling white sand dunes, which were as tall as foothills, but he found himself squinting at them. The glare of the sun hurt his solitary eye. His horse found the going difficult because its hooves sank deep into the white powder with every step. Navigating was tricky. Here landmarks no longer existed. South looked like north, east just like west. The direction ahead was identical to the direction behind. Goodnight simply followed the sinking sun, but he still had an uneasy sense of not knowing where he was, of being lost in a huge whiteness.

Since Red was exhausted, Goodnight decided to stop and make camp early. But he couldn't make a campfire because there wasn't any wood, not even any twigs, in this vast, bitter sugar bowl. The only living creature he saw was a white lizard, which he didn't notice until it moved. He found himself wondering if there were other white animals all around him, as invisible as ghosts. He kept glancing back over his shoulder, but he didn't see anything.

The wanderer ate a cold supper of hardtack, which he washed down with a gulp from his canteen. He didn't drink deeply because water was as scarce as plants in these sands. When he lay down to sleep, he found that the white sand made an excellent mattress. His hip and shoulder dug snug holes. He congratulated himself for having found the "softest" bed he had enjoyed since leaving the red canyon. He fell asleep almost immediately.

But in the night, he was awakened by a terrible pain in his one remaining eye, which he rubbed and made hurt worse. Opening his eye, he found his vision blurred. He told himself that the night was dark and his eye teary; no wonder he couldn't see clearly. In the morning, the world would come back into focus, strange though that world might be. He wanted to scratch his eye, but he knew he shouldn't, knew he mustn't. He wondered if he would have to tie his hands behind his back.

The night was an unwholesome stew composed of pain and bits of sleep and dreams of pain. And the itch. The itch was as bad as the pain: the one hurt you, the other maddened you.

The sunrise turned the dunes pink, but Goodnight could not see this wonderful tableau plainly, for his vision was still blurred. He realized now that he had been badly hurt. He wasn't sure why or exactly how, but he could feel that the sun had burned his good eye. Now he was in real trouble. He had to get out of there. But which way? Should he continue to ride west toward Hot Springs, where Loving had been seen? Or turn back? He wanted to keep going, to cross this desert, and find what he was looking for. And yet he didn't want to die in this desert that supported no life except pale lizards and white ghosts.

Goodnight saddled up and headed west. If he had turned back, he knew he would have had almost a full day's ride ahead of him before he reached familiar brown ground. He wasn't sure his sight would hold out that long. But if he kept on going straight ahead, he would probably reach the far edge of the white sand in a day at the most. Probably less. He wasn't sure how he knew this, but he knew, or thought he knew. If these white sands were any wider, he would have heard of them. Somebody would have reported them. They would be on the map. That is, if they were real.

The higher the sun rose, the darker grew his world. An ominous cloud obscured the whiteness. Goodnight realized the cloud was in his eye. He tried to ride with his eye closed, to protect his vision, but every so often he couldn't resist peeking out at the albino world. Every time he looked again, he saw less and less. By noon, his vision had been extinguished completely. The brightest place on earth had become the darkest. He was blind. He felt that he had been expecting this day ever since he had lost an eye so many years ago. And yet he still had no idea what to do.

Goodnight tried to navigate by judging the heat of the sun, but he soon became confused and disoriented. He couldn't tell which direction the heat was coming from. All he knew was that it was hot. Too hot. So he finally gave his horse its head. He hoped the poor animal could still see.

Back when he could see, he had felt disoriented because the landscape looked the same in every direction. Now he was even more confused because he couldn't tell up from down. East looked like west and heaven like earth. He found himself leaning one way, then leaning the other. He felt as if he were falling. He seemed to be tumbling through space. He was more lost than he had ever been in his life. Lost and all alone. No Revelie, no mother, no anybody . . .

That was how she found him. Lost. Blind. Wandering in a beautiful but deadly wasteland. He saw her riding beside him on a white horse as white as that white lizard. She was as lovely as ever. He had grown older, but she had remained the same. Lucky her.

"I need your help," Goodnight said.

57

"I know," said the pretty ten-year-old girl. "I been here all the time. I was always ready to help you, but you never callt on me. I begun to think you never would."

Goodnight didn't know what to say. A terrible pain stopped his thoughts. He could no longer think or see. His mind was as blind as his sunburned eye. He couldn't see outside his head or inside it either. The pain seemed to start in his eye, but then it bled back into the brain itself. And it wasn't just his brain that hurt but also his mind. His crippled thoughts wanted to shriek with pain. He wanted to say something to this young guide who had come to him, but he couldn't think what. He was so afraid she would go away if he didn't say the right thing.

"I didn't mean to scold," she said.

"No, thass all right," he stammered. "Oh, I forgot what I wanted to say."

"Take your time."

"I'm all mixed up. What's happenin' to me?"

"You're lost. You're real lost."

Then the pain drove him completely out of his mind. Riding along, he dreamed, he hallucinated, whichever. He saw a great herd of white buffalo crossing the white landscape. The herd seemed to move in liquid waves across the wavy dunes. These great shaggy beasts could have been running across the sandy bottom of the ocean. The closer he came, the slower they ran, the more liquid their movements. And then they were gone and he breathed a sigh of relief. But they were soon replaced by a herd of great white elephants. As he drew closer, curious and afraid, he saw that they weren't elephants exactly but mammoths with long curving tusks. And they were pursued by white tigers with terrible fangs.

"Do you know who I am?" a voice called to him, but he still couldn't see her plainly.

Goodnight shook his head as if that would clear it. His whole universe went blank for a moment. Is death like this? Was he dead? And then the young girl on the white horse came riding back into his void. He was relieved to have found her again, but her question troubled him. He was beginning to feel afraid of her, too.

"No," he said. "Who are you?"

"Don't you know?" she asked. "Think real hard. Take your time. I got all the time in the world."

"I'm not good at riddles. You know that."

"You're gonna have to figure this one out sooner or later. I cain't help you there. I done all I can."

Goodnight knew he knew her. He just couldn't quite call her name. It was floating around in there somewhere with all the drowned mammoths. With all his memories of what he should have done but hadn't done. He struggled to bring up the name, to force it by effort of will to float up to him from the bottom of a deep well. He seemed to see it down there. A small golden ball. A pearl. A child's marble.

That was it. The marble was a part of some memory, but he couldn't see the whole picture. How could you make your mind remember when it wouldn't? It was like trying to see when your eye couldn't. He didn't know what to do, but he figured he had better say something or she might run off again.

"Your name, it's on the tip a my tongue," he said.

"It oughta be," she said.

"Don't go," he pleaded.

"I'll hafta," she said. "I'll hafta go if you cain't remember me."

"Why?"

"'Cause if you don't remember me, I just don't exist."

"No."

"Yeah, you'll've murdered me ag'in."

Then Goodnight knew her, of course. For there was only one person who would have the right to make such a charge. He shuddered. He knew he had known her all along, but hadn't wanted to know that he knew. He had kept it from himself. It was an old, old conspiracy.

"I know you," he said in a choked voice.

"Who am I then?" she asked.

"You're my sister."

Goodnight started to cry as if he were once again ten years old and had hurt himself badly. Tears poured from his burned, sightless eyes.

Tears ran from beneath his patch and trickled down over the purple constellation. He kept expecting her to tell him not to cry. He thought she would make it better. But she didn't. She just waited patiently until his sobbing softened to a childish blubber.

"What's my name?" she asked.

He didn't want to answer. He had known the question was coming, had always known, but he was unprepared for it.

"I dunno," he lied.

"You don't know your own sister's name?" she demanded.

He felt terrible. Now he wished she had never come. Now he wanted to be alone in the whiteness again. Who needed a sister, anyway?

"I know it," he admitted. She didn't seem to understand, or was waiting for something more. "I remember your name."

"Then say it," she ordered.

"I don't wanta say it."

"Why not?"

"It'd hurt too much."

"It hurts me that you don't say it."

"Does it really?"

"Yeah, it really does, and it hurts you, too."

"It does?"

"Course it does. Don't you feel how it does? Don't you know that you're carryin' around a deadness inside a you?"

"I loved you."

"Who'd you love? Tell me. Say it or I'll leave you."

Goodnight was crying again. He was ashamed of himself. He was glad he was lost in the desert and nobody could see him. Then he remembered that somebody could see him. He felt his whole world was about to explode. He had not said the name for so long, and not saying it had worked, not saying it had kept him from going insane. Now if he said it, who knew what screaming tigers he was bound to unleash? Why couldn't the buried stay buried?

"You're feelin' sorry for yourself," she said.

"I reckon so," he admitted.

"How 'bout feelin' sorry for me and what I suffered. I don't mean to be self-centered, but I suffered, too."

"I know. I'm bein' selfish."

"Why's it so hard? I don't unnerstand. Why's it so hard to say my name?"

Goodnight took a moment to collect his thoughts.

"I reckon it's 'cause if I just call you 'my sister,' then I'm a pointin' at *me* and what *I* lost. See? *My* sister, *my* loss. Almost like you was some kinda possession I lost. I can almost stand that kinda loss. But if'n I call you by your name, then it won't be about me no more. It'll be about you. The real you. The one and only you. Not *my* anything. Your everything. Lost. Gone. Forever. Sure 'nough. All real. A real you dead. And all you mighta been. Dead. The life you coulda had. Been a mom. Had kids a your own. Done whatever. Who knows? It's the name that makes it real. Really you. Not just my sister but–but–but– No, I still cain't say it. Cain't say your name."

"You gotta."

"I cain't. I just cain't. Don't you unnerstand?"

"Course I unnerstand," she said in that way she had, "I'm your sister. I come to help. 'Cause, Jimmy, I'm lost, lost forever, but you're lost, too. And you'll go on bein' lost till you say my name. For you it's a magic name. You gotta say my name if'n you're ever gonna find your way ag'in. You hear me?"

He couldn't. He mustn't. He didn't have the courage.

"I love you, Becky," he sobbed.

"I love you too, Jimmy," she said.

58

Goodnight fell from his horse, fell through the void, really falling now, seemingly falling right out of this world, until he hit the ground. The sand was so hot it burned his hands. And his sister's name–let loose in his head after all these years–seared his brain. He rolled over and over, like a man on fire trying to put out the flames, but they burned hotter than ever. He finally came to a stop lying on his back staring up sightlessly at the sun. Then he saw Becky standing over him.

"I told you it'd hurt," he said, sounding like a kid, "and it did hurt. Real bad. You knowed it was gonna hurt me, and you made me do it anyhow."

Then Goodnight remembered the time Becky had dug a hole in the ground and then covered it over with slender branches to make a bear trap. When no bear happened along, she decided to go looking for one. And she chose her brother Jimmy.

"It's just like that time you run me over your bear trap," he complained. "You kept a callin' me and callin' me. And then I finally come a runnin' and busted my leg. You hurt me on purpose. And you're doin' it ag'in."

"I know it hurts," she said. "I wisht it didn't have to hurt, but it does. There just ain't no other way."

"Why, Becky?" he asked and shuddered. The name still hurt. "Why cain't I just pretend you're off on a visit somewheres and not dead and gone?"

"'Cause it's lyin'."

"You oughta know. You told some."

"Mebbe I did back then. But lately you been the one tellin' lies. And you been tellin' them to yourself. You been sayin', 'She's just off gallivantin'.' Or, 'I never had no sister.' Or whatever. And lyin' to yourself, that's real hard work. You cain't never rest. You always gotta be on guard. It's like draggin' a plow. It'll wear a body out."

Goodnight felt something strange happening to him. She was messing with him somehow. Then he realized she was kissing his eyes, first the patch and then the burned eye. He thought maybe her kisses would heal his sight, but they didn't, or at least not in the way he expected. He felt that he had never loved Becky more than at this moment. Which made him miss her more than ever. Which made the pain worse than ever.

"What do I do now?" he said. "You said you'd help me."

"I am helpin' you," she said.

"I know you mean to be helpin' me, but you're just makin' it worse."

"I know."

"You know?"

"It's the only way. You gotta remember me. You gotta live with my death. I know it's hard, but it's harder t'other way."

He lay in the sand and tried to be absolutely still. He tried to imagine that he was lying not just on the earth but in the earth. He wanted to know how it would feel to be a corpse–to be her.

"Becky," he said.

"What?" she answered.

"Nothin'. I was just practicin' sayin' your name."

"Good."

"Becky, Becky, Becky."

"That's right. Gits easier, don't it?"

"No, not yet."

"It will."

"Promise?"

"Promise."

Goodnight lay on his back, staring up at the sky, not seeing a thing, asking himself whether he was getting saner or going completely insane. He wondered if he was finally finding his way or lost forever. He couldn't tell whether he had already discovered what he was looking for or was further from discovering it than ever.

"Say my name," Becky said, "and I'll always be with you."

"Becky," he said again. "Becky . . . Becky . . . Becky . . ."

Goodnight knew he was raving, but he didn't try to stop. He just kept on saying her name over and over again. He was afraid that if he stopped she would go away. So he didn't stop.

"Becky . . . Becky . . . Becky . . . Becky . . ."

She was right. Her name was a magic name. It rolled away the stone from the mouth of the tomb where all his forbidden memories were buried. Now all those memories came screaming out of the dark. He wanted to roll the stone back into place–wanted it desperately–but he couldn't deny his sister once again.

59

Goodnight lay on his back staring up at a ceiling that he couldn't see. He wasn't absolutely sure that he had a roof over his head, but he figured he probably did since he had a feather mattress under his back. His sister had tended him for days as he lay on this sickbed. He said her name often. "Becky, Becky . . ." Then she would come and lay a cool cloth on his forehead or hold his hand.

"Hello," she said. "How you doin' this mornin'?"

"Fair to middlin'," Goodnight said.

"That's good," she said. "The doctor's here. He's gonna take off your bandages. Take a look at that there eye. Mebbe things'll start lookin' up then."

"No," said the blind man, suddenly frightened. "Don't."

He was afraid he would lose her if he could see again. It wasn't that he wanted to be sightless for the rest of his life. But this morning he wasn't ready for–wasn't prepared for–the visible world. Maybe tomorrow.

"It's time," she said. "The doctor needs to see how your eyes's doin'."

"No," he protested.

"You'll feel better when you can see ag'in. Your mind'll rest easier."

Goodnight felt the bed shift beneath him as somebody sat down beside him. The body smelled of medicines. Goodnight rolled away from him.

"Becky," he said, "make him stop."

"Calm down," she said, bending over him. He recognized her familiar scent. "Nobody's gonna hurt you."

"That's what you said before," he said. "But it hurt. It hurt real bad."

"What hurt?" she asked.

"Sayin' your name," he said, a little embarrassed.

"Oh, I'm sorry," she said. "But this'll be differ'nt. Hold my hand."

Becky touched his hand. Goodnight let her take it. Then he gripped hard and she gripped hard back. Her hand was strong.

"You ready now?" she asked.

"I dunno," he said.

"That's better."

Goodnight smelled medicine descending upon his face. Then medical hands touched his cheek. Foul-smelling fingers tugged at the bandage over his burned right eye. He rocked his head from side to side, making the doctor's job harder, but he didn't actually fight the medicine man.

"All right, close your eye," said the doctor, who sounded like a transplanted Yankee. "Keep it closed until I tell you to open it."

Goodnight felt the bandage being lifted away. He already missed it. He wanted it back. But it was gone. It was another loss in a long line of losses. He felt the air blowing against his bare face.

"Becky," he said, "don't leave me."

"I won't," she said.

"Promise?"

"Promise."

Goodnight gripped her hand tighter than ever. He was afraid he might hurt her, but she didn't cry out, didn't even complain. She had a good grip for a girl.

"Now open your eye slowly," said the doctor. "Very slowly."

"No," Goodnight said.

"You gotta," said Becky. "Come on now."

Goodnight slowly opened his one surviving eye. He saw a bright light. It was too bright. It hurt his eye. He closed up again.

"It hurts," he said. "You said it wouldn't hurt, but it hurts. Just like last time."

"I'm sorry," she said.

"It won't hurt for long," said the doctor. "Your eye is just very sensitive. It has to get used to light all over again. Like when you were born. You see light and you cry. But it's worth it. And the pain goes away. Try again. Slowly."

"Come on," said Becky.

Since she asked him to, Goodnight slowly opened his eye again, letting in just a crack of light, then a little more, like the lid of a coffin being slowly lifted. Light and life flooded back in. The rays of light were needles, but he could stand the pain because he saw her now with his eye open. She was real. She existed out there as well as in here. He hadn't lost her. There she was. He had her back again . . .

Then Goodnight's eye focused and he saw Loving bending over him.

60

Goodnight kept staring. He didn't believe his eye. He kept waiting for Loving to change back into Becky, but his friend remained immutable.

"It's you," Goodnight said. "I thought you was somebody else."

"I know," Loving said. "I don't mind. I was kinda flattered. I knowed she musta meant a lot to you."

"Where the hell am I, anyhow?"

"The Grand Hotel in Hot Springs. Only it ain't too grand if you ask my opinion."

"How'd you find me?"

"I didn't. Wisht I could claim I did, but tain't so. Old prospector name a Jensen come across your horse. Backtracked and found you. Lucky he come along when he did, 'cause the trail wouldn't a lasted much longer, not in that there shiftin' sand. He figured you was dead till he bent down. Then he heard you whisperin' some lady's name like it was some secret."

"Yeah, my sister–" Goodnight almost said her name, but then he hesitated. He had learned to say it when he was blind and in another world, but he wasn't sure that he could say it now that he was back with his eye open and working. Oh, well, some lessons must be transferable from one world to another. "Becky," he said, and endured the pain. He figured he was going to have to learn to live with it.

"Becky," Loving echoed.

"So how'd you git here?"

"Well, a fella I know, who knowed I knowed you, told me what happened. Said you weren't doin' no good. So I figured I'd come on over and see for myself."

"Come far?"

"Not too far. Coupla days' ride. I reckon it was worth it." He paused. "You really seemed to like me till you got your eye open."

"Yeah, well. Funny business. I was out lookin' for you, and you turn around and find me. If that don't beat all."

"You was, huh?"

"Yep. Where's this Jensen fella at now? Reckon I oughta say 'Thank you' at least."

"Oh, he took off. Afraid the gold might git away if'n he didn't hurry. I thanked him for you. You said you was lookin' for me. How come?"

"I wanted you to come back. I figured mebbe I could talk you into it. Anyhow, I was gonna try. You kin bring that there Tucson girlfriend with you if you ever found her."

"Never did. I reckon yore luckier'n me in that respect."

"Well, then, how 'bout it? Come on back. But I ain't been so lucky lately, actually."

Goodnight sensed some hesitation in his friend that he didn't understand.

"I dunno," Loving said.

"What don't you know?" asked Goodnight.

"I dunno if that's such a good idea."

"Why not? What's the matter? You got somethin' ag'inst me?"

"No, course not."

"Then what is it?"

"Well, you're a builder. I'm a drifter. We'd kinda be pullin' in differ'nt directions."

"I ain't a askin' you to help me pull a damned wagon. We ain't gonna be in harness together. So what differ'nce does it make if'n we ain't exactly twins."

"I'll think on it."

Goodnight took a nap. He was still weak from his ordeal. While he slept, he dreamed of Becky. He met her walking beside the stream near the old family fort. She hadn't been killed or even hurt. It was all a mistake. Just a bad dream. When he woke up, he was happy. Then the world came back into focus and he lost his happiness. He hadn't had that dream for years.

Goodnight wondered where Loving had gotten off to. He hoped he hadn't lost him again. He kept looking around the small hotel room as if his friend might be hiding behind the cane-bottomed chair or under the table with the wash basin. He started to feel anxious. Then the door opened and Loving walked in.

"You're awake," he said.

"Yeah, I dreamed Becky was alive," Goodnight said.

He didn't normally make a practice of sharing his dreams, but he was trying to get used to saying his sister's name. It still hurt.

"Shame to wake up," Loving said.

"Uh-huh," Goodnight agreed. "That's how come I want you back at the ranch."

"On account of you have bad dreams?"

"It waddn't a bad dream. Wakin' up was bad."

"I still don't rightly see how I can help."

Goodnight took a deep breath. He closed his eye and returned to darkness. He didn't know how to say what he wanted to say. Well, hell, just say it.

"I done lost so much in my life," Goodnight said at last. "Folks I ain't never fixin' to git back ag'in. My sister Becky. My daddy. My mama. Aunts. Uncles. A girl with a real purdy name."

"You talkin' about Revelie?" asked Loving. "You ain't lost her, have you?"

"No, I hope not. Anyhow, I was thinkin' about a Comanche girl." Goodnight hesitated. He knew he should say the pretty name, but he didn't want to because he knew it would hurt. "Her name was Lifts Something." It hurt. "She's dead, too."

"Sorry to hear that."

"Uh-huh. Well, I lost so much I cain't git back, I figured I better try to git back what I can."

Watching Loving, Goodnight began to feel that he just might win this argument after all. He hoped he wasn't just out of his head.

61

For the second time, Loving was bringing home an ailing Goodnight. They made a big detour around the White Sands.

While Goodnight had been with Revelie at home on their ranch, he had often thought about Loving, daydreamed about him, longed to have him back. But now that he was with Loving, Goodnight found himself thinking only about Revelie, longing for her, dreaming he was with her at night. In the Human way, Goodnight "felt-missing" his wife. He desperately hoped she hadn't picked up and left Texas. What would he do then?

Of course, she would still be angry at him. Still furious. Still blaming him for everything. He told himself that he could endure her anger if only she hadn't left him. If she was still there, he knew what he was going to do, what he had to do, what he now wanted to do. Well, that was stretching it. Anyway, he would win her over by doing what she had always wanted him to do: tell his story. He had made his peace with his sister, with Becky, as much peace as he ever could, so why couldn't he do the same with his wife? He promised himself that he would tell her everything at the first possible "perfect" moment.

In the foothills of the San Andres Mountains, Goodnight saw something that needed investigating. "Hold up a minute," he said. "Lemme take a look."

Goodnight dismounted in a field of pink-flowered snakeweeds. Then he started pulling them up. Their roots looked like small, twisted potatoes.

"Bringin' your wife a bouquet?" asked Loving.

"Somethin' like that."

"Might be kinda wilted by the time we git there."

"I don't figure she'll mind this time."

• • •

Goodnight kept expecting to see the canyon. He started wondering if maybe they were lost. He sure hoped not because he had had enough of losing his way. He kept reminding himself that you couldn't see the canyon from very far away. It was deep and hidden, like the future. You didn't see it until you got there.

"Don't fall in," drawled Loving.

Goodnight had been looking so hard for the canyon that he had missed it. He had been searching too far in the distance when the canyon opened almost at his horse's feet. Staring down into it, Goodnight thought his red canyon looked redder than when he had seen it last. The cedars clinging to the red walls seemed greener than when he had left them. He was surprised, but then he reminded himself that all colors had seemed brighter since that doctor had lifted the bandage from his eye and he had seen Loving. It was as though those blazing sands had burned the scales from his eye.

Goodnight reached into his saddlebag and pulled out his field glasses. He focused on the red-stone house and saw something both chilling and encouraging: the ambulance. So his mother-in-law was still in residence–but so was his wife.

"Yes!" screamed Goodnight. "Race ya!"

"Hold on," said Loving. "Don't be silly. I didn't haul you all this way for you to go an' break your neck now."

"Why, Loving, you're lily-livered."

"Race ya!"

The two horsemen dug their spurs into their mounts and charged right out over the edge of the earth. Goodnight reached up and grabbed his hat as the world fell away beneath him. He couldn't believe that they hadn't even looked to see if there was a trail here before plunging down. Now he looked and there wasn't. His horse turned half sideways and skidded down the side of a great red pottery bowl. Scree flew from beneath its hooves like bullets. Goodnight pulled back on Red's reins as if to slow him, but he knew that the horse didn't really need any encouragement to slow down: the poor animal was putting on the brakes as best it could, stiffening its forelegs, sitting back on its hind legs, but the mad slide continued unchecked.

Goodnight knew he should feel ashamed of himself. He had gone to so much trouble–been through so much–to return Loving to this red canyon, and now he was risking both their lives. It would serve him right if one of them got killed here on the actual brink of success.

He should feel guilty, but he didn't. He wasn't worried about losing Loving. No, he was worried about losing *to* Loving. He had his friend back and he wanted to play.

Goodnight was surprised at how much fun he was having. He was amazed. He hadn't felt so carefree in years. He had fallen off the edge of an old world of burdens and guilts and was falling into a new world of joy and happiness. He was giddy. He felt as if he were a boy discovering sex, falling into a woman for the first time. He didn't care if he got killed or if Loving did. Because he knew he wouldn't, just as the boy discovering physical love knows he will never die.

Goodnight lurched in his saddle as his horse crashed into Loving's mount. He felt the animal beneath him stumble. Now he was falling in a new way. He fought to regain his balance in the saddle as his horse struggled to gain some purchase on the steep wall. He was losing his fight, going headfirst over the saddle horn, when somehow the world shifted, gravity altered its angle, and he dropped back onto the seat of his saddle.

In a blur beneath him, Goodnight saw his sprawling ranch headquarters lurch into view. He tried to hold his head still long enough to search the pens and lots and yards for Revelie. When they were halfway to the bottom, Goodnight saw his cowboys spot him and begin to spread the alarm. Now Revelie should appear, but where was she? He kept on staring down into the very pit of the canyon, letting his horse find its own way. Could he be wrong? Had she abandoned him?

Then Goodnight saw her come running out of the big stone ranch house. He flinched. She still had the power to make him so happy it hurt. Now he really wanted to win the race. He was a boy again who wanted to show off for his sweetheart.

Goodnight actually spurred his horse before he realized where he was and what a dumb stunt he had just pulled. His mount staggered beneath the spur, skidded, stumbled, and then somehow managed to get its hooves underneath it.

"Sorry," Goodnight apologized, "my fault."

Looking to his left, he saw Loving. They were still running neck and neck, nose and nose. He couldn't let his friend beat him with his wife watching. That wouldn't be any way to come home.

Glancing back down at the bottom of the canyon, Goodnight saw Revelie shading her eyes and staring up at him. She looked to him a little like his sister. He had never noticed that before. Well, she didn't really look like her. It was just something about her movement, something of her vulnerability.

But he had better worry about his own vulnerability. He was getting beat up by all the bouncing around, but he was having more fun than he had had in a long time.

Glancing back into the pit, Goodnight saw his cowboys and his girl mounting up. Revelie swung up onto the sidesaddle that he had made for her. He enjoyed this secondhand contact with his wife. He saw his vision blur and he knew it wasn't the dust or the motion.

Out of the corner of his eye, Goodnight saw Loving's mount spin around on the cliff face as if it were caught up in a dust devil. But the horse was whirling the dust rather than the other way around. It finally came to a halt at the center of the red dust storm with its head pointed back up the wall and its rump pointed down toward the bottom of the canyon. The animal had evidently lost its balance and only barely saved itself and its rider by sliding into an assbackward stop.

Good! Great! All hands were safe and Goodnight was going to win. He would have slowed down a little–taken a little extra care now that he knew he was bound to win–but there was no way to slow down. He could no more put on the brakes than could the rocks that were racing him to the bottom.

Glancing back over his shoulder, Goodnight saw that Loving had his horse turned back around and was charging down the cliff again. But he was too far behind. Unless Goodnight took a fall.

Clinging to his horse with his feet and his heels and his knees and his thighs and every nerve in his body, Goodnight dropped the last hundred feet and hit the flat where his horse stumbled. The rider went headfirst over the horn and his horse's head. In midair, he told himself to roll. And when he hit the ground, he turned a somersault.

Goodnight got up dirty and bruised, but the victor. He looked around with a big smile on his face expecting to see Revelie. But she wasn't there yet. Loving rode up beside him.

"Serve you right if'n you'd broke your neck," he said. "Didja?"

"No, 'fraid not," Goodnight laughed.

He dusted himself off and climbed back on his long-suffering horse.

"Nice ridin'," Loving said.

Goodnight didn't say anything because he had just seen Revelie and her coterie of cowboys emerge from a grove of chinaberry trees. He tipped his hat to his wife and felt a big grin on his face. The canyon was redder, the leaves were greener, and his wife was prettier than when he had gone away.

"Howdy," Goodnight said almost shyly to his beautiful wife. How mad was she? How hostile?

"Hello," Revelie said, "so you're alive."

Then she turned her horse and rode away on the saddle he had made for her. He was tempted to ride after her, but he held back, hesitating. He didn't want to do the wrong thing or say the wrong thing or hear the wrong thing. She didn't look back as she cantered toward the big sandstone ranch house. Naturally, Goodnight turned to Loving. He had long imagined that Loving could heal all the wounds in the canyon. Now it was time for him to start.

"Loving, please, go talk to her," Goodnight said softly. "If I go, it'll just make her mad, but you can talk to her. You can fix it. I know you can."

Loving protested over and over but eventually gave in. Leaving Goodnight and the other cowboys hovering in his wake, he rode ahead. When he reached the ranch house, he dismounted, ground-hitched his horse, and knocked on the front door.

62

When he reached the ranch house, Goodnight dismounted and camped out on the front porch, waiting. The cowboys moved on to the corral, but the boss kept waiting and watching and consulting his gold watch, which was a Christmas present from Revelie several years back. The hands moved as if they were crippled. What was taking Loving so long? What had gone wrong? What . . . ?

This delay, this waiting, wasn't good. She must be madder than mad. Was he wrong about Loving? Maybe he wasn't the healer he had taken him for. Or perhaps this case was beyond healing. Goodnight decided he should do some work around the place and not just waste time, but he couldn't think of what to do. Summer turned into autumn; then autumn turned into freezing winter, which made him shiver on the front porch. Would spring ever come?

"Mr. Goodnight," her voice startled him even though he had been waiting for it for seasons, "won't you come in?"

He got up stiffly and entered his own home as if he were a guest. But was it his home anymore?

Goodnight and Revelie embraced politely in the big living room, but they didn't kiss. Nonetheless it was a good beginning.

He thought: That Loving sure enough had a way with the ladies. What was his secret? He must ask him sometime. That would be a secret worth knowing for sure. Where had he gotten off to anyway? He wanted to thank him.

"I brought something for your mama," Goodnight said softly.

"Something for my mother?" Revelie said a little louder. "Will miracles never cease? Did you bring anything for your wife?"

"Nope, just Loving. On the way home, way out yonder, I come across some snakeweed. Hard to find around here, but there's plenty of it out there. Thought it might help her burpin'–'less the burpin' done cured itself."

"How sweet. No, she hasn't stopped. She burps day and night. Do you actually believe you can persuade my mother to take snakeweed?"

"I'll git Coffee to brew up some snakeweed tea."

Revelie entered the sickroom followed by her husband, who was carrying a heavy, steaming mug. Mrs. Sanborn looked up, startled.

"Mr. Goodnight is back," Revelie announced, "and he has brought you some medicine. He believes it might help your condition."

Mrs. Sanborn pulled the covers up closer to her chin. She seemed to want to hide. Her hair was a mess after days in bed. Her eyes were suspicious.

"What kind of medicine?" she asked. "Have you considered that he might, *burp,* be trying to poison me to save his precious ranch?"

"Well, at least it would put you out of your misery, Mother."

"That isn't funny."

"I know. I'm sorry. He has made you some tea. Please drink it. It may soothe your stomach and make you feel better."

Mrs. Sanborn considered the matter.

"What've you gotta lose?" asked her son-in-law.

"My life. That's all."

"Not hardly. It don't even taste half bad."

"What kind of tea is it, Mr. Goodnight."

"Well, you see, it's made from snakeweed, so most folks just call it snakeweed tea."

"Snakeweed indeed. He is trying to poison me. He admits it."

"No, ma'am. Snakeweed's just a name."

"Not a very pleasant name. I hardly think it will readily replace English breakfast tea."

"Ain't supposed to. That's for breakfast, this here's for burpin'."

"Mr. Goodnight, you alliterate."

"I do not. It's the God's honest truth. Try a sip."

Mrs. Sanborn hesitated.

"Try it," Revelie said with the weight of command in her pretty voice. "Don't be silly. It won't hurt you, and it might help you. The only way to find out is to try it."

Her mother looked startled again.

"All right, Mr. Goodnight," she said, "I'll taste your snake's brew if I must."

Her son-in-law handed her the mug. Mrs. Sanborn lifted it to drink from it, making a face.

"Not so fast," Goodnight said.

"What?" asked his mother-in-law, startled once more.

"You've gotta say some words over it or else it won't do you no dang good."

"You are jesting, certainly."

"'Fraid not, ma'am. Sorry, but you gotta ask the snakeweed's permission to drink that there tea. You gotta say how come you need it. And you gotta promise that you didn't take all the snakeweed, but left plenty behind, so there'll be more snakeweed next year. Can you remember all that there?"

"I'm not an ignoramus, Mr. Goodnight, whatever you may think. But I am not accustomed to conversing with my tea. I'll just drink it if it's all the same to you."

Mrs. Sanborn lifted the mug once again, but Goodnight reached out and took hold of his mother-in-law's wrist.

"I'm serious. It won't do you no good unless you say what I said. If you ain't gonna say it, I'll just throw it out."

"Mother, say the words," said Revelie.

Mrs. Sanborn glared at her daughter, glared at Goodnight, then glared back at her only child. Then she shrugged, giving up.

"Mr. Snakeweed"–she swallowed a burp–"please cure me."

She tried to lift the mug again, but Goodnight renewed his grip on her wrist.

"Sorry, but you didn't git it just right. You gotta ask permission. You gotta say what's afflictin' you. And you gotta say you left plenty for next year. Got it?"

"All right, unhand me. Let me see. Mr. Snakeweed, I ask your permission to drink your tea."

"Good," said Goodnight.

"I need your tea because I am ill–"

"Say what's wrong."

"But this is embarrassing. I cannot–"

"Say it," said Revelie.

"I need your help because I cannot seem to stop, *burp*, burping. It is most embarrassing. You see I do need your help badly."

"Good," said Goodnight. "Now next year . . ."

"Mr. Snakeweed, I promise that my agent, Mr. Goodnight, left plenty of snakeweeds behind so that your progeny will be plentiful in the future."

"What was that?" he asked.

"She said it," explained his wife.

"Okay, bottoms up."

"I'm not quite that enthusiastic, Mr. Goodnight." But she did take a sip, making a face before and a worse face after. "I thought you told me this did not have a bad taste? It tastes like venom."

"Well, you should taste horehound tea," said Goodnight.

"I beg your pardon?" said Mrs. Sanborn.

"Keep drinking," Revelie said.

It took several minutes, but Mrs. Sanborn finally drained the large mug. She handed it back to her son-in-law.

"Nice goin', ma'am. Now we'll just wait a few minutes."

"Burp," said his mother-in-law with a scowl.

Goodnight walked over and sat on the windowsill. He looked out at his red canyon. His wife sat on the bed beside her mother.

"Burp."

Goodnight hoped to catch a glimpse of Loving getting reaccustomed to the place, but he was nowhere in sight. The medicine man crossed his legs and watched his boot twitch. It twitched for some time.

"Now try to burp," Goodnight said at last.

Mrs. Sanborn tried, but she couldn't.

In the hallway outside Mrs. Sanborn's sickroom, Revelie pulled Goodnight to her.

"Thank you," she said. "It was wonderful of you to do what you did. Wonderful in many ways."

"You're welcome," he said. "And she's welcome, too."

He sensed that in curing Revelie's mother he had also begun to heal the illness between himself and his wife.

"Thank you again," she said, lifting up to kiss him briefly on the lips. "I'm sure my mother thanks you, too."

"That's all well and good, but your mom and me, we don't hafta be best friends now, do we?"

"No, Mr. Goodnight, you certainly do not. I've never liked any man who liked my mother."

63

In honor of Loving's homecoming, they ate in the large but seldom-used dining room in the big stone house. Goodnight sat at the "head" of a large, round table. Revelie was on his right, Loving at his left, and the rest of the cowboys strung out around the table. (Mrs. Sanborn was absent, insisting she was still too weak to appear in public.) Goodnight felt a euphoria at being back where he belonged, back among the people he belonged with, back in the canyon that seemed to be the palm of God's cupped hand. God must be a red man. Goodnight just hoped he wouldn't bust out crying right here at the table. Then he saw his vision blur and he knew what that meant.

"'Scuse me," Goodnight said. "I gotta go take care of somethin'."

Getting up, he hurriedly left the table as if he had to go to the bathroom real bad and real fast. He was a little embarrassed by what he knew they all were thinking, but he would have been even more embarrassed if they had seen what a crybaby he was turning into. He managed to make it to the bathroom and to close the door before he started blubbering. He sat down on the newfangled indoor john and just bawled. His whole body shook. He couldn't get his breath and choked. He told himself to cut out this kind of behavior, to grow up, but he didn't particularly feel like growing up. He didn't particularly like choking, but he did like the way he felt all over when the spasms of crying stopped. He felt clean inside as if the tears had actually washed something away. He felt a sense of renewal as if the tears were a spring rain on parched ground. He shivered and luxuriated in the feeling.

When he felt like it, Goodnight got up, washed his face, stared at himself in the mirror, and wondered what he could do about his red eye. He splashed more cold water on it, but when he looked again, it was as red as ever. Well, he couldn't wait around until he looked like his old self again. He wasn't even sure he wanted to be his old self again. Reluctantly, Goodnight opened the door and headed back to face the family that he had gathered around him.

Entering the spacious dining room, Goodnight saw Revelie and Loving leaning toward each other talking. He stopped to enjoy the scene. He enjoyed how well the two of them looked together. He saw them as a beautiful sister and handsome brother. They even resembled each other in that they were both good-looking in the same way. Both had fine, well-made features. And they both had the same intense life burning inside them that animated them the way a candle animates a jack-o'-lantern. They seemed to belong together. And so Goodnight felt an intense pride at having brought them together here under this roof, here in the palm of this canyon.

"Mr. Goodnight," said Revelie, noticing him in the doorway, "what are you staring at?"

"The two of you," said the husband.

"What about the two of us?" asked his wife sharply.

"I cain't git over how good you look together," he said. "I just been standin' here soakin' it up."

"Really?" she said.

"You oughta see yourselves. I got the best-lookin' man and the best-lookin' woman in Texas right cheer under my own roof. I won't never need to leave home no more. There ain't nothin' more out there to look for. To quest for. Like you said."

Goodnight congratulated himself: He had fixed up things with his dead sister and now he was making progress with his wife. Anyway, he hoped so. Thanks, Becky.

"I'm glad you're feeling well," said Revelie. "I was afraid you might be ill the way you left the table."

"Oh, no, that waddn't nothin'," Goodnight said. "I'm fine. Real fine." He thought a moment. "I tell you what less do. Less kill the fat calf an' invite the whole country."

"What?" asked Revelie.

"To celebrate Loving's homecomin'. Less have a two-day, mebbe a three-day, dance. Folks sleepin' over. Fill up this here house for a change. Really raise Cain. I wanta show off my family now that I got it back together ag'in. Whaddaya say?"

Goodnight didn't think Loving much liked the idea, but he was glad to see Revelie smile.

"That reminds me of a song my mother used to sing to us when we were little," she said. "It's too bad she is too sick to be with us. The song was about Ireland, but it could just as well be about Texas. 'I am of Texas, and of the holy land of Texas. Good sir, pray I thee, on Saint Charity, come and dance with me in Texas.'"

"I'll gladly dance with you in Texas," Goodnight said. "And Loving will too. He don't look too pleased right now, but he will be."

Goodnight couldn't hear Loving's reply because it was drowned out by a sudden detonation of thunder so loud and so close that it shook the big rock house on its firm foundation. Then rain beat on the windows like small, determined ghosts demanding to be let in. The insistence of the drops seemed to wake an impatience inside Goodnight himself. He couldn't wait any longer. He wanted Revelie right now, had to have her right now . . .

"Revelie," Goodnight said, "I got an idea. Less go for a walk."

"In the rain?" asked his wife.

"Sure. You know how much I like walkin' under the rain."

64

While the storm raged, Goodnight led Revelie along an old Human trail that wound through hackberry thickets and chinaberry groves. His wife was being a good sport about this walk in the driving rain. She normally didn't even like to get her hair wet, and yet she didn't complain as the heavens poured buckets of water on her head. Her grip on his hand was warm and firm. When thunder roared, she squeezed hard. Goodnight just hoped it wouldn't start to hail. He wondered why he kept exposing the ones he loved most to dangers.

He put hail temporarily out of his mind when a flash of lightning revealed to him a dense patch of horehound plants fenced in by wild plum trees. He smiled to himself remembering how his Human father had taught him to harvest this herb that was supposed to be the friend of the barren woman. The storm was so fierce that it had beaten down many of the plants, so they formed a matting that would protect the lovers from the mud below. Anyway, he hoped so. He knew horehound was normally taken internally to be effective, but he just liked the idea of making love on top of a bed of fertility plants.

Goodnight reached for the buttons at Revelie's throat and started undoing them. She was reluctant at first, but . . . soon they only had an eyepatch between them. The lightning lit her and he saw again how beautiful she was, water dripping off her slightly turned-up nose and her slightly upturned, puckered nipples.

The husband lay down first, lay on his back, and pulled his wife down on top of him. He chose to be on the bottom because he wanted to protect Revelie. His back and not hers would touch the rough horehounds and the mud beneath. He would be her bed and her lover at the same time.

As he entered her, Goodnight stared up at the sky and saw lightning branch out across the heavens like a huge, overhanging electric tree. Then a moment later, terrible thunder shook Revelie above him, shook the earth beneath him, shook the red canyon, shook his whole world. This giant red hole in the ground magnified the thunder, echoed the thunder, made the roar last until the next great detonation, which was amplified and repeated, until the next . . .

One lightning flash was the devil's own fiery pitchfork overhead. Then another burst was God's own electric finger reaching down once more to quicken another generation of Adams with the spark of life. Then the next fiery display was a mighty electric river with many tributaries . . . the burning river above echoing the red river with its many branches down below . . . Then came a fragmented bolt that appeared to be a giant root . . . the root of an invisible tree whose leaves were stars.

The bright bursts seemed to have their own rhythm, which matched his rhythm. He felt as if he took some of their energy into his own body. He absorbed their power. He penetrated Revelie the way they penetrated the sky. The heavens thundered and Revelie moaned. He wondered why he had never made love in a thunderstorm before. He was as wild and mighty and elemental as the lightning itself. He only wished he could be as unselfconscious as the lightning as well, but he couldn't. He was aware of having gone out of his way to perform a supremely romantic act and this awareness seemed to undermine the romanticism a little.

"Turn over!" Revelie screamed above the thunder. "I want to see the lightning, too! It's my turn."

"You might git muddy," he said.

"It'll wash off," she said. "Roll over."

Goodnight rolled and Revelie rolled with him. Now she looked up at the lightning, and he saw the flashes reflected in her eyes. The rain beat hard on his bare back. It was cold. It stung. He loved it. He seemed to absorb the power of every driving drop. He was wet everywhere, and she was wet everywhere, too. Liquid moved against liquid. He was immersed in liquid. He felt as if he were back in the womb again, not just a part of him, but all of him.

"My mind cries for you," Goodnight whispered in the storm.

"My mind, uh, cries for, uh, you too," Revelie screamed into the storm.

Goodnight smelled her scent mingling with the smell of the red mud. She seemed to be a part of the red earth itself. She was as much a part of his red canyon as any tree or boulder. In making love to her, he was also making love to his canyon, to this great red womb dug deep into the earth, and in loving the canyon he loved her. He didn't think he could separate his love of this woman from his love of this place. And he didn't want to. He would always love them both more than anybody else or anywhere else in the world.

Goodnight screamed into the thunder, his cry mingling with the thunder, so he couldn't tell where one sound ended and the other began. He seemed to feel the thunder in his throat. Then a moment later, Revelie screamed too, her cry an echo of his own, both thundering down the canyon.

The husband collapsed on top of his wife, laughing softly now, no longer thundering. Afraid he would hurt her, he rolled to one side and then took her in his arms.

Lying beside her, Goodnight felt spent and weak. He hadn't made love to his wife in such a happy, fierce way in years. He thanked the storm for its help, but he felt he should thank someone else as well. After all, he had been feeling more energetic ever since his experience in those blinding White Sands. So he thanked Becky as well as the storm. He felt sure that she was the invisible maiden of honor who had led the bride and groom to this rude altar to be married all over again. His blind inner eye that had refused for so long to see his dead sister was now open. And when it opened, it saw more than his lost Becky: it saw his lost Revelie, the Revelie of old, the Revelie of the beginning, the Revelie of the first love.

Goodnight was so happy that he almost felt selfish. He wished he could share his happiness. He would have loved to have given some of it to Loving. He had more than enough to go around.

Right here, right now, in the rain, on the muddy ground, Goodnight was tempted to tell Revelie his long-guarded secrets. But the downpour had turned cold, and the mud was uncomfortable. He would tell her later. The perfect time would come.

When they returned to the ranch house, they discovered that Tin Soldier had come back. He had gotten tired of the life of a wandering cowboy-blacksmith and had come home. He had ridden in soaking wet.

Loving was working his magic.

• • •

In bed that night, after they had bathed away the mud, Goodnight realized that he had found the perfect moment to tell Revelie about his dark–his lost–life among the Human Beings. First, he had needed Becky's forgiveness. Now he needed his wife's.

"Revelie, I've got something to tell you," Goodnight said in a soft voice. "I want you to know what happened to me and what happened to my sister. I'm sorry I kept it a secret all these here years."

Waiting for his wife to respond to his emotional preamble, Goodnight heard instead a gentle snore. His exhausted wife was asleep. He felt a slight sense of pride because he had worn her out with his lovemaking. She deserved a good rest. He was sure that another perfect moment would roll around soon. Let her sleep.

The next morning, breakfast was served uncharacteristically in the dining room rather than the cook shack. At the big round table, Revelie told her mother, "We're not selling the ranch."

"Then I'm leaving," said her mother, who had not been softened by her recovery. "This country has turned you into a hard and selfish child. You don't care that I'm all alone in the world now . . ."

She seemed to be trying to burp, but she simply couldn't anymore. A burp would have nicely underscored her abandoned plight–how could you send away your burping mother?–but it was beyond her.

After several days of planning, packing, more speeches and ill humor, Mrs. Sanborn left just as the invited guests were beginning to arrive. Goodnight felt that they were actually celebrating two boons: Loving's homecoming and Mrs. Sanborn's departure from his red canyon.

With Revelie's mother in residence, Goodnight hadn't felt comfortable about renewing his effort to share his past with his wife, but now he could.

65

Goodnight stood with his back to the big stone house and stared into the bonfire that blazed in his front yard. Boys and girls of various sizes, but none much older than ten, whooped it up around the burning logs. The boys all seemed to be fighting each other. The girls clumped together in girl bouquets. Beyond the fire, horses were tied to hackberry trees and chinaberry trees and cedars. As the canyon floor darkened, the many wagons, buckboards, buggies, surreys, hacks, and two-wheel carts all melted together into a long train with hundreds of wheels. The whole country had been invited on short notice and the whole country had come.

Turning, Goodnight headed back inside, where most of the adults were congregated. He entered a living room that had been cleared of all its furniture except for chairs and benches around the perimeter.

"Where's the fiddlers?" called Too Short. "We're rarin' to go."

Soon impatient feet were stamping on the floorboards. Then the crowd around the kitchen door parted. Old Doc Wainwright (the only doctor for a hundred miles around) and Teddy Tucker (who was just a janitor who swept out the saloons in Tascosa) appeared carrying their fiddles. The doctor and the janitor touched their bows to their fiddles and couples flowed out onto the floor. These were mostly husbands and wives. Then the younger folks started looking for partners and asking and being asked to dance. The floor grew more crowded as the unmarrieds joined the marrieds.

Goodnight wondered where Revelie had gotten off to. He wanted to dance with her. He scanned the four walls but didn't find her. He figured she was probably back in the kitchen worrying over the refreshments. Well, he meant for his wife to enjoy her own party. He decided to go rescue her.

Then as he was working his way through the crowd, Goodnight looked up and saw Revelie out on the dance floor. She was dancing with Loving. He smiled to see them. They made such a handsome couple that he couldn't help staring. Most of the other dancers really didn't know how to dance, and were just chasing each other around and around in a great circle. But Revelie and Loving were actually doing dance steps–were really dancing–with a grace that matched their good looks.

Goodnight knew he couldn't dance as well as Loving. He normally just galloped around the room like everybody else. But he nonetheless wanted to dance with his wife. He wanted Revelie back in his arms. He thought about cutting in, but he couldn't bring himself to do so. It seemed somehow wrong to separate such a well-matched pair. Besides, this party was meant to celebrate Loving's homecoming, so Goodnight wanted his best friend to have a good time.

When the fiddlers stopped, Goodnight saw Revelie look around. She saw him. He smiled at her. She smiled back but her smile didn't look as big as his felt. Well, she had a smaller face.

"There you are," Revelie said. "I was looking for you. I thought you had gone outside. That's why I danced with Mr. Loving."

"I come back in," Goodnight stammered.

"Well, it's about time," Revelie said.

"Thanks for the dance, ma'am," said Loving.

He nodded slightly and retreated into the crowd.

"He's some kinda dancer, ain't he?" said Goodnight. "I never seen dancin' like you two was doin'. I was purdy near jealous. How'd he ever learn to shake a leg like that?"

"He didn't say," said Revelie.

"I hope he's glad to be home. Anyhow, I think of this here as his home, but mebbe he don't. Whaddaya think? Is he glad?"

"I think so," Revelie said. "He knows how much his being here means to you."

"But how much does it mean to him?"

"I'm sure he's pleased to be here."

"I sure hope so. He seems a little standoffish to me. Not quite hisself. But you think he's okay?"

"Yes, I do."

Goodnight was a little disturbed to hear the fiddlers tuning up again because he knew his dancing would not stand comparison with Loving's. Still, he wasn't worried enough to forgo the pleasure of tromping around the dance floor with his wife.

"Can I have this here dance?" Goodnight asked.

"I would be delighted," said Revelie.

Soon Mr. and Mrs. Goodnight took their place in the train of dancers that rumbled around and around the big, empty living room. He concentrated so hard on his movements–trying but failing to move as gracefully as his friend–that he didn't say a word to his partner. Goodnight wanted to pull Revelie close to him, to press his body to her body, but he held back. He didn't want to step on her feet or accidentally knock her down. None of the other dancers moved body to body either. They danced as couples but somehow alone. They were all accustomed to having lots of space around them, and they seemed reluctant to get close even on the dance floor. But Goodnight recalled that Revelie and Loving had danced closer and moved together as one.

"Less go find Loving," Goodnight said when the music stopped.

"I'm sure he's all right," said Revelie.

"Less look anyhow."

"All right."

With Goodnight leading the way, they moved along the walls. As they passed the cavernous fireplace with its glowing embers, Revelie paused, so her husband paused also, to look at the small children and even infants asleep on pallets by the fire. He wished–as he was sure she wished–that some of them were theirs. But that time was coming soon. After the party, he would at long last share his darkness with his wife and then . . .

Goodnight spotted Loving in a corner surrounded by cowboys. The music started up again.

"Now this here's supposed to be a dance," Goodnight proclaimed. "And that means you boys gotta dance. Loving, you show 'em how. Be a good example to 'em. Run Revelie around the dance floor a coupla times. How about it, huh?"

"I reckon Miss Revelie oughta have somethin' to say about that," said Loving.

"I am at your service, Mr. Loving," said Mrs. Goodnight. And she dropped an understated curtsey.

As Revelie took Loving's arm and moved out into the center of the room, Goodnight took a deep breath, as if he were relieved. He stood with the cowboys and watched Revelie and Loving. Their movements seemed to have an inevitability, as if they were stars in the night sky. The other dancers jerked and lurched like shooting stars, doomed meteors.

Then the husband knew what he had to do: go for a walk outside. If he stayed indoors, Revelie would feel compelled to return to him for a dance when she really should be dancing with Loving. Besides, he always liked a good walk by himself under the stars that roofed his canyon.

But when he looked up at the night sky, Goodnight saw Orion dancing with Revelie.

At midnight, Coffee rang the dinner bell. Returning to his large living room, Goodnight saw that supper was already under way. Home Ranch cowboys moved around the room passing out sliced-beef sandwiches on Coffee's sourdough bread, slices of cake, and hand-turned ice cream. Every chair and every spot on a bench was now occupied.

"If you cain't find a spot to sit down," Coffee called out to the milling crowd, "just sit on your fist and lean back on your thumb."

Goodnight looked around for his wife and his best friend. He turned all of the way around in a circle without seeing them. He shrugged his shoulders and turned a second time. He knew if he kept up this pivoting, he was going to get dizzy. He noticed an eight-year-old spinning around and around because he wanted to get dizzy. The boy achieved his goal and fell over on his side. Well, where were they?

Goodnight returned to the out-of-doors. He stretched and then sat down under a chinaberry tree. He dozed.

After so many of his guests had danced until dawn, Goodnight didn't expect many to appear for breakfast. Yet a throng crowded into Coffee's enlarged cook shack and squeezed onto the benches on both sides of the long table. Coffee, who had been up most of the night himself, supplied a steady stream of biscuits, eggs, toasted sourdough, spicy sausage, wrinkled bacon, and coffee.

Goodnight wished Revelie were with him here at the table to share in the enjoyment of his favorite meal of the day. But she hadn't come to bed until it was light out. No wonder she needed her sleep. Nor was she the only one. On his way to breakfast, Goodnight had been forced to step over several women and girls who were curled up on pallets in the main hallway. He had noticed others asleep on the dance floor, spaced at regular intervals like checkers on a checkerboard. Looking out a window to check on the weather, he had seen men and boys curled up out in the open. The rule for overnight guests was: females inside, males outside. He was pretty sure some had cheated.

Goodnight himself had been in bed a couple of hours before his wife arrived. He had turned in "early"–around 4 A.M.–because he knew somebody would have to get up and see to their guests' needs this morning. As he ate his steaming breakfast, Goodnight looked up every time somebody new entered the cook shack expecting to see Loving, but he never came. Good. That meant he had had a good time.

Lingering over his third cup of Coffee's dark brew, Goodnight told himself he had to get moving. He wanted his guests to have fun all day as well as all night, so he planned a kind of carnival. It would resemble a county fair, but such fairs were generally put on by farmers. Goodnight's fair wouldn't be a farmer fair but a cowboy fair. Farmers cared about who could grow the biggest pumpkin or bake the best cherry pie or raise the fattest pig. Cowboys cared about who could rope the fastest and ride the roughest. Farmers cared about produce and products. Cowboys cared about skill and grit. Anyhow, that was how Goodnight figured it, so he planned a whole day of contests. If folks seemed to like his cowboy festival, maybe he would do it again next year.

Goodnight and Revelie, working together, had thought hard to come up with an appropriate name for their fair. At first, she had suggested calling it a "cowboy carnival," because it alliterated, whatever that meant, but he said that was a little too cute. He told his wife that maybe the name should be Spanish since the vaqueros were the original cowboys. Cowboy hats were just Texas versions of sombreros, and lots of cowboy words were Spanish: remuda, bronco, desperado, lasso, ranch(o). Revelie said that was good, the name should be Spanish. She even pointed out that old Don Quixote might be considered the first cowboy because he rode around Spain with a big hat on his head; of course, his hat wasn't a sombrero but a barber's wash basin. Goodnight asked his wife what in the world she was talking about. Anyway, they finally settled on "rodeo" because it meant a cattle fair.

66

Goodnight smiled at what he had caused. The big corral by the barn was completely surrounded by wagons and buckboards and buggies and surreys and hacks and two-wheel carts. Every vehicle was crowded with men and women, boys and girls, some sitting, some standing up.

Goodnight crawled up on Coffee's chuck wagon and stood beside Revelie. He bent down and picked up the dinner bell. It wasn't really a bell but an iron triangle. He rang it with an iron bar. The harsh, loud metallic ringing quieted the crowd.

"May I have your attention!" Goodnight shouted. "Mrs. Goodnight has a few words to say."

The husband stepped back and his wife stepped forward.

Revelie proclaimed in a loud, clear voice: "Let the games begin."

Goodnight raised his big white hat over his head and waved it, as if he were starting up a trail drive, which was a signal to Too Short to drive over the wild broncs. Churning up a dust storm, they soon reached the big corral, where wings–built out from the gate–funneled the horses inside. They seemed to take turns bucking and kicking at nothing in particular.

"Look at them going around and around," Revelie said. "They look like a merry-go-round gone quite mad."

"I'll take your word for it," Goodnight said. "I ain't never seed no such thing. What it looks like to me is a big angry eye with a stake drove in it."

"How gruesome."

"Beg pardon, ma'am."

The stake in the eye was the snubbing post. When breaking a bronc, the first step was to lasso it and then wrap the rope around that post. That way the horse could be reeled in and controlled. Failure to get the rope around the snubbing post could result in rope-burned hands or a nasty dragging.

Goodnight loved the energy of these wild horses. They were spotted descendants of Goddogs the Spanish conquistadors had brought to this new world. There had been wild horses in this canyon for as far back as anybody–Human or inhuman–could remember. Goodnight hoped they would be here forever. The Home Ranch cowboys had rounded them up for the carnival, but after it was over, they would let them go again.

When the gate was closed behind the horses, Goodnight watched the bronc-riding contestants start climbing over the fence into the ring. The cowboys who wore guns unbuckled their gunbelts and piled them up before beginning their climb. Goodnight had decided not to enter the competition because he was afraid his cowboys might just let him win. But now he was tempted to change his mind; to take off his gun, climb the fence, and try his luck. He didn't.

"Look who's climbing the fence," Revelie said.

Then she pointed, although she had taught him it wasn't polite. Her husband was glad every time he noticed her adopting Western ways. Following her point, he saw Loving reach the top of the fence and hesitate there. Then he dropped down inside the ring.

"He didn't tell me," Revelie said, "that he was going to ride a wild horse."

"He didn't tell me neither," Goodnight said.

"I suppose he knew I would try to talk him out of it."

Loving appeared to have teamed up with a teenage cowboy who was nicknamed "Flytrap" because he often forgot to close his mouth. All the riders had helpers. The first bronc-buster who rode his wild horse to a standstill would be declared the winner and receive a special belt buckle–designed and struck by Tin Soldier–which depicted a cowboy riding a bucking bronc. Loving glanced up at his boss and the boss's wife, then looked away.

"Sure hope he wins," Goodnight said. "Show these whippersnappers a thing or two."

"I hope he doesn't get hurt," said Revelie.

Goodnight watched until cowboys stopped climbing into the ring. Then he took out his Colt revolver and pointed it up at the pale, cloudless sky. All the cowboys bunched their muscles and looked serious, even grim. All but Loving. Flytrap was so nervous he even shut his mouth.

Then Goodnight pulled the trigger, heard the report of his big

Colt, and watched the cowboys scramble. All but Loving. He took his time and moved with an economy that amounted to elegance.

Goodnight hadn't counted on there being quite so much red dust. The figures inside the corral seemed to be on the other side of a veil. He tried to focus on Loving, but he soon lost him in the dust and confusion.

"Where is he?" asked Revelie anxiously.

"I don't know," he said.

"Oh, there he is!" she said.

"Where?"

"There!" She pointed again. "On the ground! The horse is dragging him! He'll get killed!"

"No, he won't," Goodnight assured his wife. "He knows what he's doin'. But I still don't see him."

"Good, good!"

"What?"

"He's up now." She pointed. "Don't you see him?"

Goodnight tried to stare down her finger as if it were the barrel of a gun. He saw a figure who could possibly be Loving.

"You mean over there by the snubbin' post?" Goodnight asked.

"Yes, yes," Revelie said. "Is he all right?"

"How come you knowed it was him?"

"He's wearing a blue shirt."

"They all got on blue shirts."

"No, they don't."

"Well, most of 'em."

"Theirs are different," she said.

Goodnight looked but he didn't see any difference between Loving's shirt and any of the other blue shirts. Well, leave it to a woman to notice differences in clothes. It was beyond him.

Staring hard into the dust storm, Goodnight could just make out Loving looping his rope around the snubbing post. He was the first cowboy to make this much progress.

"Attaboy," Goodnight muttered.

"He's doing well," said Revelie, "isn't he?"

"I told you he knowed what he was doin'."

Loving and Flytrap were both pulling on the end of the rope that circled the snubbing post once and then ran on out to the wild horse. The post acted as a kind of brake.

"How can they breathe in all this dust?" coughed Revelie.

As if he had heard her, Loving could be seen tugging up his red bandanna to cover his nose. Soon the other cowboys were doing the same. The rodeo began to look like a tournament of outlaws. Loving and Flytrap pulled hard and steady, reeling the horse in.

"Got 'im now," Goodnight mumbled.

"You can do it!" Revelie shouted.

Loving and Flytrap had their horse almost reeled in when another cowboy showed up, tossed his rope over the snubbing post, and started pulling, too. He had a black handkerchief pulled up over his nose. Soon Loving's rope and Black Bandanna's rope got tangled up.

"They should take turns," Revelie said.

Goodnight felt an inner tremor. He didn't like the cowboy with the black mask.

"They're fighting!" coughed Revelie, clutching his arm. "He's down!"

"What? I cain't see."

Of course, Goodnight had expected some fights to break out sooner or later. They always did when this many cowboys got together. Especially if there were females present.

"Good, he's up again," Revelie reported.

Now Goodnight saw Loving, who had gotten his rope untangled from the other and was once again reeling in his wild spotted horse.

"Achew!" sneezed Revelie. "If Flytrap doesn't close his mouth pretty soon, he's going to eat up all our land. Why doesn't he put up his bandanna?"

Now Flytrap was holding the rope, and Loving stood beside the struggling horse trying to throw a saddle on its back. He lifted the saddle and hurled it onto the bronc, but the animal bucked it off. Then Loving pointed at the horse's head and evidently issued an order, but Flytrap shook his head. Loving yelled and pointed emphatically. Goodnight couldn't ever remember seeing his friend so agitated. It didn't suit him.

"What's wrong?" asked Revelie. "What's happening?"

"I dunno," admitted Goodnight.

"It looks as if they're having an argument."

"It sorta does, don't it?"

Now Flytrap, who had clearly lost the argument, was trying to do something to the wild horse's head.

"What it looks like to me," Goodnight said at last, "is Flytrap's tryin' to bite that dang horse's nose."

"Whatever for?" asked Revelie.

"Well, you know a horse's nose is real tender like. And so they say if'n you sink your teeth into it, well, it sorta gentles 'im down. Leastwise till ya let go."

"No!"

Goodnight noticed that the wild bronc was no longer kicking or bucking. Loving picked up his saddle out of the dirt and tossed it up on the horse's back. This time the saddle stayed where it landed. Loving started buckling down the straps. When he was finished, he moved up to the horse's head beside Flytrap.

"He's not going to bite him too," Revelie asked, "is he?"

Loving was buckling on a hackamore, a bridle with no bit. Wild horses didn't like bits. This hackamore had just one rein, a long one.

Goodnight felt a vicarious thrill when he saw Loving put his foot into the stirrup and swing up into the saddle. Flytrap opened his mouth even wider, released the bronc's nose, and stepped back in a big hurry. The wild horse jumped into the air and bowed its back. Loving leaned back to keep his balance and raked the horse's side with his spurs. His right hand was held high over his head while his left fist hung on to the single rein. The horse came down hard, jarring Loving. He hunched over but stayed on. The bronc jumped again and turned in midair. Loving leaned into the turn. He looked as if he had lost his balance, but he hadn't. He knew what he was doing.

"Ride him!" yelled Revelie. "Ride him! Ride him!"

"You got 'im now," breathed Goodnight. "You got 'im."

Loving fell off and lay motionless in the red dirt.

"Oh, no!" cried Revelie. "He's hurt!"

Goodnight didn't say anything, but something hurt inside. He couldn't lose Loving, too. It was his fault. These games had been his idea. Goodnight thought he saw Loving move. Yes, he was moving, a second Adam coming to life in the dirt, apparently made out of dirt himself. Red dirt. It felt like a miracle. Goodnight hadn't killed his "brother" after all. Loving was actually getting to his feet.

"Is he going to be all right?" asked Revelie.

"I sure hope so," said her husband.

Goodnight felt weak–as if he himself had suffered some sort of fall–as he watched Loving limp over to the snubbing post and fetch his rope. Then he started chasing the horse that had run off with his saddle.

Goodnight felt uneasy when another rider, a cowboy who worked for the O Bar O, swung up into the saddle. This O Bar O hand seemed to know what he was doing, too. Goodnight tried to follow them both, the one cowboy in the saddle, the other still pursuing his.

"I didn't think it was going to be like this," Revelie said.

"It never is," said Goodnight.

He saw that Loving had shaken off his limp and was once again moving with an absolute minimum of motion. The rope whirling around his head seemed to spin itself. Then it took off on its own and settled over the head and shoulders of the running horse. Flytrap appeared out of the dust and helped Loving hold on to the rope. Their high-heeled boots skidded in the red dirt. The horse got tired of dragging them and stopped.

Goodnight willed Loving to hurry. Come on. Get up there. Ride that thing. And yet at the same time, he wished his friend were out of the ring and standing safely beside him.

Goodnight felt the excitement again and the pain too when Loving swung up into the saddle once more. The wild horse jumped as high as it could and kicked out at some invisible enemy. Loving was using his spurs, trying to show the horse who was boss, but the animal had a few things to show the rider as well. The cowboy lurched from side to side like a willow in a twister. Goodnight had always thought of his friend as wiry, but now he seemed almost delicate. Wouldn't he break? How much more punishment could he take?

"I wish it were over," Revelie said. "I don't care who wins. I just don't want him to get hurt."

Goodnight lost Loving for a moment in the dust storm. When his horse reappeared, the saddle was empty. Loving was down again. Worse! He had his left foot caught in his stirrup and he was being dragged along beneath the horse. He was being trampled and couldn't get away. The bronc's right rear hoof just barely missed Loving's head.

No! The dragged man wasn't Loving. Thank God! It was the O Bar O cowboy. He had on a blue shirt, too. Loving was still all right. Still in the saddle.

The rest of the crowd went quiet. Not even the buggy springs squeaked. Goodnight stopped being glad about Loving and started worrying about the O Bar O boy. The frightened horse couldn't help stepping on him again and again. The other cowboys in the ring ran for their ropes, had to untangle them, and then threw them at the bronc. But they weren't having any luck. They kept bumping into each other, and their lassos tangled with each other in midair.

"*Achew!*" sneezed poor Revelie.

Then Goodnight saw Loving ride out of a red cloud right beside the deadly horse. The rancher hadn't exactly forgotten about his friend, but his concerns had shifted. Now suddenly Goodnight was frightened for them both, for he could see what Loving was trying to do. His reckless friend was attempting to grab the rein of one bucking bronc while he was still riding another bucking bronc. He was trying not only to ride the whirlwind but to ride it to the rescue.

"What's he doing!" screamed Revelie. "*Achew!*"

"He knows what he's . . . "

Goodnight didn't finish the sentence because he realized that he wasn't at all sure that his friend knew what he was doing. Loving gripped the pommel of his saddle with his right hand and reached down with his left trying to grasp the trailing rein of the runaway horse. He almost had it when his own horse bucked and he missed. He tried again, bending down lower, leaning even farther out of the saddle. His bronc seemed to recognize his moment of maximum vulnerability, for it gave a great leap and wheeled in the air. Loving's right foot came up out of his stirrup and he lost his seat completely. He clung to his gyrating mount with one foot and one hand.

Somehow Loving managed to pull himself back onto the horse's back. Goodnight realized how strong this delicate figure must be. Of course, strength wasn't all muscles. Loving fought to get his loose foot back in the stirrup, and he fought the horse for control. He jerked the bronc's head back in the direction he was determined to go, and he spurred him. The bucking bronc turned too abruptly and crashed against the runaway horse. Both animals stumbled. They were falling. Loving pitched forward, falling, too. But the horses somehow got their legs back under them and came back up again. When Loving came up, he had the runaway rein in his hand.

Once the two wild horses were tied together, Loving holding the rein of each, they both began to calm down. They bucked and kicked a few more times, each time weaker than the last, and then just stood there shivering.

Cowboys on the ground rushed forward to free the O Bar O cowboy's foot from the stirrup.

"He did it," said Revelie.

"He sure 'nough did," Goodnight said proudly, shaking his head.

Revelie sneezed again and then cried. Her face was still wet from tears when her husband helped her down off the chuck wagon. Then the two of them climbed the rail fence and entered the dusty arena. Revelie kept sneezing, but she recovered in time to present a prize buckle to the winner of the bronco-busting contest.

"Congratulations," Revelie said, and then she hugged and tried to kiss Loving, but she sneezed in the middle of the kiss.

Goodnight noticed that all the cowboys were looking at Loving in a different way now.

67

Goodnight—who used to enjoy riding the calves at the family fort back when he was a kid—would have loved to enter the bull-riding contest. But instead, he would be the timer. Whoever stayed on the longest would be the winner. Nobody could stay on a bull until it got tired and stopped bucking. Bulls simply weren't breakable.

Just getting on the bull in the first place would be anything but easy. To make it at least possible, Goodnight had improvised a contraption that looked like a big box or a very small pen. The Home Ranch cowboys set it up just inside the gate of the corral. It was barely big enough for one bull at a time with almost no wiggle room at all. Which was the point.

Goodnight waved his hat in the air, which was the signal to drive the first bull over. The huge stud longhorn entered the wings that funneled him down to the open gate where the box awaited him. The bull hesitated, but the cowboys behind him were yelling. Simon was even cracking his whip. Choosing the lesser of evils, the bull entered the box. As soon as the longhorn was all the way inside, a cowboy slammed a gate closed behind him. The bull could be heard banging around inside the box, but he soon discovered that he wasn't accomplishing anything and settled down. So far so good, thought Goodnight.

Then a tall, rangy cowboy from the Matador Ranch climbed the side of the box and started easing himself down on the bull. He had his bandanna pulled up over his nose outlaw-fashion because he knew he was about to kick up a lot of dust. Goodnight watched the Matador cowboy work his hand under a rope that was wrapped around the bull just behind his front legs. When the contestant was finally ready, he nodded to a cowboy on the ground. This cowboy swung open a gate on the side of the box, so the bull came out sideways and immediately started bucking and wheeling in a wicked circle. The cowboy had his left arm high in the air while his right hand clung to the rope tied around the bull. He was doing surprisingly well for a big man. Glancing down at his gold watch, Goodnight saw that the cowboy had been on the bull's back for four seconds and counting . . .

Glancing back up, Goodnight saw that the Matador hand was now in trouble. He was trying to lean into the turns–"into the well," as the cowboys called it–but the bull was turning faster than he could lean. Instead of leaning in, he was leaning out. He couldn't help it. The force generated by the bull's spinning motion was too much for him. It was the same force conjured up by a spinning rope. When you let the rope go, it would fly. And when the Matador cowboy let go, he flew, too. He landed hard on his back. Six seconds.

The bull wheeled and attacked the prostrate cowboy. The furious animal butted the man and tried to hook him. The tall, lanky cowpoke didn't try to get up, but instead started rolling toward the corral fence. The bull kept butting him as he rolled. When he finally reached the fence, the cowboy rolled right under the bottom rail to safety.

While a dozen cowboys raced to see if the bull-rider was all right, Goodnight himself climbed down off his perch on the chuck wagon. He wanted to see for himself how badly this man had been hurt. He blamed himself. Maybe he should call off this bull-riding contest. He promised himself that if the fallen cowboy were badly injured, he would end it right now.

By the time Goodnight reached the crowd, the Matador hand was already up on his feet, brushing the red dust off his torn clothes. He had what looked like an embarrassed grin on his face.

"You hurt bad?" asked Goodnight.

"Reckon I'll be okay one a these days," the cowboy drawled. "But that's more than I can say for my hat."

Goodnight looked around for the hat and discovered that it was still inside the corral where the bull was wreaking vengeance on it. Stamping. Goring. Slobbering all over it. Killing it over and over.

"I'll buy you a new hat," Goodnight said.

"Thanks but no thanks," said the cowboy. "I reckon I better buy my own hats. I'll be okay. Don't worry none 'bout me."

But Goodnight *was* worried. Not just about the bull-rider but about his bull-riding contest. He could see that it was more dangerous than he had imagined. Goodnight realized he had either to call off the competition or to come up with a way to make it safer. But how could he ever make a wild longhorn bull less dangerous? Then Goodnight surprised himself by coming up with an idea almost at once. The inspiration came from the name of the ranch on which that first bull-rider worked. The Matador.

"We gotta do somethin'," Goodnight announced. "We cain't have bulls pickin' on boys when they're down. So I figure we need some bullfighters. Boys who'll git the bulls to up and charge them insteada the riders. Maybe wave somethin' red. I reckon I'm callin' for volunteers."

Goodnight looked over the crowd that surrounded him. At first, it appeared that none of the cowboys wanted such a dangerous job, but then Too Short raised his hand. Then Flytrap put his hand up, too. Soon other hands went in the air as well. One was a very familiar hand.

"Less see," Goodnight said. "How about Too Short and Flytrap? You boys got anything red?"

"I'll do it," said Loving.

"I'd rather have Too Short and Flytrap."

"I'll do it."

"Okay, suit yourself," said Goodnight who couldn't say no to his friend. "You and Too Short. Flytrap'll hafta miss the fun this time around."

He watched his two designated bullfighters trot off to the bunkhouse in search of something red to serve as a cape. Then he ambled back in the direction of his place atop the chuck wagon. He found Revelie on the ground waiting for him.

"What happened?" she asked. "Did you cancel it?"

Goodnight hadn't even realized that his wife knew he was debating calling off the bull-riding. That was the great thing about being married for years. You knew each other's thoughts.

"No," Goodnight said. "Loving's gonna play matador, him and Too Short. They're gonna make the bulls chase them so's the riders can git away. So I reckon it'll be okay."

"What?" Revelie asked sharply. "I suppose you were the one who thought of this brilliant plan."

"I reckon I did," Goodnight said.

"You go to all the trouble to bring your friend back–you go all that way–and then you do your best to get him killed. I don't understand you. I really don't."

The husband and wife were standing side by side on the chuck wagon once again when Too Short and Loving emerged from the bunkhouse carrying globs of red. Goodnight couldn't make out what the globs were until they got closer. As they were climbing the corral fence, he recognized a faded red shirt in Loving's hand, but Too Short's cape remained a mystery. He had it all balled up. When Goodnight finally solved the puzzle, he chuckled to himself.

"This isn't funny," Revelie said.

"Don't you see what he's got hold of?" Goodnight asked. "His long underwear."

The husband noticed that his wife still didn't smile. Too Short's long johns were more pink than red. Evidently, the cowboy did occasionally scrub his underclothes, contrary to popular opinion, anyhow enough to fade them.

Goodnight took out his gold watch as another bull was driven through the gate and into the box. Then he saw a cowboy with his mouth open climbing the side of the chute. That was just like Flytrap. If he couldn't be a bullfighter, then he would be a bull-rider. Well, good luck. But the man Goodnight really wished good luck was the cowboy who had taken Flytrap's place as a matador.

"Hold up!" Goodnight yelled. "Just hold your horses."

Hurrying down off his wagon, he climbed into the ring. He walked over to the bull box–the chute–and looked between the railings at the longhorn. The huge animal seemed to be about to lose his temper.

"Excuse me, Chief Bull," Goodnight said in English even though he figured the Human tongue might work better. But he hadn't talked Human for a long time now and was rusty. He would just have to do the best he could with his mother tongue. "I have a favor to ask."

The bull looked directly at him. The cowboys were looking at him, too, with puzzled expressions. He just hoped they didn't laugh.

"This is just a game we're fixin' to play here," Goodnight told the bull. "This here cowboy's gonna jump on your back. And you're gonna pitch him off. And that'll be that. See? We're not gonna hurt you. And I'd sure appreciate it if you didn't hurt none of us. See? And then you can just go your own way back to your cows and your reg'lar life's work. No harm done, right? None to you. And none to us. I figured I'd better explain this to you or you might take it the wrong way and git after somebody. Fair enough? Whaddaya say?"

Goodnight stared at the bull and the bull stared back. Was he getting through? Had he struck the right tone with his voice? He realized how long it had been since he tried talking to an animal.

"That's about all I've got to say," Goodnight said. "I sure hope you'll think it over. We ain't gonna hurt you and you ain't gonna hurt us. I sure hope we got ourselves a deal."

Then Goodnight turned around and headed back to Revelie where he belonged.

68

Goodnight saw Flytrap nod that he was ready to ride, felt Revelie's hand tighten on his arm just below his biceps, sensed another tightening inside his gut. The chute door swung wide and the bull came out sideways, bucking and twisting. Goodnight wondered what it was about this part of the country that conjured up spinning disasters: dust devils that actually weren't so bad, tornados that could take away all you owned in an instant, and bucking bulls that could cripple or kill you. He glanced down at his watch, where the hands moved in a circle, time the worst spinner of them all, time the one that would always get you even if the others didn't. Such gloomy thoughts made his head spin.

"Flytrap still has his mouth open," Revelie observed. "I wonder what it would take to close it."

"No tellin'," said Goodnight.

But he thought he would probably have to close it if Flytrap got himself killed. Consulting his gold watch, Goodnight saw that Flytrap had been on the bull for seven seconds now. He had already beaten the time of the first rider. Old Flytrap might just win this dad-gum event. Goodnight told himself that he was likely to have to revise his impression of this open-mouthed cowboy.

"Eight seconds," Goodnight muttered.

"Come on, Flytrap," said Revelie. "Oh, no!"

Goodnight knew from experience that head-first falls were among the worst. Poor Flytrap lost his balance and dove right between the bull's sharp horns. On the way, the unfortunate cowboy probably busted his balls up against his own fist, which clung to the rope. Flytrap lay on his back with his hands between his legs, clutching the pain.

Goodnight saw the bull round on Flytrap. Saw a masked Loving run between the horns and the fallen cowboys. Saw a red shirt waving. Saw the bull change targets, forget about the cowboy on the ground, and charge Loving instead.

"No! No! No!" cried Revelie.

The wife was gripping her husband's arm tighter than ever now. Her fingernails hurt him. He was glad they hurt. He deserved to be hurt. He was responsible for the race taking place in the ring. Loving only had to get as far as the fence, which was just a few steps away. Goodnight felt as if he himself were dream-running.

"Thank God!" said Revelie.

Loving didn't so much climb the fence as run right up it. The crowd cheered and clapped, and Revelie released her grip on her husband's arm.

Goodnight was beginning to relax when he saw the bull turn and charge Flytrap once more. The cowboy was still flat on his back with his mouth open. Then Too Short appeared in the bull's path. He held his red long johns by the shoulders and shook them at the bull. The long underwear looked a little like another man, an assistant who was helping Too Short with his bullfighting. This red man danced in the face of death, really kicked up his heels. Of course, he wasn't a very modest man. Why didn't he put on some clothes? The bull charged the red man, butted him, gored him, carried him away on his horns.

"Hey, come back with my underwear!" Too Short shouted. "Hey, you stole my long johns!"

The crowd roared with laughter. After the tension, they appreciated the humor. Goodnight laughed along with the others, and he heard Revelie laughing, too.

"Come back here!"

Too Short actually chased the bull to get his long underwear back. Goodnight couldn't help admiring his bravery and his sense of humor, even though a little less of both would have been the wiser policy.

The longhorn gave his insubstantial victim a final toss high in the air and then let him float lifelessly to the red earth. Then the animal turned and looked for somebody else to kill.

The bull soon found Flytrap once again, who was now on his feet limping toward the fence. He pawed the earth a couple of times and then charged. Flytrap tried to run, but he was too crippled up by his bruising ride and fall.

Too Short ran in front of the bull's horns once more, reached down, grabbed his long johns off the ground, and threw them in the bull's face.

"He's making him mad," Revelie said. "I don't know if that's such a good idea."

"He always was short on brains along with ever'thing else," Goodnight grumbled.

Blinded by the red underwear, the bull stopped, and Flytrap made it to the fence. But Too Short didn't even try for safety. He was having too much fun to stop now. He stood in the middle of the corral and watched as the bull shook his head back and forth. When the red blindfold fell to the ground, the bull trampled it.

"Stop that!" Too Short yelled, pulling down his mask. "Them long johns've gotta last me all winter!"

Reminded of Too Short's existence, the bull turned, stared, and wondered what a man was doing standing there evidently unafraid. The longhorn charged. It was another footrace to the fence, but luckily Too Short had a good head start. He could run pretty fast on those short legs. He was running right at Goodnight, showing off for the boss, when he grabbed his leg and pitched forward on his face.

"Oh, no!" cried Revelie.

Too Short seemed to have pulled a muscle in mid-flight. Now he was down in the red dirt, like the trampled long johns. He was so close that Goodnight could smell his fear. Loving came running from his place on the sidelines.

"No!" shouted Revelie.

Both he and the bull converged upon the fallen cowboy.

"Stop it!" begged Revelie. "Don't let it happen."

Goodnight saw Loving pick up Too Short in his arms as if he were a baby. Saw the bull bearing down on them both. Saw Loving stop, not even trying to run because he knew it was too late, wanting to meet the danger head-on. Some instincts died hard. This one was about to.

Goodnight couldn't believe that he was so close and yet couldn't help. He felt impotent, useless, stupid. He couldn't just let it happen right there in front of him.

"Stop!" screamed Goodnight. *"Stop right now!"*

The bull stopped. Anyway, he tried to. He stiffened his front legs and sat down on his haunches. He still bumped into Loving and Too Short and knocked them down, but then the huge longhorn just stood over them as if protecting them. Loving and Too Short crawled out from under him. Then Loving picked up Too Short like a sack of flour and carried him from the ring. The bull just watched them go.

In the end, the O Bar O cowboy won the bull-riding contest. He was a fast healer. Revelie presented him with a buckle.

69

Only two buffalo-riders remained.

The Home Ranch cowboys had been lucky in locating a small herd and rounding up a half-dozen males. Loving, the next-to-last contestant, gracefully scaled the chute wall. So far, the longest ride had lasted just five seconds. Buffalos weren't as big as longhorn bulls, but they were harder to ride. They had odd-shaped bodies, all humps and slopes and curious angles. You couldn't even tie a rope around a buffalo to hang on to because it wouldn't stay on. The riders simply dug their fingers into the long fur of the hump and hung on for dear life.

Goodnight watched his friend settle on the furry back. A masked Loving nodded, the gate opened, and the buffalo swung out sideways. Goodnight was really jealous now: he couldn't think of anything better than riding a buffalo, except maybe flying on the back of a bald eagle and seeing what this red canyon looked like from on high. Somehow the eagle and the buffalo were tied together in his mind, probably because the Humans had such a high regard for both.

Then Goodnight saw Loving flying, but not on the back of anything. He sailed through the air, hit the fence, bounced off, and hit the ground. Goodnight looked down at his watch. Loving had ridden for ten seconds.

"Ten seconds," Goodnight shouted.

"He's the best!" Revelie said, so excited she forgot to worry if he was hurt.

"The best yet. There's one more rider."

"Nobody can beat ten seconds."

"I expect you're right, but less see."

Goodnight studied the next rider. He remembered this cowboy. It was the same one who had fought with Loving at the snubbing post during the bronc-riding. He recognized the black bandanna. As the black-masked rider lowered himself onto the buffalo's back, Goodnight examined him carefully.

"Revelie, you ever seen that there cowboy before?" Goodnight asked.

"I don't think so," she said. "Should I have? Who is he?"

"I don't rightly know, but I wisht I did."

"Why?"

"I ain't sure."

"Oh, I know who he is."

"Who!"

"The Black Knight."

"What?"

"Nothing. It was a joke."

The gate of the box swung open, and the buffalo bull charged into the center of the arena. Not wanting to take his eye off the rider long enough to glance at his watch, Goodnight counted in his head. One thousand one. One thousand two. One thousand three. Black Mask pitched forward. Good. He was going over the head. But, no, he saved himself, pulled himself back from the brink, a real feat of strength. One thousand four. One thousand five. One thousand six. Who was this guy anyway? Where had he come from? What was he? The crowd was thunderously cheering him on, but Revelie wasn't clapping. The Black Knight clung to the buffalo bull like a grass bur. One thousand seven. One thousand eight. Goodnight jumped into the air as he saw the black-masked cowboy falling sideways. Yes! Right! But again the unknown cowboy's strength saved him. He righted himself and rode on. One thousand nine. One thousand ten. No! No!! The Black Knight lurched but didn't fall. One thousand eleven. One thousand twelve. One thousand thirteen. One thousand fourteen. The spectators were going crazy. This was amazing! This was historic!

"Stop him!" Revelie cried.

"I cain't," Goodnight said. "I wisht I could."

Then the buffalo bull stopped it. He quit bucking and came to a complete stop. He was breathing hard. He was broken. The black-masked cowboy had done the impossible.

A roar went up from the ring of wagons and buggies. They loved it, and they all wanted an answer to the same question: Who was he?

"We better go find out who in hell he is," Goodnight said.

"Our friend's ride was much more graceful," Revelie said. "That should count for something."

"Well, it don't, maybe next year."

Goodnight climbed down off the chuck wagon and then helped Revelie down. They climbed over the rail fence–she being Boston-careful of her skirts–into the arena. He hurried toward the spot where he had last seen the Black Knight, on the far side of the corral, but when he arrived, he didn't see the winner. Goodnight looked around at Revelie, but she shrugged, just as mystified as he was.

"Where'd he go?" yelled Goodnight.

Nobody answered.

"Where the hell did he go?"

Nothing.

"The last rider is the winner. Will the winner please step forward."

Nobody stepped forward.

"Will the winner please step forward?"

Nobody did.

"Hell!"

Goodnight looked down and saw an "RR" scratched in the red dust of the rodeo arena.

70

After the shock, after a fruitless search for the cowboy with the black kerchief, Goodnight sat under a chinaberry tree, shaken. Loving squatted beside him. Now Goodnight wished the rodeo were already over, but there was still one event left on the schedule: the shoot-out.

"You're a good shot," Loving said over his coffee cup, the steam distorting his features. "Why don't you try your luck?"

"I figure you're a better shot than me," Goodnight said. "Just be a waste a time and lead."

"No, I seen you shoot. You handle a gun right purdy."

Goodnight was tempted, but he still figured he had better stay out of it. He had invited the others here and so owed them their fun. He shouldn't interfere.

"Well, I ain't so sure I could trust you," Goodnight said at last.

"What?" Loving looked hurt. "What's got into you, Goodnight?"

"I mean I'm afraid you'd up 'n' let me win. That's no fun."

"What give you that idea?"

"I know you. That's all."

"You mean 'cause you stopped that there bull in its tracks? You figure I'd be so grateful I'd–"

"No–"

"Well, look who's a comin'," Loving interrupted. "Less ask her what she thinks?"

Goodnight looked up and saw Revelie walking toward them, followed by several other women. He couldn't believe that Loving had seen her first. He was normally so aware of her, so attuned to her, that he always knew right where she was and what she was doing. And yet now she had managed to slip up on him without even trying.

"How do, Miz Revelie," Loving called. "We got a problem we'd like your opinion on."

Responding to his summons, Mrs. Goodnight hurried her step. She left the other women behind.

"What may I do for you?" Revelie asked when she reached the men.

"Your husband here wants to git in on the shoot-out," Loving said. "Look, it's wrote all over his face. And if you ask me, he needs some fun to take his mind off that there outlaw. This here shootin' match is just the ticket for perkin' him up."

"Then he should do it," said Revelie.

"But I'm the host."

"But this is the last event, isn't it? I believe it would be all right. Don't you, Mr. Loving?"

"Course. Less go."

The contestants and the spectators–women, cowboys, kids, and dogs–walked in a herd along the bank of the river. They stopped when they reached a bluff that overhung the water. It would supply shade as well as a backstop for the bullets. Goodnight didn't want any stray lead flying off down the canyon and killing any of his cattle, or anything else for that matter.

In front of the bluff, they found the shooting gallery already set up. Fat cedar logs had been sawed up into sections about six feet long. Then these sections were stood on end so they looked like overfed fence posts. There were six of them in a row. Goodnight had decided on the posts as a precaution to absorb as much lead as possible. Bull's-eyes had already been nailed to the posts at about the height of a man's heart.

Goodnight explained the rules: Six gunmen at a time would take their place behind a line drawn in the red sand of the riverbank. Revelie had volunteered to act as starter. She would drop her handkerchief, and when it touched the ground, the gunmen could draw and begin blazing away. The last man still shooting would be disqualified no matter how accurately his bullets hit the target. The rest would be ranked according to their marksmanship. The shooter with the highest score in each group would qualify for the next round. In the finals, the rules would change . . .

Six gunmen lined up, their legs spread slightly for good balance, crouching, their hands nervously quivering over the handles of their guns. They were all from other spreads because Goodnight believed in letting guests go first. Revelie stood off to the side down by the river. The six gunmen were all staring at her more intently than was normally polite. She raised a white, embroidered, Boston handkerchief–held it about shoulder-high–and then let it drop.

When the handkerchief touched the earth, the gunmen drew and started firing. Goodnight started worrying about his herd. He hadn't really stopped to think through how frightened they might be by all this racket. He pictured his longhorns running themselves silly up and down the canyon, confused by the echoes.

71

Looking down at his boot, Goodnight saw that the previous shooters had trampled the line into obscurity. He had to more or less guess where he was supposed to stand. He stood back a little farther than he probably had to. He adjusted his feet to about shoulder-width. He bent his knees slightly and crouched. His surprisingly nervous fingers hung two inches above the ivory handle of his big gun. He told himself that relaxation was a gunslinger's best friend, but telling and calming down were two different things. Especially when he was worried about letting Revelie down and about living up to Loving's high opinion of him.

Sensing that the others were ready and just waiting for him, Goodnight raised his head and looked at his wife. She gave him a nice smile, which made him even more nervous. She looked wonderful, but her handkerchief was thoroughly dirty by now. It was red through and through and looked like the flag of war. The crimson war flag took flight. As he watched its descent, Goodnight's fingers on his gun hand twitched involuntarily. When he saw it kiss the red earth, he hesitated because he didn't want anyone to believe he had gotten a head start. He didn't go for his gun until he saw the other shooters drawing theirs. Then he reached down and the big six-shooter jumped into his hand like an eager puppy. His peripheral vision registered a fanner to his right, but he wasn't tempted to follow suit. He thumbed back his hammer. With his gun held about belly-button–high, Goodnight stared hard at the target with his one eye. He imagined that the cedar post was Gudanuf. Pointing the barrel as if it were his finger, Goodnight remembered to squeeze rather than pull the trigger. He heard the lead thump wood, so at least he had hit the cedar post. Had hit Gudanuf. Maybe not in the heart, but he was hurting. Then Goodnight heard somebody else's bullet whistle as it ricocheted off a rock and went out looking for a cow to kill. Still pointing his metal finger, he thumbed back the hammer again, squeezed the trigger again, and heard another thump. He kept on until he was out of bullets. Each time, he heard a satisfying thump. Gudanuf wasn't having a very good day.

Goodnight let his arm drop to his side. Looking around, he saw two other gunmen with their firearms still up, so he wasn't last, anyway. Now if he had only managed to hit the paper target, Gudanuf's heart. Goodnight glanced over at his wife, who gave him another one of her brilliant smiles. He liked the smile, but her presence made waiting for the scores even more difficult. He hated the thought of losing in her eyes.

When Too Short read out the scores, it turned out that Goodnight was the only gunman to hit his target all six times. None were in the bull's-eye, but he won his heat. The husband enjoyed his wife's broad smile. She still had the purdiest smile he had ever seen in his whole life. He appreciated Loving's pleased grin as well.

"Nice shooting," Revelie called from her post by the river. "I'm proud of you."

Goodnight thought: Why did she have to go and say that? First of all, it was embarrassing. But the worst part was that he would be all the more nervous next time he stepped up to shoot. If winning made her proud of him, what would losing do?

Loving joined the final group of shooters. As Revelie raised the red handkerchief, Goodnight noticed that Loving stood straight up. He didn't crouch the way all the other gunmen had done. His feet were close together rather than spread for balance. His elbow was straight rather than bent. His right hand hung limp below his gun. He did not look like a man about to draw his weapon.

When the red handkerchief touched the red dust, Loving casually raised his hand and his pistol rocked backward into his palm. He didn't raise his gun as high as Goodnight had. He seemed to be firing as soon as the barrel cleared the holster. He was the first to finish shooting and lower his gun.

When Too Short announced the results, Loving had of course won easily with the highest score of the day. Goodnight was glad his friend had done so well. He was impressed all over again. And he could tell that Revelie was impressed, too. Goodnight couldn't help being a little jealous, even though he was still glad for his friend.

Too Short studied his dusty bookkeeping for a few moments and then called off the names of the eight gunmen who had qualified for the next round of the competition, the semifinals. The shoot-off would be held in two heats of four shooters each. The same rules would apply as before: the slowest shooter would be disqualified, while the best marksman moved on to the finals. Flytrap got a sharp-pointed stick and redrew the line in the red earth.

"First group," yelled Too Short.

"Who's that?" a cowboy asked.

"Don't matter," said the judge. "Whoever. But step on it."

Goodnight and Loving looked at each other. Loving nodded in the direction of the line. Stepping forward, Goodnight could feel his fingers involuntarily twitching again. Revelie dropped her handkerchief and Goodnight started firing. Squinting with his one good eye, imagining the gunbarrel to be his metal finger, he pointed and fired, fired, fired . . .

"It's close," Too Short shouted, "but high score goes to Mr. Goodnight."

There was a smattering of applause. He figured the hand-clapping would probably have been a little louder if one of the regular cowboys had won the round.

Seeing Loving step forward to take his place on the firing line, Goodnight stopped thinking about himself and admired his friend. Goodnight had to admit that Loving was without doubt the best cowboy he had ever seen in his life. It wouldn't be any disgrace to lose to such a man. Besides, Loving had two good eyes and it sometimes seemed as if he had even more the way they kept changing colors.

The handkerchief flew and so did the lead. Loving fired so rapidly that his gun was already hanging down at his side while the other gunmen were still lining up their third and fourth shots. Now Goodnight realized that he had no chance.

Too Short examined the targets and announced what was already obvious to everybody. The clapping for Loving was louder and longer than it had been for Goodnight. The rancher heard in this applause a preview of the ovation yet to come. Loving's victory over him would be a popular one. He was the champion the crowd wanted. He was a top hand but still a hand, and his win would be shared vicariously by all the other hands. Goodnight himself and his wife would be the only ones pulling for him to win. He looked at her, needing to be cheered up by one of her smiles, but he found her looking at Loving.

"Somebody better 'splain the new rules," Too Short called.

"Revelie, you're good at 'splainin'," Goodnight said.

"All right, these are the rules for the last round of the competition," Revelie said in a clear, loud voice. "Can you hear me?"

There was a muttered response: yes, they could hear, get on with it, let's go, hurry up.

"There are just two contestants left," announced Revelie. "This time, one of them will shoot, then the other will shoot. They will take turns. Very good manners."

The onlookers laughed.

"Tell 'em about the hankie," prompted her husband.

"Oh, that's right. As soon as I drop my handkerchief, the first marksman will start firing at the target. He must stop shooting when the kerchief hits the ground. His score will be recorded. Then the next marksman will step forward. And we will repeat the process."

Goodnight walked over to the riverbank to talk to his wife.

"Honey, why don't you rustle up a clean hankie," Goodnight suggested. "That un's so dirty, it drops just like a clod. I need all the time I can git."

"All right, I will," Revelie said. "Good luck. I never realized you were such a good shot. No, that's not quite what I mean. I knew you were good, but I didn't know you were the best."

Goodnight was caught off guard. He had impressed his wife. Even after all these years, he could still impress her. He felt a warm sense of pleasure until he saw his vision blur. That was all he needed right now. How could he shoot straight with tears in his one hardworking eye?

"I mayn't be the best," Goodnight said.

"Then one of the two best," Revelie said.

Goodnight sort of wished that she hadn't given up quite so quickly. Well, never mind. It was time to go shoot.

Turning away, Goodnight almost ran into Loving. What was he doing there? How long had he been standing there? What had he heard? Could his friend see the tears in his eye?

"Too Short wants to know how many targets," Loving said. "One or two. I tol' him just one on account of we ain't gonna be shootin' at the same time, but he said check with you."

"One's fine," Goodnight said.

Then Goodnight had an idea. His wife's good offices had been used to persuade him to enter the shoot-out, so now perhaps she could be employed once again to make sure it was a fair contest.

"Miz Goodnight, how 'bout doin' me a favor?" her husband asked.

"Certainly, Mr. Goodnight," his wife said with elaborate courtesy.

"Make Loving promise to do his best."

"Are you still worried he may let you win?"

"I don't wanna win that way."

"All right, Mr. Loving," Revelie turned and faced the graceful cowboy, "you must promise to beat my husband. Is that understood? He won't have it any other way."

"Yes, ma'am," Loving said and tipped his hat. "Cross my heart."

The two men turned and headed back toward their firing positions.

"You go first?" Goodnight said.

"No thanks," said Loving.

"It's your turn to go first."

"Ain't no turn about it. You shoot first. I'll go after."

"No, you're first." Goodnight realized that he sounded like a boy having an argument with another boy in a schoolyard, but for some reason he was determined to have his way. "I mean it."

"I thought this here party was supposed to be for me," Loving said. "The fatted calf and gittin' my way–that's what I counted on. Was I wrong?"

"No, you're right."

Goodnight stepped up to the line.

"Ready?" called Revelie.

"You bedder come a little closer," Goodnight said, "so's I can see you and the bull's-eye at the same time."

"All right," she said, "just don't shoot me."

"I'll try hard not to," he said.

Revelie moved farther from the riverbank and closer to the line of fire. She came slowly.

"How about here?" she asked.

"A little more," he said.

So she came on.

"Right there," he said.

Revelie stopped and smiled. She stood to his right and a little in front of him about ten feet away. She wasn't in any danger, or he wouldn't have let her stand there, so long as he didn't miss his aim by a dozen feet.

"Ready?" she asked again.

When Goodnight nodded, Revelie released a newly borrowed white handkerchief, which began its butterfly flight. The husband had to force himself to look away from his wife in order to shoot. The big Colt jumped into his hand. Feeling the smooth ivory handle against his palm calmed him. Goodnight pointed and squeezed, first shot. Take that, Gudanuf. He saw that the handkerchief had already fluttered down to his wife's waist. Again he pointed and squeezed, second shot, wanting to impress Revelie. Again, third shot, wanting to impress Loving, which didn't make any sense and yet it did. Point, squeeze, fourth shot. The white blur in his peripheral vision touched the ground.

"Stop!" yelled Too Short.

Goodnight lowered his gun. Then he half-turned and looked directly at Revelie, who was smiling at him. He watched her bend and retrieve the white handkerchief, which was now embroidered in red. He turned and found Loving standing behind him. He realized that in locating his wife and his friend, he was checking the points of his compass.

"Nice shootin'," said Loving.

"We'll see," said Goodnight.

"Bull's-eye!" yelled Too Short.

Goodnight wheeled around to face his target. He couldn't have heard right. But everybody was clapping all around him and this time more warmly.

"Plum in the middle," Too Short shouted. "Best goddamned shot all day."

"Don't cuss," said Goodnight.

"You cuss."

"Not in mixed company."

"Do too."

"Well, I shouldn't ought to."

Everybody laughed while Too Short studied the target more carefully. He circled all the bullet holes. Then he turned around and cleared his throat loudly.

"One smack in the center, bull's-eye, like I done said," Too Short reported. "One in the second ring. Two in the fourth."

Goodnight was amazed. Now that he had shot so well, he found it hard to look at anybody. Success made him shy, or rather shier. He glanced at Revelie, but his restless eye wouldn't stay. He didn't look at

Loving at all. He was somehow embarrassed by what he had done. Then he sensed Loving moving forward to shoot. Now Goodnight finally looked up and briefly met the glance of his friend.

"Remember your promise," Goodnight muttered.

"Sure thing," Loving said with a laugh.

Then the graceful cowboy walked up to the line and stood as nonchalantly as if he were at the bar in a Tascosa saloon waiting to be served. Goodnight wondered how his friend achieved the effect. It had something to do with the hands hanging relaxed at his sides. But it was more than just hands and fingers. It was his whole posture. But it was more still. It was his point of view, his way of meeting the world, his vision of his place in it. Well, who knew what the hell it was? Certainly not Goodnight.

"Ready?" asked Revelie.

The brim of Loving's hat dipped down and then up again. The red-rimmed white handkerchief spread its wings. Loving used the smallest motion to draw his gun and fire. Goodnight counted to himself: One. Two. Three. Four. Five.

"Stop!" ordered Too Short.

The handkerchief landed and the gun seemed to find its own way back into the holster. So Loving was faster than Goodnight was. He had gotten off more shots. But was he more accurate?

The crowd clapped in appreciation of Loving's speed and also because they liked him. This day had made his reputation and his popularity. Again, Goodnight could not help being a little jealous of his best friend on earth.

"You're even faster'n I figured," Goodnight said. "Good goin'."

Loving's hat brim bobbed slightly in acknowledgment of the compliment. He never moved more than he had to. The brim bobbed again when Revelie walked up.

"Congratulations on your quickness," she said. "That was most impressive."

Goodnight was more than a little jealous. He wanted to be the one to impress his wife.

"Thanky, ma'am," said Loving.

They were all turned, like sunflowers, facing the bull's-eye. Too Short was examining it carefully. Goodnight thought he was taking an unusually long time. Finally, he stood up straight and made a racket clearing his throat.

"Three hits," Too Short shouted. "Two in the second ring. One in the third."

Goodnight was stunned. Loving had paid the price of speed: inaccuracy. Two of his bullets had missed the target completely. Who would have thought?

"Why Mr. Goodnight, I believe you've won!" cried Revelie.

She stood right in front of her husband, took both his hands, and squeezed them tightly. She was excited. She obviously hadn't expected him to win, but that was all right. He hadn't expected it either. She looked at him in a way she hadn't in a long time. Anyway, he thought she did.

The crowd was clapping, not as warmly as they would have if their favorite had won, but nonetheless they were making considerable noise.

Goodnight had to admit that he had even impressed himself. He hadn't expected to hit the bull's-eye right in the pupil. He hadn't expected to beat Loving. But then that old fear came back to worry him. Maybe Loving had missed the target twice on purpose. He had never missed before. Why now? Goodnight turned a suspicious eye on his friend.

Would Loving deceive him?

72

The next day after everybody had left, Goodnight and Loving sat on the spacious front porch of the big ranch house cleaning their guns. After the shooting match, there had followed another night of dancing until dawn. Then the guests had piled into their vehicles or climbed on their horses–many not having slept much, if at all, for two days and two nights–and headed for their distant homes. It was all over except the cleaning up, which included the cleaning of firearms. Goodnight and Loving sat on cane-bottomed chairs that were tipped back against the stone wall of the ranch house. Their work was in their laps, which meant they were getting some oil on their clothes.

"You sure you didn't let me win?" asked Goodnight.

"Will you quit pesterin' me about that?" Loving said. "I done tol' you."

"I know, I know, but I still ain't easy in my mind about it. Somethin' seems wrong. Fishy."

"You accusin' me a lyin'? I don't take kindly to bein' called a liar, not even by you."

"I ain't callin' you a liar, not exactly."

"Not exactly!"

"Don't git so touchy. I just wanna be sure. Tell me ag'in."

"Tell you what?"

"You know, tell me you didn't let me win."

"That's right."

"No, say it. Say the whole thing. I wanna hear how you say it. I figure I could tell if you're out-and-out lyin' to me. I know you well 'nough for that."

"Okay, I didn't let you win. How's that? That good 'nough? You believe me now? Or you still think I'm lyin'?"

"I believe you, I reckon. But the hard part's believin' you missed the whole dad-blamed target. Not just oncet but twicet. That ain't like you. Not atall. That's what I cain't figure out. How'd you come to do that? Huh?"

"Do what?"

"Miss the target."

"Oh, that."

"Yeah, that. Can you sit here with a straight face an' tell me you didn't miss the target on purpose?"

"I didn't miss it on purpose. Leave it alone, okay?"

Goodnight tried to take Loving's advice, but he was still troubled by his suspicions. He wanted his win to feel as clean as his gun barrel now looked as he squinted down it. No, wait. It wasn't all that clean. There was one piece of lint way down in there. He couldn't leave it like that. He got out his swab and went to work again.

"So you're sayin' you missed the dad-gum target by accident, right?" Goodnight asked. "Nothin' more, nothin' less."

"No, I ain't sayin' that," said Loving.

"No?"

"No, not exactly. Don't go puttin' words in my mouth."

"Then what are you sayin'?"

"I ain't sayin' nothin'."

"Come on, tell me. Did you accidentally miss the target or didn't you?"

"No."

"No, you didn't miss it accidentally? You missed it on purpose?"

"No, I didn't miss the damn target. Satisfied?"

"What? But–"

"If you don't believe me, go look. See how many bullets hit the damn bull's-eye."

"What–?"

Goodnight laid down his gun, which was still all in pieces, on the floor of the porch. He got up and started walking toward the river. He looked behind, but Loving wasn't following. Goodnight felt an impulse to run, but he restrained it. He simply walked quickly. When he reached the riverbank, he turned left in the direction of the bluff that marked the site of the shoot-out. Once he was out of view of the ranch house, he did quicken his pace to a trot. When he saw the last target, still nailed to its post, Goodnight started running. Reaching the cedar post, he knelt in the red sand beside it.

With his pocket knife, Goodnight dug into the bull's-eye. He winced because the target reminded him of his own gouged-out eye. He was also afraid of what he might find.

He dug out a .45 slug.

Then he dug out another.

And another.

Three bullets in one hole. He was already trying to figure out how he was going to tell Revelie.

"If you tell Revelie," Loving said, "I'm leavin'."

Goodnight hadn't even heard him come up.

73

"You seem different," Revelie said.

The party was over. Husband and wife were lying in bed hugging each other after particularly strenuous lovemaking. Now that their bodies had been reunited so happily, he wanted their minds to be similarly joined. He told himself that this was what he had been waiting for, the "perfect" moment for the telling of secrets.

"I know," Goodnight said. "I feel different. Better."

"It's because Loving has come back," Revelie said.

"That's part of it," he said. "He's back, and my sister's come back, too. Becky's back."

"I don't understand," she said.

"You were right. I shoulda told you this here stuff a long time ago, but I buried it. Got this graveyard in my dang heart. That was wrong. Now I want you to know everything 'bout me. Gonna open up all them graves."

He paused and looked at Revelie, but she didn't say anything.

"It started to happen back when I was ten . . . "

He tried to tell it all just as it had happened, except for the rapes. He didn't think rape stories were fit for a white woman's ears. So he didn't exactly tell her everything because he wanted to protect her from the worst. But he couldn't shield himself. He remembered everything, he relived everything.

Jimmy clashed swords with Becky, knight against knight. Sir Jimmy's broadsword had been hewed out of a cottonwood branch. The hewing consisted of stripping off the bark. Sir Becky's weapon was made of sterner stuff, an oak branch, with the rough bark still on. Their armor was made of homespun cotton, which was the color of butternut. One knight wore baggy pants, the other a shapeless dress. The crash of swords rang out loud in the cool spring morning air, *whack, thwack.* It was the Golden Age: they were ten years old.

"This is the best sword fight ever," shouted Jimmy, who loved swordplay and superlatives.

"Ouch!" yelled Becky. "You hit me!"

"Sorry," Jimmy hissed happily, "but you hit me first."

These medieval knights lived in a hand-hewn family fortress in the middle of the Texas woods. The walls were made of wooden logs, sharpened on top like schoolroom pencils, standing upright side by side. The fort had been built to keep out Indians, but the red man had kept the peace for years. That morning, the only violence that concerned the fort was the battle between two of its own children, a brother and a sister, twins.

"Stoppit!" yelled carrot-topped Becky. "Stoppit! Stoppit!"

Yellow-haired Jimmy stopped his rain of sword strokes, but not because his redheaded sister asked him to. Rather it was because of something he saw. The fort's main gate, which stood wide open, framed a band of Indians. Jimmy glanced from the warriors back to his twin sister, wary of both.

"You're not supposed to hit on the head," Becky complained. "Thass against the rules."

"Hush," Jimmy ordered. "Lookeethere!"

He pointed with his sword at the warriors beyond the gate. His left hand came up and touched the birthmark on his cheek. He almost always reached for it when he was worried about something. It seemed to be the physical manifestation of all his fears, that string of blue dots that looked so much like the Big Dipper.

When Becky finally saw the warriors, she quickly ran behind her brother.

"Act like you ain't ascared," Jimmy warned. "Injuns can smell if you're ascared, like hosses."

When he looked around to see if anyone else had seen the Indians, Jimmy saw women and children running. But he noticed very few men, since most of them were working in the fields at this time of day. Jimmy felt better when he finally saw his father, Silas Goodnight, who had been working indoors, hurrying toward the open gate. Everything would be all right now.

"Daddy!" Jimmy called. "Wait!"

"Daddy!" cried Becky at the same time. "What's wrong?"

Paying no attention, the twins' father rushed past them, followed by their uncle, Ben Goodnight, and their grandfather, Elder John Goodnight. The brother and sister could hear the hurried fear in the men's voices. Then the adults paused, catching their breaths at the threshold of the open gate.

"Guess I better go see what they want," said Uncle Ben.

"I'll watch the gate," said their father, Silas. "Anything goes wrong, you come a runnin'. Unnersand? I'll slam it shut behind you."

"Wait now," said their grandfather, Elder John. "Don't go takin' no chances!"

"Got to, Pa," said Uncle Ben.

Jimmy crossed ten-year-old fingers on both hands. He saw his uncle–looking like a giant from his point of view–walk out through the open gate. And he watched his father take up his position next to the gate that never should have been left open in the first place. He saw his granddaddy fretting.

"What's gonna happen?" asked Becky.

"Shut up!" Jimmy said. "You ask too many questions. Drive a person batty."

Since he was afraid to get mad at the Indians, he got mad at his sister instead.

"I'm sorry," Becky said.

Jimmy watched Uncle Ben trying to communicate with signs and gestures. A hundred mounted warriors were milling about and screaming. Uncle Ben seemed to be addressing a red man who carried a soiled white flag.

Sir Jimmy, the fearless knight, realized he was trembling. The shivering seemed to begin in his pioneer bone marrow and ripple outward to his skin. His whole pioneer heritage told him that he now faced the greatest danger under heaven. He had been brought up to fear wolves . . . but Indians were fiercer. He had been taught to be afraid of snakes . . . but Indians were deadlier. He had been reared to tremble before the devil . . . but to fall into the hands of Indians was worse than going to hell. Indians would cut off your hair, scalp and all. Or they would cut off your balls for the fun of it. Or, the boy reminded himself, there was a good chance they would do both.

Jimmy relaxed a little when he saw Uncle Ben start back toward the fort. The boy stopped shaking and even uncrossed his fingers, which were beginning to hurt. When Uncle Ben finally reached the open gate, he huddled with the twins' father, their heads close. Sir Jimmy dropped his sword and ran toward his daddy. Sir Becky followed right behind.

"Hey, you kids, git back!" yelled their grandfather. "Go hide!"

"No, I want my daddy," whined Jimmy.

"You mind me. Go on!"

"No!"

In exasperation, Elder John Goodnight gave up for the moment and turned to greet his sons, Ben and Silas. The three grown men and two small children now huddled together.

"They're Comanches," said Uncle Ben. "Say they're hungry. Least I think that's what they're sayin'. Believe they want a coupla our cows."

"Ben, we ain't got no cows to spare," complained Elder John. "You know that."

"That's what I told 'em. Anyhow I tried to tell 'em."

"How'd they take it?"

"Not too good, don't look like. I don't trust that damn white flag. Guess I better go back and try talkin' 'em outa makin' trouble."

"No," Elder John said as sternly as he could, "less just lock the damn gate and . . ."

"I got to or there's gonna be trouble for shore."

"Now do what I say."

"Cain't."

"Nobody minds me."

As Ben and Silas turned back toward the open gate, Jimmy and Becky tried to follow, but their grandfather grabbed them and held them. Elder John wished his sons were small enough to be restrained in the same fashion. The twins' father turned momentarily to reassure his children.

"I'll be right back," he promised.

Once again, Jimmy watched his father wait by the gate while his Uncle Ben walked out to meet the Comanches. He saw red men milling and whooping and trick-riding and working themselves up into a frenzy as the white man approached. He felt a tingling in his balls. He wanted to scratch but was embarrassed, so he just touched the Big Dipper on his face and then ran his fingers through his hair.

Jimmy could hardly believe the scene unfolding before him. Viewed through the gate, it all seemed to take place on a kind of stage, like the Bible plays the family put on at Christmastime. The savage "players" wore such extravagant costumes and makeup that they couldn't be real. And what they were doing couldn't be real either. They couldn't really be plunging their lances into Uncle Ben. He couldn't really be falling. Arrows couldn't really be thumping into his writhing body. It was too far away and too colorful and too unutterably horrible to be real. Surely Uncle Ben would get up again when the game was over, just the way Jimmy and Becky came back to life after their sword fights.

Even when the Comanches started riding toward the open gate, Jimmy kept on watching as if he were witnessing playacting or game playing. The paralyzed boy just kept staring at the Comanches as they raced screaming toward him. His twin sister, suffering from paralysis too, just stood and stared beside him.

"Jimmy! Becky! Run! Run!"

Turning toward the shrill voice, the boy saw his mother, Lucy Goodnight, running toward them, coming to the rescue, charging directly toward the warriors. Her apron flapped like a frightened flag.

"Jimmy! Hurry!"

Overcoming his paralysis, Jimmy started running toward his mother. His twin sister ran with him. Looking back over his shoulder, he saw his father struggling to close the gate before the warriors could crash through. Jimmy lowered his head and tried to run faster, but then he did what that salt wife did in the Bible. Looking back, he saw a Comanche arrow strike his father in the stomach. The boy wished he could turn into salt, too, because then he wouldn't feel anything when he saw his dad fall and writhe in pain in the still-open gate. It was as though Jimmy had been shot, too. His feet seemed dead. Maybe he had turned to salt after all. He just stood there and stared at the warriors who came riding in over his father's body, dirtying it, trampling it, adding insult to death. It seemed so terrible to be killed in springtime and to bleed on the new grass.

"Jimmy!" his mother screamed. "Take my hand!"

Soon she was pulling him toward the back of the fort as more savages poured through the front gate. Jimmy saw several men rushing by to try to bar the warriors' way and thought he should join them. Now was his chance to be a knight for real and rescue damsels, but these damsels were really just his relatives. Knights didn't usually rescue their aunts and cousins and such like. Besides, he was being dragged along by his mom and couldn't get loose. Not that he tried all that hard. Looking back again, Jimmy saw two more uncles dying and his granddaddy trying to run away on legs hobbled by old age.

"Run for the spring gate," his mother shouted.

In the farthest corner, the small spring gate served as a back door to the fort. It had been cut there to make it easier to fetch water from a nearby spring. Jimmy's hand came uncoupled from his mother's, but he kept on running. He was faster than his mother and soon passed her and was even gaining on his sister. But then he decided he shouldn't run off and leave his mom, so he slowed down and waited for her to catch up.

Hearing his grandfather cry out–even in the screaming battle he recognized that voice–Jimmy looked back to see the old man on the ground. Two Comanches were on top of him. Averting his eyes from his grandfather's ordeal, Jimmy found himself staring at warriors attacking his grandmother, Granny Goodnight. The Comanche braves were tearing off the old woman's clothes. The boy had always imagined his grandmother's apron as a part of her anatomy, but now it was gone.

Jimmy forced himself to look straight ahead while his fears whipped him to run faster and faster. He saw the cabins passing. He saw the corral off to one side. He saw the tiny door, looking like a child's playhouse door, waiting up ahead. And he felt his balls beating like bell clappers between his legs.

Tripping, falling, rolling on the ground, Jimmy saw the battle inside the fort as tumbling chaos . . . blood . . . pain . . . death . . . warriors throwing his nude grandmother to the earth . . . other red men pulling the trousers from his grandfather's kicking legs . . . all seen through the misty cloud of goose feathers thrown up by the wild warriors who attacked the fort's feather beds as if these embodiments of soft civilization were their mortal enemies.

Jimmy felt his mother hauling him to his feet. They clasped hands again, but this time the boy, running in front, pulled his mother, making her go faster. He managed to cross his fingers again on the run. They reached the shadow of the picket wall, which had been so much trouble to erect and which hadn't done anyone any good at all. One after another, they began clambering through the tiny gate, its smallness making their escape feel a little like a terrible game to the boy.

Unable to resist, Jimmy looked back one last time and saw through the goose-feather fog a warrior pinning his grandmother to the ground with a lance . . . another Comanche cutting something from between his grandfather's legs and holding it up as if it were a dead ground squirrel . . .

"Don't look!" cried his mother. "Come on! Hurry! Come on!"

Jimmy was still looking back as his mother dragged him away from the little make-believe door and toward the river. As they ran, Jimmy could still hear the fighting and hurting and the rhythmic screams of his grandmother.

"What're they doin' to her?" cried Jimmy.

"Run!" yelled his mother.

"What're they doin' to Grandma?"

"Don't ask questions. Run! Run!"

Out of breath, Jimmy did keep running, pursued by Granny Goodnight's terrified, angry, hurting voice. Up ahead near the river were trees and bushes and high grass that seemed to promise a hiding place and possible safety. Jimmy was nearing this river haven when, looking back, he saw several warriors come riding around the side of the fort, chasing two young women.

Jimmy was frightened for his aunt Elizabeth and his aunt Rachel, both in their early twenties, both losing the races they were running. Rachel Plummer was slowed by the weight of her eighteen-month-old son, Billy, whom she carried in her arms. Elizabeth Kellogg ran faster, but not fast enough. With excited whoops, the Comanches rode these white women down as if they were wild game. Soon the red hunters had their prey surrounded. When Aunt Rachel tried to break out of the ring, a warrior on foot grabbed a hoe–a hoe of all things–from the ground and hit her in the face. She fell unconscious, dropping her baby. Jimmy closed his eyes as if he had been the one hit and knocked out.

Looking again, Jimmy saw warriors attacking his aunt Elizabeth, who was still standing. When they began to strip her, he was embarrassed for her–and at the same time curious and guiltily excited. So far away, Aunt Elizabeth looked like a doll being undressed. But unlike other dolls, this one fought back. This doll tried to protect its bodice with pathetic doll hands. This doll attempted to clutch its full skirt even as it was torn away. This doll didn't like being a toy, but couldn't help it. Soon all its clothes were torn off. The unwilling doll stood white and pink, humiliated and afraid. Dolls weren't supposed to feel anything, and Jimmy wasn't supposed to feel this way about dolls either.

Looking away from one doll, Jimmy saw another, Aunt Rachel, who was putting up no resistance at all because she was unconscious. But the savages were nonetheless having a hard time with her. Sound asleep, this doll was putting up a better fight than the other doll: For Aunt Rachel wore a whalebone corset that completely baffled the Stone Age warriors. They had no idea how to solve the puzzle of its tiny fastenings. It was as impossible for them to enter the corset as to enter white civilization itself. The Comanches pulled and grunted and got angry, but they didn't penetrate the whalebone armor that protected her.

When Aunt Rachel regained consciousness and began to struggle, her attackers gave up on her corset, planning to solve this puzzle later at their leisure. A brave simply dragged Aunt Rachel, who was naked except for her corset, to a nearby horse and threw her on it. Then he mounted behind her and rode off with his curiously arrayed prize. Another Comanche scooped up her baby and carried it away. A third red man dragged Aunt Elizabeth, completely nude, up onto his horse. She made a handsome trophy.

Now the Comanches, no longer diverted by the two young women, were ready to seek more victims. Seeing Lucy Goodnight and her children fleeing toward the river, they started after them. Now small white legs had to try to outrun horses. Jimmy heard the hooves and whoops drawing closer and louder. He was too frightened to look back now. The warriors overtook the mother and her children with no trouble at the edge of the small river. A circle of stone lance points fenced them in. The trapped family cringed in a clump.

The Comanche who seemed to be the leader was completely nude except for yellow paint that covered him from head to foot. All the others had their faces painted black, the color of the night, but he was the sun. All the others had long hair, but his was cut short, almost like a white man's.

This short-haired Sun Chief pointed a finger at Jimmy. The boy instinctively held up his hands as if to ward off a blow–then touched his Big Dipper birthmark. In pantomime, the naked warrior instructed the mother to place her son on his horse, acting it out. But Lucy Goodnight shook her head. No, she wouldn't give her son to this nude Comanche painted to look like the sun.

Another warrior advanced, black-faced and grim, who also wanted the boy, but again the mother refused. So the brave raised his lance as if to drive it through Jimmy. The boy was already trying to guess how much it would hurt. He saw the lance leap forward, like a rattlesnake striking, and he instinctively ducked. The spear sailed over him and plunged its fang into his twin sister. It went in her chest and came out her back. She collapsed on the grass–the way she had done so many times when they played their games–but this time she didn't get up again, no matter how loud he screamed.

"Becky! Becky! Git up! *Becky!* I'm sorry. I didn't mean to kill you."

The Comanche leaned down from his horse, pulled his spear from the unmoving girl, and aimed it once again at Jimmy. The boy felt a prickling sensation in his chest where the wound would be. The warrior with the death-black face motioned once again for the mother to hand her son up to him. This time, relenting, Lucy Goodnight bent over, grasped Jimmy under his arms and lifted him up, resigned to saving her son by losing him. The boy saw both warriors–the one painted yellow and the black-faced killer–reaching out for him. They both wanted him. Jimmy hoped his mother would give him to the warrior with the yellow war paint. And she did. At least he hadn't killed Becky.

Jimmy found himself sitting just in front of the yellow-painted brave on the back of a spotted horse. While the warrior held him tightly, the boy clung to the oversized Comanche saddle horn with both hands and stared down at his mother. He was crying and the tears fell on the purple stars on his cheek. The Big Dipper overflowed.

Jimmy saw a brave on foot rush up to his sister, grab hold of her red hair, slash, and pull hard. Becky's carrot-colored scalp came off her head with a sickening "pop." Jimmy leaned over and threw up on his mother.

Then another brave attacked his mom and began tearing at her soiled clothes. This was no doll being played with now. It was too close. It was life-sized. It was his mother. Lucy Goodnight bravely fought back, defending her apron, defending her bodice, defending her skirt, but she was no match for the warriors' hands. She was fighting for the last rag of her clothing when a loud voice interrupted her undressing.

"Let 'er go! Damn you!"

Turning to see who was shouting, Jimmy recognized the familiar figure of David Falkenberry, another of his relatives, racing toward them, brandishing a rifle. He had come from the fields on the run, out of breath.

"Put 'er down!"

Seeing the rifle pointed at him, the startled warrior released his grip on Lucy Goodnight. The mother crumpled to the ground beside her torn, crumpled clothing.

Jimmy felt the horse under him begin to run. Other white men were coming from the fields, carrying guns, firing shots, frightening the warriors. The Comanche retreat had begun and Jimmy was swept up in it.

"Mama!" Jimmy called. "Mama! Mama!"

Jimmy saw his mother falling farther and farther behind. She was calling after her son, and he was calling back to her, but her voice grew fainter and fainter.

Pursued by his mother's voice, Jimmy was carried off in the middle of a stampede of screaming warriors. Holding tight to the big horn, he was afraid of falling and being trampled. As an unknown world galloped crazily toward him, Jimmy kept looking back. He watched the family fort grow smaller and smaller and then duck behind a hill. The last trace he saw of his home was a rising cloud of feathers: the Comanches had ripped the guts out of all the feather beds.

74

Jimmy rode through a young feminine landscape. All the shapes were rounded and softened by the new spring growth. The hills rolled gently. The oak trees hung heavily over the land like great leafy breasts. The bluebonnets, which were in full flower now, made the land seem almost gaudy. Even in the midst of his fears, the boy couldn't help admiring the scenery through which he moved. It comforted him. It was so soft and gentle and nurturing that the violence he had witnessed seemed almost impossible. Cradled against this green bosom, he found it harder and harder to believe in death, which he didn't understand very well anyway, and rape, which he understood even less well, and the mutilation of his grandfather, which he understood all too well because he had seen it done to calves.

He would almost succeed in losing himself in the spring landscape and then all the horror would come flooding back over him. She was dead. The boy felt as if he had already been mutilated, as if he had already had an organ cut away, as if he had already lost the best part of himself. Yes, she was dead. He had seen her killed. He couldn't believe it, but he had to believe it. He had no right to be riding in the sunshine, no right to be enjoying the landscape that was coming back to life all around him, no right to spring.

The sun shone over Jimmy's right shoulder as he jostled in front of his warrior. They were riding northwest, away from the settlements that had slowly been moving northwest themselves. It was getting hot.

Jimmy saw his Aunt Rachel approaching, riding in front of a brave who kept his arm around her. When they were close enough, Jimmy's warrior said something to Aunt Rachel's warrior. While the two Comanches talked in their incomprehensible tongue, the nephew studied his aunt, who looked so strange dressed in nothing but a whalebone corset. The boy caught himself staring and looked away.

"Jimmy, honey, you all right?" Aunt Rachel asked. "Did they hurt you, baby?"

Even now, even here, the boy resented being called a baby. He was ten years old. He sat up straighter on the spotted horse.

"I'm okay," Jimmy called back. "How 'bout you?"

"I'm–"

The black-faced Comanche who held her put his hand over her mouth to make her be quiet. Jimmy wished he could help Aunt Rachel. He wished he could help Aunt Elizabeth, too. Most of all, he wished he could help his twin sister. But he couldn't help any of them, especially Becky. Not now. Why had he ducked? He told himself that he couldn't have known that by ducking he would murder his sister. But he had ducked! And she had been killed! He ought to have taken the lance into his own body. But he hadn't. A big help he had been. So he didn't deserve any help himself. He had it coming to him whatever they did. But what would they do?

Soon the band of Comanches stopped riding long enough to transfer their prisoners to spare horses, so captives and captors no longer rode double. This change was made not as a favor to the prisoners but to spare the animals. The captives were bound to the horses to keep them from falling off or jumping off. A strip of rawhide was tied around one ankle, passed under the pony's belly, then tied to the other ankle.

Jimmy watched his Aunt Elizabeth riding completely nude a few feet away. The boy could see his aunt growing pinker and pinker in the bright sunshine. She looked frightened and uncomfortable and so womanly. The boy felt he shouldn't be looking at his aunt this way, but he couldn't help it. He just kept staring at the exposed feminine body that rode through the lush feminine countryside. He felt all the more guilty because his sister had been a woman–would have been a woman someday–which made all women seem somehow holier. More deserving of respect and honor. And here he was gawking at his very own aunt.

Although the landscape looked soft, it was hard to cross. Jimmy began to ache in his skin, in his muscle, in his gristle. Even his own bones turned against him: they were sticks striking blows inside his body. He longed for the warriors to call a halt so he could stop riding and get down off the horse, and yet at the same time he feared a halt, for he was terrified of what would happen then. As much as he hated this ceaseless motion, this ceaseless hurt, he feared what would come next even more. And so he hoped the unbearable journey would never end.

The trip was even harder in the afternoon when the sun shone in Jimmy's face, turning his nose redder and redder. He saw Aunt Rachel's arms and legs turning the color of fire. And Aunt Elizabeth was baked crimson all over. The sun was terrible, and yet it was better than sundown, for after sundown they would surely make camp, and then . . . He didn't know what they would do, but he felt sure it would hurt. Even though he deserved to be hurt, he still stared at the sun to keep it up. Yet in spite of his stares and wishes and prayers, the sun kept sinking lower. He remembered the story–the one in his family's only story book–about the day God made longer. But where was He now?

The sun set.

By the light of the full Comanche moon, the warriors rode on and on into the night. Now the great oak trees were black and no longer comforting. The whole night seemed painted in war paint. The bushes were blackened and even the hills wore black faces. Night was a Comanche.

Jimmy need not have been so worried about sundown because the Comanches pressed their journey deep into the night. As it got later and later, he began to worry that they were never going to stop–and at the same time to fear they would.

When the Comanches finally did decide to make camp sometime after midnight, Jimmy was both thankful and terrified. Comanche hands untied the thongs around his ankles, pulled him from his pony, and threw him roughly to the ground. His aunts were thrown down next to him. Even the baby, little Billy, was tossed carelessly onto the bare ground.

Jimmy saw corseted Aunt Rachel begin to crawl toward her son, who had started to cry, but she never reached him. The Comanches attacked her as if she were a buffalo to be skinned, knives drawn, slashing away. It appeared that the warriors were murdering Aunt Rachel, but they weren't. They were simply solving the corset mystery the only way they knew how. The whalebone was too tough to tear, the fastenings too difficult to undo, so they "skinned" the young white woman out of her corset with sharp blades.

Frightened by this skinning of one aunt, Jimmy sought comfort by trying to rush into the arms of the other, but she pushed him away.

"No, don't!" Aunt Elizabeth cried out. "Don't touch me!"

"What?" stammered Jimmy. "What's the matter?"

"I'm sorry, honey. But I'm too sunburned."

Jimmy recoiled. He had hurt somebody else. First his sister and now his aunt.

Hearing a great yelp go up from the warriors, Jimmy looked back in the direction of Aunt Rachel. He saw a brave holding the corset aloft as if it were a holy war trophy. Kneeling in the dirt, his aunt looked almost as if she still wore her corset, for she was pure white where her fancy underwear had protected her–and red everywhere else. Her alabaster torso glowed in the dark, as if the moon had come to earth in the shape of a woman's body.

The Comanches, having skinned Aunt Rachel, now descended upon them all. A brave grabbed Jimmy's hands–with small fingers crossed–and pulled them behind his back. He looked and saw the others with their hands pulled behind them, too. The warriors used braided rawhide ropes to tie their wrists. The ropes were so tight his hands went numb. Would they die and fall off? And all the while Aunt Elizabeth kept crying out the loudest because she was sunburned the worst.

"No! It hurts! It hurts!"

A foot pushed Jimmy forward onto his face. He landed with a grunt. Then one by one the others fell, too. Aunt Rachel flopped onto the ground soiling her white breasts and stomach. Aunt Elizabeth struck the earth with a terrible scream. They all coughed in the dust.

Jimmy felt his feet being pulled together, felt leather ropes circle his ankles. Then the rope around his feet was tied to the rope around his hands. He was bent backward like a bow. Completely helpless, he could only move his head. Looking around, he saw his aunts bound in the same manner, as defenseless as beetles turned on their backs. And on top of all the pain and guilt and humiliation and utter terror, Jimmy's nose started to itch.

While captive hands and feet turned blue in the bright moonlight, the Comanches started their victory dance. Over a hundred warriors pranced and leapt around a bonfire as their long shadows appeared to dance on top of the captives. The warriors screamed, making sounds that seemed half language and half wild animals calling to each other.

Lying with his cheek against the cool ground, Jimmy stared uncomprehendingly at the frenzy, the blood lust. He was terrified and yet glad finally to have a moment to rest. He even closed his eyes only to open them again when he heard a particularly terrible war cry. Then a brave rushed in his direction, dropped to his knees, and shook an old familiar grey mop in his face.

"Granddaddy!" Jimmy cried.

"Hush!" warned Aunt Rachel.

The boy started to cry as his grandfather's bloody hair danced for him. Finally, the scalp was withdrawn, returning to take its place in the death dance around the fire. Then another mop of hair left the circle and advanced on the prostrate boy. It was red hair, long red hair like the knights of old used to wear, heartbreaking hair.

"Ayyyyaaaayyyyy!" screamed a boy who had become an animal. The sound told of a pain older than language. The cry was older even than mankind. It was a cry to make both rabbits and wolves shiver all across the plains.

When a warrior struck his Aunt Elizabeth across the back with his bow, Jimmy flinched as though he were the one who had been hit. Then another Comanche lashed his Aunt Rachel with a bow. Again, Jimmy's body jerked. At last, a warrior approached him and he cringed. The bow whipped him across the legs, drawing blood. It had begun, what he had feared for so long, although he hadn't known what it would be. He was finally being punished.

More and more Comanches danced around the helpless captives, striking them with their bows, kicking them, hurting and humiliating them. Jimmy cried as if he were a baby. He couldn't help it, and the baby Billy cried, too. Backs bled and legs bled and arms bled. Sunburned bodies were streaked a deeper red.

When he thought he could stand it no longer, Jimmy was given a reprieve. The Comanches lost interest in the boy as their interest in the grown women increased. Aunt Elizabeth's and Aunt Rachel's ankles were freed, and they were pulled to their feet. With a combination of horror and curiosity, Jimmy stared up at his aunts' sturdy pioneer breasts. The braves continued to beat the standing women.

Then Jimmy saw a warrior approaching his aunts with a pair of burning sticks from the bonfire. The boy closed his eyes, but he couldn't stop his ears. He heard the screams.

When he opened his eyes again–it seemed a long time later–his aunts were on the ground. Two braves held Aunt Rachel's feet spread wide while a third Comanche bounced on top of her. Four braves were needed to spread the legs of Aunt Elizabeth, who was more sunburned, in more pain, and fought harder.

"No!" Aunt Elizabeth cried. "No, don't! Please! It hurts! It hurts!"

Jimmy felt he shouldn't look, should close his eyes again, but he didn't. Although it was horrible, he couldn't help being interested. Growing up in a small cabin, he had become aware that adult men and women had some sort of secret, but he only knew enough to make him more curious. He knew there was something physical and forbidden. He even had some garbled idea about how it worked because an older cousin had told him that husbands peed inside their wives. But now these savages were giving him a practical lesson. So that was what men did to women. He was learning the arithmetic of reproduction, but the addition was set up all wrong. It should have been one plus one, but it was one plus fifty. Brave after brave mounted his aunts and rode them.

Jimmy felt their hurt almost as if it were his own, felt their repulsion, felt their degradation. But most of all, he felt the utter terror of two young civilized women who were utterly at the mercy of the Stone Age. He told himself that all of his sympathy should be going out to his aunts, but he could not help holding some back for himself, because he knew he would never be able to do *that* to a woman if they gelded him.

75

In the morning, Jimmy hated to wake up, hated the thought of beginning a new day of tortures and terrors. But he hated waking up most of all because he had been dreaming that his sister Becky was still alive. Her death had been a mistake. The lance had only just nicked her. She had lost a little blood, but she was fine. Until he woke up.

Wishing he could go back to sleep, to his dreams, Jimmy awoke to a new horror. A brave tied one end of a braided rawhide rope around Aunt Elizabeth's neck as if she were a cow, then tied the other end to the exaggerated horn of his Comanche saddle. Her riding days seemed to be over. From now on she would be led barefoot through a panorama of rocks and thorns. Another warrior tied Aunt Rachel in the same way, stringing another rawhide rope from her neck to his saddle horn, as if she were another trudging cow. The boy wondered what new game the Comanches planned to play with his aunts, who were still nude with their hands still bound behind their backs.

When the yellow Sun Chief approached him, Jimmy shuddered, but the bright Comanche did not harm him. He untied the boy's hands, which was a relief, and then lifted him onto the back of a spotted pony. But once again, Jimmy's ankles were tied to a rope that was passed beneath the animal's belly.

When they were ready to move out, the band of warriors divided, one group riding away from the sun, the other toward it. The west-riding band, led by the short-haired Sun Chief, took with them Jimmy and Aunt Rachel and her baby. But the east-riding warriors led Aunt Elizabeth away with them. The dividing of the war party meant a dividing of the spoils of war.

Looking back, Jimmy saw his aunt Elizabeth being pulled toward the sunrise. At the end of her leather rope, she was forced to run naked, bruising her feet on the rocks, tearing her flesh on the clawing bushes. Not knowing what to do, Jimmy waved goodbye to his aunt

Elizabeth, who couldn't wave back. She grew smaller and smaller. The boy kept on waving until his aunt disappeared over a hill, running naked into slavery.

Looking for his other aunt, Jimmy saw her, still red and white, running at the end of a rope a few yards away. While she ran, Aunt Rachel kept her eyes focused on the warrior who carried her baby. She should have watched more carefully where she was going, for she stumbled and fell and was dragged by the neck behind the horse. She was being hanged horizontally.

"Stoppit!" cried Jimmy. "You're killing her! Aunt Rachel!"

The woman seemed to be leaving the world the way she had come into it: pulled by forces beyond her control, helpless, headfirst, naked, and unbreathing.

Jimmy, acting by reflex, tried to get off his pony to help his aunt, but the leather rope tied to his ankles held him fast. He kicked against the rope but only succeeded in making his horse bolt in the wrong direction. When he looked back, Jimmy saw that Aunt Rachel had stopped struggling. She was being dragged along, seemingly lifeless.

At last, the rope went slack. The Comanches waited to see if Aunt Rachel would regain consciousness.

When she began to stir, a brave pulled on her rope to make her get up again. Slowly and awkwardly–without the use of her bound hands–Aunt Rachel rose to her feet. Then the rope went taut and the bleeding body began to run again.

Mounting a ridge toward evening, the Sun Chief called a halt. Jimmy, glad for a rest from the constant motion, studied a landscape that was beginning to flatten out and lose its trees. The feminine countryside of East Texas was starting to give way to the masculine country of West Texas, but at the moment it was neither one nor the other, neither round nor flat, neither soft nor hard, androgynous. Like a boy who had been cut.

The Comanche band was ready to divide again. Aunt Rachel was led off like a newly purchased brood mare toward the southwest. The Sun Chief and his followers turned northwest with Jimmy and Little Billy.

"No, my baby!" cried Aunt Rachel.

But a brave raised his whip and signaled her to be quiet. Dumbly, she followed her rope at a trot. Her nephew noticed that the unclouded sun had burned away the outline of her corset.

• • •

On the third day, Jimmy was carried into a new world. The land was more than masculine, flatter than a man's chest, harder than a man's muscles, even more unforgiving than most men. It seemed unable or unwilling to nourish anything. In this harsh place, the last harsh division took place. The Sun Chief and a dozen warriors rode north with Jimmy, while a dozen other braves carried the baby Billy due west.

"Goodbye, Billy," Jimmy whispered. "Be good."

76

After more days and nights on the trail, Jimmy found himself on the brink of a vast canyon with steep red cliffs, decorated with diminutive cedar and chinaberry trees. He had never seen anything so big, had never heard of anything so enormous, had never imagined that such a marvel was possible. He couldn't help wondering: Was he the first white man or boy to see it? The huge hole, appearing so suddenly, reminded the boy of something in a fairy tale. It was so unexpected as to be almost unbelievable. Somehow this landscape seemed incredibly old: he expected to discover dinosaurs patrolling the canyon floor. The white child stared down at what appeared to be a toy village with many hundreds of toy tepees. Comanche dolls were walking about among the toy tents. The village followed a stream for miles and miles, a vast river of tepees. In the wilderness, Jimmy gawked at the largest city he had ever seen in his life. He never knew that many people existed.

The mounted warriors began their descent of the canyon wall single file. Even they–with all their experience and ability–were careful. Eventually, Jimmy was signaled to join the line of descent. As he began his journey, moving lower and lower, he felt as if the earth were swallowing him, which, for all practical purposes, was what happened, for the village was so well hidden in the canyon that the chances of white men finding it or him were very small. Jimmy continued down into the red bowels of the earth.

As the returning band neared home, the boy grew more and more nervous as he sensed a growing excitement in the warriors and a reciprocal agitation in the looming village. Relatives and friends came rushing out to meet and escort the successful marauders. The noise and size of this welcoming multitude frightened Jimmy. He started crying, but through his tears he couldn't help noticing that all the little Comanche boys were completely naked. The little girls wore buckskin dresses, but their brothers wore nothing at all. Jimmy couldn't imagine what his new life was going to be like in this new half-naked world. He wondered if they would try to take his clothes away from him and turn him into a naked savage. Jimmy began to shake as the crowd grew larger and larger. They were all singing songs that sounded to him like the kind of songs bears and wolves would sing. The boy was fascinated and scared to death.

Random red hands reached up and touched him. He flinched in fear but was relieved to find that the touchers did him no harm. They seemed more interested in satisfying their curiosity than their blood lust. They rubbed his skin. They pointed at his pale hair, which was luckily out of reach. Jimmy seemed to be something new in this village buried deep in the earth. Villagers thronged around him as if they had never seen a white boy before. He apparently amazed them just as they amazed him. Each was evidently a new world to the other–a new red world, a new white world.

Up ahead, Jimmy saw the sun-yellow leader of the raiding party holding high a scalp pole. On it, Goodnight hair seemed to dance for sheer joy. His grandfather's grey locks were more animated in death than he had ever seen them in life. And his father's brown hair was just as active, jumping, spinning, whirling, leading the parade. And long red hair danced as if to make up for all the barn dances and hoedowns and two-steps and skip-to-my-lou's it would never have a chance to enjoy.

As the band entered the village, Jimmy saw what looked like clotheslines stretched beside almost every tepee, only these lines supported not clothing but strips of meat. Flesh had been hung out to dry. Buffalo jerky stirred in the slight wind.

Dogs ran along beside the horses, barking. There seemed to be more dogs even than people, and they were even louder than their masters. They helped to give the Comanche camp an overwhelming sense of *noise.* The captive boy, who had always lived a quiet life by comparison, was overwhelmed by the racket here in the wilderness.

Jimmy rode at the center of a huge red dust cloud raised by thousands of feet: Comanche feet, dog feet, horses' hooves, bare feet, moccasined feet, a vast multitude of beating feet that turned the earth into a drumhead. The white boy found it hard to breathe, which made him feel all the more trapped. It was as though this noisy throng had used up all the air. He was suffocating, drowning in dust.

As they passed through the village, the warriors dropped out of the procession one by one as they reached their tepees. Each departing warrior handed over his trophies to his woman and then disappeared inside his tent. Jimmy kept wondering where he would stop and what would happen to him when, at last, his journey was over.

When the Sun Chief finally reached his tepee, he turned over his pint-sized white captive to his wife. Then this magnificent yellow-stained warrior, like the others, disappeared into his tepee. Jimmy had the sense that he was being deserted. He feared his owner and yet had somehow come to rely upon him. While a crowd gathered around, the squaw carefully examined the white boy. She opened the captive's mouth and checked his teeth. She turned his head this way and that. She looked closely at his pale hands and stared into his blue eyes. A dazed Jimmy submitted passively to all this manipulation.

While she was probing him, Jimmy naturally studied her. She had short hair like her husband. The boy wondered if chiefs and their families got regular haircuts as a mark of distinction to set them apart. Her hands, which were busy exploring him, were rough and calloused. Evidently, chiefs' wives were expected to work like everybody else. Jimmy hated being touched this way, so a part of him hated the woman. But another part of him was touched in a different way by her profound sadness. He wasn't sure how he knew that she was sad since he couldn't understand her words, but he did know. In her unhappiness, she reminded him of his mother, not as he had known her, but as she must be now, having lost her twins, the daughter dead, the son carried away to who knew where. He wondered what this woman would look like if she were not so sad? He sensed beauty beneath the ravages, but he was still afraid of her.

Suddenly, a Comanche boy only slightly older than Jimmy rushed up and started beating the ten-year-old captive with a cedar stick. Nobody seemed surprised except the victim. Jimmy fell to the ground and attempted to cover himself against the blows.

77

A tall scalp pole stood at the center of a great circle of frenzied Comanches. By the light of a great bonfire, made of logs stacked like a tepee, Jimmy again recognized familiar hair. The white captive was led toward the scalps by his yellow-painted master. As the pole drew nearer, it seemed to stretch up taller and taller, a menacing giant that kept growing and growing. It appeared to shake its awful hair down at the boy. When he reached the pole, his hands were pulled behind him and bound around the great upright hair tree. Jimmy was a living scalp displayed on the scalp pole. The Comanches danced around their quick-and-dead trophies, their dance and their song building in intensity and feeling and speed. Jimmy stared at this moving circle. Then he looked above his head at the hair and the stars. He was afraid, horrified, terrorized–but also embarrassed. Jimmy had never in his life been the focus of so much attention, and he didn't like it. He wondered if he was blushing.

A young naked boy, perhaps six years old, broke from the circle and came running toward Jimmy, brandishing a flint knife. The Comanche child rushed right up to the white boy and thrust the blade at his stomach. The bound captive flinched and expected to feel an end-of-life agony, but the knife only made a small dimple in his stomach without breaking the skin. Standing on tiptoe, the Comanche boy reached up and grabbed the white boy's yellow hair and pulled it hard as his scalping knife came up. The blade grazed the pale forehead, but the child warrior was only pretending to scalp the towhead. It was a deadly rehearsal for raids and murders to come. The red boy kept on slashing again and again at the blond locks, his knife scratching the pale forehead harder and deeper, finally drawing a drop of blood. Jimmy glanced down at his distorted shadow, which looked as if it were really being scalped.

When the boy-brave retreated, another came out to take his place and then another and then more and more. All the boys in the village seemed to take a turn at the game of stab-and-scalp. They were all having a wonderful time. Jimmy began to relax a little as his yellow hair survived one scalping after another.

Then Jimmy saw the Comanche boy, the one who had beaten him when he first arrived, approaching him with knife drawn. The red boy walked with the kind of swagger that frightened the white boy even though none of the other boys had really hurt him. Suspecting that the games were over, Jimmy struggled against his bonds in earnest. He thought the Comanche boy was staring at his crotch. The white boy was even more frightened when red hands started unbuttoning his ragged, homespun pants. His trousers dropped around his bound ankles. The Comanche boy reached for his balls. Jimmy was embarrassed and terrified at the same time. It also tickled. The stone blade bit into his scrotum. The white boy closed his eyes and tried to pass out, but he couldn't.

"Kee!" shouted a familiar voice.

Jimmy opened his eyes: The Sun Chief was standing behind the red boy who was busy cutting off white balls. The Comanche boy stopped sawing. A painted yellow hand reached down and took the knife. Feeling blood running down his leg, Jimmy prayed he was still intact.

78

Jimmy limped, head down, beneath the red walls of his prison. His crotch was still sore, but it was healing in one piece. He had been sent out to gather firewood and now carried a few dry mesquite twigs in his arms. From time to time, he would daydream about running away, but then he would look around him and despair. Not only were the canyon walls steep, but they were covered with slippery sandstone scree. All around, the canyon reared up great promontories that looked like red or violet or deep purple watchtowers. From time to time, he scratched his wound and then wished he hadn't.

Squinting, searching for wood, Jimmy saw something move in the buffalo grass. He stopped, afraid. Staring, he expected to see a snake, but instead he discovered a friendly monster. A baby horny toad was looking for bugs to eat. The boy bent down and started to chase it.

When he caught it, Jimmy held up his prey in his right hand and studied it. The horny toad was so small that it covered only a part of his palm. Gazing back at him, it looked like classroom drawings he had seen of dinosaurs. Or perhaps it looked more like a toy dragon. This tiny prehistoric animal, with its armor-plated head, seemed to belong here in this ancient place. Horns rose like thorns from its skull and back and tail.

"Hi," Jimmy said.

The age-old animal blinked scaled eyes.

"Horny Toad, do you talk English? I'm lookin' for somebody who talks English."

He carefully stroked the horned back. The thorns tickled the tip of his finger.

"You do. Good," he said brightly, wanting the monster to like him. "By the way, my name's Jimmy. Who're you?"

The horny toad seemed to look at him curiously. It didn't appear to be afraid of him. It had lasted as a species too many eons to be easily alarmed.

"Oh, you're Freddy. That's a right pretty name."

Hearing somebody coming, Jimmy closed his hand over his new friend. Then he put the baby horny toad in the pocket of his rough, tattered, homespun pants. He still wore what was left of the clothes he had been carried off in. To his relief, he was considered too old–just barely–to run naked like the younger boys in the village. He felt the horny toad squirm and then relax in the warmth of its new nest.

Looking around, Jimmy saw his young tormentor, the one who had tried to cut off his balls, coming toward him. The Comanche boy, who served as the boy slave's overseer, looked disapproving. He wore a breechclout, fringed buckskin leggings, fringed moccasins, and a scowl. He had a long nose, which seemed too heavy for his face, for he carried his head tipped slightly forward. The habit gave him a scheming look.

Jimmy knew this pint-sized slave-driver better now, but he feared him no less. At first, the captive had thought the Comanche boy must be the son of the Sun Chief, but the sadistic little overseer didn't sleep in the master's tepee as a son would. So Jimmy figured the boy was probably the Sun Chief's nephew. The white boy wondered if this nephew might possibly be jealous of the slave's place in the Sun Chief's tent. After all, the white boy had always been jealous when his sister got to sleep in his mother's bed. But he mustn't think of his sister. Those thoughts made him too sad. He could stand being a slave. He could stand being separated from his people. He could even stand serving the cruel Comanche boy. But he couldn't stand to think about what had happened to her.

Drawing closer, the Comanche boy began telling the white boy to get back to work. Jimmy couldn't understand the words, but he understood the meaning. And he moved to comply, bending over, picking up small sticks. But Jimmy didn't move quickly enough to suit his young overseer. The Comanche boy hit him in the stomach and he fell. On the way down, Jimmy remembered to turn so that he wouldn't crush the dinosaur in his pocket.

A few weeks later–it was summertime and hot by now–Jimmy knelt rubbing buffalo brains into a buffalo hide. He felt sick as he watched the grey jelly ooze through his fingers. He hated this leather tanning more than any other job. He had done harder work but never messier work. He could not stand the feel or the smell or the look or the idea of brains clinging to his fingers. He was sunburned brown all over and dressed in animal skins, but he was still a white boy at heart.

Since he hated the task so much, Jimmy paused for a moment, dogging it. He looked around to see if anybody was watching him steal time. He saw lots of villagers, but they all seemed to be busy with their own chores, paying no attention to him. He tried to wipe the brains off his fingers, not succeeding very well. Then he reached into a skin bag that he kept tied to the belt of his breechclout. His hand closed around Fred, the horny toad, and he pulled him out to take a look. This archaic baby animal blinked in the bright sun for a moment. Then it started licking Jimmy's fingers. Fred loved the grey jelly. As Jimmy watched his friend enjoy the feast, he began to feel better about the brains, too.

Since he was so preoccupied with watching his pet eat his lunch, Jimmy didn't see his young overseer charging toward him. Fred saw the danger coming, turned his head for a better look, and then nestled down flat against the palm of his master's hand. His pet's curious behavior made the white boy look around just as the whip came whistling toward him–a hissing snake.

The whip was made of buffalo skin that had been cured by rubbing brains into it. Then it had been cut into strips and woven into an instrument of torture. It could be used on a balky horse or a lazy slave. The whip, rendered supple as a snake by the tanning process, came down on Jimmy's bare back. It laid a track from his right shoulder blade to his left hip.

The slave instinctively rolled into the protective ball that he had learned in the womb. At the center of his body ball, he made another ball out of his right fist. And at the center of this ball within a ball, he cradled his horny toad. As the whip blows fell, his soft flesh struggled to shield a small animal that wore plates of strong, prehistoric armor.

At last, the boy overseer seemed to grow weary of whipping the slave boy. The Comanche stopped the blows but now lashed the white boy with his tongue. The slave couldn't understand the language, but he knew that he was being ordered, on pain of even worse punishment, to be more diligent in his work.

With his pet still hidden inside his right hand, Jimmy dipped the hand into the brains again and once more started rubbing the goo into the hide. He was surprised to discover that he was crying. Tears spotted the buffalo skin. He didn't even look up as his tormentor walked haughtily away. When he felt no one watching, Jimmy decided to take another chance. He paused in his labors long enough to raise his hand, open it, and check on Fred.

"Don't cry," Jimmy whimpered to his friend. "He won't hurt you. I won't let him."

The horny toad went on contentedly licking brains.

79

The captive boy watched the captive eagle straining against its tether. The great golden bird, actually just an adolescent, had grown up a prisoner. The Comanches had stolen the eagle from its mother's nest when it was just a fuzzy eaglet. Now a rawhide rope–one end tied to a stake, the other knotted around the eagle's foot–kept it bound to the earth. The tribe held the bird in captivity because they needed eagle feathers for many of their rituals. Regretting the handsome bird's plucked tail, Jimmy would have attempted to comfort it for its loss, but he suspected that this captive would fight back.

The eagle's feathers had been pulled from its tail in preparation for the Eagle Dance that would take place later that morning. Even now, its lost plumage was being tied into the hair of the dancers who had been bathed in the creek, then streaked with war paint and rubbed with sage. During the dance, the eagle's power would be absorbed by the dancers. The great bird itself had to suffer so the Comanches could take on some of its greatness.

Jimmy knew the eagle would not be the only captive who would have to suffer on that fine festive morning. He wasn't quite sure what he was expected to do–or what they would do to him–but he doubted that he would like it very much. The Sun Chief had dressed him in new buckskin leggings that were decorated with elk's teeth. He, too, had been bathed in the creek. He, too, had been rubbed with sage. But he suspected he hadn't been so well groomed and perfumed for his own pleasure.

A half-dozen braves appeared and led Jimmy away down a ravine where they waited for the ritual to begin. Soon the white boy heard the raiders coming for him the way they had come that morning in what already seemed the distant past.

Looking up at the sky, Jimmy thought of the eagle. He almost expected to see it flying overhead, although he knew very well that it was tied to the ground. He imagined it up there and wondered if it ever imagined the same thing. He even seemed to see himself as the soaring eagle, up there in the cloudless sky, looking down on all that was happening and about to happen on earth. He saw a frightened white boy way down below.

It was as if he saw the whole ritual while floating in the sky. He saw the warriors pouring down a ravine toward the white boy, like an angry flash flood. They wore eagle feathers in their hair, and they screamed like eagles, but he knew that he was the real eagle way up in the wind.

From above, he saw them all play their parts in the ritual drama. The Comanches, who had waited with the white boy in the ravine, pretended to defend him. The raiders pretended to struggle to capture him. They fought a make-believe hand-to-hand battle there on the red-earth stage. They crashed sacred war shield against sacred war shield. They shook war axes and brandished shivering lances. Jimmy saw the white boy instinctively try to run, but a raider caught him by his blond hair–bleached almost white by the sun–from behind. It was an exciting scene. He was glad that he had such a good vantage point from which to watch.

Now the angry flood receded back down the ravine, returning the way it had come, carrying with it the white boy in the ceremonial buckskin leggings. This tide carried him to the broad bottom of the canyon floor, where the tepees rose one after the other like whitecaps. The whole tribe rushed out to welcome home the returning make-believe raiders and to celebrate the mock taking of a real captive. Watching from on high, Jimmy wondered why they went to so much trouble to catch what they had already caught.

In the forefront of the welcoming throng was the Comanche boy who was the white boy's young overseer. At the sight of him, the captive flinched. The white child seemed really to be afraid of this red boy. He wasn't pretending.

Still in the sky, looking down on the assault, Jimmy saw the Comanche boy slap the white boy across the chest with a rawhide whip. The white boy accepted the blow passively. He seemed beyond pretending, beyond struggling, beyond caring what happened to him. The red boy pushed the white boy down. Still there was no resistance. The whip rose again but stopped overhead as if it had forgotten what it was intending to do.

The Comanche boy had paused in mid-blow because he was so surprised to see a small horny toad escape from the clothing of the fallen white boy. The captive tried to scramble after his pet, but he lay in an awkward position and moved clumsily. The Comanche boy picked up a rock. The white boy reached for the red boy's arm but missed. The rock came down on the back of the small armored animal that seemed to have survived millions of years in order to die that day at the hands of a young boy.

Jimmy had seen his father killed by the Comanches. He had seen his grandfather killed by the Comanches. He had seen a Comanche spear go right through the small body of his sister. And now a Comanche had killed his last friend. He hadn't been able to fight back against the mounted warriors who murdered his father and grandfather. He had been fleeing for his own life when they were butchered. He had ducked and doomed his sister, and he hadn't done anything to avenge her death. But now he was finished with standing by helplessly and watching all that he loved being murdered. The killing of Fred was one killing too many. Now he would fight back. Now he would strike a long delayed blow for his slain father, for his mutilated grandfather, for his raped aunts, for his sister writhing on the ground.

The unarmed slave charged his tormentor, charged the whip, charged the flint-bladed knife that suddenly appeared. Jimmy kept coming, his anger blinding him to the danger. What did he care? What did he have to lose? Why cling to this slave's life? He knew he should have been the one to die at the fort instead of his sister, so now he would pay that debt and join her. But when he saw his enemy smile, he got mad enough to want to live. Why should he give this savage beast satisfaction?

Moving quickly, by reflex, Jimmy deflected the knife. The sharp stone blade sliced his palm, ricocheted off his wrist bone, and plunged into his left eye. He screamed the way his grandfather had screamed, the way his grandmother had screamed, the way his aunts had screamed. His sister hadn't screamed. She had been made of sterner stuff than he was. The Comanche boy kept pushing the knife, trying to plunge its sharp point into the brain behind the ruined eye, but the white boy's eye socket was too small to admit the wide stone blade. If he had been full-grown, he would be dead now.

With one eye destroyed and the other blinded by blood, Jimmy groped in the dark for a weapon. It was as though the God of his fathers guided his hand to the appropriate weapon, for he clutched a jawbone. Samson slew the enemies of his people with the jawbone of an ass, but Jimmy clutched the broken jaw of a buffalo. The white boy blindly struck the red boy across the left ear with his sturdy weapon made of bone and teeth. The mock ritual battle of the Eagle Dance had given way to real war.

Wiping the blood out of his right eye, Jimmy saw through a blood haze that his enemy was bleeding from the ear. The sight of all this blood–the blood in his eye, the blood of his foe, white blood, red blood–crazed the white boy. It was the blood of his father, the blood of his grandfather, the blood of his aunts, the blood of his sister, and the blood of his ancient horned pet, Fred's blood. And his own blood. He felt a blood lust for blood vengeance. He struck out again and again at the blood as if blood itself were the enemy. He wanted to hurt blood. He wanted to conquer blood. He wanted to kill blood. He wanted to destroy blood. He wanted to bury blood forever.

The eagle soaring high overhead, the one-eyed eagle who was Jimmy, looked down on a small, blood-spattered Samson who kept striking blow after blow with the jawbone. The white boy way down there had the mad strength of the insane. He had the uncaring audacity of pure lunacy. He kept waiting for the roof of the temple to come tumbling down on him, but it didn't matter because he was safe up here. Let them kill that white boy. Let them drive a lance into his back. Let an arrow pierce his side. Let him die like his sister and like Fred. Let . . .

Then his enemy fell at his feet and he was suddenly afraid. He had killed the Comanche boy and now the Comanches would kill him. He could feel the throng moving closer, constricting around him. He had a terrible picture in his mind: his hair being cut from his head, coming loose with a pop.

Jimmy saw the Comanche boy at his feet seem to come back to life, rising slowly onto his hands and knees. His enemy appeared to be starting life over again as a baby crawling. Or some lower four-footed animal. Jimmy felt simultaneously relieved and disappointed to see that he hadn't killed the other boy.

The savage white boy raised the jawbone once more. The dead buffalo seemed eager to avenge itself on the race that had killed it and so many of its relatives. Its bone struck the Comanche on the back and the shoulders again and again. As he beat the red boy, the white boy kept anticipating the feel of the lance point between his shoulder blades. He shivered.

The Comanche boy-warrior collapsed once again. And this time, he didn't try to get up. The savage white boy looked down at his beaten enemy and then around at the crowd.

Now they would kill him.

The Sun Chief stepped forward. He would perform the execution. The slave was the master's property and would die at his hands. The white boy sank to his knees. Reaching down, Jimmy's master laid hands on him, held him for a moment, and then raised him up. He lifted him all the way over his head. The master was going to kill the slave by dashing him to the earth.

The master set his bloodied slave on his shoulders. The Sun Chief paraded the small white boy through the village with a huge crowd following behind. It was a victory celebration. Looking back with one eye, the little white warrior saw a throng of Comanches all dancing and waving eagle feathers. Soaring high on his master's shoulders, Jimmy felt like an eagle leading a flock of brother eagles through savage heavens.

80

Proud of the new eagle feather tied in his hair, Jimmy reached up and touched it gently to make sure it was still there. He felt it flutter in the warm, restless summer air. Then his hand moved instinctively from the feather in his hair to the bandage over his ruined eye. Now the small purple splotches on his face, which resembled the Big Dipper, pointed not at the North Star but at his empty eye socket, as if it had always known what would happen. Squinting with his one good eye, he watched the smoke from the council fire move slowly back and forth, a grey feather as tall as the afternoon sky.

Jimmy could see the men of the village seated in a great circle, which reminded him of a huge eye. The fire at the center of the circle was the pupil. This giant eye was staring up at the heavens.

While he waited nervously for his part in the ceremony to begin, Jimmy kept turning his head this way and that as if wary of some approaching enemy. Since he had lost an eye, his field of vision was sharply reduced, and he always felt as if somebody were creeping up behind him, or on his blind side. He tried to compensate for his loss by continually pivoting his head, which was tiring and made him a little dizzy. He felt as if he lived in a wooden box and was looking out at a world through a single knothole. And the world he saw was flatter and less forgiving than it had been before. That was the bad part.

The good part was that the loss of an eye had made him appreciate what his remaining eye saw all the more. As he pivoted his head to the right and then back to the left, he beheld a paradise to which he had been blind before when he had both eyes. Of course, he had recognized from the beginning that the canyon was an extraordinary place, but he had somehow missed seeing how truly beautiful it was. Now he felt as if he were living in a fairy-tale palace with turrets and towers sculpted out of red sandstone. The beauties of his new home were made all the more touching because they seemed so fragile; not that the red canyon was likely to disappear from the world any time soon, but it might very well vanish from *his* world if his one remaining eye ever failed him. He was so moved by what he beheld that tears rolled down one side of his face.

Jimmy noticed that the women and children were gathering to watch the ritual. They formed an informal ring around the formal council circle. When he saw a certain face, he scowled, for it was bruised and battered, with missing teeth and a broken nose. But it had somehow survived the wrath of a small white warrior. Jimmy looked away from his victim, back toward the fire.

A tiny feather of smoke rose from the pipe that the men passed from hand to hand around the circle. The bowl of the pipe–which burned a mixture of tobacco and crushed sumac leaves–was shaped from red sandstone taken from the wall of the majestic canyon. The stem of the pipe was a hollow reed that was inserted into the bowl. Since the two parts of the pipe weren't welded together, the smokers had to hold them and pass them with both hands. The red pipe seemed to be a smoldering emblem of the red canyon itself.

As he watched the pipe make its way around the circle, Jimmy breathed in the slightly sweet aroma of the burning sumac and tobacco. He kept on reaching up every now and then to check on his proud feather. Touching it somehow seemed to make him less nervous. And every time he touched his feather, he then proceeded to touch his bandage, over and over, time and again, his own private ritual. When he saw a brave lay the pipe aside, the one-eyed boy reached up and held on to the feather tight.

Jimmy stared hard with his one eye as the men all rose in unison and placed their right hands over their hearts. Then they stretched out their hands to the sun. Then they covered their hearts again. Then they started walking in a slow circle, repeating their sun salute over and over again, now raising their hands, now covering their hearts. And they chanted some sort of greeting–or perhaps a prayer–to the sun. Their words and their feet made a solemn, serious sound.

When this living wheel finally stopped turning, the Sun Chief broke from the circle and walked in Jimmy's direction. The closer he came, the more the boy tugged at his feather. Reaching the blond child, the yellow-painted brave took the boy's hand, gently pulled him to his feet, and led him toward the great circle with the fire at its hub.

The Sun Chief led him inside the ring, deep into the circle, up so close to the fire that it made his face hot. The white boy stared into the flames to keep from having to look at all the faces staring at him. The aroma of the pipe was thick around him. The smoke and the heat and his nerves made him light-headed. He swayed forward as if he might fall into the fire, the blazing pupil of the monster eye, but the Sun Chief took hold of his shoulders and steadied him.

Still holding him by the shoulders, the red man turned the white boy around so that his back was to the fire. As Jimmy was trying to get used to all the staring eyes, he saw a stately old man leave the ring and approach him. He had many eagle feathers tied in his hair because he was an old respected man of magic. When the ancient shaman came to a stop directly in front of the boy, Jimmy desperately wanted to reach up and stroke his own feather, but he didn't dare move at this solemn moment.

In a deep, grave voice, the old medicine man began what seemed to be a speech directed at the white boy. Jimmy listened almost reverently although he couldn't understand a word. He heard from their tone that the words were meant kindly, and they relaxed him a little.

When he had finished his lecture, the wrinkled shaman came and stood next to Jimmy. His master the Sun Chief took up a position on his other side. The three of them now stood in a row facing the hot afternoon sun. The old shaman placed his hand over his heart, the Sun Chief did the same, and so Jimmy copied them–he placed his small white hand over his excited heart. When the medicine man raised his hand to the sun, the Sun Chief lifted his also. Jimmy did the same. Then all three hands returned to their hearts. They repeated this salute three times.

Then the Sun Chief bent down and grasped Jimmy in a suffocating bear hug as blood-curdling cries echoed through the camp. The boy gasped for breath and would have liked to cover his ears, but he was still smiling broadly. Without understanding the words, he still understood what had happened to him.

He had been adopted into the tribe. He was a Comanche.

81

In the dark, cramped tepee, the yellow-painted Comanche warrior was trying to teach his new white-haired son how to talk. He pointed to the white boy, then pointed at himself.

"Nu-mu-nu," he said slowly and distinctly.

Jimmy's face drew itself into a small scowl because he had no idea what the sound meant.

"Numunu," the new father said more rapidly, *"numunu, numunu."*

The boy's uncomprehending shoulders went up in a shrug.

"Numunu." The man pointed at the boy. *"Numunu."* He pointed at himself. *"Numunu."* He pointed back at the boy.

Jimmy was afraid his new father would be displeased with him, even angry with him, so his scowl deepened. He even cringed slightly. But his new father only grinned broadly, reached out for his hand, and led his son out of the tent. The warrior was in a hurry. He was almost running, dragging his son along behind him, in his haste to teach him. When they came upon a squaw scraping a buffalo hide, the father stopped and pointed. *"Numunu,"* he said.

They passed a warrior asleep in the shade of his tepee. The father pointed again. *"Numunu."*

They hurried on past a small band of naked boys playing a ball game. *"Numunu."*

Continuing their tour, they rushed by a group of girls in buckskin who were learning to sew with sinews and a bone awl. *"Numunu."*

Jimmy stopped. He stood in the middle of the village, thinking. Then he slowly pointed to himself. *"Numunu,"* he whispered.

As he said the word, Jimmy saw his new father nod and smile broadly. Then the boy pointed at the Sun Chief. *"Numunu,"* he repeated a little louder.

The father nodded again, still smiling.

Acting on impulse, Jimmy reversed the roles. Now the son grabbed the father's hand. Now the boy dragged the man through the village. Now Jimmy pointed at a brave mending his bow. *"Numunu!"* he shouted.

Running on, he pointed to a gaggle of old men who were telling tales, counting coups. *"Numunu!"*

When he had dragged his father to the edge of the village, he pointed to a brave on horseback. *"Numunu! Numunu!"*

The Sun Chief, his father, picked up his son and hugged him, and they called each other by that strange name over and over as if it were a love name: *"Numunu,* Human Being, *Numunu,* Human Being, *Numunu . . ."*

The new son and his new father surveyed the tribe's wealth, its horses. The great pony vault was a small box canyon that was an arm of the great canyon itself. They were a horse-rich village, which was the only wealth the Human Beings recognized. Jimmy could tell that his father took great pride in this valuable herd, so he took pride in it also.

The Sun Chief led his son in among the horses, which shied and made way for them. Jimmy was a little nervous as he looked around at all the large animals. But his father was completely comfortable, and his calmness helped calm the son. The boy stayed close to the man. Standing at the center of the herd, the father made a sweeping gesture that took in all the horses.

"Tuhuya," he said in a deep voice that was almost reverent. *"Tuhuya* . . . Goddogs . . . *Tuhuya . . ."*

"Tu-hu-ya," Jimmy said hesitantly. God-dogs.

His father nodded and smiled proudly.

"Goddogs," the red man said again.

"Goddogs," the white boy repeated.

They kept saying the word over and over to each other . . . "Goddogs . . . Goddogs . . . Goddogs" . . . until the father was satisfied that his son had memorized this all-important name.

Then the man led the boy up to a brown Goddog. The warrior patted the animal's neck and rubbed its shoulders.

"Dup-sik-ma"—the father pronounced the word slowly and clearly.

"Dup-uh-uh"—the son tried and failed.

"Dupsikma, dupsikma, dupsikma."

"Dup–sik–ma."

The boy said the word, but he had no idea what it meant, so he shrugged. The man understood and moved on to another Goddog, another brown one, and patted it, too. *"Dupsikma."*

"Dupsikma."

They moved on to a third brown Goddog, which reared as they approached.

"Dupsikma."

"Dupsikma."

At last, the new Comanche thought perhaps he understood, but he wasn't sure. He pointed to a brown Goddog, only a colt really, and tested his theory. *"Dupsikma,"* Jimmy said a little unsurely.

The Comanche warrior nodded and smiled. Yes, yes, very good.

Jimmy started pointing to one brown Goddog after another . . . *"Dupsikma . . . dupsikma . . . dupsikma"* . . . and his father kept nodding and smiling.

When the boy's enthusiasm for his new word finally wound itself down, his father led him to a light bay Goddog, whose neck he rubbed. *"Ohaieka,"* the red man said.

"Ohaieka," the white boy repeated.

Looking around, Jimmy saw another light bay. He pointed in its direction. *"Ohaieka?"* he asked.

The father hugged his son, lifting his feet off the ground. When his moccasins touched the earth again, the boy pointed at other bay-colored Goddogs . . . *"Ohaieka . . . ohaieka"* . . . over and over as if it were a new game. He was having so much fun that he almost forgot that he only had one eye.

They moved on to a reddish-brown Goddog.

"Ekakoma," said the father.

"Ekakoma," echoed the son.

Then the boy pointed to several other reddish-brown *ekakomas* and pronounced the new word carefully.

Then the father selected a yellow Goddog to pat. *"Ohaesi."*

"Ohaesi."

The father and son worked their way through the herd, the man teaching, the boy learning, the many words for the many kinds of Goddogs. At the same time, the new Human was learning how important Goddogs were to his people. He was coming to understand that one name wasn't enough for such valuable godlike creatures.

They deserved and had been given many names, *dupsikma, ohaieka, ekakoma, ohaesi, dukuma, dunaki* . . .

Jimmy could tell that the Sun Chief was proud of his new son who was beginning to sound like a Human Being.

One cool autumn afternoon, Jimmy knew the time had come for him to learn one more name of great importance. His own. The naming ceremony took place inside his father's crowded *Numu-kahni*, his Human-house, his tepee.

Jimmy thought his new parents looked proud and handsome on this special day. Both his Human father and his Human mother were letting their hair grow once again, and so they looked more Human with every passing day. Now Jimmy knew that they had cut their hair to mourn for a son who had died of a fever. To compensate in part for their loss, they had a new son who was about to receive a new Human name. His blond hair was growing out, too.

The village's wizened old shaman lit a red sandstone pipe with an orange coal from the fire. He blew pale smoke up to heaven, down to earth, and then in the four directions. Then the chief spoke solemnly in the Human tongue, but Jimmy understood only the occasional word. The old man repeated *tumarumoa,* meaning "much," so often that Jimmy wondered if his new name might be just that: Much. He was already familiar with this word because the Humans used it almost too much. Much long, much short, much pretty, much ugly, much good, much bad. Jimmy had already decided that this constant repetition of "much" was very much in keeping with Human nature: for the Human Beings were an exaggerated people who did everything much–rode much, hunted much, warred much, hated much, and now loved much a white boy.

The shaman lifted Jimmy so that the old face with two eyes stared directly at the new face with only one eye. They were nose-to-nose. And now the new Human did at last hear his new Human name for the first time. It was a much mouthful.

"Yake-Ohachahnakatu."

Jimmy had learned that *yake* meant "crying." He knew *oha* was "yellow," *chah* was "under," and *nakatu* was "forelegs." So Jimmy Goodnight had become Crying Yellow-Under-Forelegs. But what in the world did that mean? He was much puzzled.

The old shaman lifted Crying Yellow-Under-Forelegs up over his head. He held him balanced there for a moment. Then he lowered the boy, who thought the ceremony was over. But the chief lifted Crying Yellow-Under-Forelegs up again, high over his head again, then lowered him again, then raised him again, three times, the magical number. The pointed Human-house was filled with happy voices as the Humans merrily congratulated the newly named Human Being and wished his Human father and Human mother well. The boy with the new name was proud but still puzzled. He didn't have forelegs or even yellow armpits.

The Human Beings filed out of the Human-house to form a great gyrating circle around the bonfire. Jimmy's father led him into this throbbing ring. Soon the boy began to dance, trying to copy the leaps and struts of the other dancers. He felt that he now belonged to the Human circle. In the midst of the dancing, his father took hold of him and hugged him off the ground.

The circle of dancers was loud with ritual cries of joy and thanksgiving. The white Human Being let out a cry himself, trying to sound the way the others sounded, and everybody laughed.

82

Jimmy Crying Coyote–who by now had learned the meaning of his own name–tried to wipe the stinging sweat out of his one eye. It was spring again and an unseasonably hot day. The eleven-year-old boy wished he could sit down and take a break, but he had to try to keep up with his yellow-painted father: not the Sun Chief but the Sun Shaman. When he had first been adopted, he had imagined that his father was a chief, but now he knew better. His father's power flowed from another source. He was a spiritual rather than a political leader. Now that the old shaman who had named Crying Coyote had died, his father was the village's highest-ranked medicine man. The boy wondered if the Sun Shaman even knew it was hot. Maybe not. Did the sun feel its own heat? The boy sure felt it.

Crying Coyote wasn't even certain what this long, hot hike was all about. After a year in the land of the Humans–it was spring again–he spoke the Human tongue fairly well, but he still didn't understand everything. He was sure he had misunderstood what his Human father told him just before they set off on this walk. They couldn't actually be going out to talk to the plant tribes. When the Sun Shaman finally did stop, Crying Coyote sank down gratefully on the hot red earth. His father smiled at him warmly.

"We almost there?" asked the boy, still not quite at home speaking the Human tongue.

"We are there," said his father.

Crying Coyote looked around. He didn't see anything that looked like a destination.

"Where there?" he asked, still not grammatical. "I not see nothing."

"These plants," said the Sun Shaman. "We call them friends-of-the-childless-woman. That is because they can help a barren woman become pregnant."

"Not understand," the boy said.

"If a woman cannot have a baby, she makes a tea from the leaves of this plant. She drinks it. It helps her plant a baby in her stomach."

Crying Coyote looked embarrassed. He lowered his gaze. Then he looked up to study this weed with sexual prowess. Upon closer examination, it looked to him like an ordinary horehound plant. Going a little closer, he noticed something else: these horehounds were alive with bees. Crying Coyote hated bees more than anything in the world. He had once climbed a tree and disturbed a swarm of bees, which stung him dozens of times. He fell out of the tree and writhed on the ground until his mother found him . . . but he tried not to think of his white mother these days. He touched the patch over his eye–and the Dipper beneath it–as he so often did when he felt uncomfortable or threatened.

"Plants are like Humans," his new father explained. "They live in families and tribes." He pointed at a friend-of-the-childless-woman in the middle of the patch. "That one, you see, he is the chief."

Crying Coyote studied this chief. It stood about three feet tall, which made it about the same height as the other friends, no bigger, no smaller. The chief's branches were crowned with small white flowers, but all the other plants wore similar crowns. Its oval-shaped leaves were downy and wrinkled, just like the leaves of its neighbors. The chief was not particularly handsome, but he wasn't any uglier than his subjects. Crying Coyote couldn't see any evidence of high rank, and wondered what his father saw, but he took his word for it.

"This plant is also good after the baby comes," the Sun Shaman said. "It can help mothers who cannot make milk. They make a salve and rub it on their breasts."

Embarrassed, Crying Coyote looked at the ground again. This weed didn't look sexy, but it must be.

"It is also good for colds," the father continued. "For coughs." He coughed to demonstrate, to make sure his son understood. "So a woman could take it for a cold and wind up getting pregnant." The Sun Shaman beamed. "A good joke on her, do not you think so?"

Warmed by his father's sunny smile, Crying Coyote managed to overcome his embarrassment enough to grin.

"Before we gather the herbs," the Sun Shaman said, "we have to talk to them. We have to explain to them what we are going to do. We have to tell them that we need some of their leaves to help the Humans, but we will not take all the leaves. We will not kill any plants. Once they understand, they will be willing to help us. If they are not willing, then no amount of leaves will do our people any good. We must obtain their permission. So talk."

Crying Coyote just stared dumbly at the ugly horehounds and the frightening bees.

"What is the matter?" asked his father.

"I not know how talk the plant tongue," the son said.

"Just talk to them the way you would talk to a Goddog."

"I no talk Goddog either."

"But you still talk to Goddogs. You tell them to calm down. You tell them to speed up. You tell them to be good. The Goddogs do not understand your words, but they understand your tone of voice. They understand your meaning. You talk to them soothingly and they quiet down. Right?"

"Hai." Yes, that was right.

"You must talk to the friends-of-the-childless-woman in the same way. You just explain simply and directly and sympathetically, and they will understand. The worthiness of your cause will be in your voice. Go ahead."

Crying Coyote looked at the horehounds and hesitated. He was still worried that he didn't know how to talk to plants.

"Go on," his father said. "Get up close. Go among them. You must talk to the chief face-to-face."

Crying Coyote reluctantly moved a couple of steps closer to the friends-of-the-childless-woman. Then he stopped.

"You are still not close enough."

"I cannot."

"Why not? I do not understand."

"Bees sting me."

"*Kee*, they will not."

"Hai, they do. They did before. They like me much good. I afraid."

"Then you must talk to the bees, too. You must tell them that you will not hurt them, and ask them not to hurt you in return. You must ask them to share the friends-of-the-childless-woman with you. And you must promise them that we are not plant-killers, just leaf-borrowers. Speak simply and directly and sympathetically."

"Which one chief bee?"

"These bees have a woman chief, but she is not here. She is back at the bee village. So you must talk to all the bees in general."

Crying Coyote cautiously approached the bee-covered plants as if he were stalking an elusive prey. But he wondered who was actually going to end up being the hunter and who the hunted. He felt like a rabbit stalking a coyote. The horehounds were alive with bees from "head" to "foot."

"Do not be afraid," his father said. "Bees can smell fear."

When Crying Coyote reached the first horehound, he stopped and tried to think what to say.

"Keep going," said his father.

Crying Coyote moved on into the patch of horehounds swarming with bees. "Bees, I no hurt you," he mumbled, "so you no hurt me." He sucked in a breath. "I hope."

"Louder," called his father. "They cannot hear you. Talk loud enough so they can hear you, but not so loud that you threaten them."

"Bees, I no hurt you," Crying Coyote said a little louder, hoping it wasn't too loud, "so you no hurt me. Please." His skin felt cold, then it itched, then it ached in anticipation. "You no hurt me and I no hurt you." He heard the bees buzzing louder and louder, working themselves up into a frenzy. He looked back at his father, frightened.

"They are talking it over," said the Sun Shaman. "You must explain to them why they should not go on the warpath."

"Please do not go on warpath," Crying Coyote implored.

"Don't worry. Keep going. Go to the center of the plants where the chief lives."

The trip to the center of the horehound patch seemed longer than the long hike that had brought them to this dangerous ground. Crying Coyote was sure the bees were doing a war dance. And now he had bees in front of him, bees behind him, bees on his left flank, and bees on his right. He was cut off from any escape route.

"Bees, you no hurt me, I no hurt you. We be much friends."

"Hurry up," said the shaman.

Crying Coyote tried to hurry, but he was still uneasy about all those bees feasting on horehound nectar.

"Is that the way you hurry? Before you were a slow turtle. Now you are a fast turtle. Just have faith and go do your business."

Crying Coyote quickened his pace so that he covered the ground like a very fast turtle. When he finally reached the leafy chief of horehounds, he bowed his head and said nervously: "Excuse me–"

"Sit down," his father called. "Show respect."

Crying Coyote could think of nothing he wanted to do less than sit down in the middle of a war party of angry bees. Nonetheless he lowered himself slowly to the ground. He was sure he was going to sit on a bee. "You no hurt me, I no hurt you, you no hurt me . . ." The bees answered by buzzing louder and louder. Was it because he was now down among them? Or were they getting madder and madder? Glancing up, he saw bees buzzing directly over his head. Now he had stingers on all sides and even above him. The very air seemed to have turned to bees. What if he breathed one into his lungs?

"Talk to the chief," the Sun Shaman called. "Tell him what we want and why we want it."

Crying Coyote took another deep breath. "Excuse me, Chief of the Friends-of-the-Childless-Woman, I ask favor. Human Beings need some leaves."

"Tell him why."

"We need leaves to not cough." And the boy coughed to demonstrate. He was making every effort to help the chief of the horehounds comprehend his message. "Use leaves. No cough. Understand?"

The plant chief swayed ever so slightly in a gentle breeze, and the bees buzzed.

"Tell him what else," his father called.

Crying Coyote took an even deeper breath. He had been dreading this part. Now his tongue felt as though it were coated not only with danger but also with embarrassment. He coughed again.

"Excuse me," he began, "our no-child-women need leaves."

"Why?" called his father.

"Leaves make them have babies."

"Tell the chief and tell the bees that Humans do not have enough babies. Tell them much Human women are barren. Tell them that is why we adopted you. Because we do not have enough babies of our own. Tell them we need much babies."

Crying Coyote wished he could speak the Human tongue as well as his father did. "Chief, Humans need more Humans," he stammered. "Bees, you listen too, please? Much no-child-women. No much babies. You understand?"

"That is right," his father said. "But make your voice more gentle. Chant to the chief. Sing to the bees."

"You no hurt, I no hurt," Crying Coyote said soothingly. "I no take all leaves. No hurt. I no kill plants. No hurt. I leave much flowers. No hurt. They make much seeds. No hurt. Much friends-of-the-childless-woman next year. No hurt. We share. No hurt. No hurt. No hurt."

Crying Coyote was struck dumb by what he saw: the bees began moving away from him.

"Keep chanting," his father reminded him. "Keep singing."

"Humans need Humans," the son sang. "No hurt. Childless women need babies. No hurt . . ."

He chanted on and on, repeating himself over and over, amazed at the behavior of the terrible bees, growing more confident all the time. He wondered if the bees could smell confidence the way they smelled fear. The swarm of bees did not abandon the patch of horehounds, didn't pick up and move on, but they got out of his way. The insects nearest him moved to the backs of the plants, allowing him the front leaves, offering to share. The boy reached out to pluck a leaf–

"Kee!" commanded the Sun Shaman. "No, do not, not yet. You must first give the tribe of plants a gift, an offering. If you want something from them, you must first give something to them."

Crying Coyote thought a moment. "What I give? I no bring nothing." He shrugged.

"Pull out one of your hairs. Give them a golden hair from your head, and then they will give you their leaves."

Crying Coyote pulled out a hair. Ouch.

"Lift golden hair up to the sun."

He obeyed.

"Now place it solemnly on the ground."

He laid it down gently on the earth.

"Now gather your leaves."

Crying Coyote reached out slowly, tentatively, and took hold of one of the chief's leaves.

"Kee," said the Sun Shaman, "not him. Not the chief. You ask the chief's permission, but you collect the leaves of less exalted plants."

The boy turned to a plant on the chief's right and began plucking leaves. He went about his work cautiously, deliberately, solemnly.

"Taste one," his father said.

Again the son hesitated. He didn't really want to put a weed in his mouth. Overcoming his reservations, he bit off the tip of a hairy leaf and started to chew. He made a face.

"Do not worry," his father laughed. "You will not get pregnant. I promise."

Crying Coyote tried to smile. The horehound leaf tasted musky and bittersweet, with just a hint of mint. The boy thought it tasted like medicine. His tentative grin changed to a frown.

"You do not have to eat any more," his father smiled, "because you are not sick or barren."

Crying Coyote went back to picking leaves while keeping a watchful eye on the bees. "No hurt," he chanted in a soft voice. "Help us. No hurt. Help us . . ." He took a few leaves from one friend-of-the-childless-woman, then moved on to another friend and took a few more leaves. And each time he changed horehounds, the bees politely got out of his way, moved to the back of the plant, and shared with him.

"All of nature is talking all the time," the Sun Shaman told his son and apprentice. "And all of nature is listening all the time. We must try to understand nature, and we must try to make nature understand us. We owe it to each other."

While Crying Coyote went on gathering leaves and calming the bees, he began to daydream about all the other animals he would like to talk to . . . horned toads . . . rattlesnakes . . . prairie dogs . . . coyotes . . . eagles . . . and those great, shaggy, humpbacked beasts that he had learned to call Human cattle . . .

"You can even talk to rocks," the Sun Shaman said. "And rocks can talk to you."

Crying Coyote dreamed of conversations with quiet boulders and noisy brooks, with proud mountains and mean anthills, with echoing caves and calm canyons. He wondered what he would say to them, how he would introduce himself, how he would start the conversation . . .

"You talk to them the way you talk to bees," the Sun Shaman said, as if he read his son's thoughts. "The way you talk to horehounds. It does not make any difference whether it is a sunflower or the sun, you do it the same way. You talk the best you can and they will do the best they can. Hurry up. I want to go home."

83

On or about the second anniversary of Crying Coyote's coming to live among the Humans, he sat with his Human mother in their Human-house which at the moment served as a one-room schoolhouse. They were hard at work on an important task: the passing of the Human traditions from one generation to the next.

The mother's name was Wekeah. She had grown prettier as her hair had grown out and her face had gradually softened. And he had a sense that he was partially responsible for the change. Many Human females got fat in their middle years, but she still had a girl's figure. The twelve-year-old boy was proud that his mom had not let herself go. It was an almost perfect spring day.

"Tell me," Wekeah said, "what is the Human body made from?"

"From the earth," said Crying Coyote.

And so they rehearsed once again the Comanche catechism. It was also an opportunity for the boy to practice speaking the Human tongue. He knew much words by now, but he still had an accent, which he was trying to conquer.

"And Human bones?"

"From stones." He heard his accent again and winced, so he tried again, "Stones." No, it still didn't sound quite right.

"And Human blood?"

"Mother," Crying Coyote interrupted the lesson, "when will my father return?"

"When the hunt is over. Now let us continue our study."

"But I feel-missing him."

Crying Coyote used the verb *wusuwaruki*, which he had come to understand was a combination of the verbs "to feel" and "to miss." Humans found it one of the most moving words in the Human tongue. Crying Coyote missed his father, but he secretly enjoyed playing the man of the Human-house in his father's absence.

"We all feel-missing him," she said. "A family should not be apart. But let us go on. What is Human blood made from?"

"From dew."

"Hand," she said, meaning "good," and she raised her hand to underscore the compliment. Wekeah's strict schoolmarm's expression softened. "Now what are Human eyes made from?"

"From deep, clear water."

"And the light in Human eyes?"

"From the sun."

"And Human thought?"

"From waterfalls."

"And Human breath?"

"From the wind."

"And Human strength?"

"From storms."

"And Human beauty?"

"From the Great Mystery." Now his expression changed, softened into shyness, and he looked down. He told his mother: "The Great Mystery was hand to you."

"Thank you," said Wekeah, flattered but also slightly embarrassed.

"You are much beautiful," Crying Coyote said. He wanted to tell her that she was the most beautiful mother in the world. No, not just the most beautiful mother, but also the most beautiful woman in the world. But he couldn't because the Human tongue did not possess superlatives. He appreciated that this quirk of the language reduced competition, but he nonetheless missed being able to say "most," being able to bestow the ultimate compliment. All he could say was: "Mother, you are much, much, much beautiful to me."

Wekeah looked down, but she smiled. Crying Coyote smiled, too. Yes, it was good to be the male Human of the Human-house. Maybe it would be all right if his father continued his hunt for a while . . .

But a distant cry interrupted his reverie.

"The Writers are coming! The Writers are coming!"

Soon other Human voices took up the cry and spread the alarm.

"Writers! . . . *Taibos!* . . . Writers! . . . *Taibos!* . . . Writers!"

Crying Coyote had originally been amused when he learned that Human Beings called white people Writers. Having studied the invading race of pale men and sallow women, the Humans soon realized that what made these inhumans strange and different wasn't their skin color. Who cared about shades of coloring? What made the new inhumans really different was their habit of writing things down. Hearing the name now, shouted over and over, Crying Coyote was no longer amused but terrified. Because he knew the Writers were savages when they took to the warpath.

Forgetting his manners, neglecting to take leave of his mother, Crying Coyote rushed out the flap door into the bright sunshine, which momentarily blinded him. He sneezed. When his eye adjusted, he saw Human women and children running.

"Writers!" screamed the lone lookout as he rode into the village. "Writers! Writers! Writers!"

Crying Coyote saw an army of Writers crest a small rise east of the village. Unfortunately, the Humans had forsaken their canyon fortress in order to follow the Human-cattle herds, so they were vulnerable. Aboveground, on the High Plains south of the canyon, their tepees could be seen for miles. And they were vulnerable in another way also, since the men of the village were absent, off hunting the Human-cattle. The women and children had been left undefended because Writers did not normally come this far north. These onrushing Writers weren't dressed as warriors. They wore no uniforms, no paint on their faces, but rather looked like simple cowboys.

Crying Coyote didn't admire their war dress, but he was impressed by their handguns that could be fired over and over without reloading. He was terrified for himself and for his mother. He had never felt-missing his father more than now. His mother grabbed his hand and the two of them ran together. Looking back, he saw the savage Writers making war on women and children. They shot them in the back as they fled.

Then Crying Coyote heard the cavalry riding to the rescue, the Human cavalry, led by the Sun Shaman. This band of warriors rode their Goddogs into the gap between the Human women and children and the Writer rangers. Outnumbered, the Writers turned and fled. They were *pihisichapu*, running-hearts, cowards.

That evening by the light of a campfire, Crying Coyote watched a Human woman open her buckskin dress, expose her breasts, and approach the flames. She carried a flint-blade knife. The Humans within the glow of the flickering light all fell silent. The woman dangled her breasts over the fire, and orange flames reached up eager to fondle them. She used the flint knife to slash her breasts over and over again. She began to wail. Crying Coyote knew she was mourning her eight-summers-old daughter who had been shot in the back by the in-humans.

Soon other grieving women approached the fire and rained down blood into the flames. Their anguished cries grew louder and louder in the still night. Men also walked up to the fire, cut off their braids with knives, and threw them into the blaze. They grieved for sons and daughters, wives, mothers, sisters. All of the dead were women and children.

The Humans were already making plans for revenge.

84

The seventeen-year-old Crying Coyote felt a new and welcome surge of energy and purpose in the village. The Humans were once again preparing to send off their warriors to prey upon their enemies. The braves painted their faces black, the color of death. And they dreamed of captives, scalps, blood, rape, and glory.

Crying Coyote dreamed these dreams, too. He had long dreamed them in vain because he was too young to fight. So year after year, he had watched the warriors go off while he remained behind with the women and children and old men. But now at long last, he had been given permission to live the dream. He would be going on the warpath for the first time in his life.

When all was in readiness, the warriors mounted their Goddogs and pointed them south. Crying Coyote rode beside his father the Sun Shaman. They rocked along near the middle of a long column that moved across the Staked Plain like a centipede crawling across God's open hand. This column of warriors would converge with other columns at the base of the Double Mountain that rose at the edge of the plains.

But Double Mountain was an illusive destination. In the mornings, Crying Coyote could faintly see the twin humps, pale and blue in the distance, like two giant Human-cattle grazing side by side. But these great, blue Human-cattle were ghost-cattle who disappeared by noon. Morning after morning, Crying Coyote's journey seemed almost over, the end in view. But noonday after noonday, the end seemed to flee before him, to hide from him. This miracle of the mountains occurred because those peaks were magic. They had medicine. Of course, the whole world was magic. Everything in the world had medicine. But some things had stronger medicine than others. Double Mountain had medicine in proportion to its size.

After a week of pursuing the Double Mountain, the Human war

party finally caught up with it—or rather them. But the warriors never did catch the great blue-ghost Human-cattle that had been drawing them on. For as they drew near, these mountains turned back into normal, solid mountains, which were much too heavy to float in the air. And they changed from blue to brown. The newest warrior realized that he had lost the magic mountains by getting too close to them. Did all magic work the same way?

Crying Coyote and the Sun Shaman rode into a huge instant city that spread itself at the feet of Double Mountain. The new warrior was stunned by the size of this metropolis. It was four or five times larger than his home village, which itself seemed large to him. He was sure this encampment must be the biggest city in the world. It had a population of almost 500 Human Beings: warriors, warriors' wives, and even a few warriors' daughters. The Sun Shaman's band hadn't brought their women, but many other bands had. This fabulous city sprawled on broken ground that rose and fell on all sides as the plains crumbled away into geological chaos and wasteland. Crying Coyote found it much, much beautiful.

To celebrate the arrival of this new band of warriors, the city proclaimed a dance. The newest warrior Coyote dressed carefully and nervously. He owed his care and nerves to all the strange young Human females whom he had seen milling about the biggest city in the world. He had never seen so many girls in his life. He hadn't been sure there were that many girls in the whole entire world. So he was excited, apprehensive, and anxious to see what would happen. He had finally been allowed to go on the warpath and that path had led him to this unexpected capital city of girls.

He donned a breechclout, dyed blue, which hung to his knees. He stepped into leggings that were dyed red and decorated with remarkably long fringes in the Human manner. These decorative fringes were in turn decorated with beads, shells, bits of silver, and deer's teeth. He put on his dancing shoes, buckskin moccasins, made more handsome by skunk tails attached at the heels. He felt handsome, then ugly, then manly, then too young, then brave, then scared. He was a teenager.

At the center of the village, the older Human Beings formed a great circle. This ring surrounded two parallel lines of younger Humans, one row of males, the other of females, facing each other. As the drums began their mating thunder, the braves stepped forward to choose their partners.

Crying Coyote cautiously approached a girl who appeared to be about his age. She wore a pale yellow buckskin dress decorated in the Human fashion with extraordinarily long fringe at the sleeves and seams. Her teenage breasts seemed to sprout long fringe tassels. On her dancer's feet were beaded moccasins. She had gotten dressed up, too. The boy moved quietly, as if he were stalking the girl, as if walking silently would keep her from noticing him bearing down on her, as if she might become deer-frightened and run away at any moment. He was painfully aware of having only one eye, wondered if she found his patch ugly, would have liked to reach up and touch it, but didn't want to draw more attention to his deformity. Did she see the small purple stars on his cheek?

Reaching the girl, Crying Coyote designated her as his chosen partner by placing his hands around her waist. Those hands were shaking. He scolded himself for being such a timid warrior. Maybe he wasn't ready for the warpath after all. She accepted him by placing her hands around his waist. He was as thrilled as he had been when he killed his first Human-cow. Well, it was a calf really. Soon the couple were swaying together in a savage quadrille. Crying Coyote danced well. His partner was even better. For a moment, he forgot he had only one eye.

"I am called Crying Coyote," he introduced himself.

"I am called Lifts Something," said the Comanche girl.

"You have a much pretty name."

"Thank you much."

While they danced, they studied each other with quick but curious glances. She saw that his nose turned up slightly. He saw that her nose was straight. He saw a girl with hair the color of the night. She saw a boy with hair the color of the moon. He saw that she had two lovely brown eyes. She saw that he had one blue eye and a patch. He saw that she saw.

"You are beautiful," Crying Coyote said.

"Thank you," said Lifts Something.

"You are much beautiful." He had almost stopped thinking in terms of *most.* "Much, much beautiful," he added.

"Thank you much."

"You are welcome much."

Crying Coyote could see her trying to think of a way to compliment him in return. She obviously couldn't say he was much beautiful, not even handsome, not with that ugly patch.

"You dance the Human dances much hand," she finally said. But the tone of her voice conveyed more. It could not help revealing that she had not expected him to dance so well.

"Are you surprised?" he asked.

"Well, your *pui* are–is–I am sorry–is blue."

"My eye is Human," he said angrily. "All of me is Human!"

Crying Coyote stopped dancing. He turned to leave the dance circle, but Lifts Something placed her hands on his waist. He stopped, tried to think clearly in spite of the anger and hurt, then turned back around. They danced.

A few nights later, they danced their war dance. Crying Coyote stared at the largest Human circle he had ever seen. It was made up entirely of women, as if it were some giant symbol for Woman. The men danced inside this great circle of womanhood.

Yellow-haired Crying Coyote and his yellow-painted father made their way into the circle and joined the war dance. The boy searched the circle of women. He was looking for Lifts Something, but there were so many that it took him a while to find her. When he did, he danced in front of her. He jumped, he gyrated, he showed off. And inside he was jumping and gyrating and twisting, too, because he wasn't sure whether she liked him or not.

The next morning, over half a thousand Comanches rode south toward the land of the inhumans. Crying Coyote and Lifts Something rocked along side by side. He thought: She likes me! It was a miracle. The warpath was a wonderful place to fall in love. His face was painted black, the color of death. Her face was streaked with black. But their smiles belied the somber colors.

The trees grew taller and rounder and softer as the Humans rode deeper into southeast Texas.

85

The Humans camped beside the Brazos River, which was little more than a creek. As the campfires burned down to embers, the warriors began settling down for a restful night of *uhu* (blanket) *kooi* (death). But Lifts Something was not sleepy. She told Crying Coyote that blanket-death could wait because she was going to wash her hair in the river. She got up and left. Crying Coyote wasn't sure what to do. Should he roll up in his buffalo robe and drift away? Or should he go after her? Was she really interested in clean hair, or did she hope for something more?

After a long debate with himself, Crying Coyote decided that the warpath was no place for a running-heart. He got up quietly and crept nervously in the direction of the river. He heard her bathing and followed the sound. But when he reached the river's edge, when he saw her, he hesitated. Hiding himself in the shadow of a cottonwood tree, he simply watched.

But soon Crying Coyote began to grow nervous. What if she should see him seeing her? What if somebody else should spy him spying on her? Losing his nerve, he turned and began beating a silent retreat.

"*Kia!*" Lifts Something called out, indicating surprise. "Where are you going?"

Crying Coyote turned again, surprised, confused, and most of all embarrassed.

"*Hakai?*" he called back, making a question sign by rotating an uneasy hand. "What?"

"Why are you running away?" asked the girl in the river. "Are you a running-heart?"

The young warrior chose to be insulted.

"I never . . ."

"Then do not run away now."

Crying Coyote stood paralyzed. He looked so uncomfortable that the young woman laughed.

"Your hair is dirty," Lifts Something said.

He put his hand up and ran it through his hair. Then he scratched his head.

"*Kee,* it is not."

He didn't like to wash his hair too often because the dirtier it got, the darker it got, which made him look more Human.

"*Hay,*" Lifts Something insisted, "it looks dirty to me. Come down here. Come into the water. Quickly!"

Crying Coyote disrobed in the shadows and walked backward into the river. The water was shallow, only covering the bathers up to their waists. Lifts Something's young breasts stood up like pointed Human-houses on her chest. Crying Coyote couldn't believe he was this close to something so wonderful.

"Were you going to go back," Lifts Something asked, "and never let me know you had seen me?"

"*Hay,*" he said. Yes.

"Why?"

"You know."

"*Kee,* I do not. Tell me. Why were you going to go without saying hello?"

She dunked him playfully in the shallow river. He came up sputtering, with his mouth and eye wide open. He eventually managed to close his mouth, but his eye remained gaping.

"Come on." Lifts Something laughed. "How could you be so rude?"

"Because . . . because it is not proper," he sputtered.

"What is not proper?"

"For me, the boy, to be the aggressor. The girl must be the aggressor in matters such as these. You know that. You were well brought up."

"You are much old-fashioned."

"I have to be."

"Because you are not really Human?"

"I *am* Human! Do not say that."

"I am sorry. I do not mind your being old-fashioned. It is all right." She crossed her arms over her breasts. "Actually, I like it. You are a credit to your parents." She smiled. "And you are a challenge."

Lifts Something uncrossed her arms and began washing Crying

Coyote's head. He slowly began to relax. He even started to enjoy the touch of her hands. He felt a little dreamy, so he wasn't sure he heard her right.

He thought she said: *"Na-su-yake.* My mind cries for you. I love you." But he wasn't sure and so didn't say anything.

He thought he heard it again: "My mind cries for you."

But he was shy.

Lifts Something grabbed hold of his hair and pulled straight up as if she were going to scalp him.

"My mind cries for you," she said. "Now you say something."

"My mind cries for you, too," he mumbled.

She released his hair and threw her arms around him.

86

Crying Coyote stared at a miracle: a great plain made of water instead of grass. The waves rolled the way the grass on the plains rolled when the wind stirred it. He felt an urge to ride out across it to the blue horizon. He wished he had two eyes to take in so much beauty, but he also realized that he loved beauty more now that he could see less of it. Surely this watery plain was the most beautiful landscape in the world. Except it wasn't land.

Crying Coyote and the rest of the Human horde studied the panorama from atop a low green hill that allowed them to see for miles in this low country. At the edge of the blue limpid plain, they saw a tiny settlement that seemed huddled and timid. The town of Linnville was composed of only a few shacks, a couple of stores, a small church, and a huge mountain of a building that dwarfed everything else. He wondered: What in the world could that be?

Needing a friend to talk to, Crying Coyote leaned forward and spoke soothingly to his Goddog. "Run well today, Old Friend. Do not put your hoof in any prairie dog holes. Do they have prairie dogs here? Be brave, Old Friend. This is our chance to prove that we belong on the warpath."

Crying Coyote was as nervous as he had been when he was waiting for the dance to start, as nervous as he had been as he approached Lifts Something for the first time, for he was once again waiting for something to begin, waiting to see what would happen. Soon he would be charging down this bluff toward the town below, would soon be fighting his first battle, but not yet. He couldn't go until his father the Sun Shaman gave the signal. And his father wouldn't go until a venerable old warrior named Chief Iron Jacket gave the signal. But the old chief seemed simply to be enjoying the wonderful view. What was he waiting for? Why didn't he go? Didn't he know they were burning to charge? Was he too old to be eager for battle?

Crying Coyote thought: Chief Iron Jacket couldn't be afraid, could he? What did he have to be afraid of? After all, he was immortal, wasn't he, thanks to his armor? That's what everybody said. Crying Coyote's father had told him the story of the iron vest. How one of the chief's forefathers had taken it from a Spanish enemy much, much years ago. How this enemy had been a soldier in an army that wore not only iron jackets but also iron hats. How these intruders not only wore metal clothes but were looking for metal villages. How they had been crazy enough to believe that the Human Beings would make houses out of gold that would be too heavy to carry when it was time to move on. How many of these silly soldiers had lost their lives on the trackless plains and so lost their armor? The ancient iron jacket was made of overlapping metal plates that jingled merrily when in motion. But his armor was quiet now as the old man sat motionless on the top of the hill. In the bright morning sun, the old jacket gleamed as if it were gold, as if the old soldier had found the cities for which he was searching. If Crying Coyote had such a battle vest, he told himself, he wouldn't hesitate. He would–

The attack caught the impatient Crying Coyote in mid-daydream. He wasn't ready and almost lost his balance. He hoped Lifts Something hadn't noticed. He looked around for her, but he couldn't find her in all the confusion. Without warning, Chief Iron Jacket had kicked his Goddog in the ribs and charged. Which caused the Sun Shaman to kick his Goddog. Which started a stampede down the slope. Crying Coyote was caught in a vast Human wave that rolled down the green hill the way waves rolled on the new–at least to him–ocean. The red wave raced south while the blue waves raced north. The opposing waves were on a collision course. Crying Coyote was being carried along by forces beyond his control. He had not anticipated this feeling of helplessness. It didn't fit with his idea of being a warrior, for he had always imagined that the warrior dominated the battle rather than the other way around. What was happening to him? What was happening to them all? Where was Lifts Something? He kept looking around for her pale yellow buckskin dress. He longed for her as he bore down upon the inhuman town. Then he realized that he had lost sight of his father, too.

Crying Coyote rode through grass that was thicker and taller than the grass at home. He rode over ground that was softer than the baked clay at home. He even rode through air that seemed thicker than the arid air at home.

Crashing through oak limbs, Crying Coyote galloped into the garden of an isolated cabin in time to see a scene that was somehow vaguely familiar. A Writer woman was being dragged from a log cabin. He watched as one of the Human warriors tore her inhuman blouse. Crying Coyote jumped off his horse to help undress the Writer woman, but he couldn't get close enough to touch her. Stripping enemy females was a popular activity and drew a crowd. Painted warriors threw the naked Writer woman onto the back of a horse, an unwilling Godiva.

Then the warriors swarmed on toward the small town built at the foot of the great mountain of a building. Writer men rushed out to challenge them with long, clumsy rifles. They were better armed than the Human Beings but overwhelmingly outnumbered. The Humans' problem was that there weren't enough enemies to go around: only a few braves would be able to count coups because of the shortage.

Crying Coyote saw a battle that was considerably more blurred and indistinct than he had imagined it would be. He was still living in a box and was forced to look out at the fighting through a knothole. He had trouble with his depth perception, so everything seemed to happen in one plane rather than in layers. Nothing sorted itself out or stood out. He had looked forward to scenes of combat as clear and dramatic as the war stories he had heard around campfires all his Human life. But instead, his first battle was turning into a glimpse here and a glimpse there. War was too many stories happening simultaneously to be comprehended all at once. And none of them was his story because he was more spectator than warrior. He felt more confused than frightened, which surprised him.

Crying Coyote caught a glimpse of inhumans fleeing crazily toward the water, as if they thought they could run out across the blue plain. He saw them actually running into the ocean. He thought they were going to drown themselves to save themselves from a more painful death, but then he saw them getting into wooden boats. He and a dozen other braves charged after them, galloping right into the churning water, but the boats outran them. These Writers would escape because the Human Beings did not have a navy.

Crying Coyote sat on his Goddog, which was up to its chest in the heaving water, and stared about him. The ocean came at him in liquid hills, one after the other, an inexhaustible range of water mountains. This water had strong medicine and a strong taste. He was used to gentle, trickling water that made gentle, trickling sounds, but this water roared.

Crying Coyote was lost in his admiration of the fierce water when his Goddog suddenly shied. The inattentive warrior almost tumbled into the ocean. As he fought to hold on, Crying Coyote looked around and saw Lifts Something. He was startled, embarrassed–and happy. He didn't see the ocean anymore. So far as he was concerned, it had dried up.

"Come on," Lifts Something said. "We are missing the fun."

Turning their Goddogs, they rode back toward the beach. When he looked back, Crying Coyote saw the inhumans in the boats shaking their fists at him and his people. The two Goddogs splashed up onto the sand and shook themselves like dogs that weren't divine.

Then Lifts Something galloped off with Crying Coyote right behind her. She headed straight for the huge building. Now he noticed a sign on this mountain of wood that said WAREHOUSE. He hadn't seen writing for so long that he had almost forgotten not only how to read but even that he had ever been able to read–a little. He was surprised that the letters on the building spoke to him, but they did. He wondered what kind of wares were stored behind the sign.

The front door stood wide open like the front gate of a vaguely remembered family fort a long time ago, but he told himself not to try to bring that memory into focus. Remembering hurt. Keep that door closed. Closed and locked. Crying Coyote was surprised to see Lifts Something ride right through the front door of the warehouse. He rode in after her. Their Goddogs' hooves were loud on the wooden floor.

The warehouse was already crowded with Human warriors making war on bolts of red cloth, ladies' dresses, ladies' undergarments, umbrellas, and stovepipe hats. Crying Coyote jumped off his Goddog and joined the war against Writer commerce, Writer business, Writer goods. It was fun. Lifts Something joined him. They fought side by side.

Lifts Something put on a stovepipe hat and then opened a parasol that was red, yellow, and orange. She looked around to see if Crying Coyote was watching her. He was. Then she watched him as he slipped into a swallow-tailed evening coat. He added a bright red bandanna, and then he too put on a stovepipe hat. Admiring each other, Lifts Something and Crying Coyote both laughed. They were children playing dress-up together, and they enjoyed their game with childlike glee. Their laughter mingled with the whoops and yells and terrible war cries that rose from the looting army. But it seemed to them–Lifts Something and Crying Coyote–as if they were alone, playing a private game. He dressed up for her. She dressed for him. He modeled for her. She posed for him. These wild Comanches were children in the attic.

"You are much, much, much pretty," Crying Coyote complimented.

Laughing, he dove joyfully back into the goods that were spread all about him. He threw aside a bonnet . . . then wool stockings . . . then something white . . . then something pink . . . as he went on looking for he knew not what. Then his hand closed on a whalebone corset, and he held it up. He didn't remember ever having seen such an invention before, but he somehow knew it was feminine.

"Come here," Crying Coyote said. "Look at this."

"What is it?" Lifts Something asked.

"I do not know," he said. "I think it is some kind of armor."

"Try it on," she said.

"No, it is woman armor. You try it on."

"All right. Help me."

Crying Coyote tried to assist her, but he found the corset a strange and difficult puzzle. Lifts Something tried to put it on upside down, then realized it went the other way. But working together, the two Humans finally figured out how this armor worked, more or less. Lifts Something put the frilly white corset on over her pale yellow buckskin dress. Crying Coyote helped her lace it up. Then she strutted about in her top hat and corset, twirling her parasol, looking lovely and proud.

Crying Coyote found her so beautiful that he was afraid of her. He had wondered if he would feel fear in his first battle. Now he felt it. He was a coward in the face of beauty.

87

After defeating Writer commerce in the battle of the Linnville warehouse, a gaudy Human army rode north, carrying the trophies of their victory with them. They transported their booty on the backs of stolen pack mules and on stolen Goddogs. And they carried it on their own backs. A long line of wild Comanches in top hats and tails rode away from the sea. While the warriors wore Writer clothing mixed with their own, their lone Writer captive wore nothing at all. Her nude body was tied to a Goddog like the rest of the loot.

Crying Coyote and Lifts Something rode side by side dressed in plunder. He still sported his top hat and swallow-tailed coat to which he had added a necktie flapping against his bare chest. Lifts Something, who was still dressed in her top hat and corset, twirled her parasol as she trotted along. The tails of both their Goddogs were made festive by long, flowing red ribbons.

Crying Coyote loved the warpath, he loved his new finery, and he was beginning to love Lifts Something very much. So he didn't mind the hard miles on the too-soft ground. Not even the humid heat could spoil his festive mood, and it began to abate anyway toward sundown. As it slowly sank beneath the horizon, the sun turned as red as the sunburned body of the unclothed Writer woman tied to a Goddog.

It was almost midnight when the high-hatted Human army halted to make camp. They were tired but not too tired to build a towering fire and dance around it to celebrate their victory. Crying Coyote in his top hat and tails danced with Lifts Something in her corset and top hat. As he spun and leapt, his tails and breechclout stood out from his body, and her chapeau bounced down over one eye. They danced over to the ground where the female captive was being ritually raped. The Writer woman's hands were bound behind her. Her ankles were tied to stakes that kept her feet spread wide apart.

Crying Coyote looked from the naked inhuman woman to his

splendidly arrayed dance partner. He felt tempted to take his place in the rape line, but he was worried about how Lifts Something would react if he did. In spite of himself, he kept glancing back and forth from the woman on the ground to the woman dancing in front of him. Lifts Something noticed.

"Go ahead," Lifts Something said crossly. "You want to."

"Kee, kee," Crying Coyote protested, "I do not."

"You think she's pretty."

"Kee, I do not."

"Your mind cries to do it–and your body does, too!"

"Kee!"

Crying Coyote and Lifts Something were dancing away from the woman on the ground when a figure wearing nothing but yellow paint loomed up in front of them. The boy was glad to see his father, but at the same time he was embarrassed by his presence.

"Did you take a turn?" asked the Sun Shaman.

"What turn?" asked Crying Coyote.

"With the Writer woman?"

Now the boy was really embarrassed. He looked down at his moccasins. *"Kee,"* he said. Why did his father want to make his life so difficult? Couldn't he see that his son was with a young woman for whom he cared?

"You must take your turn," the Sun Shaman commanded. "You must lie on her."

"My mind does not cry to," said the son, glancing at Lifts Something, then glancing away again.

"You must prove that you are Human," his father explained. "If you do not lie on her, much Humans will say that you are still inhuman. They will think that you are only pretending to be Human. They are watching you."

Crying Coyote felt only the eyes of Lifts Something watching him, but her eyes were worse than the eyes of the whole tribe. He longed to meet her gaze, but he was afraid to. He studied the beads on his moccasins.

"Your father is right," Lifts Something said. "You must prove that you are Human. If you did not have yellow hair, you could say *kee.* But you must do it. You must."

Crying Coyote heard Lifts Something's moccasins beating on the ground. Looking up, he saw her running away into the night. He was angry with his father for embarrassing him in front of the girl he loved. At the same time, he felt a stirring of sexual excitement inside his breechclout.

"But, father, I have never . . ." He hated the Sun Shaman for forcing him to make such a confession.

"Do not worry," his father reassured him. "It will come naturally."

The Sun Shaman led his son back to the woman staked out on the ground. Crying Coyote got in line. He felt everybody looking at him, whether they were really looking at him or not, and the excitement inside his breechclout began to wane. Oh, no, this was terrible. What if he couldn't penetrate the inhuman female? What would the Humans think of him then? They would say he wasn't really a Human, wasn't even a man. The more he worried, the more he shriveled.

"It is your turn," the Sun Shaman said.

Crying Coyote stepped forward, feeling lonely and at the same time crowded, surrounded, stared at. His hopeless hand loosened the knot of his breechclout and it fell to the ground. The cool night air caressed him and his moon began to wax. Of course, it might start waning again at any moment without warning.

When Crying Coyote lay down on top of the bound woman, he felt an excitement beyond anything he had ever imagined. He entered her and was proud. He was proving himself a real Human Being and a real man. But as he continued to move, he was overcome by a crushing sadness. Why? What was wrong with him? He hoped he wouldn't cry.

88

Two armies, one Human and the other inhuman, were drawn up facing each other. The Comanches had ridden into an ambush, which was just what the Sun Shaman had feared. He had been worrying aloud to his son about how all their loot was slowing them down. Normally, raiding parties were able to escape back to Human lands before their enemies could assemble their forces to oppose them. But not this time. As they moved sluggishly north, they found their way barred by an impromptu army of regular U.S. soldiers, Texas Rangers, and armed settlers.

The Writer line was filled with grim-faced men mostly in work clothes. They wore faded blue and dirty brown. And they seemed to approach the coming battle as a job to be done. The Human line was arrayed like a war party on its way to the opera.

Suddenly, a warrior in a top hat and tails broke out of the line and charged into the no-man's-land between the two armies. Crying Coyote stared at the daredevil who pranced up and down, waving his high hat with one hand and his lance with the other, challenging the Writers to single combat. Crying Coyote was jealous of the warrior who was proving his bravery in such dramatic fashion. He longed to change places with him. He wished he were the one out there putting on a dazzling riding show, dropping over one side of his Goddog, then over the other, then pulling himself back into the saddle and tipping his top hat. When the Writers did not respond, did not pick up the gauntlet so gaudily thrown down, the warrior returned to the Human line where he was greatly admired.

Soon another Human warrior charged out into no-man's-land, screamed a challenge to single combat, put on a show of masterly Goddogmanship, and finally galloped back to the Human lines. One after another, the young braves rode into no-man's-land to prove their bravery, but the Writers continued to prove themselves running-hearts who would not fight.

Crying Coyote leaned forward and said to his Goddog, "Let us go, Old Friend. Be brave . . . be brave . . ."

Then he surprised even himself by charging out between the red and white armies. Once again, he felt all the Human eyes staring at him. He even thought he felt her eyes admiring him. From time to time, he looked contemptuously at the blue eyes across the way and screamed at them. He had become what he envied, and he wondered if the other warriors now envied him. As a finale, Crying Coyote stood up on the back of his Goddog, stood up straight in the saddle, and shook his lance at the slouching Writer soldiers. He knew he was a superior being and they were his inferiors. He felt such scorn for them all. Did they have no pride? Giving up on tempting a running-heart to fight him, Crying Coyote returned to the Human army. Now nobody could doubt that he was a real Human Being. Or so he hoped.

The next Human warrior to come charging into the space between the armies was wearing gleaming white armor: a whalebone corset. Watching her, Crying Coyote was afraid and proud and a little embarrassed all at the same time. What was she doing out there, anyway? What was she trying to prove? Why couldn't she just stay back with the other women in a woman's place? And yet his mounting irritation couldn't entirely smother his mounting pride.

Crying Coyote was relieved when, at last, Lifts Something turned her Goddog back toward the Human line. As she drew closer, he tried to lecture her with his good eye, but she saw something else as well.

"You should not take such chances," Crying Coyote scolded.

Lifts Something pointed her thumbs at her whalebone corset. "I have much medicine," she said.

"Lifts Something!"

"Do not speak to me in that tone!"

The couple seemed on the verge of having a lovers' quarrel in the middle of a war.

"I am sorry," Crying Coyote said. "You frightened me."

"Do you think Chief Iron Jacket is jealous of my battle vest?"

"I am sure."

As if he had heard his name, Chief Iron Jacket galloped forward jingling merrily. Lifts Something and Crying Coyote and all the other Humans whooped and cheered and uttered terrible war cries. Riding up and down between the red line and the white line, Chief Iron Jacket shook his war shield and lance and shouted his challenge for a white warrior to come out and fight him. But as before, no inhuman ventured out to meet him.

The Texas Rangers' unchivalrous response was to force the Human knight to joust against a rifle: a short spear against a long bullet. Crying Coyote glimpsed a small cloud of smoke and then heard the explosion. He saw the Goddog and its bright rider stagger, as if struck by an unseen lance, and then resume prancing. Iron Chief *was* immortal.

Crying Coyote saw another gust of smoke and heard another explosion. And then another. The old knight just laughed at the bullets. He was eternal. He inspired the Humans and discouraged his inhuman enemies.

Then Crying Coyote heard a volley of shots and saw the Iron Knight fall from his prancing Goddog. The magic metal jacket lay dull in the dust.

Lifts Something and Crying Coyote stared at each other. Not only had the Human Beings lost a great war chief, but the young couple had lost some of their faith in her medicine jacket. They now knew that the Writers had magic bullets that Human medicine couldn't stop. They couldn't help taking the tragedy personally.

Crying Coyote saw the inhuman army surge forward. The Writers came screaming and firing big Henry rifles and Colt revolvers and even old muskets. Crying Coyote was concentrating on the charge of the white army when he was attacked by a danger closer at hand. A frightened pack mule, heavy and clumsy with loot, crashed into the side of his Goddog. Crying Coyote felt himself falling, thought he was going down beneath trampling hooves, but he finally regained his balance, only to be hit again. Looking around frantically, he saw that he and many others were caught in a stampede of pack animals.

Before the Human army could regroup, the Writer warriors came charging into their ranks. The white men began gunning down red men and women who could neither fight nor flee because they were trapped in a whirlpool of stolen goods and terrified animals. The looters were being destroyed by their loot. Crying Coyote saw one friend after another fall from their Goddogs. They disappeared, like drowning victims, sucked down into the fatal depths. Some were killed cleanly by bullets before they fell, but many more died dirty deaths beneath muddy hooves. Human voices cried their pain above the bellows of the animals. Crying Coyote was afraid he was going to throw up.

And then he once again felt himself falling, but this time he couldn't save himself. He lurched toward a grimy extinction. His Goddog went down and he went down with it. Hooves were churning all around him. Scrambling to his knees, he started to crawl as fast as he could, crawling fanatically, crawling as if he himself were a stampeding animal. As he was jostled and bumped and splashed and bruised, the boy on all fours seemed to have lost all his Humanity. Crying Coyote crawled over a body that slowed him down. Then another fell on top of him. His enemies seemed to be trying to bury him alive under dead Humans.

"Where are you, Old Friend?" Crying Coyote called to his Goddog. "Old Friend, I need you. Where are you? Help me, Old Friend. Please, help me . . ."

Then Crying Coyote saw a hoof and fetlock that he recognized. He hadn't known how well he knew his Old Friend until that moment when so little meant so much. He started climbing the Goddog's hind leg as if it were a tree trunk.

"Easy, Old Friend," Crying Coyote said. "Stay calm. Do not kick me. You would not kick me, would you?"

In the midst of chaos, the Goddog remained still and calm until Crying Coyote could vault onto his back. Then the animal reared and plunged ahead.

"Good work, Old Friend," said Crying Coyote. "Now find Lifts Something. Find her, Old Friend . . ."

When he saw Lifts Something running in the mud up ahead of him, Crying Coyote credited his Old Friend with finding her. He knew it might have been a coincidence, but he didn't think so. Lifts Something was limping badly. Crying Coyote rode toward her, caught up with her, bent low, and plucked her off the ground. He swung her up behind him on the back of his Old Friend. Then he started to whip his Old Friend with his bow.

Looking back, Crying Coyote saw a Texas Ranger chasing him. The Writer held a Colt revolver in his right hand. The Humans had learned to fear these repeating guns. In the old days, a Human mounted on a Goddog wielding a compact bow and arrow had been more than a match for a Writer on horseback trying to control a musket. But the coming of the Colt revolver had changed all that. Now the Rangers had a weapon that was even more compact than a bow and it could shoot faster. Crying Coyote, who knew enough to be frightened, kicked his Goddog to go faster.

"Run, Old Friend," he shouted. "Run! Run! . . ."

Glancing back, Crying Coyote saw the revolver explode smoke and felt the bullet strike the girl his mind cried for. He felt her lunge forward against his back, felt her arms grip him harder than ever, felt himself being pulled from his Goddog's back. Crying Coyote and Lifts Something landed in the mud. They rolled in the mud as if they were wrestling.

"Are you hurt?" Crying Coyote asked, although he already knew she was. "Talk to me."

Sitting in the mud, he held Lifts Something in his arms. He cradled her head and shoulders.

"I feel-missing you," she said.

"Kee, kee, you'll be all right," he protested.

"I am sorry," she said. Then staring up at the sky, she began singing her death song. *"Aheya aheya ya-heyo, Ya eye heyo aheyo.* O Sun, you live forever, but I must die. O Earth, you remain forever, but I must die."

When she finished her song, she closed her eyes and did not speak again.

"Say something," Crying Coyote begged. "Do not go. Talk to me. Please do not go."

Hearing hoofbeats approaching him, he did not even look up. He heard the metallic click of a hammer going back, but he still didn't look. He had lost the girl his mind cried for and he was ready to sing his death song, too.

"O Sun, you live forever," Crying Coyote began, "but I must–"

"Don't shoot!" shouted the harsh voice of a Writer. "He's got yeller hair! He's white! Son of a bitch."

89

Crying Coyote thought the campfire was too big. Why would they need such a conflagration? Were they planning to cook and eat him? He could imagine no other reason to waste so much wood. He had a lot to learn about Writers.

He wondered what they were saying. He wished they wouldn't talk so fast. What was their hurry? Their hands flapped around when they talked like the wings of dying birds, but they didn't make any intelligible signs. Why not? He decided they weren't very bright.

When a Writer warrior put another big log on the much big fire, Crying Coyote decided he couldn't wait any longer. He scrambled to his feet and made a break for it. He ran low, crouched forward, to present as small a target as possible. He headed for the bushes, the night, the wilderness, home. He heard shouts and loud boots behind him. He couldn't believe how much noise Writers made. He felt superior to these noisy creatures, but at the same time he was afraid of them. His name had come true: he was a hunted animal who wanted to cry.

Looking back, Crying Coyote saw dark shapes struggling with the night. They looked not only less than Human but even less than inhuman. They had ceased to be Writers and had been transformed into something else even more terrible. They appeared to be monsters that had sprung up out of the dark earth. Their fathers could have been boulders. Their mothers might have been bears. They sounded like a rock slide. Who was after him? No, *what* was after him? Thank the Great Mystery, he could run faster than these heavy-footed ghouls of the night.

Looking straight ahead, Crying Coyote increased his speed. Listening hard, he heard his own lungs getting louder and louder as the monsters' steps grew softer and softer. He was pulling away from them. He was winning the freedom race. He would see his red canyon again. He would be reunited with the Sun Shaman. He would—

The sound was getting louder, not softer. A Goddog was chasing him. He normally loved the music made by Goddog hooves as they pounded on the earth, but not now. Not here. The drumbeat grew deafening.

When he looked back over his shoulder, Crying Coyote saw a lasso striking at him like a black snake uncoiling. He tried to dodge, but the snake was too quick. Snakes generally were. It coiled around his body and pulled tight. It bit hard into his flesh. Crying Coyote was jerked off his feet. The Writer's Goddog, trained for calf-roping, began backing up, dragging along the roped boy.

Then the heavy monsters of the night descended upon him, pulled him to his feet, tied his hands behind him, put a rope around his neck, and led him back to the too-big fire. They shouted and waved incomprehensibly at him and at each other. He was not too surprised when they tied his feet as well as his hands and knotted one end of the rope around an oak tree.

The second captivity of Jimmy Goodnight had begun.

Crying Coyote hated the cage. He walked up and down from one end to the other all day and most of the night. He wished they had cooked and eaten him. At least it would be over by now. Instead, he was dying slowly. No Human Being could survive in an inhuman house like this one with bars. He could see and feel that he was already wasting away toward death, losing weight and strength with every step, with every meal he wouldn't eat, with every day that passed. It wouldn't be long now.

He looked up when the stranger came in, but he didn't stop pacing in his jail cell. The Writer was dressed in a black suit, was tall and thin, and had a mop of white hair that would make a handsome scalp. The captive tried to ignore the newcomer–to lose himself in his pacing–but he couldn't completely. He was drawn to this inhuman by a sense of familiarity, but that was impossible. Still there was something about that long face, that strong nose, those sad blue eyes. The old creature studied him and he studied the ancient one. While one paced and the other stood still, they looked each other up and down. The Writer said something to Crying Coyote, but he couldn't understand. The inflection of the voice indicated questions, but they were as incomprehensible as always. What did this white-haired man want to know?

Who was the old man anyway? Crying Coyote almost recognized the old one's features, but not quite. There was something wrong. They were familiar, and yet they weren't. He had seen them before but not arranged in quite this way. They were like a reflection seen in troubled water.

That was it. That inhuman face reminded him of a Human face that he had often seen reflected in streams and ponds. The old face reminded him of a young face that he knew well. He might have been looking at his own future, at the way he would look many summers from now. Was this old creature a ghost? Humans feared almost nothing, but they did fear ghosts. He shivered and stopped pacing.

Trying to make sense of the apparition before him, Crying Coyote pointed at his own strong nose, then at the old one's nose. The ancient one smiled and nodded and copied him, pointing at his nose, then at the boy's. Crying Coyote pointed at his single bright blue eye, then used two fingers to point at the old one's pair of faded blues. The old mouth laughed and wrinkled hands clapped. Crying Coyote recoiled. His aged double stopped clapping and started asking questions again.

Concentrating hard on the sounds, Crying Coyote finally thought he recognized something. It set up a distant echo in his mind. He decided to try to give voice to this echo.

"Juh, Juh, Juh," he tried to copy what the old one said.

The white-haired one got excited.

"Juh, Juh, Jim–"

The ancient one waved his arms all over the place. He was so lively that he looked younger.

"Juh, Juhimmy," Crying Coyote said.

The old one was so happy that he didn't look bad for a Writer.

"Jimmy," the boy said.

The ancient one was laughing. Crying Coyote smiled back. He couldn't help it.

"Jimmy," he said again since the old one liked hearing it so much. "Jimmy, Jimmy, Jimmy, Jimmy."

The old one stopped laughing and started crying. Crying Coyote wondered what he had done wrong. He still had a lot to learn about Writers.

90

Jimmy Goodnight entered Weatherford, Texas, riding in the midst of what looked like a victory procession. The whole town had turned out to welcome him, but so far they had only succeeded in frightening him, waving flags and shouting. The wooden Goddog paused in front of a wooden house painted white. The boy had been kidnapped seven years ago from a log fort, but now he was returning to a home built of sawed lumber. He was growing up and so was Texas.

Jimmy saw a white welcoming committee lined up in front of the white house. Some of them looked a little like the white-haired old man who had found him in a jail and gotten him out. By now, he knew that the ancient one was his uncle, Isaac Goodnight, and he guessed that the others were probably relatives, too. Some of his memories of his pre-Human life were beginning to come back to him, and he could even remember a few words of the Writer tongue.

Jimmy understood his uncle Isaac when he said "Welcome home." The wild boy stared at his new family. They were smiling. He grinned shyly back. He understood that he was being introduced to his uncle's wife and son and two daughters, but he couldn't make out the strange Writer names.

They all went into the house. Jimmy watched the women putting food on the table. It smelled strange. The foreign aromas suggested that these people didn't know what was good to eat. Soon the whole family was sitting around the table. Uncle Isaac bowed his head and closed his eyes, then all the others did the same, all but Jimmy. Uncle Isaac mumbled some sort of speech, but his nephew didn't understand a word. When he stopped talking, they all opened their eyes and started reaching for food.

Jimmy's aunt put a chunk of meat on his plate. It resembled Human-cattle flesh, but it was more fine-grained. He wished it smelled better, but he was hungry enough to eat anything. He picked up the meat and ate it with his hands. Grease ran down his chin and dropped onto his chest, where it stained his new homespun, butternut-colored Writer shirt.

That night, Jimmy discovered that he had been assigned his own blanket-death room. He was lonely in his own bedroom. He missed having other bodies close to him. He couldn't understand why Writers wanted to live in such big houses. These structures must be hard to pick up and carry when the time came to move the village. He didn't like this room, but he was tired enough to sleep anywhere. He lay down on the floor beside the bed and surrendered himself to a good night's blanket-death.

91

The rooster crowed and chores beckoned. Jimmy had been allowed to rest for a couple of weeks when he first came to live with his uncle Isaac, but as soon as he had relearned enough English to take orders, he was put to work. He didn't mind doing his share, but he didn't like the way they were always pushing him to work harder–to prove that he hadn't turned into some shiftless savage. He knew the Human Beings worked as hard as any Texas farmer, they just didn't plant and hoe and milk. But try to explain that to a Writer.

Jimmy got up out of his feather bed, shivered in the cold air, got dressed as fast as he could, and headed for the cow pen. He had milked in the summer, milked in the fall, and now he was milking in the winter. He had learned that winter milking was the worst. His hands were so cold it hurt to close them around the cows' fat tits. And imagine how much the cow liked it! The cow was an old guernsey with just one horn. Since he just had one eye, he considered that they were even. Maybe that was why he kept worrying about how the cow was feeling.

When he finished milking, Jimmy stood up a little too quickly and felt light-headed. As he swayed there for an instant–momentarily vulnerable–he remembered his mother Lucy. He had been told how she had died of a "broken heart" shortly after she had lost her whole family: husband killed, daughter killed, son carried away. She wouldn't eat and grew weaker and weaker. Regaining his balance, Jimmy managed to put his dead mother out of his mind as he headed for breakfast.

Jimmy got up earliest, so he was the first one at the kitchen table. His aunt Orlena was at the stove frying eggs, frying bacon, frying hot cakes, baking biscuits, and boiling coffee. Soon his cousin Jeff came in with eggs stuffed in all of his pockets. Jimmy had been hoping for seven months that one day he would forget to take the eggs out before he sat down for breakfast, but so far it hadn't happened. Next, Uncle Isaac came in rubbing his cold hands together. Jimmy wasn't really sure what his uncle did when he got up and headed outside every morning. As an apprentice "Writer," maybe he wasn't yet old enough or white enough to understand a farmer's ways. Cousins Rhoda and Naomi, both redheads, were already trying to sweep the dirt out of the house. Piles of it had collected in just twenty-four hours. The pretty white home wasn't very tightly put together. And the wind always blew in Texas. Uncle Isaac was fond of saying, "One day the wind stopped blowing and all the chickens fell over."

When Aunt Orlena started putting platters of food on the table, Rhoda and Naomi scrambled to take their places. Uncle Isaac bowed his head and prayed. Then everybody reached and grabbed. Jimmy thought breakfast was the best meal of the day, and the biscuits were his favorite part of his favorite meal.

"This is shore good 'nough to eat," Jimmy said with his mouth full.

"Thank you, Jimmy," said his aunt Orlena with a grateful smile. "Glad you like it."

"Wheat's dyin'," Uncle Isaac mumbled into his eggs. He meant his crop of winter wheat. "Damn, wisht it'd rain."

"Don't swear," Aunt Orlena said. "Not in front of the kids. Not before Gawd."

The mood at the table changed. The wilting wheat now set the tone rather than the good food. Jimmy wanted to rescue the good feeling before it died along with the winter crop. Besides, breakfast made him feel optimistic.

"Texas ain't farmin' country," Jimmy said. "It's ranchin' country."

"It's Gawd's country," said Aunt Orlena. "That's what country it is."

"Amen," said Uncle Isaac.

"I know, I know," Jimmy said. "But if we was to go up to that canyon I done tol' you 'bout. Now that's real Gawd's country."

"Don't blaspheme," said Aunt Orlena.

"I'm not blasphemin'," said Jimmy. "It's the Gawd's truth. Wait'll you see."

"Don't start that again," said Uncle Isaac. "Stop pesterin' me about that damn canyon."

"Don't swear," said Aunt Orlena.

"But Uncle Isaac—" Jimmy began.

"I mean it," his uncle interrupted sternly. "I don't wanna hear no more o' that crazy talk. I swear, you ain't got good sense, boy. So just pipe down."

"It ain't his fault," said his aunt. "The heathen got holda his mind."

After breakfast, Jimmy and his cousins set off for school. It was a four-mile walk, which seemed longer in the winter. They followed a dirt road that got wider and wider as it approached town. The schoolhouse had just two rooms, one for grades one through six, the other for seven through twelve. The room for the little kids in the lower grades was considerably more crowded than the room for the big kids in the upper grades. But the school did manage to graduate one or two almost every year.

The closer they got to school, the worse Jimmy felt. His breakfast-table optimism gave way to schoolhouse pessimism. His shoulders sagged. His head dropped lower and lower. He hated having to study with the little kids rather than the big kids. He was now eighteen years old, but he was only in the second grade. His years with the Human Beings had taught him a lot but not how to read. He had even forgotten what little reading he had learned before he was taken. So he more or less had to start all over at the bottom. When he and his cousins reached the schoolhouse, Jimmy entered the first room with eight-year-old Rhoda and six-year-old Naomi. But fourteen-year-old Jeff, who was four years and three months younger than Jimmy, got to go in the second room with the big boys and girls. It was a daily humiliation for the eighteen-year-old second-grader.

"Take out your readers," said Mr. Dobbins, the skinny, bald-headed teacher.

Jimmy had come to hate the tattered old book by William McGuffey. He couldn't even read the title of this reading book. What did *Eclectic Reader* mean, anyhow? It was discouraging to take out a book day after day and not be able to read the very first word on the cover.

"Turn to page fourteen," Mr. Dobbins said, and then started calling on different "scholars" to read aloud.

Jimmy hated reading out loud more than he hated milking in the cold, more than he hated just about anything. Afraid to look up–he might get called on–he studied a drawing of a boy walking along with books under his arm. Jimmy thought: Poor boy, he's on his way to school.

"I once knew a boy," read a seven-year-old girl named Sally who had huge freckles even in winter. "He was not a big boy."

The big boy in the second grade wondered if everybody was looking at him. He didn't dare look around to find out.

The teacher called on his cousin Naomi to read next.

"If he had been a big boy," redheaded Naomi read perfectly, "he would have been wiser."

Jimmy was even more embarrassed now. Big boys were supposed to be wise, but this big boy couldn't even read. He felt even worse when he heard Mr. Dobbins call his name.

"Buh, buh, but he was a, uh, a, luh, luh–" Jimmy tried but got bogged down.

"That's right," Mr. Dobbins said. "Sound it out. You can do it."

"Luh-eye-tuh."

"No, the *I* is short. Like in 'big.'"

Jimmy flinched. "Luh-ih-tuh, tuh, tuh–"

"Somebody help him," said Mr. Dobbins.

Naomi raised her hand and got called on.

"'Little,'" she said.

"That's right, Naomi. Very good. Go on, Jimmy."

"Buh, but he was a little boy. He was not much uh–"

He heard somebody laugh.

"'Taller,' Jimmy, 'taller,'" said Mr. Dobbins. "'He was not much taller than a table.'"

Jimmy wished he were like that boy, that little boy, no taller than a table, no bigger than the rest of the kids. Or else he wished he were in the big kids' room. Or better yet, he wished he were in the big red canyon. He heard the teacher say something, but he didn't pay any attention. He thought Mr. Dobbins was talking to somebody else. After all, he had already had his turn reading.

"Jimmy," Mr. Dobbins said more sharply, "I'm talking to you. What's the matter with you?"

"He's daydreamin' about his canyon ag'in," said Naomi. "The biggest canyon in the whole world."

All the kids laughed. He knew they thought he wasn't quite right in the head. He would show them. But how? More and more, he felt as if he really might be going crazy, like everybody thought he was. Someday he would show them.

92

Revelie was crying. She had always wanted to hear the story, and now it had made her unhappy. She was not shedding the kind of tears that one weeps at the end of a sad tale. She was sobbing as if her child had died—even though she had no child. She cried uncontrollably, hysterically.

"What's wrong?" asked Goodnight.

"Nothing," said Revelie.

"Really, you can tell me," he reassured her.

"It's nothing," she sobbed.

"Now who's got secrets?" Goodnight said with a laugh, meant to cheer her up.

She just kept on crying, her body jerking, breathing as if she were choking.

"I thought that's what you wanted," he said.

"I did," she sobbed.

She pulled him close to her, wetting his cheek and chest.

BOOK FOUR

CLAWING

93

When Goodnight emerged onto his front porch just after daylight, he scanned the great red walls of his fortress, as he did every day. He saw, coming down the north wall, a lone rider. He was tiny in the distance, but the rancher already had a bad feeling about him. The stranger was carrying something over his shoulder as he rode, which made him resemble a scorpion with its tail curled over its back. The rancher shrugged and wondered what this newcomer wanted. The ranch didn't need any more hands just now.

Goodnight couldn't understand his feeling about the stranger because he generally cherished visitors. They brought news and gossip from the outside world, and they provided diversion for Revelie. Besides, in this cruel country, everybody had to help everybody else or they would all be defeated. But nonetheless, he felt hostile to the approaching horseman. Well, he wouldn't be here for a while.

Remembering that he was hungry, Goodnight headed for the cookshack to have breakfast with his cowboys. Soon he smelled coffee and bubbling grease, which made him hungrier. Entering the small whitewashed building, Goodnight sat down beside Loving on a long bench at a long table. When Coffee appeared and put three bowls of scrambled eggs on the long table, the sleepy hands woke up and started grabbing for their share. Then the cook put out platters of bacon, which provoked more reaching.

After breakfast, the cowboys, sleepy again, shuffled and stumbled to their horses as another workday began. Goodnight mounted up and rode out with them. They happened to head up the canyon on a course that would intersect with the stranger's. Most of the herd was well up-canyon at the moment. Goodnight and Loving rode side by side at the head of the pack. After they had been riding for a little over half an hour, Goodnight saw the stranger approaching along the canyon's flat floor.

"Company," said Goodnight. "What's that over his dang shoulder, huh?"

"I dunno," said Loving, squinting. "Kinda looks like a damn ax. Funny way to ride, ain't it?"

Goodnight nudged his horse into a fast trot to go out to meet the stranger. Loving spurred his horse, also, but the others trudged on behind. The newcomer kicked his horse, too. When Goodnight raised his hat in greeting, the stranger lifted his ax and waved it over his head.

"I reckon that's one way to say hello," said Loving. "Not my favorite way, but one way."

When the three of them met beside the red river, Goodnight tipped his hat again, and the stranger wobbled his ax. The newcomer turned out to be not much more than a boy. He looked to be about fifteen or sixteen.

"Hello," Goodnight said.

"Hello," said the stranger.

"I couldn't help noticin' that there ax. How come you're ridin' around the country with an ax over your shoulder like that?"

"Truth is, I like axes. And I heard you liked 'em, too. So I figure we got somethin' in common there. Thought it might do as some kinda introduction."

Lifting his ax off his shoulder, the stranger drew back and threw it overhand, hard, so that it went spinning in the air. Then the blade bit and dug into the broad trunk of a nearby cottonwood tree. It hung there quivering.

"Nice throwin'," said Goodnight.

Then he reached down and pulled his ax from the scabbard that was built for a rifle. He lifted it over his head, took aim, and threw. The ax somersaulted toward the cottonwood tree. It hit so close to the other ax, cheek-to-cheek, that it knocked the other blade out of the tree trunk. The stranger's ax fell to the ground.

"Nicer throwin'," said the stranger.

"Thanks," said Goodnight. "You're a long way from home, ain'tcha, mister?"

"I ain't got no home," said the stranger. "But I'm sorta lookin' for one."

"Well, you'll be our guest for as long as you wanta stay." Goodnight hated to make such an open-ended offer, because he didn't trust this scorpion, but he owed it to his Code of the West. Strangers simply couldn't be turned away. "We got a fair-to-middlin' cook and good beds. Anyhow, we think so. The cook's name's Coffee. He'll give you breakfast."

"Uh, well, I was hopin' to be a little more'n a guest."

"I'm real sorry, but we done got enough hands. Sorry, but thass how it is."

"Well, see, I was hopin' to be more'n a hand."

Goodnight looked at the stranger quizzically. He thought maybe he had misheard.

"What?"

"Well, look at me."

"I *am* lookin' at you. I been lookin' at you for some time. Whaddaya mean you wanta be more'n a hand? You applyin' for the position of foreman or somethin'? I don't git you!"

"Take a *good* look at me, and tell me"–the stranger paused in mid-sentence–"don't I look familiar?"

Goodnight shrugged and continued to study the presumptuous cowboy. Was there something familiar about the boy, something he seemed to have seen before, some sleeping memory that refused to wake up?

"Don't you know me?" asked the stranger.

"Cain't say as I do," Goodnight said.

The longer he stared at the unrecognized face before him, the more uneasy he felt. Maybe he was one of the Robbers' Roost boys. He studied the cowboy's hands. Were the thumbs busted? No, he was too young. But there was something strange about the fingers. The right hand was perfectly normal with the right number of fingers, but the left hand was another matter. There were just–one, two, three–three fingers. Not only were there too few fingers, but they were twisted. The left hand looked like a claw.

"Don't you know me? Really?" said the stranger. "I'm your son."

"You're a liar," Goodnight said. "I don't have no son."

"You raped my mama."

"What?"

Goodnight's mind reeled. He knew it couldn't be true. Knew he hadn't ever raped anybody's mother. Knew he had never raped anybody at all. Knew he wasn't that kind of man. And yet his innocent brain was nauseous.

"In Linnville," said the stranger. "When you was a heathen savage. You done carried off my mama, and you raped her, and you left her for dead. But she didn't die. Not then."

Goodnight hung his head. "What?" he asked again.

"You all done raped her. The whole tribe. But I'm yours and nobody else's. No mistake about it. Else I'd be a half-breed. Do I look like some half-breed?"

Goodnight looked into the stranger's blue eyes. Familiar eyes in a familiar face.

"No," he said in a low voice.

"And she was your own cousin. Your cousin Sarah. Sarah Goodnight."

"No, no. She told you–you mean–she said it was me?"

"No, she never told me nothin' 'cause she done died birthin' me. But I done worked it all out. Who my daddy was and how and how come."

Goodnight felt infinitely tired and weak. Did this poor boy owe his deformed hand to inbreeding, cousin on cousin? Was it possible? The old taboo.

"You're hired," said Goodnight. "Put your stuff in the bunkhouse."

"Thanky kindly," said the stranger.

"You've got the advantage of me. You know my name, but I don't know yours. What do folks call you."

"My full name's Silas Ben Goodnight, but ever'body just calls me Claw. I didn't like it at first, but I've got used to it. Call me Claw."

94

Goodnight sat in his big living room with the *Tascosa Times* in his lap, but he was having a hard time paying attention to the stories. He usually loved to read the weekly newspaper. It was normally a treat, since copies of it rarely made it all of the way out to the Home Ranch. But he owed this particular copy to the stranger who claimed to be his son, and that was the reason he couldn't concentrate. He appreciated the young man bringing it out to him, but he didn't know what to do with a "son."

Goodnight glanced at Revelie, who was sitting nearby reading a book of poetry. She had told him that it was written by somebody named Tennyson, whoever that was, and it was about some king or other. The husband kept glancing at his wife because he couldn't decide what to tell her about the new hand that he had hired that morning. Should he confide the whole truth right now? But who knew what the "truth" was? He certainly didn't. What if his "son" was lying? What if he had made up this story because he had designs on inheriting the Home Ranch? What if? What?

"What's in the paper?" asked Revelie.

"Oh, I don't know," Goodnight said, startled. "I mean it looks like the same old stuff. Nothin' interestin'."

"Mr. Goodnight, what is the matter? You generally love the 'same old stuff.' You know good and well you do. Something must have 'put you off your feed,' as your cowboys say. What's wrong with the old stuff tonight?"

Goodnight felt trapped. How did she know he was trying to hide something from her? Again? Well, he wasn't really trying to hide it, he told himself, he just hadn't quite decided when and where and how to tell her.

"Well, I guess I'm figurin' on somethin'," he said at last.

"That's what I thought," said Revelie. "Can I help?"

"No, I don't think so."

"Mr. Goodnight, you know how I hate it when you refuse to share your problems with me."

"I know, I know."

"So!"

Revelie stared at him. He wanted to be anywhere else. Maybe he should just get up and go somewhere else. But where could he go? Because he not only wanted to hide from her, he wanted to hide from himself. What had he done? And why had he done it? He couldn't imagine himself, as he knew himself now, doing what he had done then. And yet he could not deny his own memories.

"Mr. Goodnight?" Revelie prompted.

"Well, I been puzzlin' out how to tell you," he said and then fell silent.

"Tell me what?"

"About this new cowboy come today."

"A new cowboy? I thought you said we had too many already, but you didn't want to let anybody go. Why do we need another cowboy?"

"We don't, not really."

"So?"

Goodnight kept trying out sentences in his head, but he didn't like any of them. He simply didn't know how to tell her.

"So!"

"So he claims he's my son."

"Your son!"

"Thass what he claims. He's prob'ly a damn liar."

"Probably?" He could see her doing math in her head. "You mean he might be your son?"

"I doubt it." Goodnight was looking down at his boots.

"You doubt it? You mean it's a possibility? Were you married before? You just forgot to tell me? Maybe you're still married? Are you a bigamist, Mr. Goodnight?"

"No, not hardly."

"Then you deflowered some poor girl and then deserted her?"

"No, not really, not like that."

"Not like that? Then how did you desert her?"

Goodnight felt that his mind was a wolf trapped in a cage. It ran back and forth, back and forth, looking for a way out, but there wasn't a way out.

"Answer me."

"I didn't know I was deserting her."

"What!"

"Remember I told you about going on the warpath, you know, back when I was living with the Comanches."

"Vividly."

"And 'member me telling you about the raid on Linnville? When we went all the way to the ocean?"

"Of course."

He paused. He looked down at his dusty boots and shook his head. No, he just couldn't . . .

"Don't go bashful on me, Mr. Goodnight."

"This ain't easy to tell."

"Go ahead."

"Well, he claims we–they–took his mama captive."

Revelie took a moment to think through this latest revelation. Her husband studied her with rising apprehension.

"You mean you raped his mother?"

"Maybe it wasn't his mama. Maybe he made that part up."

"But you admit you raped somebody!"

Now Goodnight's tongue was truly tied. He just sat there staring at his wife. How could he admit to her that he was a rapist? Her view of him would be changed forever.

"Everybody did."

"Who did?"

"All the warriors."

"All of you! You gang-raped her?"

Goodnight shrugged and then didn't say anything.

"You all raped her and that makes it all right? That's worse. That poor woman."

Goodnight got clumsily to his feet and headed for the door. In the doorway, he paused and turned: "The boy claims she was one a my cousins." Shaking his head, he went on out.

You can't let him sleep in the bunkhouse," Revelie said in bed a few days later. "You have to invite him to live with us here in our house."

"But he'll upset you," Goodnight protested. "He'll be a constant reminder that–"

"Invite him to live with us. Tell him to live with us. It's only fair. He's your responsibility."

"No. I don't even like him."

"But he's the son I haven't been able to give you. He's the child we've never had. That's been so hard for me. I thought maybe it was your fault, but now I know it's mine. He's your one and only son. You must embrace him."

"For my sins?"

95

The next morning, Revelie accompanied her husband to the cookshack, where the cowboys were eating breakfast. She had come to meet Goodnight's "son." When she entered the small room, all the cowpokes stood up quickly, knocking their benches over backward. They all mumbled greetings. Some called her Mrs. Goodnight, others wished Miss Revelie a good morning.

"Mr. Goodnight, would you kindly introduce me to our newest cowboy?" Revelie said.

"Course," he grumbled. He walked down the line of cowboys on one side of the long table and stopped at the new hire. "Miz Goodnight, this here's Silas Ben Goodnight, or so he says."

"Call me Claw," said the cowboy. Then he reached out with his good hand and shook hands with her. "Pleased to know you, ma'am."

"The feeling is mutual, Silas," Revelie said. "I have come to issue you an invitation. Mr. Goodnight and I would be pleased if you would move into the ranch house and live with us. It only seems appropriate. Would you please accept our hospitality?"

"My pleasure," beamed Claw.

So Goodnight's putative son moved into the big sandstone house and slept in a bedroom across the hall from his supposed father and stepmother. This room had originally been intended as a nursery, then had become a sewing room, and now finally a son inhabited it.

Goodnight hoped he would get to like the boy better as he got to know him better, but he didn't. Claw still insinuated something cruel, something in fact like a claw, a claw bent on tearing and shredding. Goodnight told himself that it was unfair to pick on the boy's handicap, his disability, but he couldn't help it. He distrusted Claw, distrusted his story, distrusted his motives.

Now in the evenings, there were three of them in the big living room passing the time until sleep. Goodnight read the newspaper or bent over the ranch's account books. Revelie kept on reading Tennyson. Claw didn't read.

"Listen to this," she said one night. "'To strive, to seek, to find, and not to yield.' Isn't that beautiful? Do you hear the beat, ba-bump, ba-bump, ba-bump?"

"Anything you read," Goodnight said, "sounds purdy to me."

Having satisfied her hunger for poetry for one evening, Revelie put down the thin Tennyson and picked up a fat Trollope. She owned several of his novels as well as volumes by Scott. She had these books–usually pirated editions printed with double-column pages–shipped out to her from Boston.

Claw passed his time cleaning his six-shooter over and over again.

"The Robbers' Roost boys are in the paper again," Goodnight said. "Looks like they stuck up a stage, robbed ever'body, stole the horses, and burned the stagecoach. Now why'd they wanta do that. Just pure meanness."

"Robbers' Roost?" Claw asked. "What's that?"

"Just a buncha outlaws that don't like us too much. And we don't like them right back. Their leader's done promised to nail my cut-off ears to the swingin' saloon doors in Tascosa."

Sensing disapproval, Goodnight glanced at his wife.

"Would you mind dispensing with such talk?" Revelie said.

The trio fell silent once again. Goodnight made the most noise rattling the pages of the *Tascosa Times.* Revelie's pages turned almost noiselessly, while Claw's cleaning and oiling made even less racket. Coming to the end of a chapter of Trollope's *He Knew He Was Right,* Revelie paused, looked up, and studied the two men in the room. Noticing something, she put her book aside, got up, and approached first Goodnight, then Claw, examining them carefully.

"Mr. Goodnight, I would like to point something out to you," Revelie said. "I don't know why I didn't notice it earlier."

"What?" asked Goodnight.

"Look at your ears," said his wife. "No, I'm not that silly. I know you can't see your own ears. But reach up and feel them."

"Why?" asked her husband.

"Because you've both got a little bump on your right ear. Right at the edge. It looks like a pimple, but thankfully it isn't."

Both Goodnight and Claw reached up and felt their right ears. Then they looked at each other, then back at Revelie.

"See, you've both got the same bumps. They make your ears look a little peaked, as if you were descended from elves. But just on that one side. The other ear is normal. You're half elves. Surely that proves one of you is descended from the other."

"Thanks," said Goodnight.

96

In the morning, Revelie got up before Goodnight, which was unusual. She shuffle-stumbled to the "night jar" and vomited. The sound of her retching awakened her husband.

"Revelie, what's wrong?" Goodnight asked.

"I've got a queasy stomach," said Revelie. "Go back to sleep."

"I cain't go to sleep if'n you're sick."

"It's nothing."

"It ain't nothin'. It's the third mornin' in a row."

"Maybe I ate something."

"Ever'body else ate what you ate. And nobody's sick. We bedder harness up and head for Tascosa."

"No–" She threw up again.

"Yes!" Goodnight rolled out of bed, ready to make all the preparations. He hurried to his wife and held her head.

"No!"

"But–!"

"I know what it is. Well, no, that's not quite correct. I know what it probably means."

"What?" asked the innocent.

"I think I may be pregnant. Morning sickness is a symptom."

"Hoooraaayyy. No, I don't mean hooray because you're sick. Don't misunderstand me. Please. I don't want you to be sick. But the reason, that's good news. Wait'll I tell the cowboys."

"No, Mr. Goodnight, don't tell the cowboys. Please don't. First of all, I'm not completely sure. It could be something else. But mainly, a woman doesn't like to have herself talked over when it comes to such matters. It should be a very private condition. I implore you not to tell anyone, not until we know for sure. No, not until I begin to show and we can't avoid people knowing. Will you promise me, Mr. Goodnight? I implore you."

"Course, if you put it that way. I'm just so happy. I'm bustin' with happiness. But I won't bust if'n you tell me not to."

"Please don't burst, Mr. Goodnight."

97

One morning about a week later, as Goodnight emerged from his great sandstone house, Claw got up from his seat on the porch and joined him on his walk to the cookhouse. The presence of his "son" still made him nervous in spite of the new evidence that he was indeed this misshapen boy's father. Goodnight congratulated himself that he would soon have a new child who would of course supplant this unwanted son.

"Good mornin'," said Claw. "Is Miss Revelie all right?"

"Of course," Goodnight said tartly.

"Good, 'cause I thought I heard her early this mornin'. She sounded sick. Like she was throwin' up. Thass an awful sound. An awful feelin'. I was worried about her."

"She's doin' fine. Just fine."

"But this ain't the first mornin' I heard that there retching sound. I'm just across the hall and I hear a lot."

"I'm not interested in what you hear. Please, less talk about somethin' else. See them clouds over the north rim? Looks like rain today."

"No, what it looks like to me, what it sounds like, is Miss Revelie is gonna have a baby. Now ain't that so?"

Goodnight's face reddened. He stopped walking and turned on his "son." Claw stopped too and faced his "father."

"That ain't none of your concern," he snapped angrily.

"Ain't none a my concern–?" Claw protested aggressively.

"Thass what I said and I mean it."

"It shore as hell is my concern. Because that there bump in her belly that's makin' her so sick might just be my little baby brother or little baby sister. Ain't that so?"

"No!"

"No? You mean it ain't gonna be kin to me?"

"I just mean no. Shut up about it. If'n you wasn't–"

"Because if he ain't kin to me, then he ain't kin to you. If it ain't my baby brother, it shore as hell ain't yore baby boy. Or if it's a girl, it ain't your baby daughter if it ain't my baby sister. So it must be my concern. Gotta be."

Goodnight wanted to swing at his son. He wanted to break his teeth.

"No, no, just shut up!"

"Course, maybe you mean it ain't none a my concern on accounta you ain't the papa. Then I'll shut up 'cause it ain't got nothin' to do with me. Who you figure the papa is?"

Goodnight swung, hit his son in the mouth, and knocked him to the red earth. Out of the corner of his one eye, the angry man noticed his wife emerging from the big sandstone house. He also saw Claw spit out some blood and then smile.

"It's Loving's, ain't it? You know it's Loving's, don'tcha? When you're gone, I hear him and Revelie acrosst the hall. Huffin' and puffin'. Just like I heard her throwin' up this mornin'. I hear a lot."

Goodnight tried to kick his son in the mouth, but the boy turned away, so the boot glanced off a shoulder. Then the father staggered backward.

"Tell you what you oughta do," Claw said. "You oughta tell her you're gonna go huntin' overnight. Or you're goin' to Tascosa on business. But you don't go."

Goodnight kicked his son in the ribs.

"You hide out."

The father kicked his son in the stomach as he was trying to get up.

"Then–you–circle back," Claw managed to sputter, "and you'll catch 'em."

The father kicked his boy in the mouth and broke teeth.

"Stop it!" screamed Revelie, running toward the father and son. "Mr. Goodnight, please stop."

Goodnight had drawn his boot back to deliver another blow when Revelie tackled him. She wrapped her arms around him and pulled him back from his victim.

"Git off my land!" Goodnight hissed.

"He doesn't mean it," said Revelie.

"Git off my land or I'll hang you," he said. "And I sure as hell do mean it!"

"No, he doesn't," she told the cringing Claw while she continued to hold her husband. "This just proves we're a family. Families fight."

98

"I'm going to Tascosa," Goodnight told his wife one morning several weeks later. "I've gotta do some business at the bank."

"Be careful," said Revelie, who was barely beginning to show. "Come back safe."

His wife smiled at him. It was a beautiful smile. The pregnancy seemed to make her more beautiful than ever. The happy smile that lit her beautiful face made her husband wonder if perhaps she was a little too happy. Was she glad to see him go?

It was late morning before Goodnight rode away from his ranch headquarters heading in the direction of Tascosa. But he had no intention of going to town. As his horse trotted along the bank of the shallow red river, he hated himself for finally doing what Claw had suggested. Getting rid of Claw had been easy: he had just chased him off the place. But getting rid of the suspicions he had kindled, that was harder. Mistrust and jealousy were flint and steel in his chest, striking sparks, making fire. At last, Goodnight had decided that he just had to find out one way or the other. He couldn't go on wondering.

As horse and rider climbed the north wall of the great canyon, Goodnight told himself that Claw had probably been lying. Of course he had. He had lied about Revelie. He had lied about Loving. He had lied about being his son. He had lied about everything, top to bottom.

But what if he hadn't been lying?

No, no, but he was. He had to be. Otherwise life was just too cruel. He couldn't bear it. If Revelie was really betraying him with Loving, then he hoped the canyon walls would fall in on the ranch and the rancher. The canyon itself should be filled in and exist no more.

When he reached the top of the wall, Goodnight rode along the north rim, just killing time, waiting for dark. He was wasting a day and it pained him. There was so much to be done on the ranch. He blamed Claw for all these wasted hours. Why had he ever listened to that monster anyway?

Goodnight wondered: Who did he hate more, his son or the Robbers' Roost outlaws? Well, by now maybe they were one and the same. As he was being evicted from the Home Ranch, Claw had promised to find Gudanuf and join his gang. Was it an empty threat? Probably. At any rate, he was gone and good riddance. Thankfully he wouldn't be there tonight to see his drama played out.

Goodnight sat on the bed in Claw's room, spying the way Claw had spied. He was no better than his despised son. His body wanted to lie down, but he was afraid he would fall asleep. He had returned under cover of darkness–the moon was black tonight–and had crept into the big sandstone house by a back door. He hated being sneaky. He hated everything about this night. Of course, he hated Claw, but he also hated himself for giving in to Claw's accusations. He hated Revelie and Loving in advance, as if they were already guilty. And he hated himself doubly for not being able to suspend judgment.

It was getting late. He couldn't see his big pocket watch in the darkness, and he couldn't light a lamp without giving himself away, but it seemed to him that it must be almost midnight. Of course, he couldn't be sure. Sometimes time passed slower when you couldn't watch it go. Still he was fairly sure that it was past his bedtime. Working ranchers needed their rest.

He dozed sitting up.

Unnnhh, unnnhh, unnnhh, unnnhh, unnnhh, unnnhh."

The sound roused Goodnight from his shallow sleep. Shrugging and rubbing his eye to wake himself up, he recognized those moans. Oh, no. Why had he played this trick? Standing up, he rocked back and forth clumsily. Wake up!

"Unnnhh, unnnhh, unnnhh."

He raised his shoulders again and then let them sag. He reached up and touched his eye patch, and then reached down and touched his six-gun tied to his leg.

"Unnnhh, unnnhh, unnnhh."

Then he lurched forward. He reached for the doorknob, turned it, and pulled the door open. Standing in the bright hallway, lit by oil lamps, he listened.

"Unnnhh, unnnhh, unnnhh."

Disaster lurked only a few feet away behind another door. He paused in the hall that divided the two bedrooms to try to collect his faculties. What would he do? What should he do? He didn't want to know for sure–it was the last thing in the world that he wanted to know–but he had to know.

"Unnnhh, unnnhh, unnnhh."

Goodnight stumbled groggily forward and grasped the doorknob of *his* bedroom door. He quietly opened it and stood there staring. The bedroom was dark, but he could see well enough, or rather too well. Loving was on top of her.

Claw was right! It hurt like that flint blade in his scrotum so many years ago.

99

As he reached automatically to draw his gun, Goodnight wanted to hurt the woman whom he had wanted to shield from pain all these years. He knew he would never again be able to love his greatest loves. Goodnight thumbed back the hammer of his six-shooter and pointed the barrel–as if it were a deadly finger–at the lovers who hadn't even seen him yet. They were so busy fucking, they hadn't noticed the danger they were in. He pulled the trigger. The gun made the loudest sound he had ever heard in his life. He had never fired a fieldpiece, a cannon, but he couldn't believe one would make any more noise. The sound trapped inside that room seemed to shake the earth, shake the whole canyon, but perhaps it was only him that it shook.

Goodnight saw Loving roll off Revelie and sit up. He was naked. Still lying on her back, the unfaithful wife pulled her discarded dress over her breasts. Now she felt that she had to hide her nakedness in the presence of her own husband.

Goodnight, who had officially "won" the title of fastest and most accurate gunman in these parts, had missed his target. He wasn't sure just why, but lots of reasons occurred to him. Now he felt embarrassed standing there with a smoking gun, as if he were the one who had done something disgraceful. Had seeing his best friend fucking his wife driven him to bad manners? Was taking a shot at them bad form–a word his wife had taught him?

"Git dressed," Goodnight ordered. "Then we'll settle this. I cain't shoot nobody nekked." He started to turn and go, but then hesitated. He stared at his best friend. "Come out with your gun strapped on, and we'll finish this up."

Goodnight was furious at Revelie and Loving, but he was also angry at himself. He damned them, but he also damned himself. They were too perfect–at least as he saw them–to be entirely at fault. He was the imperfect one, the flawed one, who had somehow allowed the betrayal to occur. He had given his permission without knowing it. He had worshiped them both and so put them on a higher plane where they had naturally turned to each other. He hated himself as much as he hated them. He wanted to kill himself as much as he wanted to kill Loving. By now, he already knew that he couldn't kill his wife. Maybe he would rather kill himself than kill Loving. He deserved it more because he had somehow betrayed his best friend and his wife into betraying him. Or was the terrible pain behind his eyes–the one eye blind all the time, the other often enough–simply driving him mad?

Turning, he fled the bedroom.

Outside in the corridor, Goodnight felt that everything had changed forever, changed in a moment, changed utterly. It was as if he had returned his ax to the block of iron where he had found it. He had lost his magic. Lost his powers. Lost his belief in himself, which was the greatest magic of all.

"Don't shoot," Revelie's voice reached him from inside the bedroom. "Don't shoot, I'm coming out. All right?"

Goodnight desperately willed her to be ugly, but when she emerged from their bedroom–still naked–she wasn't. She was as lovely as ever. Lovelier. Her beauty hurt him. Now it seemed a fierce beauty, a primeval beauty. At the same time, she was soft, pleading, frightened. She was as gorgeous as the setting sun that is at its finest just before it deserts you. She was one person more in his life that he had lost and he couldn't stand it.

"Don't fight him," Revelie begged.

Goodnight didn't say anything.

"Please, don't, because he won't fight. He'll just let you kill him. I know it."

Goodnight half-turned from her.

"Please, just go," Revelie implored. "Leave him alone."

"Shut up," Goodnight said in a small voice.

"Don't kill him. It wouldn't be right. Please. I beg you."

The more Revelie pleaded, the more Goodnight wanted to do just what she was asking him *not* to do, for she was taking *his* side even now. Of course, why wouldn't she? But somehow it surprised him that even after the betrayal had been discovered, she would stick to Loving. She remained more her lover's than her husband's. Goodnight wanted to smash her lover, to destroy his rival, to make her pay by making him pay.

"Come on out," he called into the bedroom. "We gotta settle this thing. Sooner the better."

Goodnight strained to hear the slightest movement, but he neither saw nor heard anything. He might just as well be talking to God. Or the Great Mystery.

"You don't come out," Goodnight said, "I'm comin' in." He took out his gun and fired it at the ceiling. "I'm serious. We gotta do this."

"No! Please!" cried Revelie. "You can't kill him in cold blood."

"Maybe he's gonna kill me," the husband said, studying his wife. "You ever think a that? Or don't you give a damn?"

Even now he felt a pang at swearing in mixed company.

"He won't. He'll just let you win again."

Oh, so she knew about that, too.

"How do you know what he'll do?"

"Because he's your friend."

"Some friend."

"Well, he is. He loves you."

"Awful funny love. Didn't stop him from takin' my wife. If'n he'd do that, he'd do anythin'."

"No, that's different."

"How come?"

"I don't know."

"But I thought you was such an expert when it comes to him."

"Stop this. Stop it before you do something terrible."

"Too late for that now."

"Why?"

"Just is. You know that." Goodnight turned. "I'm comin' in!"

As he moved toward the dark doorway, Revelie grabbed his left arm and tried to hold him. He angrily pushed her away. To hell with her.

Stepping inside the dark bedroom, Goodnight saw his best friend standing in the middle of the room. He was dressed now. He was so graceful that he had somehow pulled on his clothes without making any noise. He even wore his gun.

"I won't fight you," Loving said.

"You gotta," said Goodnight, his hand quivering above his gun.

Goodnight tried to hate Loving and he succeeded to some extent.

He was glad the familiar face remained obscure in the darkness. He picked out a spot on the dim chest as his target. He doubted that he would live to pull the trigger, but he was certainly going to try.

"Go ahead and shoot me if it'll make you feel better," Loving said. "But I ain't gonna draw."

Something in the tone, in the attitude, infuriated the wronged husband. He wanted to shut Loving's eyes forever so they wouldn't see his degradation, his embarrassment, his smallness. A husband who couldn't keep a wife was such a pathetic thing.

"Don't do me no favors," Goodnight said angrily. "I don't need no damn favors from you."

Loving didn't say anything.

"I'm gonna kill you if'n I can, I'm warnin' you, so you better try an' kill me first. That's all there is to it."

"Ain't nobody stoppin' you."

"I mean it."

"Hurry up and git it over with if that's what you mean to do."

Now Goodnight could see a little better. The features were beginning to sketch themselves on Loving's blank face. That was too bad. He was more real. More recognizable. His betrayal now seemed more personal. And killing him would be more personal, too. Goodnight told himself he should have drawn and fired right away before the shadow turned back into his best friend. He hadn't then, but now he could–he would–before the face grew even brighter. It wasn't going to get any easier, just harder. Then he heard boots climbing up the front-porch steps. The gunshots had alarmed the cowboys. He had to do this before they got there to stop him. Goodnight reached for his gun.

"No!" screamed Revelie. "You can't shoot him in cold blood."

Her voice stopped Goodnight. His revolver remained in his holster as he glanced back over his shoulder at her. Squinting, he saw his wife come rushing into the bedroom carrying something heavy. He thought for a moment that she was going to run over him, try to knock him down, tackle him. But instead, she squeezed past him and hurried to the side of her lover.

"He won't fight you," Revelie said, "but I will."

Now Goodnight recognized the weight in her right hand. It was a gun. He had given her that gun one long-ago birthday.

"What's the matter?" asked Revelie. "Afraid to fight a woman?"

Goodnight didn't say anything.

"It's my fault. I'm the one you should be gunning for. I'm sorry I don't have a holster, but I can hold it like this." The naked woman whom he loved lowered the gun to her side so that it pointed at the floor. "Will that do? Then what? Shall I count three? I'd drop my handkerchief, but I don't have one."

"I ain't fightin' you," Goodnight said. "Right now my quarrel's with him."

"But he won't fight you," she said. "And you won't fight me. So there we are. This game of yours isn't working out, is it? Maybe you should just leave. Go away!"

The more she talked, the more she took *his* side, the more Goodnight hated her. And the more he hated her, the more he wanted to kill Loving. His right hand trembled in anticipation.

"This is between me and him," Goodnight said. "Ain't but one of us gonna come outa here alive. You hear me, Loving?"

Revelie raised her gun again and pointed it at her husband's stomach.

"If you try to shoot him," the wife said in a controlled voice, "I will shoot you first. I promise. You know I don't break promises."

The boot noise was in the hallway, coming on fast, almost on top of him. He couldn't wait any longer.

"You broke one," said Goodnight and reached for his gun.

The roar of the gunshots shook him so violently that he did not know he had been shot until he was already lying on the floor. He heard voices above him, but he couldn't tell what they were saying. Now he was not only half-blind, but deaf, too. Seeing Loving still on his feet, Goodnight knew that even as a gunfighter he had failed. He was relieved and at the same time angry at himself. Angry both at his failure and at his relief. He thought Loving had shot him until he saw the smoke curling lazily from the barrel of Revelie's gun. Was he relieved again? Was he glad it had been her instead of him?

"He's dead!" cried Too Short. "You killt him."

"No," Goodnight choked. "I ain't dead yet."

He started trying to sit up.

"Simon," Too Short sobbed. "She killt Simon."

The bullet had gone through Goodnight and hit the unlikely cowboy who had turned out to be a top hand.

100

Goodnight rolled down Main Street in a contraption hammered together by Tin Soldier. It was an overstuffed easy chair with four wheels attached. The two larger wheels came from a buggy, while the two smaller ones had been borrowed from a couple of wheelbarrows. Tin Soldier, who pushed from behind, was panting but smiling.

"Get a horse!" yelled a passerby.

"Go to hell!" Tin Soldier shouted back good-naturedly.

Goodnight suspected that the cowboy-blacksmith enjoyed finding his invention, this curious wagon-chair, the object of so much attention. But the man in that chair had very different feelings. He knew that the whole town–the entire country hereabouts–had been gossiping about him and his wife and his wife's lover. Now he could see the townspeople turning to each other, talking him over. Some were even bold enough to point at him as he passed by.

He couldn't help comparing this trip down Tascosa's Main Street to that long-ago visit when he had seen Revelie for the first time. He had saved her then–anyhow, saved her thumbs–but he wouldn't be able to save her now. She would have to face judge and jury on her own.

The chair-wagon hit a bump and Goodnight winced. He was still too weak to walk. Just standing up made him break into a sweat and feel dizzy. She had almost killed him, but he had been lucky. Lucky the bullet passed just beneath his heart. Lucky it went right through and came out his back. Simon Shapiro had been the unlucky one. He had been buried beside Suckerod on the Home Ranch. Now he would be a part of the red canyon forever. Goodnight sure felt lucky, all right. Real lucky. Lucky enough to get one of his cowboys killed. Lucky enough to lose his wife and his best friend. Lucky enough to feel real sorry for himself. He told himself he had to snap out of it. He hated self-pity. He ended up pitying himself for not being man enough to escape self-pity's clutches.

Reaching the front door of the courthouse, Tin Soldier turned the wheeled contraption around and pulled it up the steps backward. There were only five of them. Then all too soon, Goodnight was inside the courtroom. Some fifty or sixty chairs–most of them cane-bottomed–had been arranged in rows.

"That's far enough," Goodnight said. "I wanta sit in back."

Tin Soldier positioned the wagon-chair so that it became one of the chairs in the last row. Then he sat down beside his boss.

"This okay?" asked Tin Soldier.

Goodnight grunted.

He knew that no matter how far back he sat, he would still be at the center of the case. His eye searched the room and found Loving sitting in the front row. He would be seated right behind Revelie when she arrived. Goodnight was jealous of Loving's position, so close to her. Finding himself staring at Loving, Goodnight looked away self-consciously.

He studied the floor, which was grimy. She shouldn't have to be tried on a dirty floor. It wasn't right. She was better than that. He started to tell Tin Soldier to get somebody to clean the floor, but then he remembered that he wasn't in charge here, so he just seethed helplessly. He wondered if they had failed to scrub the floor on purpose. He knew by now that many people resented his wife's supposed airs. He had heard talk about the great Boston lady finally getting her comeuppance. He wished he could protect her from such spitefulness.

Hearing a rustling just behind him, Goodnight half-turned and found himself staring at Revelie. He couldn't breathe. He almost wished he were blind again. He realized now that he had hoped that a couple of weeks in jail would mar her beauty, but instead it had just made her seem more vulnerable–more fragile–which made her all the more lovely. He desperately wanted to protect her. Their eyes met and then she looked away. Had she averted her eyes out of guilt or abhorrence? Did she blame herself or him? Who was more guilty? The wife who betrayed her husband? Or the husband who drove her to pull the trigger and kill somebody? Loving had only made her an adulterer. Goodnight had made her a murderer.

Revelie was accompanied by Sheriff Dub Martin, who had arrested her and who had recently been her landlord. After the shooting, Goodnight had been too delirious to decide whether Revelie should be shielded from the law or turned over to it. So Tin Soldier had taken it upon himself to ride from the red canyon all the way to Tascosa to lay the facts before "Sheriff Dub." Then Black Dub had ridden to the Home Ranch, where he took Revelie into custody. Fortunately, Loving had been away from headquarters at the time, off alone somewhere trying to make sense out of what had happened. Otherwise there might have been a fight. Goodnight was the one who had wanted law and order in this country, and now that law threatened to take his "wife" away from him. He was having second thoughts about getting what he had asked for.

As everyone stared, Revelie swept by her husband and moved to the front of the courtroom. She sat down at the defense table beside her attorney, Hank Wallace, the only lawyer in town, whose office, located at the corner of McMasters and Main Streets, was no more than a shack. His suit was shiny, but his shoes weren't. His eyes were too close together, which made him look unreliable. Goodnight thought Revelie deserved better. She should really be tried in Boston, where the people would understand a woman like her. Her husband stared hard at her back, hoping she would turn.

And Revelie did turn. Goodnight was happy for a moment. He thought she was looking for him. But her gaze stopped before it reached him. She had been looking for Loving. Goodnight saw their eyes meet. She smiled warmly.

Now her husband wanted to hurt her. He had been informed that he couldn't be forced to testify against his wife. That was the law. But he could take the stand if he so chose. He had told the prosecutor, John King, who made his living running the drugstore, that he had no desire to testify. But now he felt himself changing his mind. Now he wanted to take the stand and tell the jury that the woman who was smiling at that cowboy was a killer, a murderer, a . . .

Calm down, calm down. The doctor had warned Goodnight that he shouldn't get excited. He looked away.

When he looked back, Revelie had her back turned once again. Goodnight found himself studying the back of Loving's neck. He wondered what Loving thought of him. Why did he care? But he did.

The judge–a circuit judge who passed through Tascosa every month or so–entered the courtroom and everybody stood up. Everybody but the crippled Goodnight. His Honor struck a table with a wooden hammer and everybody sat back down.

Circuit Court Judge Sam Rawlins pointed at the prosecutor and asked: "You ready?"

"Yes, sir," said John King, whose job was to get Revelie hanged.

"Good." Then the judge pointed at Hank Wallace: "You ready?"

"Yes, Your Honor."

"Then we better git started. Time's a wastin'. You"–he pointed again–"call your first witness."

Goodnight wondered if the judge had trouble remembering names.

"I call Mortimer Jones," said John King.

Leaving his place beside Goodnight, Tin Soldier reluctantly got up and headed for the witness stand. Actually, it was a chair that sat beside the judge's table. Tin Soldier's face was a deep brown, but his forehead was white where it was normally shaded by his steel hat.

Henry Kimball, who happened to be another blacksmith, did the swearing in. He handed the witness a heavy Bible and asked, "Do you swear to tell the truth, the whole truth, and nothin' but the truth, so help you God?"

"Yeah," said Tin Soldier.

John King, the prosecuting druggist, stood up and approached the witness chair. He wore a black suit, a string tie, and was completely bald, with a freckled head.

"State your name, please."

"Mortimer"–Tin Soldier looked embarrassed–"Jones."

"And where do you reside?"

"The bunkhouse at the Home Ranch."

"All right, I reckon that'll do. Where were you on the night of June twenty-fourth?"

"The bunkhouse."

"Well, what happened?"

Tin Soldier cleared his throat. He looked around the courtroom as if searching for an escape route. His eyes met his boss's and focused. Goodnight felt sorry for him.

"I'm waitin'," prompted John King.

"Well, we heard a shot and come arunnin'," said Tin Soldier. "And we heard Mr. Goodnight tellin' Loving to draw. But he wouldn't fight him. And so when the boss there pulled his gun, Miz Revelie shot him. And she shot my friend Simon Shapiro with the same bullet. And he fell down dead." He said it all without taking a breath.

Goodnight discovered that he resented Tin Soldier for trying to hurt Revelie. He knew the poor cowboy didn't really have any choice. Everybody in town already knew the story–gossip being what it was–so poor Tin Soldier couldn't very well make up some new chain of events now. Still, Goodnight liked his cowboy less. He couldn't help it.

When Revelie glanced back over her shoulder at Loving, Goodnight discovered that his opinion of Tin Soldier was improving.

101

Loving seemed to sit as easily in the witness chair as he did in the saddle. Goodnight studied the cowboy's well-made features for an answer to the only question that mattered to him: How could his friend hurt him so? But all he discovered was how much it still hurt. First he had lost his sister, and now he had lost his brother. He felt that he couldn't stand it anymore and looked away.

He tried not to listen as Loving swore to tell the truth. Goodnight wished he could stop his ears, but he couldn't keep out the sound anymore than he could stop the feelings. He sat helplessly in his wagon-chair and was drenched with sweat. He couldn't help wondering if anybody noticed. He wiped his forehead and tried to stop sweating. He couldn't do that either. He couldn't keep the sound out or the water in.

"Well, what happened?" asked the prosecutor.

Goodnight longed to pass out. His chest hurt where he had been shot, as if the wound were brand-new. He thought he was bleeding again. Looking down, he didn't see any blood. He felt a blinding pain behind his eyes, the good and the bad. He wanted to get out of there. He had never run from a fight, but he was ready to run now.

"Mr. Goodnight and I quarreled," Loving said easily. "He threw down on me. I was faster'n he was. My bullet went clean through him and killt Simon Shapiro, who didn't have no part in our fight. I'm real sorry for that, and I'm ready to take my medicine."

Goodnight felt dizzy, delirious, sick. His head was a crudely carved block that balanced precariously on his shoulders. He actually felt as if it were about to fall off. He fought hard not to throw up. It seemed to him that Loving had betrayed him once again by usurping his role, the husband's role, as Revelie's protector. Goodnight hated Loving for what he was attempting to do. And loved Loving for it. And resented him. And admired him more than ever. And was deeply, deeply jealous.

"Hold on," said John King. "You mean you did the shootin'?"

"Yes, sir," said Loving calmly.

Goodnight had to admit that this cowboy even lied well.

"Remember," said the prosecutor, "you're under oath."

"That's why I'm tellin' the truth," said Loving.

"No!" screamed Revelie. "I did it. I killed that poor man." She pointed at Loving. "He didn't do anything. He's lying."

Goodnight wondered if his wife would ever have sacrificed herself in this way for him. Oh, maybe once. Maybe a long long time ago. But surely not now. And this hurt. Revelie had opened another wound. And this time she hadn't missed his heart. His shoulders hunched and he bent forward. He looked down and saw that the front of his shirt was slowly turning red.

102

Goodnight thought he smelled smoke. He lay on a narrow bed in a back room of the Exchange Hotel with its huge, steep roof. The hotel was full tonight–a very unusual circumstance–because so many people from all around had come to town to see the hanging. The unmarried cowboys, who had come riding in for the show, mostly slept on the ground, but the married men and their wives and daughters naturally wanted a roof at night. Goodnight was surprised at the number of womenfolk who had made the trip to see another woman die at the end of a rope. He supposed it was a measure of their resentment of his Boston wife. These Western women wanted to see the Eastern lady dance her last dance with her feet off the ground. Perhaps what he was smelling was the hatred in the air.

No, something was really burning. Goodnight couldn't see anything from where he lay. If he wanted to satisfy his curiosity–possibly even save himself from burning–he was going to have to get out of bed. But could he? Ever since his relapse in the courtroom, he had rested in this bed day and night.

Goodnight told himself that he had to get to the window. He was worried about Revelie locked in her cell. What if the jail was on fire? He was also worried about himself. What if the hotel was burning? If Revelie was the one in danger, he would wake up the town. If he was the one, then he would just tumble out of his ground-floor window. But probably it was just some bonfire lit to celebrate the woman-hanging.

Goodnight eased his feet over the edge of the bed and they dropped of their dead weight. Then he started the hard job of trying to push himself up into a sitting position. He told himself that he wouldn't mind dying before Revelie died, but he didn't want to be burned alive. The frightening odor was growing stronger. Climbing down off this bed seemed harder and more dangerous than the precarious climb down into his red canyon. He looked dizzily down at the floor that loomed a mile or more below. Stand up! He just sat there. *Stand up!* Pushing with his hands, he shifted his weight to his feet and rose slowly. When he reached his full height, he ceased to exist. He was gone. He died. He was falling. Then he came back to life just in time to regain his balance. He swayed, light-headed, but remained standing. Then he began the long trip across the room. The floor stretched in front of him like the White Sands. He took small steps with wooden feet. His side hurt. He had never worked harder or been so tired. He was sweating again. He felt as slippery as a fish.

When he finally reached the window, which looked out of the back of the hotel, Goodnight saw the scaffold that had been erected in a vacant lot next to the jail. It momentarily distracted him, so he forgot the reason for his long trip.

Then he saw a yellow flash. The scaffold was on fire. Good. No, it wasn't good. It wasn't the hangman's platform burning. It was the jail. His first fears were confirmed. Revelie was locked inside a burning cage. She would be burned to death. He couldn't imagine a more terrible fate. Gripped by panic, he started clawing at the window, trying to open it, trying to get out, desperately trying to escape, as if he were the one locked in a blazing building. He had to get to her. He had to save her.

The window opened and he half-jumped and half-fell out. It was like being born anew. He was completely naked. Except for his bandage, his eye patch, and the six-gun he held in his hand.

103

Goodnight lay on the ground, dazed, but only for a moment. Then he started struggling to his feet. He felt as if somebody were stabbing him just below his heart. He touched the stabbed place, expecting to get blood on his fingers, but there was none. His chest was damp but only with sweat. He took a deep breath and then began his endless journey to the fire. The blaze was brighter now.

"Fire!" screamed Goodnight, and then aimed his pistol at the stars and pulled the trigger. The gun roared. No stars fell. "Fire! *Fire!* The jail's on *fire!*" He squeezed off another shot. He was embarrassed to call so much attention to himself when he wasn't dressed for it. Wasn't, in fact, dressed at all. Still he kept up the alarm. "Fire! Fire! . . ." And he emptied his gun shooting at heaven.

Soon his howling was accompanied by a ringing bell. It seemed to make a frightened sound. It was so loud that he stopped shouting. Somehow the clanging seemed to be going on inside his head. His skull was the bell and his brain was the clapper. He felt as if the bones in his head were about to crack like the Liberty Bell. He wished the ringing would stop. His nerves couldn't take any more.

People were now pouring into the street. Goodnight could see dark figures silhouetted against the bright flames. As he fought to reach Revelie, limping badly, he was haunted by Suckerod, the shaking cowboy. How many of "his" people was he going to have to lose to fire? The ground felt hot beneath his bare feet.

Goodnight just hoped that somebody had the sense to unlock Revelie's jail cell and let her out before she was burned alive. But what if they couldn't reach her? What if the jail was already too hot? What if they couldn't get in and she couldn't get out? He thought he heard her screaming, but it could have been his imagination. He tried to listen harder. Was the noise coming from his wife or from the fire itself? Was the inferno howling?

As he drew closer to the burning jail, Goodnight could see the gathering crowd more plainly. Some people were carrying buckets of water, but they seemed to move in a haphazard fashion. There didn't appear to be any organized fire-fighting. He imagined his wife dying for lack of an orderly effort. He knew how to give orders if he could just get there in time.

But would the town take orders from a naked man? Goodnight felt as if he were moving in a nightmare, for he had often dreamed of coming to town nude. But he always woke up . . . until now. Thank God the fire had everybody's attention at the moment, but he knew somebody would eventually notice him. He put his hand over his crotch as if that did much good.

Goodnight forgot his embarrassment when he saw Revelie emerge from the jail. Dub held her by the arm as if to keep her from escaping. Her husband thought that was uncalled for, but at least she was safe from the fire. He could see coughs shaking her whole body. She looked pitifully pale in the light cast by the bright fire.

"Rev–"

He stopped his shout when he remembered that he was nude. He wanted to see her, but he didn't want her to see him. That would teach him to sleep in the nude. He had gotten in the habit in his days as a Human Being.

"Revelie," he whispered from afar. "Thank God you're all right." He breathed her name over and over again. "Revelie, Revelie, Revelie, Revelie . . ."

Goodnight almost hoped the intensity of his stare would make her look in his direction, make her see him, but if she did, he would really die of embarrassment. He felt not only as naked but also as weak as a newborn baby. He sank to his knees and covered his nakedness with both hands. His vision blurred so he knew he was crying. Well, he didn't need to be strong now. She was safe–at least until morning, when they would hang her.

Looking for someplace to hide, Goodnight selected a small mesquite that grew about five yards away. He felt too tired, too drained, to stand up, so he crawled, like a baby. Fear once again gripped him, not for his wife, but for himself. What if somebody saw him? The news would spread as fast as a runaway fire, and soon everybody would be staring at him. And laughing at him. Including Revelie. Moving along on all fours, he felt like some lower animal, a dog, even a pig. Not a cat. He wasn't as graceful as a cat.

When he finally reached the cover of the small mesquite, Goodnight felt as if he had been saved. Like Revelie. But somebody would eventually see him, and come daylight, somebody would hang Revelie. This saving business didn't seem to save very much for very long. He just wished he could rush over, grab her up, carry her off, and hide her from the hangman. He wished it so much that he could almost see it. He imagined himself riding a strong horse down McMasters Street. He had his clothes on and he bent down and–

His wish was made flesh, but unfortunately not his. A rider was galloping down the dusty street. People scrambled to get out of the way. It was Loving riding furiously. Good for him! Save her! Please! He couldn't thank Loving enough, but at the same time he couldn't help being jealous. Now this graceful cowboy was not only his wife's lover but also her savior.

Goodnight bit the inside of his cheek as Loving bent down and pulled Revelie away from Sheriff Dub, who was certainly strong enough to have put up a fight if he had wanted to. Loving lifted her up onto his saddle, where she lay across the pommel. It wasn't a graceful position–nor a comfortable one–but it surely beat a hanging. Goodnight wondered if Loving hadn't set the fire on purpose to force the sheriff to unlock Revelie's cell. He wouldn't put it past him.

Loving and Revelie–the people he loved best in the world, the only two people who had ever shot him–galloped away from the light and soon disappeared into the darkness.

Nobody fired a shot.

BOOK FIVE

QUEST FOR VENGEANCE

104

1880s

On a lovely spring morning, Goodnight sat on the front porch of his beautiful rock house feeling bad. He had never quite regained his strength after his wife shot him. He wasn't sure which had crippled him the most, taking the bullet or losing Revelie and Loving. It had been years now and he still hadn't healed. He got tired more easily, so he worked fewer hours. And when he wasn't working, he generally sat right here on this porch. Now that he was alone, the house behind him was too big for him, so he resisted going inside until he had to. But the porch was different. It wasn't too big. It was half indoors (because it had a roof) and half outdoors (because it didn't have walls), so it belonged to the canyon as well as to the house. He had installed a store-bought rocking chair, and he spent many hours in it, with his back turned to Revelie's mansion, his face turned to *his* red-walled home.

As he rocked, Goodnight noticed Too Short coming toward the house. Something about the way he moved suggested reluctance. Goodnight supposed his new foreman–new since the departure of Loving–must be bringing bad news. The rancher felt his shoulders slump as if they were about to receive some heavy weight. He was thoroughly tired of bad news.

"Howdy," Goodnight said.

"Howdy," Too Short returned the greeting.

"What's wrong?"

"How'd you know?"

"I reckon I'm gittin' to be a pessimist."

"Well, here's how 'tis, I brung somethin' for you to read. I don't much think you're gonna like it."

Too Short handed over a single sheet of paper folded several times. Goodnight patiently opened the folds and then stared down at the writing done by an unfamiliar hand. He squinted at the paper with both eyes–his new glass eye and the one that worked–and remembered how much he hated being called on to read during his brief school days. He was glad he didn't have to read out loud anymore unless he wanted to.

Goodnight read silently: *We, the undersigned cowboys of the Panhandle, do by these presents agree to bind ourselves into the following obligations, viz. . . .*

"'Viz.'? What's 'viz.'?" Goodnight asked.

"Don't ask me what it means," Too Short said. "Tommy Harris done wrote it. I guess you'd hafta ask him."

"Who's he?"

"He's wagon boss over to the LS."

"Why's he writin' me a letter? I don't even know no Tom Harris."

"It's to all the ranchers hereabouts. Harris said to show it to you first on account of you're head a the Cattlemen's 'Sociation."

Goodnight nodded and went back to reading: . . . *viz.: First: That we will not work for less than $50 per mo. and we farther more agree no one shall work for less than $50 per mo. after 31st of Mch.*

"This Harris fella," Goodnight said, "he's got sorta a roundabout way a puttin' things."

"Uh-huh," said Too Short.

Second: Good cooks shall also receive $50 per mo.

"How about bad cooks?" Goodnight asked.

"I dunno," said Too Short.

"Looks to me like us ranchers could save a passel a money by hirin' nothin' but bad cooks. How'd all them fifty-dollar-a-month cowboys like that, huh?"

Too Short shrugged.

Third: Anyone running an outfit shall not work for less than $75 per month.

Goodnight glanced up at Too Short, then looked back down at the letter.

Anyone violating the above obligations shall suffer the consequences.

"What consequences?"

Too Short shrugged again.

Those not having funds to pay board after March 31 will be provided for 30 days at Tascosa.

"This here Tom Harris a rich fella?"

"Not that I know of."

"So how's he gonna pay for all them thirty days? Figure it's gonna run him two bits a day for ever' cowboy, huh?"

"He gonna pass the hat, I reckon."

Goodnight then read over a long list of signatures at the bottom of the letter. Some were easier to make out than others, but all were decipherable, with patience.

Thos. Harris	*J. A. Marrs*
Roy Griffin	*Jim Miller*
J. W. Peacock	*Henry Stoffard*
J. L. Howard	*Wm. T. Kerr*
W. D. Gaton	*Bud Davis*
B. G. Brown	*T. D. Holiday*
W. B. Boring	*C. F. Goddard*
D. W. Peepler	*E. E. Watkins*
Jas. Jones	*C. B. Thompson*
C. M. Hullett	*G. F. Nickell*
A. F. Martin	*Juan A. Gomes*
Harry Ingerton	*J. L. Grissom*

Goodnight scratched his head and checked the list again. Several of the names were familiar to him, but only vaguely.

"I don't git it," he said. "What's this here got to do with me? Ain't none a my cowboys signed this here paper, right? Ain't none a you involved?"

Too Short got reluctant again. He used his right hand to scratch under his left armpit. He glanced up at the sky to see if there was any chance of rain today. There wasn't.

"Well, um, them there's just the boys that was around when they wrote the damn letter," Too Short said at last. "Happened somethin' like this. There was these three outfits out lookin' for drift cattle and so on."

"What outfits?" asked Goodnight. "None a mine?"

"Well, I reckon it was the LIT, the LS, and the LX boys. And what they found besides some scrawny cows was each other. Sorta bumped into each other, don'tcha see? And they ended up havin' supper together. And you know what happens when a bunch a cowboys git to talkin'. Purdy soon they was complainin' about this and bitchin' about that. And this here Tommy Harris come up with this here idea for a union of all things. He's from back East where they got that sorta thing. So he knowed all about it. And first thing you know, they'd written this here letter to all the ranchers in these here parts."

"Includin' me?"

"Yes, sir, includin' you."

The "sir" bothered Goodnight. Too Short never called him "sir." So this matter must be serious.

"So what if'n the cowboys don't git their fifty dollars a month? What happens then?"

"We're gonna go on strike, I reckon."

"Hold on, whaddaya mean by 'we'? You're done gittin' a hunderd dollars a month, ain't you?"

"Uh-huh."

"And this here union's only askin' seventy-five dollars for outfit bosses, right? So how come you said 'we,' huh? Just a slip a the tongue, I hope?"

"Not exactly. I figure I better stick with the boys. If'n they're strikin', I reckon I'm strikin'."

As always, when there was trouble or the threat of trouble, Goodnight missed Loving.

105

When Goodnight entered the Exchange Hotel on March 29, two days before the cowboys' deadline, he saw that most of the other ranchers were already there. The boards, which creaked beneath his feet, were a part of the first wooden floor put down in Tascosa. He knew that these timbers had often squeaked on happier occasions, for the hotel had become a real social center, a dancing center. This floor was accustomed to the waltz, the glide polka, the schottische. It wasn't used to strikes. By now, most of the houses in town had wooden floors, and cowboys considered themselves working stiffs. They were all going to have to get used to living in a new and different world.

As president of the Panhandle Cattlemen's Association, Goodnight had called this meeting. He had conceived the idea of an association a few years earlier when his only problems were rustlers. It was in March of 1880 that the ranchers all met and elected him president. They had pledged to battle the stock thieves collectively rather than individually. The association even posted a standing reward of $250 for anybody caught rustling. These efforts seemed to have slowed down but not stopped the loss of cattle. Back then, Goodnight's association had simply been a part of his ongoing effort to bring law, order, and, in particular, justice to this untamed and often unjust part of the country.

But now the cattlemen's association was convening to attempt to deal with a problem it had never anticipated. Goodnight felt that he knew what the others were feeling. Double-crossed by their cowboys, by the times. Or was it just him? Maybe he was simply preoccupied with betrayal after all that had happened.

Looking around the hotel's combination lobby and dining room, Goodnight checked attendance in his head. There was Moss Hays, who owned the Springer Ranch. Will Lee, owner of the LS. Jim Cator of the Diamond K. Jim Evans of the Spade Ranch. Jules Gunter of the T-Anchor. And a dozen or so others. Everybody seemed to be here now, so it was time to get the proceedings under way. Lacking a gavel, Goodnight used his fist, tapping lightly on the hotel's fragrant cedar dining table.

"Okay, let's git started," Goodnight said in a loud drawl. "Ever'-body just take your seats."

The ranchers shuffled–their spurs jingling–up to the long table and sat down. The president of the association solemnly regarded them all with one blue eye that worked and a bluer eye that didn't. Now that he had given up his patch, he was even more acutely aware of his Big Dipper birthmark. Maybe this glass eye hadn't been such a good idea, after all. When he sent off for it, he had been trying to be modern, but now he was no longer sure he liked new-fangled modernity.

"Well, y'all know why we're here," Goodnight said in a businesslike way. He was in a hurry to get these proceedings over with and go home again. "Let's put the cowboys' demands to a vote. All those in favor of acceptin' their terms raise your right hand."

No hands went up.

"All opposed."

They all raised their right hands except John Dunhill, the owner of the Matador Ranch, who had lost his right arm fighting for the Confederacy. He raised his left hand. Nobody seemed to mind. Goodnight didn't raise either hand.

"How 'bout you, Goodnight?" asked Will Lee, the boss of the LS. "Where do you stand on this thing?"

"Pres'dent just votes to break ties," Goodnight said.

"Since when?"

"Since now."

Goodnight felt that he was losing control of the meeting. He had thought that his not voting would lead to a more peaceful get-together, which would be fairer at the same time. But now his very evenhandedness was disturbing the peace.

"Okay," Goodnight announced, "these here demands"–he waved the cowboys' letter–"are hereby rejected. The floor's open for suggestions."

"How many are threatenin' to strike?" asked Moss Hays of the Springer.

"They claim two hunderd-fifty," said Goodnight.

"Cain't be that many," said Lee of the LS in an accusing voice.

"Well, the point is," said the association president, "what're we gonna do no matter how many of them there is. Anybody got any ideas? Huh?"

"There ain't but one thing to do," argued Lee. "I ain't gonna pay no highway rob'ry to my cowboys, and that's all there is to it. And I ain't gonna feed nobody who ain't workin', and that's all there is to that, too. No damn work, no damn fodder. They can starve for all I care."

"Are you makin' that a motion, Will?" asked Goodnight. "Or are you just talkin' to hear your head rattle?"

As soon as he said it, he regretted it. He had promised himself to be a calming force, and here he was picking a fight at the first opportunity.

"Hell, I'm makin' it a motion if that's how you want it," Lee said angrily. "You and your fancy Boston ways. I call for a damn vote."

The mention of Boston hurt Goodnight as it was surely meant to do. He had long suspected that the LS boss was jealous of him, envying his position as the first rancher in these parts–first chronologically and first in influence. Now, Lee had found a wound that he would continue to bother without mercy.

"Not so damn fast," Goodnight said. "Any second to the motion?"

He looked around the table hoping nobody would support Lee in his implacable stance.

"Second," said Hays.

"Okay, okay, all in favor."

Goodnight counted five raised hands. He was pleased to see that the motion had not carried. Lee glared at him.

"Anybody else got any thoughts?" Goodnight asked.

While he waited for a response, he tried for the thousandth time to come up with a solution in his own mind. He could afford to pay the cowboys what they were asking, but he knew that some of the other ranchers couldn't. He also believed in this association that he had founded, and so he favored united action. Still, he admitted to himself he didn't know exactly what to do. He wondered if his thinking might have been sharper before he had gotten shot under the heart. He wished he could ask Loving or Revelie what to do?

"How about offerin' a little more," said Jim Cator of the Diamond K, "but not too much more?"

"We'd be cavin' in," said Lee.

"How much you got in mind?" asked Goodnight.

"Well, I dunno, how about, say, thirty-five dollars for hands, and, I dunno, maybe sixty-five for the foreman?"

"That's too much," argued Lee.

"Let's vote," said Goodnight.

"How 'bout a second, huh? You fergit your damn rules already?"

"Okay, okay, any second?"

"Second," said the one-armed Dunhill.

"All in favor or whatever."

This motion received only three votes.

"Well, okay, less make it less," suggested Cator. "Less say thirty dollars and sixty dollars. How about that?"

"That's just sayin' 'uncle,'" said Lee.

"Second?"

"Second."

"All in favor."

He counted the same three hands. The trend did not seem hopeful.

"Less try it this way," Goodnight said. "Ever'body in favor a any kinda raise atall. How 'bout it?"

"Not if'n we know what's good for us," said Lee.

The same three ranchers put up their hands. Goodnight felt tired and discouraged. He believed that in his prime he could have forged an agreement–almost any agreement–by sheer force of will and optimism. But now he had lost faith. Betrayal would do that to a man. He could no longer make something happen just by believing in it. He sat there feeling as useless as a glass eye. Meanwhile, he could see with his good eye that the others also felt his impotence.

"We ain't gittin' nowhere," complained Lee. "You want me to make that there a damned motion?"

Goodnight shook his head. He hated to agree with Lee about anything, but in this case he knew the hot-tempered rancher was right. All they could agree on was nothing.

"You ain't makin' it no easier," Goodnight said.

"You tellin' me to shut up?" asked Lee.

"Just take it easy. Okay?"

"That's the problem. You're takin' it too easy. Seems like you done gone soft on us, huh?"

"What?"

"Anyhow, that's what your wife done tol' me." Will Lee laughed at his own humor. "You wanta put that to a vote?"

106

Goodnight lay on his back staring up at the ceiling of the mansion he had built for Revelie, feeling miserable. He had lost his wife and his best friend, and now he was losing his cowboys. They were all on strike, and one by one they had started to drift away from the ranch. Some would eventually come back, he believed, but not all. It was as if his family were disbanding. He blamed himself. Somehow he must have driven Revelie into Loving's arms–perhaps by loving them both so much–and now he was driving away his cowboys.

Raising his clenched fist, Goodnight stared at it for a long time. This knotted hand, which hung above his face like some sort of threat, did not seem to belong to him. He felt he couldn't control it and wondered what it was going to do. The fingers were squeezed together so tightly that they turned white. He was afraid of them. He was sure they were up to no good. And he was right. The clenched fist started hitting him in the eye, his good eye. The blows were struck mechanically one after the other and seemed to keep time to some slow music. He told himself to dodge the onrushing fist, but he couldn't move. He just lay there and took the beating that he so richly deserved. He wondered if he would keep it up until he blinded himself permanently.

Then he heard a knock at the front door and felt embarrassed. Goodnight stopped hitting himself and lay quietly on the floor barely breathing. He hoped his visitor would become discouraged and go away, but instead he heard a familiar voice calling his name. In the old days, before the strike, Too Short would have just walked in, but such familiarity between management and labor was evidently no longer possible.

"Coming," Goodnight called back.

Getting to his feet, he felt stiff and old. He touched his eye and found it swollen. He wondered what Too Short would think. Actually, he wasn't sure what to think himself. He shuffled across the big living room and opened the door.

"What happened to you?" asked Too Short.

"It's a long story," said Goodnight. "What's up?"

"Coupla boys just rode in lookin' for work. Figured I'd better tell you. Don't know what you'll wanta do."

"We don't need no new hands."

Too Short just shrugged.

Goodnight desperately wanted to say something that would make matters better on the Home Ranch. His mind struggled to find some solution, but his brain felt as bruised as his eye. He had just about given up when an idea occurred to him. He rushed right into it.

"So you cowboys say you want fifty bucks a month," Goodnight said. "But do you figure ever' cowhand on this here ranch is really worth that much?"

Too Short shrugged again. "Well, I dunno. Some're worth more'n others, I grant you."

"Right." Goodnight smiled. "So here's what I'm willin' to do. You tell me whichuns are worth the full fifty, and that's what I'll pay 'em. But you gotta give me your word they're really worth it. Okay? We got a deal?"

"Well, what about t'others?"

"They'll still git twenty."

"That don't hardly seem right."

"Okay, I'll make it thirty. And I'll pay you one ten. How's that?"

Too Short looked as if he were in pain. Goodnight sympathized because he recognized the expression as one he himself had worn most of the time since the strike began.

"Well, it's temptin'," Too Short said at last. "Real temptin', but I dunno, don't hardly seem fair to pay some boys one thing and t'other boys somethin' else. When we started this here union thing, we said we was all gonna be in it together. Sorta took a pledge. So I don't reckon I can help you there. Sorry."

Goodnight was surprised at how angry he became. He had thought he had found a way out of this bedeviling problem, and his foreman had rejected it out of hand.

"Well, at least, think on it," Goodnight said.

"Thinkin' on it won't make it right," Too Short said. "Wisht I could, but I cain't."

"But you yourself said they aren't all worth fifty."

"Is that what I said?"

"Good as."

Too Short shrugged.

Goodnight felt his face filling with blood as if it were one giant bruise. He knew he was turning red. He clenched his fists and wanted to strike out at Too Short for being so unreasonable. He squinted angrily at the cowboy out of his partially closed eye.

"You're fired!" Goodnight said.

"If that's how you want it," Too Short said in a maddeningly matter-of-fact voice.

"Get off my property."

"I'm goin'."

Too Short turned and walked unhurriedly away. Goodnight stared angrily after him. He wanted to pick up a rock and throw it at this cowboy of many years' service who didn't seem to mind getting fired. Goodnight even picked out a rock in the front yard, but he left it alone. His anger at Too Short was already subsiding.

Or rather Goodnight was transferring the rage from his fired foreman to himself. He realized that he had driven away yet another old friend. What was wrong with him? When would he be satisfied? When he was completely alone in his wonderful red canyon?

Closing the front door, Goodnight returned to the empty living room and lay down on his back in the middle of the floor. He started hitting himself in the eye again.

107

The cowboy strike was almost a month old. Goodnight once again took attendance in his head. Yes, there was Hays of the Springer Ranch. And Cator of the Diamond K. And Evans of the Spade. Gunter of the T-Anchor. And a dozen or so others whom he knew less well. But so far Lee of the LS was missing. Goodnight devoutly hoped he wouldn't come. He had seen and heard enough of Lee to last him forever. Just being on Lee's side of this strike made him feel that he might very well be on the wrong side. He kept glancing at the door of the Exchange Hotel, then at his watch, then back at the door, then once more at his ever-so-slow minute hand. Since Revelie had given him the timepiece one Christmas, it now seemed to burn in his hand. The meeting of the Panhandle Cattlemen's Association had been called for 8:00 P.M., and he intended for it to begin on time with–or preferably without–Will Lee.

At 7:59 P.M., the boss of the LS walked through the hotel's front door. Goodnight figured Lee must have been standing outside in the dark staring down at his watch, too. Goodnight thought: How childish of him. Well, how childish of them both.

Goodnight banged an empty coffee cup on the long table to call the meeting to order. As he watched his fellow ranchers take their seats, he couldn't get over feeling disappointed that Lee had shown up at the last instant. He rapped on the table again with his cup to call for silence. Then he cleared his throat. It always seemed to need clearing these days.

"Well, you all know why we're here," Goodnight said. "You know what we're up against. Any suggestions?"

Sometimes he didn't half-blame the cowboys for what they had done, not the ones exposed to the likes of Will Lee. He knew Lee had told his hands that if they didn't work they wouldn't eat. The son of a bitch had simply shut down his chuck wagon and invited his hands to starve. When hunger didn't cause any change of heart, he ordered them off his land. With new cowboys drifting into this corner of Texas all the time, Lee had not had much trouble hiring a new lot of hands. Strikebreakers. Cowboy scabs. Goodnight was learning a whole new vocabulary against his will.

Some of the other ranchers had been almost as bad and threatened worse. Goodnight knew that Jules Gunter had stockpiled buffalo guns–Human-cattle guns–out at the T-Anchor. He had even placed kegs of gunpowder in all his outlying buildings–blacksmith shop, barn, stables–so he could blow them up if strikers tried to take them over. Goodnight figured the strain must have driven Gunter a little crazy.

Other ranchers had continued feeding their cowboys but wouldn't let them touch ranch horseflesh, which left many of them afoot and more or less emasculated. Others had offered raises of $5, $10, $15, even as much as $20 per cowboy–but the hands had turned all offers down. They were holding out for the mystical $50 a month. Maybe the strain was getting to strikers, too, making them somewhat unrealistic.

After his failure at negotiating a bargain with Too Short, Goodnight had withdrawn into his stone house and done very little except wait and see. He hadn't cut his cowboys off the chuck line or denied them mounts. He felt guilty about being so passive, but he didn't know what else to do. If he had had the backing of Loving and Revelie, maybe he could have done more. Somehow he just didn't feel up to dominating events any longer.

"We need more firepower," Will Lee told the association. "Hire us some gunslingers. Stand up to these damn thievin' hooligans."

Goodnight just shook his head. He seemed to feel some unseen presence in the room–the way he used to sense Becky there just beyond the limits of his vision–but this new illusive visitor frightened him. It had come to harm rather than help him. He turned his head quickly but saw nothing. Still he was sure that evil was there standing just behind him. Did it have a claw?

"I dunno," Goodnight said. "Might just be makin' matters worse. Cure worse'n the disease."

"We gotta do somethin', dammit," said Lee. "Hell, they're robbin' us all blind. Plum blind."

Goodnight wondered if "blind" was aimed at him since he had just one working eye. The word rankled him, and yet he knew, much as he hated to admit it, that Lee had a point. Many of the striking cowboys had turned to rustling. At first, Goodnight had figured you couldn't blame them much because they had to do something or starve. But the losses to rustlers had grown steadily and had become alarming. Goodnight had to confess that he was worried. There was even talk that some veteran outlaws had joined forces with the striking cowboys. His mind naturally ran to the Robbers' Roost boys.

"The point is," Goodnight said, "I ain't partial to bloodlettin' if'n it can be helped."

"You're losin' your nerve," said Lee. "I'm sorry to hafta say."

Goodnight suspected that Lee was interested in more than just this strike. He cared about more than hiring a bunch of trigger-happy killers. He was out to accomplish a power shift in the Texas Panhandle. Lee surely wanted to replace Goodnight as the leading rancher in these parts. The owner of the LS wanted to be the new king. Goodnight had never really wanted to dominate this corner of the country; rather he had accepted leadership as a kind of burden. But now that somebody wanted to take that burden away from him, he didn't want to let it go. The crown was heavy but hard to give up.

"Well, I ain't losin' my common sense," Goodnight said. "Violence just makes more violence." He paused wearily. "My whole adult life, I been tryin' to bring some kinda order and some kinda justice to this here God's country. And I ain't about to chuck it all when things git a little tight. I'm warnin' you."

"Stop," said Lee. "You're sceerin' me to death."

"Good, then maybe you'll pipe down."

"Don't count on it. I mean what I say. And I say we gotta build up our firepower. That's all there is to it."

"That ain't all there is to it. There's lots more. Nobody knows how much more. Not me. Not even you."

"Then put it to a vote. That's all I say. Less vote."

Goodnight just shook his head again. He didn't know how to get rid of this saddle burr. He felt betrayed again but perhaps just out of habit.

"Hold your horses," said Goodnight. "Anybody else wanta say anythin'?"

He looked up and down the table.

"Well, I was just sorta wonderin'," said the T-Anchor's Gunter, "what Will's got in mind exactly. Where we gonna find these here gunfighters for rent?"

Goodnight smiled.

"I've got a line on some boys," Lee said. "They're good and they're willin'."

"You done talked to these boys?" asked Goodnight, trying to calm down, trying to stay in control of himself and the meeting.

"Yeah, I done talked. What's the matter with that? I ain't gonna sit around and wait for this here problem to take ceere of itself."

"Where are these boys now?"

"They're some of 'em out at my place right now. You mind? That all right with you?"

"No, it ain't. It ain't atall. You're draggin' us into a fight willy-nilly without even a 'by your leave.' Ain't that so?"

"What's so is I ain't waitin' around for no do-nothin's to lead the way. How's that suit you?"

"Let's vote," said Gunter. "This arguin' ain't gittin' us nowhere."

"I second that there motion," said Lee.

"You cain't second," said Goodnight. "It's your idea."

"Oh, come on," Lee said. "All in favor raise your right hand."

Goodnight was amazed. Lee had stolen the meeting right out from under him. He cleared his throat to protest–

"Motion carries," announced Will Lee. "Good. We're fixin' to fight back and that's all there is to it."

108

Goodnight sat in the lobby of the Exchange Hotel staring at the bright glass chimney of a kerosene lamp. This source of light resembled a woman in its shape. Its hips contained the fuel while the flame burned in the middle of its breast. Its swelling glass bust shimmered gaily. Catching himself in the middle of this reverie, Goodnight had no trouble figuring out which woman he saw transformed into a lamp. He still missed her. He didn't suppose he would ever stop missing her. He wondered if he shouldn't just go to Boston and try to win her back. He shifted restlessly in his rocking chair.

Dinner was over and the hotel's lobby dining room was deserted except for Goodnight. He had been living in the hotel for weeks now. He had temporarily removed himself from the Home Ranch because he found it too depressing. The rock house was too big and too empty. The red canyon was too idle. The cowboys were still striking, so he wasn't really needed on the spot to supervise work that wasn't being done. Rather than sit on his front porch watching his ranch slowly decay, he had ridden into Tascosa to rock in a hotel lobby.

Goodnight kept in touch with the Association's band of "rangers" mostly by rumor. He had heard that they had lynched three cowboys supposedly caught in the act of rustling. All three were striking LS hands. Perhaps Goodnight should have been reluctant to criticize–to "throw the first stone," as the Bible said–since he himself had been known to hang some outlaws. But that had been a long time ago. He had thought this country had progressed beyond that sort of vigilantism. Now this land of promise was backsliding into chaos and breaking his heart. Breaking it again.

Goodnight had heard rumors about the strikers, too. Some said that the outlaw Gudanuf had thrown in his lot with the striking cowboys. There were also stories about a new outlaw leader, the most cold-blooded killer since Billy the Kid, a young gunfighter known simply as the New Kid. He seemed to be somebody worth worrying about. Several steers had been found shot dead with their eyes gouged out. Maybe Gudanuf was putting together a new collection. Or this new perversion could be the signature of the new badman. Goodnight wondered what sort of man would attack eyes. He took such an attack personally. Reaching up to touch the familiar patch, he found the glass eye, so he just touched the Dipper on his cheek.

Deciding he was sleepy enough to justify a walk to his room, Goodnight wondered if he would dream about the Kid again tonight. He certainly hoped not. Nightmares about getting your one working eyeball punched out were as bad as–maybe worse than–dreaming your balls were cut off. Still, you couldn't compromise with sleep. You either surrendered to it unconditionally or not at all. Ready or not, here came your nightmares. He got stiffly out of his rocker and headed down the hall to his rented room. For some reason, his left knee was stiff. He felt as if he were decaying right along with his poor ranch.

Twisting the knob–he never bothered to lock his hotel door–Goodnight entered. He kept the door open to light his way to the kerosene lamp–another emblem of Revelie–beside his bed. Grasping the transparent bosom, he lifted the glass chimney, struck a match, and lit the wick. He replaced the bright bust and went back and closed the door.

Getting undressed down to his red long johns, Goodnight lay down under a sheet and a patchwork quilt. He had stopped sleeping in the nude. Of course, he would have been happy to go back to his former habit if only that glass Revelie had been flesh and blood. Oh, hell, shut up and go to sleep. The long johns actually felt good on this cool March night. It would be spring tomorrow, according to the calendar anyway, but it was still winter tonight.

Goodnight wasn't surprised when he didn't go right to sleep. He had been having trouble sleeping ever since Revelie was taken from him. His insomnia got worse when he came to town. There were fewer ghosts but more loud noises. Anyway, they sounded loud to him since he was accustomed to the peace of the red-canyon night. He heard every slow-footed horse that passed on Main Street. Worse still were the hell-raising cowboys partying the night away at the Cattle Exchange Saloon which was right next door to the Exchange Hotel. And several doors down was the Equity Saloon, which sounded almost as loud. These bars seemed to be filled with cowboys all night, hands who didn't have to get up in the morning because they weren't going to work anyway. Goodnight wondered how these unemployed cowpokes could afford so much partying. Then he called himself stupid for not remembering how they could pay for it.

Goodnight wondered if Gudanuf was in town. He hadn't seen him, but then he didn't get around much lately. And what about the New Kid? The eye-gouger? Goodnight rubbed his eyes, the one that worked and the other one. He hated thinking about Gudanuf and the Kid when he was about to doze off. Why couldn't he wool-gather about something more cheerful? But what? He had once been a gifted leader, but now he couldn't even lead his own mind: it paid no attention to him and went wherever it wanted to go.

"No! No! Not my eye! Don't–"

Jeering voices in the street woke him from his eye-gouging nightmare. It sounded like trouble, but he was glad for the trouble since it had awakened him from worse.

Listening hard–not at all ready to go back to sleep–he heard challenging tones. He couldn't quite make out what they were saying, but he was pretty sure that striking cowboys were yelling at Association rangers, and vice versa. The voices got louder and he was able to distinguish a few swear words.

Goodnight decided to get out of bed and go take a look. It was better than lying there under the covers waiting for some nightmare to dig his eyes out. (He wondered if the Kid had any glass eyeballs in his collection.) The floor was cold on the bottom of his feet. Holding his watch near the window where the moonlight would strike it full, he saw that it was a little after two o'clock in the morning. Getting dressed in the semidarkness, the first thing he put on was his hat and the last thing he put on was his gun.

Moving quietly, not wanting to wake up the house, Goodnight left his room, crept down the dark hallway, and crossed the squeaking wooden floor of the dining-room lobby. He walked outside and felt a cool wind hit him. Chilled, he rubbed his upper arms with his hands.

Looking around, he saw a group of rangers standing in the middle of Main Street. He knew them: Fred Chilton, Frank Valley, John Lang, and Ed King. But not well. Goodnight was somewhat surprised to see a young woman standing with the hired gunslingers. Her name was Sally Emory, and she looked almost beautiful in the flattering moonlight. She reminded him for an instant of his Revelie who wasn't his anymore. Ed King had his arm around pretty Sally.

The four rangers were shouting at the cowboys lounging on the front porch of the Equity Saloon. Goodnight didn't know all of the cowhands, but he did recognize some: Louis Bousman, Charley and Tom Emory, Tim Oliver, the Catfish Kid, and Lem Woodruff. Lem was the tallest cowboy and appeared the maddest. It took Goodnight a moment to recall hearing that Sally was Lem's girl. Well, evidently not any longer. Goodnight knew how that felt. He found himself on Lem's side even though Lem was a striking cowboy–maybe even a rustler–while Ed was one of *his* rangers supposedly protecting *his* interests.

"Hidin' behind a woman," Lem Woodruff taunted. "Just like a damn 'Sociation scab."

"I ain't hidin' behind nothin'," Ed King protested. "I ain't scared of the likes of you."

"Then come on over here if'n you're so brave."

"My pleasure."

Sally tried to hold her ranger back–and Goodnight silently prayed that she would succeed–but her new love shook her off and started walking toward Lem. He moved slowly, unhurriedly, his hand near his gun. Goodnight found himself thinking: No, stop, stop, stop. Ed King stopped.

"This close enough?" asked the ranger.

"Come up here on the porch," Lem said. "I got somethin' to tell you."

"No," said Sally.

Goodnight agreed with her. Please, don't go. Don't. He was talking to himself again.

Ed King hesitated, thinking it over, but then he headed for the porch. Not all Sally's cries nor Goodnight's lame wishes could stop him.

The ranger stepped up on the porch and a shot rang out. It seemed to come from inside the saloon.

109

Association Ranger Ed King seemed to jump backward off the porch. It was as if some prankster had roped him and pulled him back. When he hit the ground, he raised a cloud of silver dust that shimmered in the moonlight. Goodnight felt something in his own gut pull as if he had been roped also. Another love triangle had ended in a shooting. Another body lay in the dirt. Goodnight almost felt as if it were his fault, as if he had brought this disease to his corner of Texas. He didn't want to look, but somehow he couldn't turn away as Sally rushed forward and knelt over the man she now loved. Goodnight could feel an old wound opening again as he also sank to his knees. He was in the perfect posture to pray, but he didn't know what to say and wasn't sure Anybody was listening.

Lem Woodruff shuffled off the porch and approached his former girlfriend. He drew his six-gun and pointed it at her.

"Don't!" Goodnight shouted. "Stop! That's enough."

Lem lowered his gun.

Goodnight thought: Good.

Then the gravely wounded ranger tried to get to his feet. Seeing his struggle, Lem walked over and shot Ed in the back of the head. His whole skull exploded. Sally was covered with blood and brains. Goodnight, like some damned greenhorn, threw up. He felt sick and embarrassed.

Wiping his mouth on the right sleeve of his long underwear, Goodnight watched Lem turn and run back through the saloon's swinging doors. The other cowboys on the porch wasted no time in following him. The walls were thick adobe, which made the saloon a strong fortress. While the doors were still swinging, the lights inside the saloon went out. Muzzle flashes lit up the inner darkness.

Goodnight realized that he had switched sides emotionally. He hated Lem for coaxing his rival into stepping into an ambush . . . despised him for shooting a man who was already down . . . blowing up a defenseless man's head . . . soiling his own supposed love with a stain she would never be able to wash out. But hadn't he stained his own loved one? Stained her character? Who was he to throw the first stone?

The rangers in the street turned and ran for cover. Goodnight decided maybe he should do likewise. Still stunned by the sudden violence, he started backing up, retreating toward the Exchange Hotel. Then he turned and ran. This wasn't his fight. Why get killed over somebody else's unfaithful girlfriend? Not paying close attention to where he was putting his feet, he stumbled, almost went down, almost regained his balance, then fell heavily in the dirt. The collision with the ground knocked the wind out of him. He lay in the dust just trying to breathe. His left leg hurt terribly. Reaching down, his fingers felt warm, slippery blood. He had been shot and this wasn't even his war. Or was it? He somehow felt as if his wound had been intended rather than just a stray bullet. Could Gudanuf have been hiding in the dark? Or the New Kid?

While he lay helpless in the street, Goodnight watched the gunfight. The gunmen in the saloon fought from the cover of darkness and seemed an unseen evil force. Bullets out of blackness. Bullets from the underworld, from hell itself. The rangers in the street were occasionally visible as they peeked from behind posts or leaned around buildings.

Frank Valley, who had taken cover behind a shack, sprang from hiding and seemed to dive headfirst into Main Street as if it were a river. The ranger lay in the dirt kicking his legs and moving his arms as if he were swimming. He swam for what seemed a long time before he gave up and drowned.

Unable to stand because of his wounded leg, Goodnight decided to try to roll to safety. Over and over. He was getting dizzy. His world was tumbling, now right side up, now upside down. He saw another ranger fall . . . and another . . . and another . . . or was it all the same ranger glimpsed again and again? Then he had the impression that somebody was shooting at him. Again? Was the world going crazy? Or was he? Bullets kicked up dirt all around him. He still had a long way to go. Over and over. He was never going to make it. Over and over . . .

Then Goodnight felt himself being lifted in strong arms. He

thought his savior was Loving–once more carrying him to safety–but as his head cleared, Loving turned into Sheriff Dub. Goodnight lay his dizzy head against Black Dub's great chest.

They had almost reached the cover of the Exchange Hotel when the sheriff dropped Goodnight as if he were too heavy. Then Dub collapsed on top of his old boss, almost crushing the life out of him, but shielding him at the same time. Goodnight was in too much pain to be grateful until later.

110

Goodnight was worried about the funerals. The rangers would certainly ride into town to pay their last respects to their brothers in arms, Ed King, Frank Valley, and Fred Chilton. And an even larger force of cowboys—they considerably outnumbered the rangers—were certain to crowd into town to hear words said over Tim Oliver, the only cowpoke killed in what was already being called the "Big Fight." He had been found slumped in front of the Equity's long bar with no nose because a bullet had crashed head-on into his face. With so many cowboy-hating rangers and even more ranger-hating cowboys on hand, the odds favored another fight, an even bigger battle. Not only Goodnight but the whole town was concerned. No women or children would be attending the funerals for fear they might get caught in the cross fire. Instead, most would be gathering at a hastily arranged picnic—the object of which was to get them out of town—to be held on the north bank of the Canadian River. Tascosa was probably going to need a sheriff today more than ever before, but it didn't have one. Not anymore.

Standing at his Exchange Hotel window looking out, Goodnight was dressed only in his long johns and a leg bandage. His restless gaze finally came to rest on a vacant lot where a shack had stood the night before. It had always been something of an eyesore. So far as he could remember, this old shed hadn't been much account for years. It certainly hadn't done Frank Valley much good last night. The bullet that had killed him had gone right through the shack's weathered timbers and hit him in the throat. Well, next time he would know better and hide behind some adobe. Goodnight felt his mouth twist into a wry smile. The shack was missing now because there hadn't been enough loose lumber in town to make up five coffins, three for the rangers, one for the lone cowboy, and the last for Sheriff Dub Martin. Goodnight hated to think of his old friend being laid to rest in a box made from the remnants of an ugly, worthless old shed. Maybe when they ran out of shacks, they would have to start making coffins out of adobe. His lips twisted wryly once again. Might be a good idea at that.

Using his new crutches, Goodnight limped back to his narrow bed and lay down to rest his injured leg. The bullet had hit him in the calf, luckily missing bone. Goodnight dozed for a little while. When he got back up and returned to the window, he could see that the crowd was already gathering. He was surprised to see several men wearing bandannas over their faces, which caused him to worry all the more about a new outbreak of violence. Why in the world were they masked? Who were they, anyway? Rangers? Striking cowboys? Outlaws? Were they planning to mourn the dead by treeing the town?

Goodnight decided it was time to get dressed. His new black suit was draped over a chair in the corner of the room. He hadn't brought any dress-up clothes to town with him, so he had bought new duds this morning at Wright & Farnsworth General Store. He sat down on his bed to pull on the trousers. The right leg went in easily enough, but the left one with its bandage was more clumsy. He put on a clean white shirt that the hotel had washed and ironed for him. Then he pulled on his coat. As he was tying his black string tie, he wished Revelie were there to see him in his new suit. He wondered if he should bring his gun. It seemed in the wrong spirit for a funeral, but this burying might well be different from others. He decided to strap on his gunbelt. His six-shooter made his new suitcoat hang awkwardly on one side. Too bad.

He glanced back out the window where Main Street seemed to grow busier by the minute. Looking down at his watch, the gift from Revelie, he saw that it was five minutes until two, time to go. Hooking his crutches under his arms, he headed for the funeral. As he moved awkwardly along, he noticed that he was short of breath.

Crutching himself out the front door of the Exchange Hotel, Goodnight found a buggy waiting for him. He had rented it from Mickey McCormick's livery stable earlier in the day for the trip to Boot Hill. He had never liked that name–Boot Hill. He thought it somehow mocked the dead. Besides, the good citizens of Tascosa had just been copying Dodge City. But in this case–these cases–he had to admit that the name was apt, for all five of the departed had certainly died with their boots on. He untied the reins from the hotel hitching post and clambered awkwardly up into the buggy, trying not to hurt his sore leg more than absolutely necessary.

From his seat in the buggy, Goodnight was high enough to see all of Main Street from one end of town to the other. He noticed more masks than ever now. They irritated him in part because he thought they showed a disrespect for the dead. One of the masked men, who walked slowly with his head down, looked familiar. He was short but powerfully built. He looked like he would make a good hand.

"Hey, Too Short!" Goodnight yelled.

The masked cowboy turned around.

"Hello, Mr. Goodnight," said the former foreman of the Home Ranch. "How's your leg?"

"Fair to middlin'. How come you got your face covered up? You boys plannin' to cause trouble?"

"No, sir. Some of the boys just figured it'd be a good idea."

"How come? What boys?"

"I dunno."

"Sure you know. It was them boys in the fight, waddn't it? They don't want nobody to recognize 'em, huh? 'Fraid somebody might try'n even the score."

"I said I don't know."

"Them boys killt Black Dub. You're sidin' with them ag'inst him?"

"No," Too Short said, pulling down his mask, "I reckon not."

"Good."

"Good to see you, Mr. Goodnight."

"You, too. When all this is over, look me up. We'll talk."

"Yessir."

Goodnight jiggled the reins and the rented horse edged out slowly into the crowded street. Up ahead, three buckboards were lined up side by side. The one on the left held three coffins, the one in the middle just one, and the one on the right also a single wooden box. The trio of boxes must contain the three slain rangers. But which of the two single coffins held the dead cowboy? And which one cradled Dub?

Naturally, the procession to Boot Hill—that terrible name—didn't start right on time at two o'clock. Goodnight kept expecting violence to break out as so many sworn enemies crowded into Main Street side by side. If he had been running this show, he wouldn't have had all the funerals at the same time. But the burying had been arranged to fit the crowded schedule of Circuit Court Judge Sam Rawlins, who would read over the bodies. Fortunately or unfortunately, the judge happened to be in town holding court. Tascosa didn't have a preacher or a church. It wasn't that kind of town. So a circuit court judge was about the best they could do for somebody to preside at funerals. When the judge wasn't around, Henry Kimball, the blacksmith, usually did the honors. Since the whole town always closed down for funerals, Goodnight figured the good merchants of Tascosa had also been in favor of doing all the burying at once and as quickly as possible. Get them all over with and then open up for business once again. Make some money while the funeral crowds were still in town.

It was close to two-fifteen by Goodnight's pocket watch before the buckboards that served as hearses started to roll. And even then they didn't move very fast, which was fitting, but he still wished they would pick up the pace a little bit. The longer this burying took, the longer there would be for something to go wrong.

The funeral procession was unlike anything Goodnight had ever seen. There must have been five hundred or more mourners. Merchants. Cowboys. Saloonkeepers. Rangers. Even a few farmers, which was something new in this part of the country. Men on horseback. Men in wagons and buggies and hacks. Men and even a few boys on foot. All these boots and hooves and wheels were kicking up a mighty dust storm that made Goodnight sneeze.

He kept "chomping at the bit," wishing they would all move faster–when something happened that stopped him completely. A masked cowboy placed himself directly in his buggy's way. Why was he doing such a thing? Did he want a job? No, that couldn't be it. Nobody went job-hunting wearing a mask. Goodnight pulled back on the reins to keep his horse from running over this curious fellow.

"What's the matter?" Goodnight raised his voice. "What's wrong?"

The masked man took hold of the buggy horse's bridle as if he were afraid that Goodnight might suddenly shake the reins, or lay on with his whip, and make a run for it. Couldn't he see that nobody could make a run for anything in this mob?

"Take a good look at me," the masked cowboy said.

"What?" asked Goodnight.

"Do I look familiar?"

"I cain't tell with that damn mask on."

"Take a good look."

Goodnight studied this presumptuous cowboy. Then he knew. Of course! He should have recognized him by the voice alone. Goodnight drew back his whip and then lashed out at the masked man. Claw released the reins and dodged away from the whip.

"Good!" shouted Goodnight's son. "Wouldn't be no fun if you didn't know me."

Claw slapped the buggy horse on the foreleg and made it rear. Goodnight pulled back on the reins to try to get the animal under control. He was afraid somebody was going to get kicked or trampled. When the horse calmed down, Goodnight looked around for the all too familiar cowboy, but he was gone.

Goodnight wiped his forehead with the sleeve of his new black coat. He told himself to calm down. Take a deep breath and try to look normal. Think funereal thoughts. Get back in the funeral mood. Remember why you're here. Look sad. As soon as he felt his mouth twist into a frown, he couldn't stop the sadness. It hit him like a flash flood. He was drowning.

I've lost another one. I've lost another one. I've lost another one. He couldn't stop saying the sentence over and over again in his head. He told himself not to be so selfish, not to dwell on his loss, but upon Dub's loss of life itself. *Dub is dead. And it's my fault. I made him take that job. And he was trying to save me. Dub is dead and I killed him.* But he knew he was being self-centered again. He was feeling sorry for himself rather than mourning Dub. *Dub is dead. Dub lost everything. Dub is dead, dead, dead, and I miss him.* That was about the best he could do. His vision went out of focus and slippery drops rolled down both his cheeks. It still surprised him after all these years that both eyes, the one that worked and the one that didn't, could shed tears.

Disoriented by the blurry landscape and strong feelings, Goodnight felt a welcome presence at his side, just creeping into his watery field of vision. Was she riding a white horse? He was glad to see her or almost see her. He knew she had come to comfort him in this time of pain. He tried not to look, begged himself not to look, but he couldn't help looking. When he turned to his left, she fled as she always did when he tried to "catch" her. Now he was all the sadder for having lost not only Dub but also Becky again. He couldn't stop crying. What would the town think of him?

Almost blinded by his own leaky emotion, Goodnight thought he saw another phantom, this time on the other side. Once again, it was a welcome presence. Once more, he felt comforted. But it wasn't her this time. It was him. He told himself not to look, begged himself, pleaded with himself, but of course he looked.

And there was Loving riding beside him.

111

Are you real?" Goodnight asked.

"Reckon so," said the vision. "Leastwise nobody never told me no differ'nt. Anyhow, not lately."

Goodnight looked away, doing a kind of test, to see if the vision would still be there when he looked again. Turning back, he found Loving still there.

They moved along side by side in silence for a while, the one in a buggy, the other on horseback. It was as if they did it every day, as if they didn't have anything of any importance to say to one another. They just seemed to be comfortable companions. They acted as if nothing were out of the ordinary, but more and more people began to look at them as if they were indeed something unusual.

"I reckon we're causin' a fuss," Goodnight said at last.

"Yeah," said Loving, "they're waitin' to see if'n you'll kill me."

"I 'spect so."

"Prob'ly layin' odds."

"Uh-huh."

They fell silent again. People kept looking at them expectantly.

"Heard you were in Californy."

"That's right. Purdy country."

"That so? You come back for the funeral?"

"Not exactly. Black Dub just got killed last night. I'd've kinda had to hurry to ride over from Californy and git here in time for today's festivities."

"'Spect so."

The silence returned for a while.

"Then how come you to come?"

"Well, I'd heard some rumors."

"What kind?"

"Oh, I heard there was some trouble hereabouts."

"Yeah, some, off-'n'-on."

"Even heard maybe you was in trouble."

"Do tell. Nothin' I cain't handle."

"So you don't need no help."

Goodnight spat on the ground.

"Trouble is, I remember how you helped me before."

Loving didn't say anything.

Goodnight tried not to let on how confused he felt inside. When he first saw Loving, he had been shaken by a spasm of pure happiness. But when the spasm passed, he remembered how angry he was at Loving, how badly he had been hurt by Loving, how much reason he had to hate him. But he found he couldn't hate him, not cleanly, not purely. He hated him and loved him at the same time. It was a little like the way he had felt about his sister Becky back when she was alive. Not that he had ever actually hated her, but she had been good at making him mad. He wondered if he loved Loving so much because he had lost his sister. He hadn't loved Revelie like a sister, didn't want to, because grown-up, man-woman love complicated the emotions. But he could and had loved Loving like a brother. And now he desperately wanted him back. The only trouble was, he hated him too much.

Up ahead, the three buckboards bearing the coffins came to a halt, but the rest of the procession continued to move forward. The cowboys and rangers were pressed ever closer together as they all tried to get close enough to the graves to see the burials. As the boxes were being unloaded, Goodnight felt cheated because he still didn't know which one held Black Dub. He kept looking from one to the other trying to guess. He knew it didn't really make any difference, and yet it did. He didn't want to get all misty-eyed staring at the wrong coffin.

Goodnight was so withdrawn into his own thoughts–about Black Dub, about the coffins, about Loving–that he didn't notice the first signs of trouble. He was roused out of his reveries by shouting. Then he saw pushing and shoving at the very edge of the graves, as if cowboys and rangers were trying to bury each other alive. He found himself wishing that Black Dub were there to flash his star and break it up with his incredible strength.

His disgust turned to anger when the shoving and pushing reached one of the coffins being borne aloft on the shoulders of six pallbearers. The grey weathered wood, which looked as if it had already been buried for years, swayed back and forth precariously. The pallbearers staggered, trying to keep their balance, their struggle made more difficult by their heavy load. The coffin bounced about above the mob like an old grey rowboat trying to ride out a violent flood. Could it stay afloat? It was sinking. No, it bobbed up again. It capsized. No, it righted itself again. Then it sank beneath the "waves" and didn't come up. Goodnight heard a crash and wood splintering.

Anger turned to a fury that burned his stomach. They were trampling on the body of his friend (if it was his friend). He reached automatically for his gun–now he was glad he had brought it along–pointed it up at heaven and pulled the trigger. He hoisted himself up to a standing position–*damn,* his leg hurt–and fired again. And he still wasn't even sure whose casket had fallen.

"Git back!" Goodnight shouted. "Git outa the way! Move back!"

He saw dozens of curious faces turned in his direction, but nobody moved. They seemed to be paralyzed.

"Move!" he screamed. "Go! Git outa there!"

If he weren't crippled, he would have jumped down off this buggy and waded into the middle of them. He would damn well make them move. He fired into the air once again.

Looking around, trying to decide what to do next, Goodnight saw Loving reach out and grasp the buggy whip. When he cracked it over his head, it sounded like a gunshot.

"You heard him," Loving raised his voice. "Move! Git moving!"

Then he rode forward into the mob, flailing about him with the whip as he advanced. His blows convinced the crowd to part. Cowboys and rangers started running to get out of the way.

"Hurry!" he shouted. "Git the hell outa here!"

Goodnight had never heard Loving actually yell. He had never seen him so excited or angry.

As the unruly sea parted, Goodnight caught a glimpse of the broken coffin, but he still couldn't identify the body. Urging the buggy forward, he got a better look. It was Black Dub. He was wearing a brand-new black suit just like the one that Goodnight wore. Then he saw something much colder, much more disturbing: a masked cowboy kicking the body. He looked like the same masked boy who had stopped the buggy: Claw.

In spite of the pain in his leg, Goodnight scrambled down from the buggy. He was too upset to mess with his crutches. He tried to walk on his bad leg, but it hurt too much, so he started hopping on his good leg toward Black Dub. But the masked boy saw him coming and melted into the mob. When he reached the busted box, Goodnight stood over it, looking around at the cowboys and rangers, hating them all, daring them to do any more harm to Black Dub.

Loving dismounted and stood with him.

"Okay, now, bow your heads!" Goodnight shouted. "Show some respect!" He fired in the air again. "I mean it. Bow your damn heads. And take off your damn hats."

Glaring at the surrounding men, Goodnight saw a couple of hats removed, then a few more, then lots more. And heads started bowing.

"That's better," Goodnight said. "Now somebody find a hammer and fix up this here box."

He figured there had to be a hammer in one of the many wagons now cluttering up Boot Hill. He was right. Soon Henry Kimball came running, waving a blacksmith's hammer. Well, that wasn't exactly what he had had in mind, but it ought to work anyway. The blacksmith went to work binding up the coffin. Goodnight watched him closely to make sure the job was being done right.

Looking around, Goodnight saw that there was one cowboy who hadn't removed his hat: it was the same masked boy who had kicked the body. He was standing there at the front of the mob: Claw.

Now, Goodnight was sure who had killed Black Dub. Anyway, he thought he was sure. Pretty sure. Well, sure enough to pursue the matter to some sort of conclusion. He couldn't let Black Dub's murderer go unpunished. Black Dub had brought law and justice to this part of the country. It would be too cruel, too unfair, if the law failed to punish his killer. Goodnight vowed it wouldn't happen.

112

Goodnight sat at a large round table in the Exchange Saloon holding a council of war. Loving sat at his right hand. The others around the table were Will Lee and the rangers hired by the Association. Goodnight didn't really feel comfortable with the rangers, but he told himself that he needed firepower and he didn't know where else to get it. He couldn't very well recruit townspeople to make war on the striking cowboys' camp: they would either turn and run or get slaughtered. What other choice did he have?

The brass star on his chest still seemed out of place. He believed in law and justice, but he had never intended to be a lawman. Yet here he sat, the duly sworn sheriff of Tascosa, because nobody else wanted the job. Not now. Not under these circumstances. And he was bound and determined that acts of murder should not be forgotten or forgiven. If nobody else would bring in the killers, then he would.

"I dunno," said Loving. "I'm not sure them boys're gonna hand over those fellas just 'cause we ask 'em to."

"I never figured they would," said Goodnight.

"And if'n they don't, chargin' into Strike Town, well, I'm not sure that'd be much fun."

The striking cowboys, along with their outlaw allies, had set up a large camp on the north bank of the Canadian River about seven miles west of town. Some of the women who normally worked at the Equity and the Exchange saloons were now living and working in Strike Town. The camp had grown and grown until it was almost a rival town. Most of the inhabitants slept in the open under the vast plains sky with their heads on their saddles, but more and more tents were being put up. Even a few shacks had been nailed together with wood that might come in handy for more coffins if Goodnight decided to go charging in after the guilty parties. Well, he was aware of the dangers, but he wasn't just going to drop this matter of murder.

He had recruited Black Dub to be sheriff of Tascosa, so he bore some responsibility for what had happened to him, and even more responsibility for punishing those who had done it.

"You don't hafta come," Goodnight said.

"I know I don't hafta," said Loving. "That ain't the point." He paused. "The point is that some a our good friends're in that there damn camp. Too Short's in there, for God's sake. You don't wanta git in no damn gunfight with him. How'd you feel if'n you killt Too Short?"

"I ain't gonna fight Too Short."

"You don't know that. You cain't never tell what's gonna happen oncet the shootin' starts."

"I've gotta do somethin'. I ain't gonna just let this thing go. I cain't."

"I know. I don't like what happened no more'n you do. But maybe we oughta just not rush into nothin' right away. Give it some time. This strike thing cain't last forever. You kin do your arrestin' when it's all over with."

"They'd be gone clear outa the country by then."

"Mebbe. Mebbe not."

"I ain't takin' that chance."

"Could be you'd be takin' a chance on somethin' a good deal worse. You're thinkin' 'bout Black Dub, but there ain't much we kin do for him no more, way I see it. I'm thinkin' about Too Short and maybe Flytrap and who knows who all else. Maybe I'm even thinkin' a you. Stranger things've happened."

"I know, I know."

Goodnight hated to argue with Loving like this. Now that he was back, Goodnight almost seemed to be trying to drive him away again. Well, maybe it would be for the best if he did succeed in driving him off. At least, Loving wouldn't end up getting killed charging into Strike Town with guns blazing.

"Let's sleep on it," Loving said.

"That'd just be puttin' off," Goodnight said.

"That's the idea. There's always gonna be plenty a time to die. Ain't no reason to rush it."

Goodnight felt frustrated and irritated. Why couldn't Loving just get out of his life and leave him alone? But was he sure he wanted him to? Could he stand to lose him again? Besides, he had never been any good at saying no to Loving, and he didn't seem to be any better at it now, not even after all that had happened.

"Okay, we'll sleep on it," Goodnight said.

As he was getting up from the table, ready for that night's sleep, Goodnight felt Will Lee tugging at his elbow.

"Less burn 'em out," said Lee. "Less burn 'em good."

113

Goodnight couldn't believe that he was beginning his career in law enforcement by rustling. He had carefully planned a sneak attack not upon Strike Town itself but upon the strikers' remuda. He reasoned that if he stole the new town's horses, then he would be in a position to bargain for the surrender of the wanted men. He would trade horseflesh for murderers. Anyway, he hoped the striking cowboys and their allies would agree to such a swap. But first he had to steal the horses.

Only about half of the some three hundred cowboys owned their own–or maybe had stolen their own–mounts. The rest had ridden ranch-owned horses back when they were working and so were afoot now. They were as forlorn as sailors marooned on shore. Anyhow, Goodnight figured swabbies were forlorn on dry land. What did he know? But he was sure cowboys were forlorn without horses to ride. So he would steal the camp's last 150 mounts–maybe more, maybe fewer–and see how they *all* liked being stranded on the ground. He suspected that taking the horses would cripple the cowboys' very identity. With nothing to ride, they would be no better than farmers. They might just as well call their little settlement Clodhopper Town. Well, he needed some kind of lever–didn't he?–to pry those killers out of Strike Town.

Sheriff Goodnight and his gang of thieves approached the remuda at around three in the morning. It wasn't a big gang, just Goodnight, Loving, and three Association rangers who seemed the most sympathetic. Lefty Smith was a left-handed gunslinger, Johnny Johnson a potbellied sometime killer, and Reb Brenner a grey-bearded veteran of the Civil War. Goodnight had chosen them because they didn't seem quite as bloodthirsty as the rest of the rangers. And yet he still wasn't sure how far he could trust even them to keep their firearms cold in their holsters.

"I don't want no shootin'," Goodnight told them firmly once again. "Shootin's just gonna wake up the whole damn camp, and I don't like them odds. They only outnumber us I'd say sixty, maybe seventy, to one. So we just slip in quiet, grab them ponies, and git the hell outa there. Understand? I ain't just talkin' 'cause I gotta purdy voice."

"He means it," said Loving. "His voice ain't all that purdy."

As they approached the horses, the Goodnight gang was armed with dirty socks full of dirt, which were supposed to serve as clubs. Someplace he had heard that the nicest, safest way to knock folks out was with an earth-weighted sock. He didn't want any skulls crushed.

The rangers' sock-saps looked misshapen because none of them turned out to have any socks without holes in them. So they had tied knots to keep the sand from running out. Goodnight was afraid those socks were probably so rotten that they would just explode like sand bombs on impact.

"I feel silly," said Reb.

"Then go on home," said Goodnight.

"Aw, hell, I was just jawin'."

"We're supposed to be sneakin' up on somebody, so just keep your jawin' to yourself. Okay? That goes for the rest of you, too."

Lecturing his gang, Goodnight felt more like a schoolmarm than a dangerous leader of thieves. He smiled in the dense darkness. He had chosen a night when the moon would be a black face in a black sky.

Glimpsing movement up ahead, Goodnight held up his hand and all the riders stopped. He couldn't yet see anything that looked like a horse, but he was sure the remuda lay less than half a mile up ahead. Then beyond the remuda would be Strike Town itself.

"You know what to do," Goodnight said in a low voice. He knew they knew, but he couldn't resist telling them again anyway. "Wait here till you see two matches light up side by side, right? Then come ridin' in real quiet like. Now don't go gittin' impatient, you hear?"

Then Goodnight and Loving dismounted. They handed over their reins to the rangers and started out on foot. Goodnight's gunshot wound, now a little over two weeks old, still hurt him, but he was able to walk–or rather creep–on it. He wished he had on quiet moccasins instead of noisy boots. He tried to walk carefully, keeping the disturbance to a minimum, but it seemed to him that his feet were making a terrible racket. Meanwhile, Loving wasn't making any sound at all.

How did he do it? Goodnight found himself both admiring and envious all over again. He redoubled his efforts to be quiet, but he still sounded like a cautious freight train. He wanted to blame his injury, but actually he didn't figure it had much to do with it. He just wasn't as graceful as Loving and never would be.

Goodnight had been watching the remuda from hiding for the past several nights and so knew that a single cowboy was assigned to guard the horses every night. On a ranch, three cowpokes would have shared this duty, taking shifts, but Strike Town was different. They were in a state of rebellion against the ranches and so were determined not to act like a ranch. Maybe they figured they had nothing to fear from thieves since they had already formed alliances with the outlaws. Anyhow, people said they were allies. Occasionally, the remuda's single guard would mount up and ride around the makeshift corral–a single strand of barbed wire held up by rather flimsy posts–but most of the time he was content to laze beside a small campfire. If all went well, he wouldn't be hard to find, for that fire would light the way for the ambushers.

Goodnight, who liked operating aboveboard, was distressed at how sneaky he felt. He was glad it was so dark nobody could see him–which was of course the idea anyway. Foolish thoughts. He was pretty sure Loving wasn't wasting any mental energy doing this kind of crazy thinking.

As he drew nearer the weak glow of the fire, Goodnight began to make out the features of tonight's watchman. He realized he didn't know the man and was glad. This keeper of the horses was a young cowboy, probably only in his teens. His elders had obviously wanted to get their sleep and so had assigned this youngster to watch the herd. But he was sleepy, too. His head was bowed and he appeared to be dozing. Now Goodnight felt even worse about his plan, which called for creeping up on this sleeping teenager and beating him senseless. Some hero he was turning out to be. Some brave defender of law and order.

Goodnight started worrying that Loving was getting too far ahead of him. He tried to speed up, but then he made more noise, so he slowed back down again. Then he saw that Loving had stopped to wait for him. He was relieved and irritated at the same time. Who asked him to wait? Just as Goodnight was about to catch up, Loving started out again. Well, if he was going to wait, why didn't he wait? Did he enjoy keeping his lead? Foolish thoughts. Crazy thinking.

Loving stopped again. Waited again. This time Goodnight caught up. They nodded silently to each other. As they rested for a moment, Goodnight realized he could hear his heart beating. He stared at Loving's chest to see if it too was heaving, but of course he saw nothing. Well, it was dark.

Goodnight pointed at the watchman and they moved off once again. This time, they advanced side by side. Well, that was good. Soon the new sheriff was close enough to hear the boy breathing. His breaths came slowly and regularly. He was almost snoring.

Raising his dirt club–and feeling like a very poor sport–Goodnight advanced the last few feet and brought his weapon down hard on the back of the boy's sweat-stained hat. The sock exploded, throwing dirt in the sheriff's eye. He was not only stunned but also embarrassed. It occurred to him that if Revelie had still been around his socks would have been in a better state. The blow–instead of knocking the poor kid out–only succeeded in waking him up. Startled, the boy turned his head and stared at Goodnight. It evidently took him a moment to figure out he wasn't dreaming. Then he opened his mouth to scream.

At that moment, Loving hit him a crushing blow on the back of the head with the butt of his revolver. Well, so much for the great sock caper. The teenager crumpled and fell too close to the fire. Goodnight pulled him back so he wouldn't get burned–or cooked.

Then the sheriff and his favorite deputy retreated into the dark, got out matches, and struck them side by side. They watched them burn until their fingers were in danger of burning. Then they dropped them to the ground and stepped on them.

Soon they saw a dark mass approaching slowly. This mass then divided into three horsemen leading two riderless horses. Goodnight and Loving went to meet them. Before long, they were back in the saddle.

Goodnight reached down and pulled his ax from its scabbard. Then he took the lead in attacking the single-strand barbed-wire fence. Leaning down, he swung his ax and struck the barbed wire near where it was nailed to a slender post. The sharp blade cut the wire in two. Looking more closely, he could see now that the wire was badly rusted.Goodnight thought disapprovingly that the cowboys hadn't used very good material to build their fence. Moving along the perimeter of the herd, he rained destruction on the no-account fence. As his furious blows fell, it was as if he were making war on barbed wire itself and all it stood for.

While he continued to swing away, Loving and the rangers started driving the horses through the gaping hole in the fence. Now the raid got noisy. The animals, who had been dozing standing up, started to neigh and whinny. They reared and snorted. And when they started running through the gap in the barbed wire, they were as noisy as a train with hooves.

Hearing shouts coming from Strike Town, which was only a hundred or so yards away, Goodnight sheathed his ax and joined the others herding the horses. They drove the animals away from the river. The rangers turned out to be pretty fair cowboys. They kept the herd bunched.

Turning to look back, Goodnight saw dark running figures. Then a muzzle flash and an instant later the report of a rifle. A bullet whistled overhead. Well, people usually shot high in the dark. He just hoped they kept on shooting that way. Another flash, report, and whistle.

Then Goodnight heard the sound of much closer gunfire. The rangers were shooting back, directly disobeying his orders. He was angry, but at the same time he realized that it was hard for men to get shot at without wanting to return fire. He just hoped his side was shooting high, too. He was afraid a stray bullet might hit some camp whore or maybe even the whore's kid.

The dark, chasing, firing figures ran desperately, trying to keep up, but they were on foot. And they would remain on foot for some time unless they were willing to surrender the killers among them. Goodnight and his gang, well mounted and driving more than a hundred other mounts before them, began pulling away from their pursuers.

Then Goodnight heard a scream. It came from the direction of the camp. The voice was high-pitched, but that might have been because of the pain, so the hurting sound had not necessarily come from a woman or a child. But it might have.

"Hold your fire!" Goodnight shouted into the night.

The rangers didn't hear him or just didn't pay any attention. They kept on shooting.

But as the pursuers fell farther and farther behind, the firing slowed and then ceased on both sides. The Goodnight gang had made rustling look easy. The leader of the gang felt an unexpected surge of elation. This was fun. The new sheriff actually enjoyed riding on the wrong side of the law. No wonder there were so many outlaws.

114

Goodnight's idea was to approach Strike Town with a large force—all but one of them Association rangers—under a flag of truce. He wanted to be taken seriously, but he didn't want any violence. Not if he could help it. He was simply going to state his proposition and then pull back and let them mull it over. But without a significant show of force, he figured they would just kill him. After all, a lot of them still figured horse stealing was a capital offense. Now he just hoped somebody in the camp had sense enough to know what a white flag was supposed to mean.

As he bore down the tent town, the scene reminded Goodnight of one that had been burned into his brain and soul a lifetime ago: a band of warriors approaching a new settlement under a flag of truce. But now all the roles were reversed: this time it was Goodnight himself who carried the white flag. Would there be another tragedy? Would he have to keep reliving the past until he got it right? He wondered: Was there a ten-year-old girl in the camp who resembled Becky? Probably. He hoped he would not be the agent of any harm coming to her, but he knew he might be. His resolve almost failed him. Was he about to do unto others what others had so cruelly done unto him?

"You sure you wanta go through with this here?" asked Loving, who rode beside him.

Goodnight was startled. It was as if his friend had overheard his thoughts. He looked at Loving suspiciously.

"I don't wanta," Goodnight said, "but I gotta."

"I mean this here's likely to be easier to start than to finish. They're l'ible to be purdy mad about them ponies."

"We been all over this."

"If you say so."

As he drew closer and closer to Strike Town, Goodnight kept glancing down at the ground to look for tarantulas. And every time he looked, he saw several. He had first noticed them early that morning when he was on his way to Mickey McCormick's livery stable to fetch his nineteen-year-old horse, Red. Hundreds of the huge spiders were crawling across Main Street. He had encountered this phenomenon before and never understood it. For some obscure reason of their own, all the tarantulas in this part of Texas had picked today to go for a damn walk in the sun. They all crawled up out of their holes and headed for some unknown destination.

Looking up, Goodnight saw a small party of cowboys emerging from Strike Town. There were only five of them, and they were on foot, of course. Beyond them the camp itself was now bustling with activity. He figured everybody was cranking live rounds into their breeches and preparing for a fight.

"Hold up," Goodnight said in a commanding voice, raising his right hand.

His sixty-odd deputies obeyed.

"Loving, Lefty, Reb, let's see, Johnny Johnson, come with me. The rest of you wait up. If'n they try anything funny, come a runnin'."

Then Goodnight nudged his horse and moved forward again. Loving, Lefty, Reb, and Johnny followed him. The rest stayed put as they had been instructed to do. The two armies were now arranged in a fashion that recalled the battle in which the immortal Iron Jacket had lost his life. The memory made Goodnight even more nervous than he already was. Well, he had no illusions that he was immortal. He intended to be careful.

As the emissaries drew nearer, five from one side and five from the other, Goodnight recognized one of them: Claw. Aw, hell's bells! But he had to go through with this parley, didn't he?

"You see who I see?" asked Loving.

Claw was carrying an ax.

"I'm sorry," said Goodnight.

"Don't say you're sorry."

"I'm–"

As the five spokesmen, including Claw, drew near, Goodnight dismounted. He was putting himself on the same level they were on. Following his lead, his four deputies climbed down off their horses.

When Goodnight put weight on his sore leg, he winced. He hoped his adversaries didn't notice.

"How you doin', Crip?" asked a familiar figure.

Goodnight recognized the voice–and the older face. It was Gudanuf, who wore gloves to hide his busted thumbs. He stood shoulder-to-shoulder with Claw as if they were father and son. Goodnight was jealous of Gudanuf, who seemed to be his son's other father, while at the same time he hated that son.

The two parties on foot advanced to within five yards of each other and stopped.

"Goddamn you!" Claw yelled. "You stole our horses!"

"I took 'em into custody," said Sheriff Goodnight.

"You what!?"

"I arrested 'em."

"You cain't arrest horses."

"Looks like I can."

The horses, 136 head in all, were now in "jail" at Will Lee's LS Ranch. Goodnight hated leaving them there, but the LS was closest to Tascosa, and the rangers used Lee's spread as their headquarters. It would have been too far to drive them to the Home Ranch. Besides, he didn't particularly want to get his home mixed up in all these troubles.

"You're a damn thief, Daddy!" Claw accused.

"Yeah," Gudanuf echoed.

The rangers exchanged looks. The cowboys did the same. What was going on here?

"I'm a damn sheriff and I can arrest whoever or whatever I like," Goodnight told Claw. "And you're no son of mine. Not one I'd claim, anyhow. But tell you what. I'll trade them horses for murderers."

"Go to hell!" said Claw.

"You better think about it. Talk it over. I'd settle for just Lem Woodruff and you."

"Me?"

"Yeah, you. We got suspicions about some others, but you and Lem, we figure we got dead to rights."

"Who'd I kill?"

"Sheriff Martin."

"Prove it."

"I know it. That's good 'nough for me."

BOOM!

The gunshot startled Goodnight, frightened him. What had gone wrong with his plan? Looking to his right, in the direction of the sound, he saw Reb dancing a jig and pointing his six-gun at his own feet.

"Spiders," Reb yelled. "Spiders is eatin' me alive."

He fired again and again, but he would need all the bullets fired at Gettysburg to kill all the spiders on the move that morning.

"Hold your fire," Goodnight ordered.

Reb shot again. He was in danger of shooting some of his toes off. It was almost funny the way he was dancing and firing down at his own feet.

Goodnight caught a glimpse of Claw lifting his good hand. The cripple clutched a big, black gun that was swinging up in Goodnight's direction. But surely Claw must understand what was happening, must see that poor Reb was scared of tarantulas, must realize that he didn't mean to break the truce declared by the white flag. And yet Claw's gun kept on coming up. Goodnight was momentarily paralyzed. He couldn't believe that all his careful planning and plotting had come to this. He didn't know whether to dodge to the left, dodge to the right, duck, or try to draw. And so he did nothing. Just stood there waiting to be killed. He could see his son thumbing back the hammer on his gun.

115

Goodnight felt something slam into his side that emptied his lungs. He thought he had been shot, but then he realized that the force that had hit him was Loving. Then he heard the sound of the gunshot. Knocked sideways, Goodnight saw his friend grab his own face. Oh, no! Not that! The blood spurted from between Loving's fingers. Then he went down.

Goodnight thought: He won't be so pretty no more.

Then he couldn't believe he could be thinking such a terrible thought. He hated himself. He would have to make up for the way his crazy mind worked. He must somehow atone.

Suddenly, a blood anger drove all other thoughts from his mind. He just wanted to kill the Claw! Destroy him! He hated Gudanuf, too, with a new energy. Avenge blood with blood!

Letting his own momentum carry him to the ground, Goodnight rolled and drew his gun at the same time. He fired and rolled. Fired and rolled. He was a damn tumbleweed spitting mean lead.

He was amazed: Claw and Gudanuf turned and ran. He thought in the Human tongue: They are running-hearts.

Now Goodnight realized that everybody was shooting. Not only the up-front rangers–Reb, Lefty, and Johnny–but the sixty-odd backup rangers were also blazing away. And all of Strike Town seemed to be shooting back.

Realizing that he would never catch Claw or Gudanuf in a foot race, not with a bad leg, Goodnight turned back to his horse. He grabbed the horn and pulled himself back up into the saddle and set off after his blood foes, riding directly into a driving storm of bullets. Goodnight galloped into Strike Town, the bullets dodging him, right into the midst of the "enemy."

He was so focused on his pursuit of his monstrous son–and his son's new "father"–that he didn't notice the hot, blazing wildfire until it roared at him. His horse reared. Then he realized that cowboys were fleeing all around him. Flames were chasing at their heels. The strikers were in too much of a hurry to bother with killing him. Goodnight hadn't seen how the fire got started, so it might have been lit accidentally by the flame from a gun barrel, but he doubted it. He remembered Will Lee's wanting to burn down Strike Town and figured one or more of the rangers had probably done his bidding. Goodnight felt guilty. He hadn't even succeeded in controlling his "own" men.

And yet the blaze might well have saved his life. It certainly gave the cowboys something to do besides shoot at him. They weren't just fleeing from the fire itself but also from all the critters fleeing the fire. Tarantulas and rattlesnakes and rats moved in a wave in front of the wave of flame. The fire chased the varmints, who chased the out-of-work cowpokes. Naturally, a lot of God's creatures, including the strikers, lost the race. Goodnight heard screams of pain and imagined cowboys being bitten by rattlers. Or struck by bullets from the continuing gunfire. Wounded, would they be able to keep going, or would they fall and be burned in the fire? Worse yet, not all the cries seemed to come from cowboys. Surely some of those wails came from women and their children. Some of them were losing the race, too.

Goodnight saw a young boy–he looked to be no more than ten years of age–trying to outrun the flames that burned the clothes on his back. And the back itself! No matter how fast he ran, he would never outrace that fire that rode and spurred him so brutally. Goodnight saw a ten-year-old girl running with her red hair on fire. Somehow all the children seemed to him to be ten years old. All frightened. Some of them doomed. And Goodnight realized that he himself had loosed this Judgment Day, this fire-next-time storm.

The fire raced through the grass, charged deep into Strike Town, and then slowed somewhat. It seemed to want to take its time and do its job thoroughly. It was as if it relished its work and wanted to make it last, wanted to savor it. Now tents and crudely built lean-tos and shacks were in flames. Bedding was burning. Carefully hoarded supplies were on fire.

Then Goodnight had a terrible vision: Loving on fire. Gravely wounded, but perhaps not yet dead, he was back there in the flames. Helpless to save himself, he was being burned alive. Cooked. Roasted. Now Goodnight smelled the terrible stench of human flesh burning.

It was a sweet, suffocating odor like no other. Was he smelling the flaming body of Loving?

Goodnight realized that he had lost sight of Claw and Gudanuf–the fire had taken his entire attention–but he couldn't worry about them now. He had to get back to Loving, had to pull his burning body from the fire, had to save whatever was left to save.

Goodnight turned his horse and spurred it directly into the flame. The animal reared and snorted, but the habit of a lifetime, the custom to obey, was stronger than the instinct to flee from fire. The aging Red charged the blaze, Goodnight spurred him to jump, and he cleared the wall of flame. The horse–singed but not ablaze–came down on the smoldering grass behind the fireline. Hoping its hooves would protect it from the embers over which it trod, Goodnight rode off toward the spot where Loving had fallen.

When he reached the spot, he rode back and forth, criss-crossing the ground. He saw smoking snakes twisting in agony, saw burned-out tarantulas, saw cooked ground squirrels and roasted rats, saw a blackened, grotesque Reb who had survived Shiloh but hadn't lived through this fire and firefight. But Goodnight didn't see Loving. He must be around here somewhere. Goodnight became frantic. He was afraid he wouldn't find Loving and even more afraid he would. What had he done to his friend? Where was he? Maybe he had managed to drag himself off somewhere to burn and die. Perhaps this wasn't even the right place. He had figured it was because he had seen poor Reb's body, but Reb wasn't necessarily killed at the same time or in the same place as Loving. Who knew what had happened to Reb?

Goodnight spurred Red. He raced up the fire line searching for Loving. (He reminded himself that Revelie would have called it a quest.) Not finding his best friend, he galloped back down the fire line. Where was he? What had happened to him? He could already feel the grieving beginning. Luckily, he had had a lot of practice. Oh, no, don't think like that. Keep looking. Keep hoping. Keep trying. Keep striving. Keep on seeking. And keep on not yielding. Hell! Where? Where? Damn it, where!

Turning Red, a little too sharply, Goodnight headed back down the fire line once again. Where was Loving?

"Loving!" Goodnight screamed above the roar of the fire and guns. *"Loving! Loving! Loving!"*

Turning Red once again, Goodnight once more patrolled the

steadily advancing fire line. Was Loving already dead? Was that why he didn't answer?

"Loving! Loving! Where are you, Loving! Loving! Loving! LOVING!"

Out of breath, Goodnight stopped shouting. He felt guilty. Why couldn't he keep on screaming when his friend's life was at risk? Why was he so tired?

"Boats!" an excited voice cried. "They're gittin' away in boats!"

Goodnight glanced in the direction of the river and saw men scrambling into rowboats. These small craft were normally used as ferries for crossing the flood. He reined in his horse, used his right hand to shade his good eye, and stared at the river's edge in search of the monster, his son. It was hard to make out faces–much less hands–at that distance. Still, Goodnight thought he saw a familiar figure. And was that Gudanuf in the boat with him? He wasn't sure, but if it was Claw, if it was Gudanuf, he couldn't let them get away. Reluctantly leaving Loving to his fate, Goodnight turned his horse and spurred it toward the water.

116

Once more, Goodnight lifted old Red and they jumped the wall of fire. In midair, the heat burned him right through his boots, so he knew the horse beneath him was suffering. As he landed, he noticed that a cowboy was pointing a six-gun at him, but he really didn't pay much attention. He was in too big a hurry to worry about bullets. He heard the sound of the gun going off, but he didn't feel anything. He was a little disappointed in the cowboy for not being a better marksman. These striking cowpunchers just weren't sharp anymore. They hadn't guarded their horses properly. Now they weren't shooting worth a darn. He expected better of the cowboys of the South Plains. It was as if they were letting down the country. Pretty soon, this corner of Texas would have a reputation for shoddy work. Oh, hell, more crazy thoughts. Why couldn't he keep his mind on what he was supposed to be doing?

His horse shied and reared above a snake. Goodnight took a shot at it and hit it in the head. He knew it was a lucky shot, but it still gave him a smug, warm feeling. Now if he could just get his hands on the other snakes that he thought he had glimpsed down by the river. Where was Claw? Where was Gudanuf?

Goodnight galloped past the big saloon tent that was now on fire, charged on down to the river's edge, and splashed in. The churning water was cold on his legs. Soon his horse was swimming. Goodnight already relished his revenge. Now he realized that he hated his son even more than he hated Gudanuf. Now that misshapen monster would pay for killing Black Dub from ambush, would pay for murdering Loving under a flag of truce, would pay for killing Becky. No, that wasn't right.

The men in the boats were shooting back, but Goodnight paid the lead no attention. He was focused. The bullets only got his attention when one of them hit poor old Red in the neck. Had Claw or Gudanuf fired the shot? Whatever the truth, he blamed them. Miraculously, Goodnight's horse kept on swimming, but he was hurting. No, not now, don't stop now, don't die now, Goodnight silently begged the horse beneath him. Please, please. But the wounded animal's legs moved slower and slower until they couldn't move at all. Then the horse began to sink and turn sideways. Goodnight grabbed his ax from its scabbard and floated clear of his old friend. Then he clamped the handle of the ax tightly between his teeth and started crawling hand over hand after Claw. He swam through blood–human blood, horse blood. His hands and arms and even his face were sticky with blood. He raced through a red river after his enemy.

Wading ashore, he couldn't find them. Had he just imagined that he had seen Claw and Gudanuf in that boat? Were they some sort of mirage? Had they just evaporated the way mirages did? He wished more than ever that he had two eyes to search for them. Staring through the knothole in his skull, he couldn't find them. Without knowing where he was going, Goodnight tried to run, but his bad leg quickly pulled him up short. How could a one-eyed cripple ever chase down those demons? He blamed himself for his injuries. He blamed himself for letting them get away. He blamed himself for everything. Maybe he should just put his gun in his mouth and pull the trigger. He pulled his six-gun out of its holster, probably just bluffing, and saw that he was out of bullets, unless there was still one left in the chamber. He checked. Bad luck..

Then Goodnight saw them. He was surprised to find them quite near. Was it another mirage? There was Claw. There was Gudanuf. There was Loving! What was *he* doing here? How had he crossed the river? It must all be a mirage. A dream. Loving was supposed to be on the other side of the river, gravely wounded, probably dead, his body burned and smoking. Goodnight's eye blurred with tears. No! He had to see clearly. He tried to focus. Yes, he was right. He was thrilled that Loving was still alive, but then he realized that his friend, although alive, was about to die.

Gudanuf was holding Loving while Claw prepared to chop his head open with an ax. Goodnight told himself that the outlaws could never have controlled this prince of cowboys if he weren't wounded. Still Loving struggled. Good, fight them. Yes! He broke free and tried to run, but the two outlaws easily caught the crippled cowboy once again. Loving seemed to give in and accept his fate. Claw's back was to

Goodnight as he raised his ax to split Loving's skull, his brain, his life. Now Goodnight wished he hadn't already used up his bullets. They were not only gone, but they had been fired to no effect–except for that snake.

Goodnight had only one weapon left. Gripping it tightly, he cocked his arm, took careful aim at the back of Claw's head, and threw his lucky ax. As the blade left Goodnight's hand, his terrible son ducked. Could he see behind him? No, he lowered his head because he was beginning his own mighty blow.

A horrified Goodnight realized that his ax was going to miss Claw and kill Loving instead. Had he half-wanted to murder him all along because he had dared to love Revelie? Could it be? In his mind, Goodnight saw his weapon turn over and over in slow motion. Glimpsing the ax in flight, Loving was smart enough and fast enough to dodge. The blade missed Claw and Loving and split the skull of Gudanuf. One startled eye went one way and the other eye went the other. The handsome nose cracked in two. Teeth and brains spilled all over Loving. Goodnight's old nemesis was dead, but instead of elation, the victor felt nauseous.

The two, Loving and Gudanuf, both crumpled backward just as Claw delivered the blow with his ax. He missed, and the blade buried itself in the red ground. Claw just stood there staring, stunned, perhaps even sorry for what had happened to his new father figure.

While his son paused, Goodnight lurched forward, limping, staggering, as best he could. He saw Claw grin as he pulled out his pistol. The son took careful aim at his father and pulled the trigger. Goodnight started to sing his death song:

"O Sun, you live forever, but we must die. O Earth, you remain forever, but we must die . . ."

117

Click. Claw was out of bullets, too. Like father, like son. Seeing his crippled daddy bearing down on him, the boy threw away his empty six-gun and reached for his ax. He had struck with such energy and power that he had trouble pulling his blade from the red earth. Good! His hate had handicapped him.

Reaching Gudanuf's body, Goodnight pulled his own ax from the outlaw's skull just as Claw managed to free his from the red clay. Father and son faced each other. They circled one another, the father limping, the son hopping from foot to foot.

Goodnight swung his ax and his enemy used his own to deflect the blow. Goodnight swung again. Claw once again warded off the stroke with his ax. Goodnight had a flash memory of the sword fights in the old family fort. Sir Jimmy against Sir Becky. The memory made him want to kill Claw more than ever, as if the boy had been responsible for what had happened to her. Even with his crippled hand, Claw was a surprisingly good swordsman. Goodnight kept swinging away, hitting nothing, blocked every time. After the hard swim, all this chopping made his arms tired. He was working hard and breathing harder. He even began to wonder how much longer he could keep it up. Revenge was turning out to be a real chore. Goodnight retreated a couple of steps to catch his breath.

"What's the matter, Daddy?" the son asked. "Gittin' tired?"

"No," Goodnight said, wheezing.

"I'm gonna kill you, Old Man," the boy hissed, "and then I'm gonna finish off your buddy."

Goodnight stepped forward and attacked again. He tried swinging from below, but his blade only bit into the wooden handle of another ax. He could see Claw's strategy: wait for the old crip to wear himself out and then cut him to pieces. And the plan was working. Almost as much as he wanted to kill Claw, Goodnight just wanted to sit down.

"You don't look too good," the son taunted. "Your face is all red. Look like you're about to have a fit and fall over dead."

Goodnight decided to put all he had left into his next blow. He raised his ax over his head and swung down with all his might. Once again, all he hit was wood, but this time his blade bit deeply. Claw's ax handle snapped in two. Moving quickly to exploit his advantage, Goodnight swung his ax like a baseball bat and caught Claw right in the gut. The sharp blade sliced open his middle, and intestines came rolling out. Claw sat down hard and stared at the tangled tubes in his lap. Goodnight took a step forward and raised the ax once more to put the monster out of its misery.

"You done killt your own son," Claw said.

"I know," Goodnight said, and then hesitated before adding, "and good riddance."

"But I ain't quite done yet," his boy croaked.

Claw pulled a Derringer from the sleeve just above his claw, pointed it at his father, and shot him in the chest.

"Die, Daddy. Go to hell."

When Goodnight opened his good eye, he saw Loving looking down at him. His friend, whose left cheek had been shattered by a bullet, wasn't as good-looking as he had been, but he was still a welcome sight.

"I thought you was–" Goodnight whispered.

"No, I ain't dead yet," Loving said.

"Looks like I am. Anyhow purdy soon."

"No."

"Sorry."

Goodnight was surprised to see tears in his friend's eyes.

"I love you," Loving said.

Goodnight couldn't believe he had heard those words. Maybe he was hallucinating as he sank into death. But he didn't think so. Loving had said it all right. Goodnight had always felt that he was the one who loved, but who remained unloved. He had loved both Revelie and Loving in different ways, but they seemed not to return his love, for they had betrayed him. And yet now Loving spoke of loving him. The world was even more complicated than Goodnight had imagined, and some of those complications were good, but he had learned this lesson too late for it to do him much good in this life.

"Me, too," Goodnight gasped. He saw Claw lying motionless beside him. "Is he done for?"

"Yeah," Loving said.

"I reckon there ain't no gittin' away from the past nohow, huh?" Goodnight said. Or maybe he didn't actually say it. Perhaps he only thought it. He wasn't sure. "The past'll git ahold of you somehow and just won't never let go for nothin'. I guess I shoulda known. Becky tried to tell me."

Loving was saying something, but Goodnight could no longer make out the words.

118

Loving wrote Revelie what had happened, and she came as quickly as she could. She also came quietly since she was still a wanted woman in Texas. Loving met her at the railhead in Abilene, Kansas. He brought with him a bay mare carrying the old sidesaddle that her husband had made for her. Unexpectedly, Revelie brought something with her, too, a small son, so another mount was needed. Loving bought a pony for him to ride. The boy was already strikingly handsome. People disagreed about whether his eyes were brown or blue.

The trip took almost two weeks. Revelie hated the new scar on Loving's left cheek at first–but had come to like it by the time they finally reached the Home Ranch.

She found the place little changed. She had expected it to feel empty and listless, but it didn't. The strike was over and the cowboys back to work. They had all survived the battle and the fire except Flytrap, who caught a bullet in his open mouth.

In his optimistic will, written long ago, Goodnight had left his share of the ranch to any children who might survive his marriage. Moreover, Mrs. Sanborn, who had recently died, bequeathed her estate to her daughter's offspring. And Revelie, a fugitive from Texas justice, had deeded her share over to her son, so the state wouldn't confiscate it. Now the boy with the changeable eyes owned all of the red canyon, its steep walls, its river, its twining history.

Loving walked Revelie to the hackberry thicket where Goodnight was buried. The grave lay in a small clearing at the center of thorns. When she caught sight of the tombstone–an impressive monument made of granite shipped in from somewhere–she stopped and stared. The blade of an ax was imbedded in the headstone.

Revelie walked forward slowly, knelt, and kissed that blade. When she stood up, she was smiling, but from her lips trickled a drop redder than the canyon walls.